AMONG SPIES

Tony & Dixie

With many many thanks

for your help.

Wally

AMONG SPIES

A NOVEL

JOHN WALLIS CREIGHTON

Elderberry Press, LLC
OAKLAND

Elderberry Press, LLC
1393 Old Homestead Drive, Second floor
Oakland, Oregon 97462—9506.
http://elderberrypress.com
E-MAIL: editor@elderberrypress.com
TEL/FAX: 541.459.6043

All Elderberry books are available from your favorite bookstore, amazon.com, or from our 24 hour order line: 1.800.431.1579

SAN: 454 - 4288
Library of Congress Control Number: 2004108691
Publisher's Catalog-in-Publication Data
Among Spies/John Wallis Creighton
ISBN 1-932762-05-1
1. Mexico—Fiction.
2. WW II——Fiction.
3. Nazi——Fiction.
4. Women——Fiction.
5. Spies——Fiction.
6. Suspense——Fiction.
7. Murder——Fiction.
I. Title

This book was written, printed, and bound in the United States of America.

John Wallis Creighton

South China born and cultured, experienced in Central and South America, John Creighton has been a building contractor and has managed sawmills, veneer mills and furniture factories. As a professor and department head at Michigan State and Colorado State universities and the U.S. Naval Postgraduate School, he completed many research contracts.

Among Spies, his third novel, starts Maggie Magodon's foreign service career at the U.S. Consulate in Veracruz, Mexico where she becomes a counter-espionage agent assigned to expose Nazi spies during World War II.. Film rights have been acquired for **Waring's War,** based on his World War II experience in Ecuador procuring balsa wood for the manufacture of the British Mosquito Bomber, and for **Aira in Red,** in which Aira and Barc strive toward their own and each other's success.

Following retirement from the U.S. Naval Postgraduate School in Monterey, California, he has devoted his time to writing. He lives in a house he designed and built in Carmel, California.

Chapter I

"Párese ya, Stop right now," the guard bellowed. "You can't go there."

Maggie Magodón slammed shut the gate and, red rain cape flapping, dashed across the Mexico City airfield. She heard boots pounding the runway behind her — closer, closer, but focused on the runway ahead and shouted in Spanish, "Leave it be. Don't move that ladder."

"Come back," roared the guard. Inspection — customs."

"Out of my way,"Maggie yelled, swinging high her purse to get a crewman's attention as he pulled the boarding ladder from the DC-3 airplane. "Hold it! I've got to go — Veracruz." She brushed past the man, scrambled to the top and leaped across a three-foot gap into the plane.

The steward blocked her way. "You're too late, Señorita. All the seats are taken."

"The airplane is here, Señor. I am here so I'm not late. Tell those *carabineros* out there to leave me be." She pointed out the hatch. "I have a diplomatic passport so I bypass customs."

She heard voices on the ground and saw the boarding ladder pushed back to the airplane. "I have priority and reservation. Look." She pulled documents from her purse. "See, July 3, 1941. That's today." She waved the papers in front of the steward's eyes and squeezed past him into the passenger cabin.

"Get that woman," the guard shouted as he mounted the ladder.

Maggie wheeled. "Call the captain," she yelled, and just then he emerged from the curtained pilot compartment.

"What's the trouble?" he asked the steward in English.

American, good, Maggie thought. Determined to win his favor, she toned down her voice. "I got bumped off my flight in New Orleans and I'll not get bumped again. I came all the way from there today and I've got a priority."

"Everybody on board has a priority, Miss. Weight's the question." The captain looked her up and down and made a quick estimate. "Where's your baggage?"

"Checked through to the Veracruz consulate," Maggie said.

"Let's just take a look at your priority." The pilot held out his hand and she held out the documents. "You're Margaret Magodón?"

"Who else could I be?" Had she just imagined that he'd flashed her a smile? "I've just got to get to Veracruz," she said, as the captain took the passenger list from the steward. She racked her brains to come up with arguments to hold her place, but her hopes sank as she watched the pilot's head turn slowly from side to side.

Finally he marked the list, returned it to the steward and gave her a quick glance. "Have a good flight," he said, and escaped behind the curtain.

Maggie saw the guard stare at the steward whose eyes were fixed on the curtain, and decided to explain the captain's decision herself. *"El capitán dice que . . ."* she said, and went on to tell the guard that she would take the flight and that the captain would greatly appreciate the guard's cooperation if he would escort the evicted traveler back to the terminal. When he nodded and smiled, she turned to the steward. "Will you show me to my seat, please?"

Maggie swept a glance over the passengers, all men except a woman wearing a scarlet raincoat, and knew at once that she would be the one to lose her seat. She steeled herself against pangs of guilt when the woman erupted, screaming. Her white uniformed companion objected, too, and passengers craned their necks to see the cause of the commotion. A tall blond man in the front row rose and headed back toward the fracas.

Maggie blocked his way. "This does not concern you, Señor," she said in Spanish. "I can handle it." When the man tucked his chin into his neck, lifted a hand and was about to speak, she cut him off. "Back off. I mean it."

The man shrugged and went back to his seat.

Like the boss I had at Douglas Aircraft, Maggie thought — so courteous, helpful, then demands return favors only a woman can give a man. Finally, the raincoat-clad woman was ushered out, and the steward readied the airplane to take off.

Maggie sat down, snapped on her seat belt. Getting on board was a minor victory, but one she needed, she thought as the plane taxied forward. She'd kow-towed to men for eight years in the male-dominated aircraft factory, and was determined to keep all men at bay from now on — control her own destiny. Still, she felt sympathetic toward the evicted woman and the man beside her. She turned toward him. "I'm sorry," she said. "Is the young lady your wife?"

The man in uniform glowered and chewed his cheeks the way that boy in Torreón had done years ago just before he spit in her face. She opened her purse to get a hanky, but he just swallowed and picked up a Mexico City newspaper.

She couldn't help noticing a heading— AIRLINE CRASH. He flipped the paper over. "Oh, no, TANKER TORPEDOED," she burst out as a giant headline caught her eye.

The man jerked the front page up between them, but she'd caught the gist of another subheading. A Mexican oil tanker had been sunk by a German submarine in the Gulf of Mexico just east of Tampico.

"Tampico — three hundred miles from Veracruz," Maggie murmured, squirming to quell the shivers in her back, "about like from St. Louis to Chicago. Hmm." Had the State Department bigwigs back in Washington known the Nazis were active in Mexico? That must be why they'd added a week with the FBI to her orientation program? Shivers? No, she felt her shoulders tense with a thrill of excitement at the prospect of pitting her ingenuity against Nazis. What a relief that would be to temper the boredom of a humdrum, shuffle dollar job.

Maggie remembered that in Washington, she'd mentioned *Investigative Finance,* as her favorite college course. The remark had resulted in her assignment to the Veracruz consulate where financial accounts were reported to be in shambles. Now that she'd been trained by the FBI, with the war so close, would she also be a spy?

The DC-3 zoomed, stalled, sideslipped, and plunged. Maggie gasped and held her breath. The wingtip outside her window barely cleared a boulder-strewn Sierra Madre ridge. "Scary!" she exclaimed as the plane banked away.

"

Qué miedo!" The young man beside her burst out at the same instant.

They both laughed as the plane leveled and bounced up and up until it broke through the cloud cover.

"You're from the States?" he said in English.

"You live in Veracruz?" she asked in Spanish at the same time.

"Sí," they responded as one.

She held out her hand. *"Mucho gusto."*

"También." He grasped it, irritation from his companion's ouster apparently put aside. "I'm Victor Dalpica, home from university in the States."

"I'm Margareta Magodón." She saw that he had straight white teeth and the corners of his eyes crinkled.

Just then the plane banked. He looked across her and out her window. "We're going north around Popocatepetl and the storm."

"Popocatepetl, hmm, I like the name. My father spoke of the volcano and the other mountain with the strange name.

What was it? Cit — Cit —"

"Citlaltepetl, the highest in North America," he chipped in. "We call it Pico Orizaba, too. Do you have friends in Veracruz?"

"I have a job at the American Consulate," she said, and went on to tell him she expected someone from the consulate to meet her at the airport. "You are in uniform. Are you in the military?"

"*Sí*. Public relations, Mexican Navy. I'm an engineer, but I once worked for the family newspaper, *El Dictamen,* so the Navy sent me to the States to study journalism and public relations." He paused and looked sideways at her. "Your Spanish is excellent. Have you been in Mexico before?"

"I was born in Torreón, my mother's home. Then, fifteen years ago, when I was ten, my mother was killed in a car wreck. My father took my sister and me back to the States. He died five years later, so I had to go to work." Knock it off, she told herself. He's just a stranger trying to be polite — good at it, too. She looked out the window. "Oh, look. That mountain is awesome."

He leaned across her. *"Pico Orizaba."*

Maggie regarded the massive peak, green, its snow cap golden in the setting sun, a dazzling island in a sea of white clouds. The DC-3 banked slowly east, dipped, and clouds enveloped the cabin in a gray pallor.

She shuddered, apprehensive in the darkness. Tomorrow her career would begin. Was she ready? What would the job be like? Had the Nazis stepped up their operations in Mexico? Might she encounter German agents?

She'd reviewed Mexican history while in Washington, particularly that of the state and city of Veracruz where her father had participated in the 1914 United States invasion. She'd been fascinated by his pictures, and spellbound by his stories. Delighted by her assignment, she'd requested further details about it. Mr. Albert Williams, the American consul, will tell you what to do, she'd been told.

In St. Louis, before going to Washington for training, she'd heard Charles Lindbergh speak against American involvement in Europe where Adolf Hitler and the German armies were on a rampage. She'd agreed with Lindbergh, and local sentiment had seemed to back him, too. Now she wasn't so sure. Nazi forces had crushed Norway, Denmark, and the low countries. British forces in France had escaped total defeat by their retreat through Dunkirk. Mussolini, Italy's dictator, had joined Hitler to form the Nazi-Fascist axis.

The DC-3 descended through murky clouds to burst into the gray of dusk. Through the window, cross-veined by rain, she made out fishing trawlers on leaden Gulf of Mexico waters, and the black columnar outline of a tall volcanic neck on the flat coastal plain a short distance inland.

"*Cerro Hermal,* " her seat mate said. "In the sixteenth century, Hernán Cortez kept a lookout on top to warn him when ships approached."

The plane swung south over vessels docked in the harbor, circled past the city, touched down on a macadam strip, and taxied toward a low building. Maggie took a deep breath. "Ugh," she muttered, as the tall blond man rose from a seat ahead and fixed his eyes on her.

"*Siéntese,* Sit down," someone shouted. "Wait until we stop."

The man approached. Aryan, and too old now, she thought, but just the type Hitler recruited for his Jugend, the Nazi Youth Corps. He stopped at her row and leaned across Victor.

"May I be of assistance, Miss? My car will pick us up."

"*Con perdón, Señor Buehler,* " her seat mate cut in. "She has made other arrangements."

"*Qué lástima,* " the man said, clicked his heels, and turned away.

How had he known her name? Oh, sure, the embarkation list. Before leaving Washington she'd been warned to avoid such approaches. He's probably German, she thought, but aside from zizzed "s's," he sounded almost American.

The man's manner and posture reminded her of Fred Dilgaard, who had tried to rape her the day after his marriage to her sister. Was this man a Nazi? Fred would have supported Hitler, she was sure, had he lived in Germany.

Mr. Buehler pushed open the curtain to the pilot's cabin and stood there until the plane stopped. Maggie saw him speak to the captain, then follow him out. He must work for the airline, she decided, joining other passengers to stand and clap their thanks to the captain for the safe journey.

She put on her rain cape and hat, bid Victor goodbye and descended the ladder to splash through the rain to the dimly lighted baggage pick-up shed.

After missing several flights, she was sure her luggage had not arrived, but she waited to make sure then left directions to have it delivered to the United States Consulate. On the street, she saw the door of a long black car open and the tall blond man step out.

"Miss Magodón," he called. "This way, hurry."

A taxi door opened. *"Señorita Magodón?"* The driver beckoned. *"El consulado de los Estados Unidos?"*

Maggie waved to Mr. Buehler, then dashed to the taxi and clambered in. "How did you know my name?"

The driver chuckled. "The consulate told me to be on the lookout for a pretty woman at the airport, and no other passenger was more beautiful than you."

"Gracias. It must have been hard to pick me out," she said, "because I was the only woman passenger among twenty-four men."

They both laughed, and Maggie felt at home to be speaking Spanish again after so many years in the States. The driver was friendly and had merely answered her question, so she didn't think he'd been presumptuous.

The rain stopped as they approached the harbor on *Calle Montesinos* and swung south on *Avenida Independencia.* They passed the Arches and the *Plaza de Armas,* the central square, known as the *Zócalo.* Driving east again on *Calle M. Arista,* the driver slowed and pointed at a large house behind a masonry wall. "There's the consulate," he said, "and the consul's residence is around the corner on the Malecón, the seawall street."

The entry was in the center of the building. Long, tall windows on the right
side indicated a spacious hall or ballroom, and Maggie supposed from the lighted windows on both floors on the left, that someone kept late hours.

"Are those coconut palms?" Maggie asked as they turned onto the Malecón, a boulevard where palms towered over a median strip, and a narrow park separated it from harbor waters.

"Sí, cocos," the driver answered.

She couldn't see much through the residence gate. Around the corner, the south wall on *Calle E. Morales* had no breaks, but a chipped corner revealed the wall's construction: red brick, plastered and painted white, with broken glass protruding from a cement cap. Farther on, landscaped gardens caught her eye through the driveway gates on *Avenida General Figueroa.*

The apartment reserved for her was three blocks away, so she directed the driver to take her there to register, then bring her back to the consulate.

"Cuánto, por favor?" she asked when they returned. "I'll take a taxi to my apartment after I let them know I've arrived."

"Nada. The consulate will pay," he said. "But if you need a ride later, I will
be near."

Maggie thanked him, took a deep breath, and squared her

shoulders. Heart pounding, she pushed open the gate just as church bells sounded eight o'clock. She mounted the steps and grasped the entry knob. Locked.

She knocked, pounded, and tried the door again, but it would not budge.

"Anybody here?" she shouted. No answer.

Was she at the right place? A plaque beside the entry read, *Consulado de los Estados Unidos.* Lighted windows indicated that someone was in. Shouldn't the gate have been locked, too, if they locked the front door?

"Scary," she mumbled, then stood still long enough for crickets to resume their shrill. A frog garumped. The rain had stopped, but the air was hot and musty. Her blouse stuck to her body and she plucked it free. Creepy — feels like eyes watching me, she thought but, looking about, she saw no movement except flurries of harbor insects attacking the street lamp on the Malecón corner a half block away. A bat wing flicked her rain hat and she flailed her arm at it. Settle down, she told herself. Just then she saw two men rise from squatting against the lighthouse wall across the street and saunter toward her. Midway, they broke into a run. She jumped down the steps, slammed the gate, and threw the bolt just as a body slammed against the heavy gate planks.

She heard cursing, then all was quiet, even the frogs and crickets. The
thumping in her chest seemed to pick up the distant beat of marimbas from the central square. Three mournful blasts gave notice of a ship's departure. Maggie leaned against the heavy gate to wait for some sign of the men's departure.

"Vámonos," she heard one of them whisper, then held her breath until the sound of bare feet slithering over wet pavement faded.

There had to be a back door and a path to get to it, she thought, and followed flagstones through lush plantings. Save for sounds of droplets shaken from the foliage, far away marimba music and the squish of her loafers on the rain-soaked earth, she heard nothing. The path took her around a screened veranda, and along the rear to the service entrance.

Locked.

The back door was locked, too. Banging on it and pressing the bell button brought no response.

She backed away from the consulate in order to see upstairs windows, but froze as she heard bushes rustle behind her.

"*Qué quiere?* What do you want?" a voice behind her demanded.

Good, a watchman, she decided, and was about to answer when she heard a muffled response, the creak of gate hinges, a dull thud, a gasp, a groan, branches breaking, a crash — silence.

She ducked under low branches, tucked her purse into a tree crotch, and waited. At last a frog croaked, and crickets resumed their shrill. She took a chance and crept through dense shrubbery as cold droplets off rain-soaked foliage showered her. She parted branches and, peering through, saw that the driveway gate was ajar and, next to it, the gatehouse was dark and its door open. She hid again when she heard two voices, whispered *esses*, a growl, the sound of a scuffle. Then a man emerged from behind shrubbery and darted her way, but he veered toward the driveway where another man joined him, then both disappeared.

She waited, but nothing happened. A lone peddler barked his wares on the Malecón. Bursts of laughter and muffled voices from the consul's residence beyond the property wall reached her. She heard a guffaw, a loud response in English, and decided to go next door to the Williams residence. Faint light came from an enclosed passageway connecting the consulate to a pergola and continuing to the wall between it and the consul's house. Might Mr. Williams use the passage to go to his office? Might there be a door she could enter? It was much closer than to go out the gate and around to the front entrance.

Maggie heard voices, a piano, singing, then the cicadas drowned the human sounds with their own crescendo. It was a good time to move, she thought, and parted branches to peer back at the consulate. Movement under a window caught her attention and she saw a man push another man through a window. Burglars! She'd have to warn the consul — right now.

Maggie burst from cover, stumbled and, off balance, reached out to brace herself against a tree. It gave way, and she was sprawled face down into a puddle under a thicket.

Calle E. Morales

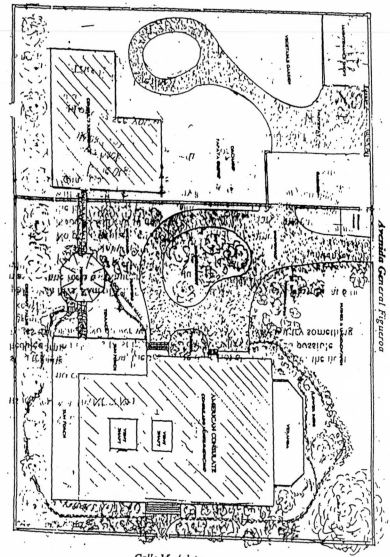

Calle M. Arista

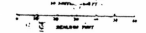

Chapter 2

No noise— I mean it. Don't move, Maggie told herself but, gasping, she'd sucked in yucky water and she just had to spew out the gunky stuff in it. Those thugs must have heard her fall. She lay still, hoping they wouldn't pry. She lifted her head, squeezed water from her eyes and stared. What? Half a face? Where was the other half? Buried in mud?

She reached out with trembling fingers and touched a forehead — cold. Was it a garden statue? Then she felt the a chin — beard stubble — a real man, but where was the body? Was that what had given way, causing her to fall?

She rose to her knees and looked up. "Oh-my-God!" she burst out under her breath, as a shaft of light from a distant consulate window fell on a body hanging upside down, its back against a tree. It had to be the watchman and, if he weren't dead already, he'd suffocate with his face half buried. Hands trembling, she dug mud and rotting leaves from his mouth and nostrils. "Dear God, I hope I'm not too late," she murmured. *"Señor. Señor,"* she whispered.

No response.

She grasped his shoulders to ease the strain on his twisted neck, could not move him, then saw that his arms were extended around the tree behind him.

She peered about to make sure she wouldn't be seen, then crawled around the tree and groped for his hands. She found them bound together, each wrist wrapped with rope and knotted so tightly that her muddy fingers could not loosen them.

Remembering the pen knife in her purse, she rose to get it. Careful to make no noise, she backed away from the hanging man but tripped over another rope and fell again. "Come on," she murmured, as a squall rustled the trees and rain muffled the slosh of her fall. She got up and followed the rope to a tree where she untied the knots and gently lowered the body to the ground.

Maggie parted branches to peer through the foliage, and saw one of the burglars catch a dark packet tossed from a consulate window. Then came a low call for a rope. When the man with the packet wheeled and started toward her, she hid under dense shrubbery. "Mmm." Maggie sniffed — gardenias.

"Por Dios!" she heard the burglar growl when he reached the watchman. He cut the rope, then rolled the body over with his foot. *"Bien, bien. Estás muerto* – good, he's dead," he muttered.

Peering from under the bush, Maggie saw him hide the packet behind a corner of the gatehouse, then coil the rope and return to the consulate.

She went back to the watchman and felt for his pulse. Her fingers were too muddy to feel anything, but his arm jerked so she thought he was alive. Help him, and get a wiggle on, she told herself. Call the police. Surely there would be a telephone in the gatehouse.

Maggie backed away from the body, crossed the driveway, and snatched the packet from its hiding place. Inside, when she groped for a telephone, her hand brushed something onto the floor. She jerked back bumping her elbow, and felt her funny bone go crazy and the packet fly from her grasp. Lunging to catch it, she upset a stack of garden tools, and thought she'd never heard such a loud crash when they hit the floor. There was a faint ding — the telephone. Think, Maggie, think. Forget the funny bone, call the police before the burglars get here.

Joggling the earpiece hook, she barked into the mouthpiece, *"Hola, hola."* — nothing.

"Hola, hola, hello, operator," she shouted again. *"Policía, de prisa. Consulado, Estados Unidos,* hurry!" Might the burglars run off to avoid the police? Maybe, but she doubted it. They'd seemed to know the packet would be in the consulate, had come for it, got it, and wanted more. Why else did they need the rope unless they planned to take something larger.

She heard the *splat-splat* of bare feet. She reached for a weapon — anything — and grasped a long-handled shovel off the floor. Crouching low, she raised it barely in time to strike as a head appeared as a silhouette in the open doorway. The blade rang: her hands stung from the impact, and she saw him fall.

Heart pounding, she poked him with the shovel, but he lay still. Where was the other burglar? Would he come, too? Dragging the shovel, she dashed out, intending to hide in the bushes. Too late. There he was, and she felt her legs wobble like mushy noodles.

"Párese ya, stop right there!" she screamed. The man veered right and plunged into the shrubbery. "Yippee, get out of here!" she shrieked, her strength surging back. Brandishing her shovel, she went after him.

"Espérate, wait!" She heard from behind her, and she wheeled, raising her weapon.

"Bravo, Maggie!" yelled a black-clad figure as it burst past her, and she saw the flash of a long blade in his hand.

Should she follow him? she wondered. Her long shovel was no weapon for fighting in undergrowth, so she gripped it with both hands ready to strike if the burglar emerged.

How did the man know her name? He must be from the consulate, and it was about time he showed up. The consulate expected a Margaret to arrive, but Maggie?

She heard a branch snap, a groan, bodies thrashing, and just then felt the shovel torn from her grasp, and a hand clamp over her mouth. She kicked, twisted, tried to bite his hand as he dragged her into the thicket near the hangman tree. How could she have forgotten that burglar in the gatehouse?

"Where's the box?" the burglar hissed.

Maggie raked her fingernails across the hand gagging her, twisted her head free and screamed. Lurching forward, she jammed her elbows back into her assailant's ribs with all the force she could muster, and broke away.

He lunged at her, stumbled, fell, and she pounced on his back, but he struggled to his feet and scraped her off against a tree just as the black-clad figure appeared from nowhere and plowed into her attacker.

Confident that the man in black would be the one to return, Maggie took a deep breath, suddenly aware of quiet in the warm Veracruz night. The shush of foliage embracing the rain and pavement repelling it calmed her. The sounds of Zócalo marimbas, harbor noises, faint voices and laughter from the consul's house, brought her back to reality. Was the watchman alive? She went into the bushes to look for him just as she heard a call.

"You okay, Maggie? You did great!"

"Dear God, English! I'm okay. Did the burglars get away?" she called back. Then the man in black came up the driveway, and she saw by the row of white teeth glowing in the darkness that they had not.

He gestured, "There's one of them on the driveway."

How could he act as if nothing had happened? She stared at the dark mass. "You mean — you — is he —? " Gritting her teeth, she knew she had to get busy to steady her quaking knees. "Help me with the watchman," she said. "Don't want him dead, too."

They found the man lying on his side with a hand on top of his head. "I'll take care of him," Maggie said, jabbing a finger toward the gatehouse. "The burglars stole a package about the size of a cigar box from the consulate. It's in there on the floor. Can you return it?"

The black figure left, and Maggie knelt beside the watchman. "Can you hear me? Can you sit up?" she asked.

The watchman groaned, turned onto his back and tried.

"There's no hurry," she said, putting an arm about his shoulders to help him up. They'd reached the driveway when gatehouse lights came on and the man in black emerged from it.

"I straightened up the gatehouse," he said, taking the watchman's free arm. "The racket those tools made brought me on the run."

Together, they took the watchman to the gatehouse and helped him into the toilet room.

"Thank God you showed up," Maggie said. "Who are you?"

"José Alvarado. Remember? We've met before."

His voice was familiar, but where had she met him? "How do you know me?"

"Miguel told me you were here."

Keep him talking, and don't you dare risk a glance at that body on the driveway, Maggie told herself. "Miguel?" she repeated. "Who's he?"

"The taxi driver who brought you from the airstrip. You surprised all of us. I was in Mexico City this morning to meet your flight. Lucky you weren't on it."

"Lucky? I got bumped off. Call that lucky?"

"Yeah. It crashed. No survivors."

"Dear God! Everybody? Are you sure?" Maggie saw him nod, but the vision in her mind was that of the blue-eyed little girl who'd bumped her from her seat. She looked up. "I'm so sorry! There was a little girl who —" She broke off and went out the door. "I'll be a minute," she said. Outside, she turned her face up to the rain. "Please God," she said, her voice solemn, "never again such a tragic day." As she bowed her head, the vision of the black heap on the driveway returned. She wheeled and went back in. There was work to do.

Inside again, she found her champion slumped onto a folding chair. "You're hurt," she said, seeing that he was covered with bloody mud. A sleeve and pant leg were in tatters, and cuts on his head, left arm, and thigh dripped red. Dizzy, she shook her head, snatched up a rag and tore it into bandages.

"Water hose outside," he said, got up, and staggered out the door.

Maggie dragged the chair out. He sat down and she turned on the water.

"Jeepers, you look greeby," she muttered, as she hosed him off.

"Aren't you a sight, too?" He forced a chuckle. "I'd never have recognized you."

How could he laugh and tease at a time like this? Still, it took her mind off the gory task and she supposed it relieved his tension, too. "You know me, but I haven't a glimmer about you," she shot back. "You look worse than me." She glanced down at herself, rain cape torn and muddy, blouse and skirt soaked, muddied, rumpled and awry. "Come on, who are you?"

"José Alvarado, St. Louis, Washington University — you gave me copies of your résumé and application for government employment after Thompson chased you out of the interview room."

"Oh, yeah, and who would ever have thought I'd meet you here?" She tied a bandage on his arm just as the watchman staggered out.

"His turn," José insisted. He took off a shoe and sock, wiped mud out of the shoe with grass and put it back on without the sock. "I've got a lot to do." He rose, swayed for an instant, then hobbled slowly toward the consulate.

Should she stop him, urge him to rest? Somehow Maggie knew he'd do as he pleased, and watched him go, one leg stark white in contrast to his black getup. "My purse, hat, and shoes are somewhere out there, Mr. Alvarado," she called. "Mind picking them up if you find them?"

"I'll look, but call me José."

"*Macho, muy macho*, a real man," she murmured.

"*Sí, Señorita, muy macho,*" the watchman said softly.

She urged him to sit down so she could examine the cut on his head. There was a walnut-sized lump but nothing serious, she decided, when he picked up the garden hose without staggering. He'd stripped to shorts, and she was hosing him off when José returned and, just then, she heard a car pull up outside the iron gate.

"It's Miguel with my car," José told her. He opened the gate, the car came through, and he beckoned the driver to follow him down the driveway.

José seemed better, Maggie thought when the car stopped beside the dark mound and José heaved it into the rumble seat compartment. How awful. Why didn't he call the police and have them remove the bodies? she wondered, as she cleaned the watchman's wounds.

"Do you know who the burglars were?" she asked.

"*No, Señorita.* A man outside the gate said he had a message for the consul. That's all I remember."

Do you lock the front gate when the consulate closes?" Maggie asked, remembering that it had opened with a light push when she arrived.

"*Sí, Señorita.*"

So one of the burglars must have unlocked it after hiding inside the walls during the day as part of a planned burglary. Scary! Maggie forced her thoughts back to the watchman. The cut on top of his head had almost stopped bleeding, so she stuffed crumpled newspaper into a visored cap she found in the gatehouse and put it on his head to control the bleeding.

The car returned with José behind it, limping. "Ready?" he said, "we've got to go."

"Shouldn't we call the police?"

"What would you tell them, Maggie?" José leaned against the door jamb and rubbed his chin. "You could say that two men forced their way onto United States property. You tell them that and the watchman will lose his job. Or tell them that two local citizens died on that same property? Think what the newspapers would do with that." José pushed himself erect, went around to open the passenger door and beckoned. "Come on."

"Váyase. Go." The watchman nodded vigorously.

"My purse. It's out —"

"Got it already. It's in the car. Shoes and hat, too."

Miguel leaned out of the driver's window. *"Buenás noches de nuevo, Señorita.* Good evening again."

Maggie hesitated. She recognized the car as a Model A Ford coupe. The rumble seat lid was closed, but were there two dead men in there?

José still held the door open. "Hurry, get in!"

"You crazy? Me get into a car with four strange men, two of them dead? I'll go over to the Williams's house." She headed for the gate.

José cut her off. "No, Miss Magodón, you will not. Mrs. Williams would never forgive you for dragging mud into her house, not even into the service entrance. Just what would you tell the consul and his guests? Can you even imagine that Mr. Williams wants the notoriety of two deaths on consulate grounds? It's just too bad if you can't take the sight of a little blood. Get in!"

"Who do you think you are, Mr. Alvarado? Blood? I've handled worse than this mess. Well, okay, but don't you dare imply I'm a gutless lily liver!" She shouldered past him and climbed in.

Miguel drove out the gate. José closed it and got in. Maggie thumbed over her shoulder. "What are you going to do with them? They'll stink pretty quick in this heat."

"We'll manage. A bit of advice, Maggie," José said softly. "You'd be wise to forget what happened tonight. I mean it, Maggie. Forget all of it."

Maggie shuddered. "I heard you, but . . ." She let her sentence dangle, thinking years back to the accident when, with a broken ankle and only ten, she'd crawled up to the road to get help, then ridden on the bed of a truck into Torreón with her screaming older sister, mangled father, and lifeless mother. She forced her mind back to what José was saying.

"Never expected to welcome you to Veracruz quite this way," he said. "What's it been, five weeks?"

"More like seven." Was José using small talk to distract her from thoughts of their cargo, or to relieve his own tension? Whichever it was, she welcomed it. "You were with that crumb — you know, strawberry jam hair?" She remembered well what she'd thought of José that day: the image of a Spanish Don, tall, slim and graceful. How his eyes had shone when he caught on to her trick to land that job interview.

"Uh-huh, Nolan Thompson, my roommate back at the University of Minnesota." He chuckled. "Fraternity brothers called him Fireball, and not just because of his hair. Fidgety, hot-tempered, spoiled rotten, but a nice guy most of the time. His mother's hair's the same color."

Miguel stopped the car at a corner near the Zócalo to let a string of burros pass, and José shooed a beggar boy away from his window. "I seem to meet you under unusual circumstances," he said.

"Come again? What's strange about a college student interviewing for a job?"

"You tricked a Miss Ortiz – took her appointment, I believe."

"Misrepresentation, that what you mean? Alphabetically, my name comes before hers, and she wouldn't have gotten the job anyhow."

"But she did, Maggie. Thompson hired her and, even now, doesn't know you work for State."

"Oh?" Surprised, Maggie thought hard for something to say. "You took a copy of my résumé, tricking me into thinking you had a job to offer — a position, as I recall?"

"Precisely the job you got — position, rather. I gave the application to a guy I know in the State Department. Thompson turned you down for Treasury."

"You mean —" A thought struck her. "I know you're not the consul. You a vice-consul or something?"

"I'm in business — a silversmith, a jeweler. I don't work for the consulate."

Maggie thought a moment. "So you're to blame. You got me to Veracruz for this? What a job! Look at me — mud, hair all stringy."

"That's just it. What's better than a mud bath for strawberry hair? I found you mixed up in a burglary and hiding in the bushes. I don't meet many women that way."

"Speak of the pot and kettle." Maggie couldn't help herself, and retorted with a chuckle. "There you go. I meet you diving into slime for a refreshing rollabout. Besides, murder's worse than burglary."

Miguel turned into a dark lane and stopped the car.

"My place," José said, opening the door. "Out we go."

"No we don't," Maggie said. "I've got an apartment and the driver knows where it is. He can just take — "

"*Señorita,*" Miguel cut in, "it was broken into just after you registered. There's no furniture. I'll put a good lock on the door tomorrow.

"Come on." José grasped her hand. "You'll be safe here. Miguel and I will be busy all night." He pulled her hand for a moment, but let go, then unlocked a tall iron gate set into a masonry wall. "Careful, it's wet and muddy."

* * *

"You first." José indicated a bathroom in his apartment. She entered, quickly locked the door and heaved a deep sigh.

Moments later, when she looked out to ask for a towel, she saw him take the black packet from under his shirt, wipe the mud from it, and put it in a wall safe. A gash above and behind his right ear was still bleeding, and blood oozed down his neck and under his collar. He was leaning to the left, seeming to favor his right leg. He staggered, shook his head, straightened, locked the safe and hung a picture on the wall to cover it. Maggie closed the door without a sound.

Why hadn't he returned the packet to the consulate, and why had he hidden it from her? She determined to find out what was in it. Probably nothing was wrong. Still, she'd follow up on it. "Do you have another towel handy?" she shouted from inside the bathroom.

"One moment."

Presently he knocked, and she reached out for the towel.

"Take your time," he said. "Miguel's waiting, and I've got to get something from the car. Keep the door locked."

When she left the bathroom a few minutes later, she saw a note on a chair directly in front of the door. She read:

Sleep here tonight. Can't risk burglary at your place.
Left a shirt out. Use it. Best I could do.
Camila will wake you at six-thirty. Breakfast at seven.
Leave your clothes beside the door. Camila will clean and
    return them.
If you need help, press the button on the right side of the
    desk.
No one. Please. Nobody must know you were here tonight.
Explain later. Destroy this.
    Bravisima.   —   JA

"Wretched jerk!" Maggie burst out, face flushing from the rage rising within her. Why hadn't he told her he was leaving? She read the note again. Well, he did have to dispose of two bodies, and why shouldn't she stay? There really wasn't much choice. She'd wanted to be alone in her own apartment, but certainly not if it had been broken into. Besides, José's note indicated he would not return.

Wrapped in a towel, she walked through the apartment There was a bedroom, another bath, a living room, office and a kitchen. How strange — each room had a window secured with iron bars opening onto a central ventilation shaft, but none opened to the outside.

She glanced back at the bed. The quilted spread was emblazoned with a life-sized figure of an Aztec warrior. She was tempted to stretch out on it, but went back to the office.

Taking care not to let her soiled purse smudge anything, she emptied its contents on José's desk, then gathered her soiled belongings to put them outside the door. It would not open, and suddenly she felt all hollow inside.

Locked in! Why did I ever let that man talk me out of going to the Williams's house, Maggie thought, raising her fist to pound the door. Then she let it fall, remembering that José's note mentioned an emergency button. What reason did she have to open that door right now? None. Without clothes, what could she do? Best get the day behind her, she decided, and flopped down on the Aztec warrior.

Chapter 3

Four - five - six. Maggie rolled onto her back just as she'd done years ago in Torreón when six peals from the church bells served as the household wake-up call. She'd always been dressed before her father knocked to make sure she was up. Might José do it, too?

She threw a towel around herself and hurried to the entry. It opened. Good, she wasn't a prisoner, but what could she wear? The soiled laundry she'd left beside the door was gone, so she didn't even have that. Oh, for something to eat, anything. She got a Coca Cola from the refrigerator, drank it all, but was still hungry. What had José's note said about breakfast? She picked it up and read. Camila would bring breakfast and her clothes, but where was she? How could the woman do everything in such a short time? Maggie shredded the note, flushed it away, and took a shower.

She slipped into José's shirt after her bath and looked into the mirror. "Might as well wear a tent," she muttered, and sniffed, "mmm coffee, and my hair can wait." She hurried into the bedroom and saw covered dishes laid out on a wheeled serving table.

What a jewel Camila must be, she thought, and called out the door, *"Gracias,* Camila."

No answer. Should she go find her? Not yet — not wearing José's tent.

She went back to the table and removed a plate cover.

"Oooh, swell!" she exclaimed, and fingered a bacon slice to her mouth. She lifted another cover. "Omelet — queen's breakfast, no, kings," she said, when she saw fried potatoes and sausage. She slit a roll, tucked in a steaming link, and took a bite. "Truck driver's breakfast. Queen would get too fat." She wolfed a few bites, then settled down to enjoy her meal and wonder just what kind of man José Alvarado might be. The sumptuous breakfast just didn't fit the fastidious José she'd encountered in St. Louis. But last night's José? Yeah, just right for such a man. Gotta find out more about him, she decided, getting up from the table.

She went to the bathroom to comb her hair and, returning, saw that the breakfast cart was gone, the bed made and her clothing laid out upon it. Even her blouse, torn the night before, had been neatly mended, and her purse and shoes looked almost new.

She couldn't help wondering who Camila might be and why she was so secretive. There was something mysterious about José, too, especially his demand that no one know she'd spent the night with his warrior. She couldn't help chuckling at how he'd insisted that she use his apartment, and wasn't that an invitation to poke around? Why were there no outside windows? The gray light from ventilating shaft windows failed to do justice to the exquisite furnishings. She sat at his desk and gazed over the office. Was he married? Did he have a family? She looked for pictures of women — none, and the photographs on the walls were of rodeos and bullfights. One showed José dressed as a toreador with a bull pawing up great clods of turf in the background. Was he a *macho,* a real man? Somehow the image didn't fit her concept of a jeweler. What else might he be?

Books in cases lining the walls told a different story. Encyclopedia Britannica, Harvard Classics, Shakespeare, dictionaries, professional journals, reference books. An entire shelf was devoted to metalcraft, stone cutting, geology, and mineralogy. Aside from the pictures, the office supported his claim to be a jeweler, but was it his primary profession? Might he be a high-class thief? Why had he put the packet they'd salvaged from last night's robbery in his safe?

Slots in a pen holder contained business cards: *Alvarado Silversmiths, El Paso, Texas, José Alvarado, Vice President*, was one. Another read, *Fábrica Alvarado, Platero, Veracruz, Méjico, José Alvarado y Valdez, Presidente.* No wonder he hadn't taken the packet into the consulate. He really was a private businessman, and had he entered the consulate to return the packet the night before, he'd have been considered a burglar himself. Still, she wondered what would become of the packet. Why not ask?

There was another puzzle, too. He'd said that arrogant, red-haired Thompson had rejected her application, and that he'd submitted it himself. Something was fishy. In St. Louis he'd seemed to be debonair, almost happy-go-lucky. He was a fraternity brother of Thompson's and Fred Dilgaard's, who'd dumped Thompson, soggy drunk in her apartment. With friends like that, she'd supposed José was a lush, too. Even then, he'd seemed a cut above the others. Who would have imagined that a jeweler would take on two burglars, even kill them in hand-to-hand fighting? Now the precise organization of his apartment marked him as a man with exquisite taste.

She dressed, opened the door to thank Camila, but the door across the entry landing was locked. She tapped. No answer, so she shouted her thanks and that she was going to the American Consulate.

She secured the door behind her, went down the stairs, and slid open a barred gate opening into a foyer. On her right there was a plaque beside a glass door similarly barred which read, *Platería Alvarado.* She admired the ornate silver craftware in display cases, and pressed her cheek against the wall to get a better view of a filigree bracelet. Her eyes brimmed from thoughts of the hours she'd worked on similar pieces with her mother, a filigree artisan. This wasn't the time to reminisce — not on the first day of a new job.

"Escobas." She heard the vendor's cry when she stepped onto the street, but where was the consulate? The growl of the lighthouse horn cutting through low clouds and drizzle reached her. The consulate was across the street from it, so she set off to follow its groaning.

Maggie found herself on *Avenida Arista,* the consulate street, and saw the building and the coconut palms on the Malecón beyond. A street vendor waved his arm. She raised hers in return, and smiled as she saw him dip milk from a small tank and fill a woman's container — shades of home, like Torreón, she thought.

She sniffed the salt in the gulf air and, exhilarated, quickened her pace past the consulate to the Malecón parkway. Something *thunked* to the ground close by. "Hmm, my first coconut," she mumbled. Stooping to pick it up, she heard the rapid patter of running feet come to an abrupt stop. Turning, she saw a barefoot urchin standing still, eyes glued to her prize.

"Do you want the coco, Chico? What's your name?" she said and saw the boy's eyes widen.

"Paco."

"Here, Paco, take it," she said, then watched him hug it to his chest and scamper off.

She took a last look at the harbor and saw a freighter, its trail of black smoke hugging the water surface as it departed. Where was it going — New Orleans, or maybe to a port in Europe with cargo to support its raging war? She shivered and, turning back toward the consulate, saw Paco and his coco disappear.

Paco was still on her mind when she pushed open the consulate gate. She took a final look at the coconut palms, the ocean beyond, and felt a surge of pleasure. It just might be a swell place to work.

She paused to examine a red bougainvillea espaliered on the consulate wall, then grasped the door latch. Locked. On Thursday at nine o'clock, why would the consulate be closed?

"Oh. Fourth of July," she murmured, thinking it strange that the consulate would be closed when it wasn't a Mexican holiday.

She heard a machine start up inside, thought the gate must have been opened to admit workmen, and knocked.

"Go to the back door," someone shouted in Spanish.

Use that scary path again? Not after last night. Well, maybe, she thought when she smelled gardenias and stepped along the path to admire white blossoms set off by deep holly-green foliage. Farther on, she saw more gardenias along a bowered way, poinsettias and hibiscus arching overhead, other lush plants, their blossoms a maze of color. Picturing how it would look in sunshine, she chanced getting her shoes wet again.

The path took her past a service door then the rear entry. Inside was a wide, dimly-lit hallway reeking of stale kitchen odors. She left the door open behind her for fresh air, and looked in at the first door on her left — a large kitchen. Three women at the far end were shouting in tones of a minor rebellion, each trying to drown out the others and claiming specific instructions from *el patrón* about preparations for an upcoming event. She frowned, remembering she'd been told that neither the consul nor his wife spoke Spanish. Whoever *el patrón* might be wasn't much of a supervisor, she guessed, proceeding to the front entry.

She heard the drone of a machine, then *whap-whap-whap-clunk,* and looked into a spacious room — reception room, she supposed, and saw a man bent forward, fists on hips, staring at a floor polisher.

"*Qué tal*, how's it going?" she asked, lifting her hand.

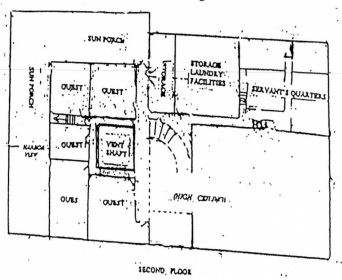

SECOND FLOOR

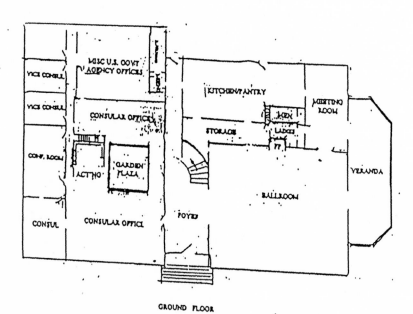

GROUND FLOOR

AMERICAN CONSULATE
VERACRUZ MEXICO

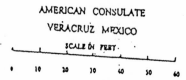

SCALE IN FEET

0   10   20   30   40   50   60

The man straightened, threw out his hands, shook his head, and waved her away.

She grinned and, turning, saw a brass wall plate indicating the consular offices. Suddenly she felt like sitting down, or better yet, running away. Where was the welcome she'd expected? Instead, she'd encountered burglars, death, foul odors in the workplace, bickering, equipment breakdown. What an insufferable place to work.

Maggie forced herself to take in her surroundings. Opposite the front door, a broad marble stairway with gold-painted, wrought-iron railings rose in a quarter circle to the balcony surrounding the vestibule. Across from the offices, and separated from the foyer by a high wide archway, was the high-ceilinged room where the workman was polishing the gleaming terrazzo floor. She strolled in, careful to avoid the machine's power cord. What a grand ballroom this could be, she thought, and wondered what furnishings might be available.

Glancing about, she frowned. Why had the architect spoiled the room with the high, narrow windows which seemed to reject rather than invite brightness from outside? Even the bladed ceiling fans and black wrought-iron chandeliers with their bare lamps had a deadening effect on the gray walls.

A shout from the office area broke into her thoughts. "There's no time for that." A man's voice. "You should have done it yesterday." Maggie heard a woman snort, and the man exploded again. "Governor Gutiérrez will arrive early with that niece he told me about. Food and drink period. Forget the decorations!"

"But . . . but . . ."

"No, and that's final."

Uh-oh, bicker-bicker, and just then Maggie heard the woman grumbling and the slow click of heels over the rumble of the polisher. She peeked around the corner and recognized the plump woman from a photograph she'd seen in Washington as Mrs. Williams, wife of the U.S. Consul.

Maggie approached her. "Mrs. Williams?"

"Yes?" Head bent forward, the consul's wife glanced sideways at Maggie.

"I'm Margaret Magodón, and I've just arrived."

"Oh yes, Margaret, I'd heard you were coming. Could you possibly come back tomorrow? My husband will want to welcome you then but, with our Fourth of July reception this afternoon, he'll not. . ." The polisher roared close by and she shouted, "Boy! Workman! That's enough! Stop that racket!"

The man looked up, grinned, nodded, and went on with his work.

Maggie called out, *"La Señora dice que. . . "* She went on in Spanish to explain that Mrs. Williams thought the floor was very well polished and that he should stop. The man shrugged, shut down his machine and took it away.

Maggie turned back to Mrs. Williams. "If you're entertaining this afternoon, I'd be glad to help. I wouldn't want to intrude, so as soon as guests start to arrive, I'll slide out the back door and be out of your way."

Brow raised, Mrs. Williams stared at her. "That man understood what you said, didn't he? Well, you might help me after all. By the way, child, what do I call you?"

Child. Maggie cringed, but answered pleasantly. "The people here will probably call me Margareta, but friends in the States usually call me Maggie."

"Margareta. How nice. The name lends a distinguishing touch to an office in Mexico, doesn't it? Yes. Margareta. Very nice. Come, I'll introduce you to the servants." Maggie followed her into the kitchen.

"This is Margareta. She will tell you what to do," Mrs. Williams told four women and a young man.

Maggie shook hands with each. *"La Señora quiere que. . . "* She explained that she was to help with preparations, spoke briefly to each person, then returned to the foyer with Mrs. Williams. "You must have a lot to do to get ready," she said, "so let me work with the help to do what I can? How many people will —"

"They're all right here." Mrs. Williams interrupted, handing Maggie a crumpled wad of paper.

"Do you have any special instructions? For instance —"

Mrs. Williams shook her head briskly, darted a glance at the office door, then spoke softly. "This room is like a factory. I want it to look nice, but my husband — well, he —" She broke off abruptly and, traipsing off toward the office area, called back, "See what you can do, child."

Then Maggie heard her call, "Albert, our new girl is a godsend. She even speaks Spanish, and will be such a help for me, I'm sure."

"Child," Maggie hissed under her breath, "new girl, helpful to her. I'd better look out. If she makes me her favorite, every demigoddess in the office'll come at me green-eyed and claws bared. Oh well, better than being on her blacklist."

Who besides the governor might come? What did she have to do? She spread out the crumpled paper, looked and mumbled, "Hmpf, some list — Elsa, Jean, Monday bridge, Governor, usual receiving line, check with Helen." Maggie crumpled it again. Better figure sixty.

She checked in the kitchen — gobs to eat and drink. But the ballroom — god-awful, stark, in spite of a basic elegance. She went into the kitchen and beckoned to a young man drinking coffee. "Come with me," she said. "You're going to help me make that ballroom look like a garden."

* * *

Maggie dumped trash into a container, wiped garden mud from her shoes, and went back into the consulate. She wished she could relax her aching body in a hot tub, but slumped onto a chair instead. She ran fingers through long strawberry-blond hair and plucked her sweat-soaked blouse free of her body. Feeling grubby, she knew she looked a mess as she gazed at what she'd done. Would Mrs. Williams be pleased? Why hadn't the woman even made an appearance to see how the work was going?

Maggie checked her mental list. Wicks had been trimmed, and sconce lamps lighted. Thanks to help from the watchman and errand boy, flowers and

potted plants from the veranda and garden, and furnishings from the offices and storeroom had been arranged so that people might cluster after passing through the reception line. Lamps were positioned to cast soft light through exotic foliage and across the glistening terrazzo floor. Oh, but the floor shouldn't shine. She wished it looked more like sand. Maybe there was too much light.

She got up, closed the draperies and turned off the chandelier lights, causing the depressing black fixtures to almost disappear. Much better. She considered turning off the ceiling fans to get rid of their annoying drone, but dropped the idea. Their noise would be smothered by party chatter.

Time to escape, she decided, but just then someone opened the draperies on the window closest to the foyer.

"Open all the drapes," a sharp-nosed, sandy-haired woman ordered.

Maggie felt the eyes of the woman coursing over her bright tousled hair, mussed blouse, cranberry skirt, and mud stained loafers

"No, leave them closed," Maggie demanded in Spanish.

"Just who are you?" the woman said.

"Maggie Magodón. I just arrived from the States, and I know you're not Mrs. Williams."

"I'm Mr. Williams' secretary," the woman said, and stalked to the next window.

Just then the consul's wife arrived. "How wonderful, Margareta," she exclaimed, bustling up to Maggie. "You've done the ballroom just as I told you to. And yes, the effect with closed draperies is enchanting. Isn't that so, Helen?"

"Certainly, Mrs. Williams." The secretary snapped her eyes at Maggie, then handed Mrs. Williams a sheet of paper. "Here's the guest list," she said. "There will be the governor, senator, congressmen and their wives, and everyone of importance in Veracruz."

"Oh, dear me." Mrs. Williams's hands fluttered. "So many?" She swung around to face Maggie. "Margareta, you're not dressed. Hurry. Guests will be arriving at any instant."

The consul entered the vestibule wearing a tuxedo, and Maggie wished she'd escaped while she had the chance. She had not yet met Mr. Williams, and this was hardly the right time. Both his wife and secretary wore cocktail dresses, and gleamed with gold and jewels.

"But I can't, Mrs. Williams," she begged. "The airline lost my baggage. I don't have anything to wear other than what I have on right now."

"Nonsense, my dear child, there's no reason for you to change. Nobody will pay any attention to you." She stepped back to survey Maggie's attire. "Just go upstairs and freshen up a bit." Head high, she jiggled her portly frame off to the kitchen.

Purse slung over her shoulder, Maggie dragged herself upstairs thinking to tidy up a bit then leave by the service entrance. Aside from the servants, Mrs. Williams and Helen were the only ones who even knew of her presence. Surely, they'd not miss her. She paused on the balcony overlooking the foyer. From there she could see much of the ballroom. Not bad, she thought. The decorating left much to be desired but, considering its former starkness, it looked pretty good. She imagined it filled with people. Stiff-necked men in tuxedos, black ties, piercing eyes, and lofted chins — ladies in shimmering gowns, glittering jewels and hair coiffed high — a regular poodle party.

She giggled and shook her head. It would be fun and she hated to miss it, but surely there would be other such occasions.

She went into one of the bedrooms and stood before the mirror. Could she possibly make herself presentable enough? Hair? Awful. All she could do for it was comb and brush it. And her clothes? She could borrow an iron, she supposed, and perhaps if she waited until people were mingling and personal scrutiny had run its course, she might not be too conspicuous. No, it was ridiculous even to consider. Exhausted, she sighed, kicked off her shoes, stretched out on a chaise longue and dozed.

* * *

A woman's whisper awakened her.

"Señora, it's Señorita Magodón, *peliroja,* hair of fire. The house staff think she's wonderful, and she speaks Spanish."

Maggie sat up. *"Buenas tardes,"* she said. "Am I in the wrong room?" She saw a maid in the doorway beckoning to someone outside, then stared, thinking the person who entered was the most beautiful woman she'd ever seen. Black hair, dressed in black velvet, blue eyes and sapphires sparkling, the woman approached with hands extended. Maggie rose to grasp them.

"I'm Irena Gutiérrez y Montoya," the woman said, "and you must be Margareta Magodón. How nice it will be to have someone in the consulate who speaks our language. But come. One as beautiful as you should be with the guests."

"Oh, Señora, thank you, but I can't go. If only I could look like you."

Smiling, hands clasped, they looked into each other's eyes. Maggie gestured toward her shoes. "See those, and what I'm wearing? It's all I have. I brought a cocktail dress from the States, but the airline lost my baggage."

Irena stepped back, pursed her lips and stroked her chin. "I have it." She rummaged in her purse for pen and paper, and made a list. "Here, Pía," she told the maid, "bring these from the house and take one of her shoes to see if my niece's are nearly the same size."

Maggie couldn't take her eyes off the woman. Señora Gutiérrez seemed genuinely delighted with the prospect of providing a dress. Hmm, Gutiérrez. Might she be the governor's wife?

"Don't just stand there, Margareta — Marga, what do I call you?"

"Either is fine. Mostly I'm Maggie."

"Magi. Como magia. Like magic." Irena cut her name short, as if spelled *mah-gi,* the "g" sounding as in go. "We thought you were lost forever, then heard you'd missed your flight, and now it's magic that you have come. In there. A bath. Your hair, and dry it, *en seguida,* quickly. Pía will help you dress when she returns."

"But Señora Gutiérrez," Maggie protested, "you —"

"No, no, Magi. I am Irena. The gown Pía will bring is very beautiful. You are just right for it, and I am not. My husband does not like me to wear it because it. . ." She raised hands to

John Creighton

her breast and wiggled her fingers. "It is too — too . . . It has not enough dignity for the wife of the governor."

Maggie looked down at herself, then into Irena's eyes. "And what will it make of me, a . . . a . . .? Oh, you know what I mean."

Chapter 4

"Oh my gosh — beautiful — but I can't wear it," Maggie exclaimed, her gaze fixed on the emerald-colored gown draped over the bed as she emerged from the bathroom.

"Si-sí, Señorita," Pía said, turning to her and extending a high-heeled gold slipper. *"Véase,* see, maybe they fit, but how can you compare its size to your shoe with no heel?" She held the shoe up against Maggie's beige loafer.

Maggie tore her eyes from the gown. It was simply gorgeous, and maybe with a few stitches she might — hmm. She reached for the gold-colored shoes, determined to get them on her feet. Her own were just too bourgeois to be worn with the gown Pía had brought her. Just then Irena came back into the room and stood beside Pía. Maggie felt the hush of their waiting, and shared a flush of pleasure from their squeals of delight when her foot squeezed in. She grinned to assure Irena that the shoes were not too snug, determined to wear them no matter how much they pinched her toes.

"They're perfect, Irena, but I don't know if I can walk in such high heels." She put the other shoe on, stood up, and willed her knees to stop quivering as she extended her arms into the dress Pía was holding. Could she keep her balance? She looked down to take a step, gulped, jerked a hand to her breast and slumped her shoulders. "Oh-my-God. I'll nev — I don't dare —"

"No-no, Maggie, never, never do that." Irena snatched

Maggie's hand down and tipped Maggie's chin up with a soft touch. "That's it. Always a regal look, head high with pride, shoulders back, and you will be a delight to every man, and the envy of every woman — especially me. Here, hold still."

Maggie stared at the image of herself in the mirror as Pía put up her hair. Strawberry blond, it complemented the emerald green of the gown. Highlights scintillated on lustrous silk, accentuating her figure and her every movement. Entranced, she hardly noticed as Irena clasped a golden bracelet set with emeralds on her wrist, an emerald pendant around her neck, and emeralds in her ears. Pía finished styling her hair, then applied final touches to her makeup.

What should she do? Maggie breathed deeply. "Oh, Irena, I love it, the dress — everything, but — but —"

Pía, too, ah'd her delight. Irena gazed over hands folded at her chin, admiring her creation. "Just wait until Benancio sees you." She lowered Maggie's hand again. "You are embarrassed, no?"

"I will be when I —"

"No-no." Irena shook her head. "Think only to balance on high heels. In seconds, self-consciousness will be gone. One instant looking into the eyes of the guests and you will glow and be glad for such a gown." Eyes shimmering, head cocked, Irena murmured, "Benancio and I have had no children. But now might we have a daughter? Margareta Gutiérrez y Magodón? Hmm, how would you like that, Margareta?"

"How can I ever thank you? I've never dreamed of wearing anything like this."

"Of course you like the gown. But our daughter?"

"Oh. You're teasing. You hardly know me and your husband doesn't —"

"You would be surprised by what we know about you," Irena interrupted, "especially my husband. Pía, please ask don Benancio to come upstairs. He must be acquainted with his daughter when we present her to Mr. and Mrs. Williams and their guests." Irena picked up her purse. "You have made the dress beautiful, Maggie, so it belongs to you. I cannot wear it. Benancio would be upset if I were to give you the jewels, but we will find others for you."

"But — but — I don't —" Maggie stammered.

The door opened and Pía entered. *"Ya viene*, here he comes."

Irena went out to meet her husband. While she was gone, Pía applied perfume to Maggie's throat and behind her ears. "The men must know you are near," she said, as Irena returned with the governor.

Maggie extended her hand, but Governor Benancio Gutiérrez grasped both of hers. She felt an immediate bonding from their touch and the strength and warmth of his smile. As if by magnet, her eyes held his, and she read in them that he liked her for herself and not just that she was gussied up. I like him, too, she thought.

"My wife told me you were beautiful," he said finally, raising her hand to his lips, "but she scarcely did you justice."

"Gracias," Maggie said. "She's been so good to me."

Still holding her hand, he put an arm around Irena. *"Querida mía,* she's everything you promised — and more." Releasing both, he urged them toward the door. "Many are waiting for us in the office. Come. We'll use the private stairway."

"Gracias, Pía," Maggie whispered, giving the maid a quick hug before following.

They just oozed importance, and no wonder he was a governor, Maggie thought, appraising them from behind. He looked dignified and proud, just as she'd imagined a governor would. His eyes were deep brown and glowing, his mustache and brows black, and his hair iron-gray in color. Dressed in black with a short jacket, white shirt, string tie, and sporting a broad red cummerbund, he fit her image of a Spanish don.

She stood between them at the balustrade overlooking the foyer as Irena indicated a doorway leading to a storage, laundry, and servants' quarters area on the other side of the stairway. She described other features of the second floor, enough so that Maggie was certain that the packet now in José's safe had been thrown from a servant's window. Might a servant have been an accomplice?

"There are five guest rooms around this ventilating shaft," Irena explained, taking Maggie by the elbow. "Mrs. Williams visits with her friends in that nice little alcove above the front entrance."

Governor Gutiérrez urged them to the back stairway. "There's a rather distinguished group of guests waiting for us in the conference room," he said, "a United States senator, two congressmen and their wives."

Maggie held back. "Shouldn't I just meet you downstairs later? Mrs. Williams didn't say anything about —"

Governor Gutiérrez reached for her hand. "I will tolerate no such thing. They are waiting, and a surprise has already been announced. Come."

Maggie followed slowly. Would Mrs. Williams be offended by her appearing in a lovely gown after being told that she had nothing to wear? How would she herself feel? Betrayed, that's how. Would Mrs. Williams ever forgive her? In Washington she'd heard that Mr. Williams was a bit stuffy, but that his wife was something else. A toffee nosed snot, one woman had said. Why had she allowed Irena's flattery to go to her head? What price would she have to pay? Oh, well, too late to turn back now. She'd just have to stay in the background.

The scent of fresh flowers buoyed her spirits, and her thoughts turned to the attractive couple ahead. She hoped the governor would turn out to be as congenial as Irena. She'd noticed a bulge in his cummerbund, and remembered that her father had always had a pistol tucked behind his waistband while in Torreón. Would all the men here carry guns? Ought she to have one, too?

"Remember, Maggie, head high," Irena whispered over her shoulder.

Maggie felt her chest tighten and her confidence ebb with each step as they descended the stairs toward a babble of voices. When they entered a small reception room, chatter ceased, and a wave of self-consciousness engulfed her. She held on to Irena's words — head high, shoulders back, smile. Was she dreaming? No, her toes hurt too much. There were only a few people in the room, all smiling, and when she heard Irena introduce her as their daughter, her anxiety faded.

"Join the crowd," greeted a bald man, heavy and red of face.

"Charmed," the slender woman beside him exclaimed.

Mrs. Williams approached with hands outstretched, and Maggie felt a surge of alarm. The consul's wife had not recognized her and had to be warned. "Good evening again, Mrs. Williams," she said.

"You're most welcome, Margareta," Mrs. Williams said. "May I present — Oh, my goodness." Her hand flew to her mouth. "Margareta. Oh yes." Recovering her composure, she took Maggie's hand. "I believe you have not met my husband. Albert, this is Margareta, the new girl I was telling you about."

"Welcome to Mexico and Veracruz, Margaret," the consul said, shaking her hand. "This is quite a surprise." He introduced Senator Johnson, Congressmen Tyler and Smith, and their wives. "We'll begin the receiving line in the ballroom right away. Governor, you and Mrs. Gutiérrez will be next to us, then you, Senator, and the others."

"I thought you had no children, Mrs. Gutiérrez," Mrs. Williams said as they proceeded to the ballroom.

"Our nieces are like daughters to us, especially Margareta," Irena answered. "And do you not include your family in your parties?"

When Mrs. Williams declined to answer, but turned on her heels and led the way through back halls and the kitchen around to the ballroom, Maggie wondered if Irena might have found a way to contend with the consul's wife. Thinking about it took her mind off her pinched toes and exposed appearance for the moment, but as the receiving line formed, Mrs. Williams pulled her aside.

"That was a cheap trick," she hissed, barely loud enough for Maggie to hear. "Nothing to wear, you said." She jerked a thumb at Maggie's bosom. "Then this! I told you to come as you were. Just you wait. You'll not hear the end of this."

"My blouse was ripped and I . . ." Maggie gulped and clenched her teeth. Just who did this woman think she was to imagine that anyone would attend such a reception in dirty work clothes. And Irena was to blame, too, for upstaging the wife of the American Consul by using a consulate employee to create a scene. Still, Mrs. Williams had no cause to be uppity. Oh well, she thought, as Mr. Williams positioned her in line between his wife and the governor, to pop off would just make matters worse, and she'd better just go along with the governor's daughter sham.

Mired in self-pity, Maggie barely heard Helen announce the first guest, and numbly shook hands until a woman grasped her hand firmly and whispered, "Chin up, Miss Magodón. You're gorgeous, and let's see a big smile."

Maggie forced a smile, saw the woman wink, and just then felt herself pulled back from the line.

"I'm Kyna, Senator Johnson's wife," the woman said as Maggie faced her. "Feel wretched, don't you? Well, Margaret, you just buck up. These shindigs aren't staged for fun. They're work — hard work. All these people are here with a purpose. Now get back in line and do your job."

Job? Maggie watched her sidle in beside her husband, and

just then heard a guest greet the consul in Spanish.

"Thank you for coming," Mr. Williams responded in English.

"So nice of you to come," Mrs Williams echoed.

The man moved on and joined a cluster around the American dignitaries where Irena and the governor were bridging the gap between Spanish and English. Maggie heard a portly guest and his wife, round, rosy-cheeked and even chubbier than Mrs. Williams, introduce themselves, then ask who the visiting dignitaries might be?

"Sí, sí. Mucho gusto," Mr. Williams said.

What a stupid answer, Maggie thought. How can — Oh-my-God, don't be a ninny, she scolded herself. Mrs. Williams had pulled her into the reception line to be an interpreter, and not to punish her.

Maggie spoke briefly to the guests in Spanish, then turned to the consul. "This is the mayor of Veracruz, and I just told him who your American guests were. He and his wife offer to help make their visit pleasant in any way they can."

"Yes, yes, of course. Very nice people. We've met before," the consul said.

"His wife just loves your gown, Mrs. Williams," Maggie told her, "your brooch, too, and wants to know if you purchased it locally."

Mrs. Williams beamed, and Maggie felt a glow of confidence when the consul flashed her a broad smile. From then on, he introduced her to guests as the Gutiérrez's daughter, even to the consulate staff, none of whom had been included in the receiving line. Uh-oh, trouble ahead, she thought. Helen and the others had barely been polite.

"Bellísima, beautiful." José's voice in a whisper.

Eyes alight, Maggie wheeled. "Thank you. I was —"

"Mucho gusto, Señorita. I'm José Alvarado," he sad, clicking his heels and lifting her hand to his lips. "Nicely done,"

he whispered across her hand, "for your own sake, don't let on that we've met before." Louder, he said, "Charming, exquisite, *Señorita*. I look forward to meeting you again."

"Thank you," Maggie said. What might he be doing here? She'd seen him in the room, but why hadn't he come through the receiving line? Why the secrecy? "However I look this evening," Maggie said, "I owe to Señora Gutiérrez." Remembering Irena's advice, she threw back her shoulders, then couldn't help laughing when his eyes widened in response. She took his hands, stepped back, and looked him over. "No one's going to beat you at looking distinguished, but do I detect a slight limp? However did that come about, and how cleverly you brushed your hair to hide the results of your many activities? I trust you were victorious."

"Lay off, Maggie." José's eyes flashed. "I warned you. For your own safety, forget last night."

"I promise," Maggie said, and saw the crinkles return to the corners of his eyes, "but I can't help wondering why."

"Easy," José replied. "Think about how you would answer questions about your arrival last night? Think. With this reception you've won a battle — a conquest — abrupt entry into the elite circles of our city. Don't let that image of your arrival be pushed aside by shady gossip about events of last night."

"Okay, José, but I'm completely bewildered by everything." She waved at Victor Dalpica, who was approaching from the veranda.

"Good evening, Señorita, Señor Alvarado," Victor said, as they shook hands. "A famous silversmith, this *caballero,* Maggie. You must see his work — most exquisite."

"Victor pointed out the sights as we flew in," Maggie explained, after the officer left them. "Who's that tall blond guy talking to Mrs. Williams? He tried to hustle me at the airport yesterday. Uh-oh, he's headed our way."

"Adolf Buehler." José turned to the newcomer. *"Buenas*

noches, Adolf.   May I present Margareta Gutiérrez."   To Maggie, he went on, "Señor Buehler is the Central America agent for the Valparaíso Steamship Line."

Adolf Buehler bent over Maggie's hand. "Adolf Buehler at your service, Señorita."

José took Maggie by the arm. "Now if you will excuse us, Señor, Señora Gutiérrez beckons."

"First, a message from Mrs. Williams, Señorita," Adolf said. "She wishes your attention at once. *Hasta mañana.* I will see you on our cruise tomorrow."

"Thank you, Mr. Buehler," Maggie said. "Please tell Mrs. Williams I'll be just a moment?"

"We're joining Mr. and Mrs. Williams for dinner," Irena said looking up from under furrowed brows as Maggie and José approached her. "You are not invited, but perhaps it is —"

"Whew! What a relief," Maggie cut in. "Is Pía still here? Can I change and leave the dress with her?"

"No-no, Maggie, the dress is yours," Irena said, and faced José. "Suppose you bring Maggie to dinner on Sunday?"

"With pleasure." José bowed.

"But the jewelry?" Maggie said. "I have no place to keep it until then."

Irena hugged Maggie, then backed toward the offices. José will keep them in his safe. *Hasta el Domingo.* Mrs. Williams insists that you work tomorrow, and we must be in Jalapa."

Maggie left José nibbling on leftovers at the buffet table and hobbled on aching feet to Mrs. Williams. "Congratulations," she said. "Your reception was a tremendous success. What may I do for you?"

"Thank you, child." Mrs. Williams jerked her chin toward José. "I want you to tell that man to leave at once. He was not invited, and is never welcome here."

"But — b — b —"

Maggie clamped shut her mouth.

Mrs. Williams waved at the ballroom. "I expect all this to be cleaned up before you leave tonight. Everything must be just as you found it this morning. After all, tomorrow is a work day here." She turned toward the office door.

"Mrs. Williams," Maggie said quietly.

The woman paused, but did not look back. "Yes, child."

"That's so considerate of you, Mrs. Williams, but I suggest you go straight to hell."

Chapter 5

Ingrate! You wretched jerk! Maggie mouthed the words as she watched Mrs. Williams waddle off. Trouble was, she was swaggering, and Maggie felt that she'd belittled herself to the consul's wife. Of course she should not have popped off like that. Still, she'd landed a punch, and supposed the bitch might goad her into doing it again. She kicked off the gold slippers. If her toes hadn't hurt, would she have sassed Mrs. Williams? What difference did sore feet make? No excuse, really. She stalked barefoot into the ballroom, and put them in a corner.

"Something wrong?"

Maggie glanced up. José was nibbling on an hors d'oeuvre and holding an empty plate for her. She didn't answer, but took it and stabbed a toothpick into a tray of shrimps.

"I heard what you said." José offered a bowl of meatballs swimming in a fiery red sauce. "Better watch what you say to Mrs. Williams. She's Madam Big here and if you —"

"I can handle it," Maggie cut in, sure José would never support her against the consul's wife. She waved off the bowl. "What's good? I had no lunch and no time to gorge on these." She gestured at depleted dishes on the long table, then helped herself without waiting for an answer.

"Bang-up reception," José said. "The watchman told me you decorated the ballroom. Won yourself a friend for life."

"He was a big help. All the house staff were, and the best thing was that Mrs. Williams didn't butt in and claim credit until everything was done. Maggie sat down and wiggled her toes. "Oh, that feels good. The shoes belong to one of Irena's nieces, and don't fit."

"Poor girl. Died about a year ago. She was a big disappointment to Irena and the governor, but don't tell anyone I said that. Champagne?" He picked up a bottle.

She shook her head. "Punch, please." She reached for the glass he handed her. "I'm glad you told me about Irena's niece. No wonder Irena was so upset when she heard I'd crashed."

"Something else you should know." José put his empty plate on the table. "I'm not welcome here at the consulate. Mrs. Williams saw us together, and she'll make you pay a price if it happens again."

"She just told me to kick you out. Why?"

"Long story. I'll tell you sometime. Ready to go? I'm going to Jalapa tonight, but will drop you off at my apartment."

"No, thank you. I'll go to my own after I clean up here."

"Let's not go through that again," José cut In. "There's still no lock on the door." He backed toward the door. "Tell the watchman when you're ready to go. He'll have someone take you, and Camila will let you in. I'll pick you up Sunday at your apartment, say eleven-thirty?"

"Wait. The jewelry." Maggie unclasped the bracelet.

"Leave it in my desk drawer for tonight." He wheeled and was gone.

Maggie put the bracelet back on and surveyed the deserted ballroom. How could she possibly move chairs, tables, lamps, and potted plants back to where they'd come from? She hoisted herself up to sit on a table, and let her shoulders slump and feet hang limp. Why had she left a steady job at the aircraft factory to come to this, where she'd already been involved in a robbery and the death of two men? Back there she'd had to ward off men's advances, but was that worse than being ordered about by José and Mrs. Williams? She shook her head and the sensation of emeralds bobbing against her neck was new and swashy. Her fingers caressed the emeralds in the bracelet and necklace, and she burst into laughter. Just imagine, a cleaning lady adorned by thousands of dollars in jewels.

She looked about the room again and thought it looked passable. With a few touches, it could be swell. She'd seen bookcases full of books, magazines, table covers, and knickknacks in the storeroom. She closed her eyes and conjured up images of a game area, one for friendly groups, another where visitors might relax rather than sit on straight backed chairs lined up against the wall. Yeah, why not, she thought. Don't put everything away, just rearrange it.

A servant arrived and began to clear dishes off the tables. Good, she thought. That was one thing she wouldn't have to do. She slid off the table and went to the back door. *"Guardia necesito ayuda.* I need help," she called.

"Ya mismo. Right away," came the answer.

*   *   *

It was two o'clock in the morning when Maggie strolled through the rearranged ballroom, and glanced at what she and the watchman had done. Long serving tables under dark green covers displayed magazines, books, assorted tourist information, and even a set of children's books. Folding screens set aside a waiting room and spaces for group conversation, each furnished with items from the stock room and potted plants from the veranda. The far end was a mini-theater, with a screen, a frontal table and rows of folding chairs.

"The watchman called me," a man's voice came to her from the foyer.

"In here." Maggie stepped from behind a screen. "Oh, Miguel. It's you. What's so funny?" She felt his eyes course over her as he roared with laughter. He turned to take in the room, nodded approval, and looked back, chuckling.

"Ready to go?" he said, then burst out laughing again.

How could such a scrawny little man make so much noise? She caught a glimpse of herself in a long mirror and exploded, too. Sweat splotches marred the emerald green dress,   strands of hair, freed from tortoise combs, hung across her sweat beaded brow. The emerald ear drops, necklace, and bracelet still spangled her.

People sleeping. The thought struck her and she clapped a hand over her mouth. "Shush," she said through parted fingers. "People are asleep upstairs."

Maggie couldn't fault him for laughing, and thought he'd avoided being too familiar quite well. She picked up the laundry bag containing her clothes. "José went to the capital," she told him. "I'm to leave the emeralds in his apartment."

Miguel took the bag from her. "José told me. The governor went, too, but not Señora Gutiérrez. She will pick you up at José's apartment at seven-thirty tomorrow morning."

* * *

"*Gracias,* Camila," Maggie called into the hallway as she left José's apartment the next morning. How did the woman do it? Breakfast, clothes cleaned, she'd done everything as she had the day before except that the stained ball gown had not shown up. She stopped again at José's barred showroom gate to admire his displays, then went out to the street just as Irena's long black Cadillac arrived.

"How did the dawn greet you?" Irena asked, as Maggie climbed into the limousine. She slid open the glass partition to the front compartment and told her chauffeur to go to the consulate, but not to arrive before she signaled.

"Dawn came too early," Maggie answered. "But thanks to Camila, I had a good breakfast, and my clothes were cleaned again. I can't imagine how she gets it all done."

"She's quite remarkable and talented as a silversmith, but cannot talk. Speaking of remarkable, you are, too, Maggie. Everybody loved you last night." Irena closed the compartment panel and leaned back.

"Thanks to you, Pía and the dress. But I upset Mrs. Williams, I'm afraid."

"No-no, think nothing of her. Yes, the costume was a nice touch, but I refer to your poise and friendliness. There wasn't time for us to explain that plans had gone wrong. You see, José was supposed to meet you in Mexico City two days ago, introduce you at the American Embassy, then bring you to our house. We gave up hope when reports of the plane crash listed no survivors. You were fortunate to catch a different flight."

"I was delayed a day — got bumped off the plane in New Orleans."

"We did not know that. When Beno accepted —"

"Beno?"

"Beno, yes, Benancio, my husband. When he accepted Mr. Williams' invitation to the reception, it was on the condition that our niece would be invited, too."

"Niece?" Maggie leaned forward and looked back at Irena. "What do you mean? Surely —"

Irena lifted a hand to interrupt. "When we arrived at the reception, Mrs. Williams asked about our guest. I explained that our plans had changed."

"I don't get this." Maggie continued to stare at the woman beside her. "Did you really expect me? My orders don't include a stop at the embassy."

"José made all the arrangements. He believed it was important to warn you of the conditions at the consulate."

"Why should he warn me? Shouldn't I find out for myself? Why should I trust his advice?" Maggie edged back into the seat corner. "I should think Mr. Williams, certainly not José, would be the one to break me in. José doesn't even work there."

"Trust me." Irena leaned over, her eyes on Maggie's. "José must be in Jalapa today and tomorrow, but he will explain everything on Sunday. Trust him, Maggie. He's not what you think."

"Of course I'll listen." Maggie stifled a yawn. "But I'll have to do the work Mr. Williams assigns."

"You must be tired, and today will tax your patience." Irena pursed her lips as she gazed out at rain-glistened streets. "You were born in Torreón, no? And your mother's name was Gutiérrez?"

"Irena," Maggie cut in, "I thought you were just being nice to me with your talk about daughter and niece at the reception. Yes, I was born in Torreón, and Claudia Gutiérrez was my mother's name. But she was fair skinned and blue eyed, and her hair was the color of mine." Maggie shook her head. "Besides, she was an American citizen."

"Ask José." Irena tapped the signal for the driver to proceed to the consulate. "Did he tell you that Adolf Buehler is a favorite at the consulate? José wants you to find out all you can about the man and his business."

"Oh?" Maggie glanced sideways at Irena. "Why? Is he jealous? Why doesn't he tell me himself? I'm not here to work for José, Irena. After I get started at work, I'll have a talk with him."

Maggie thought of her first night in Veracruz. José had helped her, perhaps even saved her life. But he and Irena had embarrassed the consul and his wife. Had they compromised her chance to succeed in her new job? After all, she was employed by the U.S. State Department, and it would be a serious breach of duty to spy for a Mexican businessman or political figure. Might this niece business be a ploy to gain favor from the U.S. government?

The limousine stopped. Irena leaned toward her and they hugged. "Until Sunday, Maggie. José will pick you up at your apartment."

"I feel like a bean bag, Irena, thrown about without an

inkling of what's going on. Doesn't it seem strange that I should feel at home and welcome in Mexico, but a stranger among the people from my own country?"

"Not at all strange. You did not try to bring your culture with you as most Americans do."

The chauffeur opened Maggie's door and she got out. "Oh." She looked back. "José said I wouldn't be safe at my apartment. Do you know why?"

"Burglars, the two rooms next to yours, Pía told me. Miguel will install new locks today. *Hasta el Domingo."* Irena pulled the door closed.

Miguel again — the man or his name kept popping up, Maggie thought, as she watched Irena's limousine roll away. She pushed open the consulate gate wondering if there might be more than one Miguel, and if Governor Gutiérrez really was her uncle.

* * *

"Good morning, Helen," Maggie said to Mr. Williams's secretary as she entered the consular office.

"Mr. Williams will see you at once," Helen said without even a pause in her typing.

What a welcome for the start of a new job! At least she knew where Helen stood — the consul's eagle eye, honed and probing.

"Good morning, Mr Williams," Maggie said, entering his office. "You wished to see me?"

He waved her to a chair on his right as he picked up a folder. "Yes, sit down, please."

His voice sounded pleasant enough, but Maggie thought it strange that his eyes seemed glued to the file pages.

"Your record shows an examination for Certified Public Accountant," he said. "Did you pass?"

"I'm sure I did very well, but I don't expect to know for another month or two." Why hadn't he looked up at her? He hadn't been evasive like that during the reception.

"Our staff is closely knit, Miss Magodón, each member mindful of the character and deportment of the whole. Hmm." He flashed her a glance, then shifted his gaze to look out the window. "Your room wasn't occupied last night. This morning you arrived in a chauffeured limousine."

Maggie could hardly believe what he'd said, and thought by the way he held his pencil while he tapped it on the desk that he might be a drummer.

"Well?" he said, still avoiding eye contact.

"I'm not aware that you asked me a question, Mr. Williams." Maggie slid forward and, elbows on knees, spoke with quiet deliberation. "I'm twenty-six years old, Mr. Williams, and have supported myself since I was sixteen. I'd like to think you had not made those remarks. As this is our first work conference, I'll try to avoid a confrontation. You're right on both counts. The lock on my room was damaged so I did not stay there last night. Señora Gutiérrez dropped me off here this morning." She pointed to the folder on his desk. "Is that my file?"

He did not answer, but when he covered the upper portion of the front page with his hand, she was sure that it was hers.

"Perhaps you overlooked something," she went on. "My parents met in this country, at Torreón. Governor Gutiérrez was originally from there."

He removed his hand to examine the file again.

Maggie stood up so she could see, too. "My mother's name . . ." She pointed. "Right there, see, Gutiérrez, Claudia Gutiérrez. By Mexican custom, my name is Margareta Magodón y Gutiérrez." She sat down again.

He nodded, then leaned forward, fingers steepled. "I must have missed that. Yes, I see, but Governor and Mrs. Gutiérrez left the dinner early last night to go to the gapitol."

Maggie shook her head. Okay so he was wrong, but this

was her first day so maybe she'd better retreat a bit. Mr. Williams may have backed off a little, too, but he was still scowling. She waited until he met her eyes before answering. "I don't know how you get your information, Mr. Williams, and I don't expect this subject to come up again. But if you must know, the governor did go to Jalapa last night, but Mrs. Gutiérrez did not. She's on her way right now and was kind enough to bring me to work before she left."

He leafed the folder again then looked up. "Well, well. Now that we've cleared up that matter, I suppose you'd like to get started." All smiles, he stood up. "Helen will show you the account files. They're somewhat confused, I'm afraid. Your predecessor was not a skilled bookkeeper. There's one more thing. I want you to spend a substantial amount of time with Mrs. Williams. You'll find it somewhat difficult to adjust to a foreign country. You've impressed her most auspiciously and, since she's already taken you under her wing, she'll be a wonderful advisor for you." He pressed a button.

Maggie heard a buzzer sound in the outer office and stood up. "Yes, sir, whatever you suggest, Mr. Williams." Hold your tongue, Maggie, she told herself, fighting back a retort. "I shall value her guidance, sir," she said.

Did he even know what auspicious meant, Maggie wondered, as she left his office. If his wife had been impressed, wouldn't she have shown at least some appreciation? Or was she one to gloat over the discomfort of those below her social status, believing it boosted her own stature? In that case, Maggie decided, she'd just make sure not to pop off to the woman again.

Helen was on the telephone when Maggie reached her desk. Wasn't she on a high horse though, looking over at her with tilted chin and tight little smile. A fink, that's what she was, the boss's spy, the sort to tattle for her own self-interest. Well, she'd given herself away, and Maggie decided to stay on guard.

She looked over the office and saw that all the desks were occupied save one near the cabinets on her left. It would be hers, she supposed. She'd met two interpreters at the reception, a man and a woman, and the American at the desk in front of Helen. There were four other people: another secretary, a clerk-typist, a receptionist, and an errand boy. Finally Helen hung up.

"Mr. Williams suggested that I —"

"Yes, I know." Helen indicated the filing cabinet corner where the two interpreters had just traded the vacant desk for one of the others. "You'll be over there. Get yourself oriented, and find the entertainment account files." The buzzer sounded and she picked the telephone receiver off its hook. "Yes. I'll tell her," she said, and hung up. "At eleven o'clock you're to take the files I mentioned up to the balcony alcove where Mrs. Williams will go over them with you."

Maggie approached the file cabinets and nodded to the interpreters. "Good morning." They both smiled and the woman took out a cigarette. The man lit it and a cigar for himself, then spoke to the woman. Russian, Maggie thought. The woman answered in German, and Maggie caught the gist of what she said: *"We'll just let her highness have my filthy old desk."*

They both laughed, and the man went back to his work.

Maggie opened a bottom drawer intending to put her purse in it, recoiled at the tobacco odor, and slammed it shut. She got bicarbonate of soda, a bucket of water and rags from the kitchen, and plunked them on the desk in front of the woman interpreter. "Your choice," she said in French. "Make that desk smell and look like new or trade the desks back to where they were. She slapped the man's shoulder. "I understood you, too," she said in Spanish. "Hop to it, *ahora mismo,* right now!" Would Helen interfere? Maggie stared at her, saw her rise, sit down again, and avert her gaze.

* * *

Maggie acquainted herself with the files and, as eleven o'clock approached, carried a box of documents to the stairway.

"Perdóname." It was the errand boy. "I'll take them upstairs for you."

"Gracias." She followed him up, tripped on the top step but recovered. Get your mind on your job, Maggie, she cautioned herself. Tired, sure, but this is your first day and don't you dare flub it.

Maggie was sorting documents into accounts when she heard Mrs. Williams's voice, "She'll be our interpreter so you can ask her about her emeralds on the way."

Maggie looked up from the jumble of ledgers. "Good morning, Mrs. Williams, Mrs. Johnson, Mrs. Tyler. Did you waken refreshed?" She thumbed at the desk. "Mrs. Williams, I'll need your help to unscramble these accounts."

"Not now, dear. You're going with us to get acclimated to Veracruz. We'll dine at a fabulous restaurant north of the harbor — just us four. Mrs. Smith is recovering from the party and won't be with us, and the men will be busy into the evening."

"How wonderful for all of you, but I should get busy here." Maggie waved at her desktop. "Besides, I'm not dressed for it and my baggage hasn't arrived."

"Tut-tut. Your outfit will be just fine and my husband insists that you become familiar with the area. Come along, dear." She swept Maggie's work aside and beckoned Maggie and the others to follow her.

Maggie took a deep breath, blew hard, and trailed along.

Outside the back door, Mrs. Williams indicated a red bougainvillea trellised against the building. "Isn't that beautiful? And look at these." She led them to a cluster of gardenia bushes.

Tangled undergrowth away from the building reminded Maggie of her experience two nights before. She shuddered.

Somewhere back among those bushes, she'd been attacked. She saw a flicker of light, a reflection, and moved closer. Black and shiny, an object protruded from under dead leaves. She glanced at the others. The gardener, rake in one hand, was explaining how he took care of gardenia plants. Casually, Maggie left the path, ducked quickly between bushes and snatched up the object — a pistol. Was it José's? Should she leave it for the gardener to find? No, she'd give it to José or keep it.

Startled by the blare of a horn, she slipped the gun into her purse and looked up as a long black car pulled into the driveway. "Transportation's here," she called.

"Maggie," Mrs. Johnson said when the women drew close, "I asked Sarah if the earrings you wore last night were real. Do you mind if I ask where you got them?"

Maggie chuckled. "Real? The earrings, yes. But the emeralds aren't mine. I believe they're real, but I really don't know."

"Muy buenos días," Margareta." It was a male voice. "You may be sure they are genuine and of most exquisite quality."

Maggie wheeled. Adolf Buehler, who'd tried to intercept her at the airport was opening the doors of his car.

Chapter 6

Maggie backed away to avoid Adolf Buehler's reach and motioned to Mrs. Williams. "You should have the front seat beside Mr. Buehler."

The consul's wife bustled forward and got in.

Careful not to meet their host's eyes, Maggie opened the rear door. "What about a window view, Mrs. Tyler?" she said. "I'll sit in the middle, Mrs. Johnson, because I'll have lots of chances to see the sights."

"Thank you, Maggie," Mrs. Johnson said as she climbed in after Maggie. "Let's forget formalities, shall we? She's Daitha, and I'm Kyna, but just call me Ky."

"Ky it is," Maggie said, thinking that the other two women would never have suggested the use of first names. In terms of husband status, Ky outranked them both, so what could they say?

Adolf closed the door, then glared in at Maggie as he got in. Maggie met the challenge in his eyes with an indifferent stare. Somehow she'd upset his plans, and had irritated Mrs. Williams, too, for she sat stiff backed, chin high, and stared straight ahead as Adolf drove from the grounds.

"Maggie, is there a mystery about your emeralds?" Ky asked. "Don't you know if they're real? They'd be perfect with the dress my husband gave me on my birthday, and I told him I wanted earrings just like them."

Maggie chuckled, thinking that Ky was trying to ease the

tension, and asked, "What did he say?"

Daitha laughed. "Bet he said, 'fake.'"

"Well, not exactly, but his answer was encouraging."

Daitha clapped. "You're kidding. Just what did he say?"

"He said, 'why not, they're just baubles.'" Ky touched Maggie's knee. "What about it? They are real emeralds, aren't they?"

"They're not mine." Maggie flashed Ky a quick smile and leaned forward. "Mr. Buehler, last night Mrs. Gutiérrez lent me some emerald earrings. I heard you say they were genuine. Do you know anything about them?"

Adolf Buehler kept his eyes on the road but cocked his head sideways. "Yes, yes, the very best. My sister's lapidarist in Ecuador cut them. For his wife's birthday present, I got for the governor a very low price."

"Did you come from Ecuador, Mr. Buehler?" Daitha asked.

"Argentina," Mrs. Williams broke in, "and there's his yacht, the *Riesa*." She pointed out a cabin cruiser as the yacht harbor came into view.

"I have a surprise for you, Donna Sarah." Adolf indicated a larger craft moored beyond it. "The *Hedda* just arrived from South Africa — a beautiful ship."

"How wonderful, Adolf." Mrs. Williams craned forward to see better. "But isn't it here a week early? You told me —"

Maggie heaved a sigh of relief and settled back. Mrs. Williams had come off her high horse, so maybe the day wouldn't be so bad after all.

"Yes, yes, so I did," Adolf answered. "I was surprised when she arrived yesterday."

"Oh," Maggie said, but broke off, doubting that the arrival was unexpected. She saw him whisper something to Mrs. Williams, heard a giggled response and, at once, questions she'd had at the reception about the friendship of the two popped into her mind. He had reason to curry favor, but romance?

Ridiculous on his part for a dumpy arrogant woman at least ten years his senior. A glance at the mirror showed Adolf's eyes riveted on her and she piped up, "Watch where you're driving."

She couldn't help grinning when he jerked the car back in line, but suppressed it when Mrs. Williams swivelled to scowl back at her. Ha-hoo — good to know, she thought. Adolf wants concessions from America, but he won't get them if he fans Mrs. Williams's jealousy by making advances toward me.

Maggie smiled when Adolf scurried around to open Mrs. Williams's door after parking. She had to admit that he was handsome, Dark glasses and a navy-blue jacket trimmed and buttoned in brass, together with yellow ducktails spilling from under his jauntily pitched officer's cap really looked natty as he ushered them aboard and into the *Hedda's* salon.

When he excused himself to go up to the pilothouse, Maggie stepped back onto the afterdeck to help get the cruiser underway. She heard the engines start and, when Adolf looked out from the bridge, she called, "I'll throw off the lines."

"Get aboard, Margareta," Adolf shouted.

Maggie paid no attention. "I'll cast the stern line," Maggie called to the deckhand, a barefoot bare-backed boy. He cast the bow line, Maggie, the stern, then both leaped aboard and the craft headed to the open harbor. She picked up the line and, lazily coiling, gazed back at the receding city. Where might — there. She felt a surge of elation as a stained glass dome, one of her father's seven world wonders, rose into the city's rooftop profile near the church on the central square. She'd —

"Señorita."

Maggie turned and saw the deckhand gesture toward the cabin. *"Gracias,"* she said, wishing he hadn't broken into thoughts she cherished, and mounted the steps to the salon where Adolf, perched on the closest bar stool, was talking.

"Specially for you, Margareta," he said, indicating the stool between himself and Mrs. Williams, then went on talking.

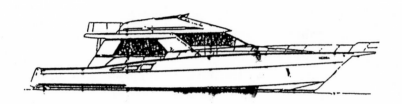

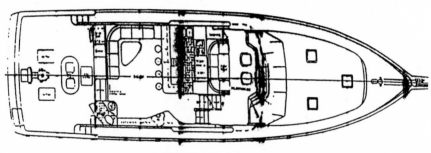

MAIN/PILOTHOUSE DECK

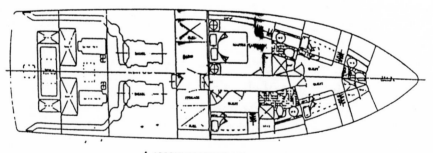

ACCOMMODATIONS DECK

THE CRUISER – *HEDDA*

Sit between him and triple-chin? Uh-uh, Maggie thought, backing against the starboard window with the tray the steward gave her. Munching, she observed the others. Quite a figure, that Adolf— no wonder Mrs. Williams was attracted to him. He spoke easily on subjects the three older women introduced without offering his own point of view, and seemed especially interested in comments regarding activities in Washington, D.C. After all, as the agent for the Valparaíso Steamship Line, whose major cargoes were either destined for U.S. ports or were shipped from them, it must be quite an opportunity for him to influence U.S. government officials through their wives. She steeled herself to stare back in defiance whenever his eyes roved her way. What use could she be to him? He hadn't known of her connection to the consulate when he'd first accosted her, so his interest in her had to be as another skirt to charm and use for his own pleasure. Well, that was then, but now? She'd been introduced to him at the reception as the governor's daughter. Might he now consider her as an intermediary through the governor to influence Mexican business interests, politicians and socially important people?

Adolf was aping President Roosevelt's show of teeth and long cigarette holder, Maggie noticed, as he put a long, straight-stemmed pipe into the corner of his mouth and pointed it up at a jaunty angle. He swivelled on his bar stool with one foot on the floor while describing the island fortress of Ulua at the harbor mouth.

Maggie was finding it difficult to keep her eyes open when she suddenly felt all eyes focused on her, and Adolf speaking around the pipe stem. "It will be a special experience for Margareta, and you may be sure I will see that she enjoys every moment."

Maggie hadn't heard what he was talking about, but his leering eyes and snickers from Daitha and Mrs. Williams put her on guard. Ky's left eye was squinting at her from under a furrowed brow, and Maggie took her quick head shake as a warning to let the remark pass. How dare that man make suggestive remarks.

Bristling, she shot back, "Why don't you light your pipe?"

That got him, she thought when Ky's eyes sparkled. Adolf blushed. The pipe jerked higher and he lifted his chin. He was silent a moment as the *Hedda* swung north, then he gestured at a small island off the starboard bow.

"Sacrifice Island," he told them. "Many years ago, the people avoided epidemics by feeding the dead to the sharks from that island."

Who could ever believe that, Maggie wondered. They'd dump bodies off a boat, not an island. Well, maybe they would if people died there.

"How disrespectful," Daitha exclaimed.

"That's terrible," Sarah Williams added. "Margaret. You're smiling."

What's wrong about smiling? Maggie wondered, but she spoke up. "I was just thinking." She glanced from Mrs. Williams to Adolf. "It had nothing to do with your account, Mr. Buehler, but I remembered that I used to tell wild stories about Mexico to American kids. I was only ten years old and didn't speak English very well." She returned Ky's smile. "My mother had just died and my dad crippled, so I suppose I needed some way to get attention." Disregarding Mrs. Williams's frown and waggling finger, she said, "Someone told me that one of your captains had trouble with the customs office recently, Mr. Buehler. Is he still in jail?"

"False arrest," Adolf snapped. "They could prove nothing." He went on to explain the smuggling charge, arrest, conviction and subsequent pardon of his captain.

Oh-oh. Ky was tapping her lips in warning, and Maggie realized that her backtalk to Adolf must have sounded impudent. She rose, excused herself, went up to the pilothouse, and slid onto the seat beside the helmsman.

"Buenas tardes," she said.

"Good afternoon," he responded in broken English. "Me Afrikaans. No Spanish. Come Africa."

"Magnifico!" Maggie exclaimed, looking about and thinking the pilothouse must be equipped with everything imaginable. An upholstered booth directly aft of the pilot station could seat five or six people who would have broad views through the windows. Adolf must have decided that his guests would prefer to sacrifice panorama for the luxurious salon, galley and bar.

A craft like the *Hedda* would be just what Adolf would need to conduct shipping line business in Gulf and Carribean ports, Maggie supposed, so his duties must require a lot of travel. Had she misjudged him? Might he really have a major role in the Valparaíso Steamship Line organization?

Only hours ago, Irena had told her that José wanted her to find out everything she could about Adolf and his business. Why would Irena think she might spy for José, a businessman? Confusing — sure, she'd find out everything she could, not for José or anyone else, but for her own protection.

Thinking about it, she pursed her lips. Would there ever be a better time to explore Adolf's cruiser than right now? She tapped the helmsman's shoulder, then went through the motions of scrubbing her hands and washing her face. Then she spread out her hands and raised her brow.

The helmsman grinned, jabbed a forefinger downward twice, and turned back to his job.

"Veilen dank," she said in German, not knowing how to say 'thank you' in Dutch or Afrikaans. She went down past the salon where everyone was looking out the far window, and heard Ky ask if an inlet was the place where Cortez had first landed in Mexico.

Maggie missed Adolf's answer and went down into a

gloomy, carpeted companionway on the accommodation deck. She paused a moment to let her eyes adjust, then turned left down three steps and opened the door on her left — storage, no head. Across the passage, she knocked on a door. When no one answered, she opened it and flipped on a switch — telegraph keys, instruments, glowing dials, radio and all kinds of mysterious stuff no cruiser she'd ever seen would ever need. She backed out and closed the door. The throb of diesel engines and a jumble of voices shouting German and Spanish came from farther aft. Don't get into that, she told herself, going forward past the ladder to knock on the first door on her left — no answer.

She entered just as the rattle of keys reached her from the radio room. Quickly, she closed the door then flipped a switch illuminating dim bedside lamps. "Hmm, luxurious," she murmured, hurrying through to the head. When she came out moments later, she paused to examine the cabin. She'd never seen such a large bed. It was high, mounted on drawer cabinets, and the spread was embroidered with two warriors clashing in battle. She turned on a dome light and looked back. The figures looked like the warrior on José's bedspread — Aztec. Why Aztec, when the cruiser had just arrived from South Africa? Maybe José would know. She thought the wardrobe, bureau and woodwork were crafted in teak, oil finished and hand rubbed.

Suddenly she spun about. Was someone watching her? She checked the shower and the shadowed corner beside the bed — nobody. Then she turned, gasped and tumbled backward onto the bed. A face, scary — "My God!," she rasped, as she sat up, "Only a picture. Hideous!"

One eye was monstrous, pale blue and round, the other black through slitted lids, and both were set in deep sockets under protruding brows. Maggie felt trapped, caught snooping by the owl-like eye, with the other poised to enforce the strictures of justice. The man's head was a white dome, hairless except for an arrowhead shaped tuft over the bulbous forehead. He looked like a space demon in a Flash Gordon cartoon, she thought. The lips were scrunched to the side in a taunting sneer. Who could he be?

Heart thumping, she pushed herself off the bed and picked up the golden picture frame. A black plate mounted on it read in golden letters, *Ragnorak Holz, December 25, 1940.*

"Christmas, only half a year ago," Maggie murmured. Christmas present? That? Only a mother could want it and, as old as that man looked, she'd have to be dead. Maggie backed out of the cabin feeling pursued by the owl eye until she closed the door behind her.

Shivering in spite of the muggy heat in the companionway, she paused to compose herself, then looked into two cabins near the bow — crew's quarters. There was still one unexplored cabin, and she opened its door. It was another stateroom, but smaller than the first, and a picture of Adolf hung on the wall. Adolf's cabin, what might she find out about him here?

She opened a drawer — nothing. If this was Adolf's cabin, he was only number two, and not the big shot in the area where the *Hedda* would operate. The master stateroom must belong to the Ragnorak man, and the creature must be Adolf's boss.

A scraping sound outside the cabin door brought her back to reality. She'd been below deck too long and dreaded being caught snooping. Adolf would wonder where she'd been, and may have sent someone to look for her. She sucked in a quick breath, switched off the light and stepped into the companionway. As she closed the door behind her, she heard a click, wheeled, and saw a shaft of light from the master stateroom snuffed by a closing door. Had the person been listening outside her door? Might someone else be spying on Adolf? Someone was in that stateroom. Might El Ragnorak be on board?

She took two steps up to the salon but paused when she

heard voices and the rattle of telegraph keys.

"What does it say?" a man asked in Spanish.

"*El Ragnorak!*" another man exploded. *"No! Nunca! Never!"* Just then a man burst from the radio cabin, swung onto the steps and crashed into her. A piece of paper flew from his hand and she grabbed it.

"Por el capitán," the man squawked, grabbing at it.

"Bueno, I'll take it to him," Maggie said, and scampered up to the salon. Empty. Before going on to the pilothouse, she looked at the message — dots and dashes — nothing.

"Where in God's name have you been?" Sarah Williams demanded when Maggie joined her group in the pilothouse.

"Radio room. That's where I got this." Maggie waved the document. "Mr. Buehler." She pretended to read it as he swung around to face her.

"Yes, Margareta?"

"A message for you. I guess El Ragnorak's coming. Just who exactly is he?"

Adolf's eyes flashed. "Do you understand Morse code?"

Maggie lifted a shoulder and smiled. "Lots of Girl Scouts learn Morse Code," she said, handing him the message.

Chapter 7

Adolf snatched the message, scanned it and swung the cruiser east into the Gulf of Mexico. "Hold it on that compass point," he barked, as he pulled Maggie to the helm-seat then bolted down below.

The scree of gulls, swash of the prow and the rhythmic throb of the diesels engulfed the cabin, the sounds swollen by contrast to the abrupt silence following Adolf's departure. Maggie felt a surge of elation, of power from Adolf's reaction and the response of the cruiser when she veered starboard then port and back to the course.

"Well, Margaret," Mrs. Williams said. "We're waiting. Just what was that all about?"

Just don't let that woman spoil the moment, Maggie thought, answering with only a shrug.

"Do you really understand Morse code?" Ky asked, rising to stand beside Maggie.

Maggie shrugged again and mumbled, "I was a Girl Scout."

"So what?" Ky looked at Maggie from under raised brows, and lowered her voice when Maggie brushed a finger across her lips. "You have a foxy way about you. You mean no, don't you?"

Ky was smiling, and Maggie whispered, "I can tap out S O S. I'd just heard a man say he was afraid of El Ragnorak. The message I gave Adolf was all dots and dashes, and I must have hit the right button when I guessed what the message was about." She relinquished the pilot seat when the helmsman took control and swung the craft to its former course.

A short time later Adolf returned. "What luck," he said, relieving the helmsman, who went up to the boat deck. "Catrina, my sister, is arriving on one of our ships this evening."

Ky leaned forward. "Is your sister the emerald lady I've been hearing about, Mr. Buehler? I want to meet her."

"Yes-yes, emeralds, Catrina's favorite. We will meet the ship on the return to Veracruz this evening. My sister will be happy to make your acquaintance. Most charming lady, and very beautiful."

Maggie heard a dull *thump* as if a heavy object had fallen onto the boat deck above them. What could the helmsman be doing up there? She'd counted only a crew of three, the steward, helmsman, and deck hand. Might there be a fourth, an engineer doubling as a radio operator? Adolf could probably handle the cruiser himself, but would need at least one and probably two crewmen to keep the vessel shipshape.

Maggie was looking out the window thinking about the advice she'd received from the FBI in Washington to keep her eye peeled for any Nazi activity when she saw the helmsman climb down and disappear aft. He was Afrikaans, and had just told her he'd brought the *Hedda* from South Africa. Why would he bring it to Adolf, a German born in Argentina, and working for a Chilean steamship company? Who was El Ragnorak — Ragnorak Holz? The timing of the *Hedda's* arrival suggested that it was intended for El Ragnorak's use, and not Adolf's. How come Adolf's sister was arriving at the same time and on the same ship? The way Mrs. Williams was fawning over Adolf might mean that she was in cahoots with him.

There were so many questions, but was there a connection to Nazis? Still, she couldn't believe that so many things happening at once could be a coincidence, and decided to discuss the matter with Mr. Williams. Dare she trust him when his wife was so openly chummy with Adolf? Maybe it was best to say nothing, a lesson she'd learned back at Douglas Aircraft in St. Louis when nosing into executive matters had cost her two promotions. You'd better mind your own business, she thought, and forced her mind to consider what she might wear at the governor's mansion on Sunday.

But the ghastly face in the picture came back to haunt her. Did José Alvarado know of El Ragnorak? Obviously Adolf did, and might his connection with the man be what José wanted her to find out?

She stood up and looked out the window, but couldn't shake the doubts in her gut. Adolf's sister employed lapidarists, essential to the jewelry industry. José was a silversmith, manufactured jewelry, so might be associated with Catrina, Adolf, or both? Might José be trying to drive a wedge between brother and sister, or might his interest be romantic?

She excused herself, and crossed in front of Ky and Daitha to look out at the jungle shoreline.   .

"We will turn into Rio Antigua where those fishing boats are clustered," Adolf told her, motioning to the others to approach the window. "Cortez landed in 1519 about a kilometer up the river. You will see the ruins of his house in Antigua, and the first church built in the Americas."

The cruiser rounded a sand spit into waters muddied by the rain-swollen river. Maggie wished she had a camera to get a picture of the helmsman on the foredeck swinging the sounding lead with a flock of white egrets rising from a marsh in the background. The egrets circled southward, leaving a great blue heron poised on one leg as a lone sentinel.

"Well, I declare," exclaimed Daitha, as a dwelling atop bamboo poles came into sight on a low plain on their left. "Do you suppose people really live in that?"

"Oh yes," Mrs. Williams said. "See, there's the woman hanging up her laundry. She does her wash in the river, too."

Hardly in salty tidewater, Maggie thought, noting a winding stream near the shanty. Let it pass, she decided, and called Ky's attention to the coconut palmed riverbanks. Farther upstream, the river narrowed to about sixty meters and foliage took on the deeper green of the predominantly ceiba forest. "Quite a place – acres and acres," she said as a clay colored wall appeared on the north shore.

"Adolf." Ky pointed. "Who owns that hacienda?"

Adolf gave it a quick glance. "Probably an old family in Mexico City."

Maggie sat down again and dozed to the sound of pursuing gulls, murmuring voices and the diesel's rhythm. Presently the engine throb slackened, the gulls lifted their scree to an even higher pitch, and the women stopped talking. Maggie roused herself to look out the window. A walled compound with a landing on the north shore caught her attention as Adolf took the cruiser past, then swung around to approach against the incoming tide.

"Antigua," he announced, maneuvering the *Hedda* close to shore.

The deckhand shoved a plank ashore, then crossed over to hold the craft with a pike pole while the women disembarked. Adolf spoke softly to Mrs. Williams before helping her up the bank to a plaza paved with keyed brick flagstones, and bordered by vendors' bamboo shacks.

"Look over there, ladies." Adolf indicated a reposing elephant-like gray hulk bending up into a tree at its end. "That is the very ceiba tree to which Cortez moored his ship when he landed in 1519."

"Rope that long must have tripped a lot of people," Maggie said.

Sarah Williams cleared her throat.

Maggie flicked a glance that way then at Adolf, who had wheeled to face her.

"The tree was close to the river at that time," Adolf growled.

Prickles of pleasure flowed through Maggie at the thought that she'd rubbed raw nerves in them both, and she turned toward the Cortez tree to hide a grin.

"Watch it, Maggie. That wasn't funny," Ky whispered, taking her by the elbow. "You didn't pay attention when Adolf explained that the river has moved about two hundred feet south since Cortez's time, and the gulf shoreline is about a kilometer east of where it was then." Ky hustled Maggie toward the giant ceiba. "If you expect to live the life of a diplomat, you'd better act like one. Sarah's burning up, and Mr. Buehler just stumped stiff legged back to the cruiser."

Maggie felt her face burn, and murmured an excuse. "Adolf's so arrogant. He reminds me of a man I detest, and her highness has been riding me ever since I got here."

"You're missing the point, Maggie." Ky spoke in a low tone while taking in the grotesque shape of Cortez's tree. "Sarah and Adolf are predators and thrive on mistakes others make. Every time you rise to their bait, you give them a victory."

"I never thought of it that way because I've always had to fight for everything." Maggie pretended to read a sign describing the tree, but was thinking that she had much to learn from Kyna Johnson about how to get along with politicians. "I suppose you're right," she said. "I'll try to patch things up."

She beckoned to an urchin selling postcards, bought one, and approached Daitha and Mrs. Williams. "Would you like a postcard of the tree?" she said. "The little boy over there has several views of Antigua, but all the captions are in Spanish. I'll be glad to translate for you."

Daitha wiped her brow with a handkerchief. "I'd like to see those cards. My gracious, it's hot. We'll just sit here and look at them."

Maggie glanced at Mrs. Williams, who was watching the

Hedda pull away from the dock. She couldn't believe that the two women would tolerate the noise and persistence of hawking children much longer. An old building with a Hotel Ceiba sign just past the Cortez tree had shaded tables in a courtyard surrounded by a low, white wall. "Would you care for something cold, Mrs. Williams?" Maggie said. "It's shady in the hotel courtyard and these little hucksters won't bother you there. Come on. I'll order something for you."

The women followed her to a table, and Maggie went into the hotel to find a waiter. When she returned, she heard one of three men seated at a nearby table make an off-color remark about gringo women. The men laughed, and Maggie paused beside their table.

"Buenas tardes, Señores," she said, and went on in Spanish. "Would you like me to translate your story for my friends?" She couldn't help grinning when the taleteller's face turned crimson and he started to rise. "Please don't get up," she said, motioning him to remain seated. "If you tell my friends about Antigua and this hotel, I will be glad to translate for you."

"Gracias, Señorita," another man said, chuckling. "All of us speak some English. What would you like to know?"

A waiter came to take orders. The men pulled their table closer, and conversation flourished. Maggie felt both surprise and shock a few minutes later when Mrs. Williams said, "This old hotel is so picturesque. As often as Adolf has taken me to his hacienda, why hasn't he brought me here?"

Ky pushed back her chair. "I came a long way to call on that old war-horse Cortez. If you'll excuse me, I'll —"

"Me too," Maggie broke in and, when Mrs. Williams waved them away, got up to go with Ky.

Maggie could hardly wait to get away. "Wasn't Mrs. Williams disgusting?" she whispered. "Can you believe she'd be so brazen — practically bragging that she was playing around with that man.

"You mean what Sarah just said?" Ky paused to let a football bounce past.

"Quite clever."

"Clever?" Maggie drew up short.

Ky stopped, too, then went on. "I mean it, Maggie. She's a strong woman in spite of her frumpy appearance. She does and says things that seem childish, thoughtless or rude, but over time she gets her way." Ky indicated a bench shaded by an immense banyan tree. "Let's sit here a moment."

"I was shocked," Maggie said as they sat down. "What could be clever about the wife of the American consul announcing that she's fooling around with that skirt chaser?"

"Maggie." Ky got a postcard from her purse to fan her face. "Sarah knows Mr. Buehler's a womanizer and she can read you like a book. She was telling you to steer clear of him because he's dangerous, he's hers to deal with, and if you don't toe the mark, you're gone."

"She didn't say anything like that, Ky."

"Real meaning usually lies between the lines, Maggie. With that remark, Sarah told all of us that she can get away with anything. Adolf will hear a blown up-story about it, and know that he has a price to pay if he's to expect favors from our country. Daitha knows that Sarah's open to schemes to bring herself advantages and that the door's open for her to gain, too. The three locals know she can be reached and can be persuaded to give favors, but probably not much more than that. For herself, she's let the local people know that they'll answer to Adolf unless they cater to her. That's about it."

Maggie shut her mouth, barely aware that she'd been listening while looking like a dimwit with her jaw hanging loose. She leaned forward, forearms across her knees, and turned her head to Ky. "I'd never have dreamed any of that. But you haven't told me what you understood."

"I've seen your files and know about your mother." Ky

pressed Maggie's shoulder to straighten her up, nudged her knee and, when Maggie brought her knees together, went on. "Your mother was Mexican and would have urged you to sit and walk and talk with dignity. No, I haven't told you what Sarah's words meant to me. You're not going to drop the subject, are you? I'd rather not believe my thoughts, but here goes. Albert Williams has the title, but Sarah is the real consul in Veracruz. She's your real boss, and she won't let anything get in her way."

After a moment of silence, Ky went on. "You've got a great deal going for you, unusual poise, and you're a striking woman. You've gotten yourself dumped into the world of diplomacy, international to an extent, and full of intrigue. May I suggest that if you're to survive, you'll have to learn to smile through your anger and laugh through your tears. That's the first step. Now let's have some fun. I've wanted to see this place for ages."

They got to their feet, and strolling the cobblestones beside Ky, Maggie felt proud to be her friend.

"Look at that, Maggie," Kyna exclaimed as they approached the Cortez ruin surrounded by a low, jagged wall. "Isn't nature something to grow trees beside those high walls so they won't fall down."

"Banyans — upside-down trees," Maggie said. "My dad told me that the mama tree sends roots down from its branches. The roots swish around until they find a nice piece of dirt where they'd like to live. If they can dig in, they become baby banyans, and mama suckles them while they send out their own little rooties and grow into banyan kids."

"How delightful! You must have loved your father very much."

"My mother, too, Ky — both of them born to teach." How nice of Ky to say that, Maggie thought as they passed a weathered Spanish cannon in front of the ruin. "I'm not sure," she said, "but I think my mother met my father here in the

Cortez house when she tripped and dad caught her as she fell. I'm going in."

"Me, too, but don't fall," Kyna teased. "There's no dashing cavalier to catch you."

"Oh, you," Maggie said, laughing as they went in to explore.

Presently they left the ruins and went down the cobblestone street to a small white structure, where a plaque read, *Ermita del Rosario*, and Maggie translated a description claiming it as the first church in the Americas. It was surrounded by a wall which dipped to about four feet high in a series of swaybacks between six-foot-high pillars. The side windows of the church were arched, as was the central entry. A bell tower above the entry had two bell ports at one level, and another centered above them under an arch at the top. In the courtyard, they counted out the fourteen steps of the way to the cross, a mosaic crafted of Talaveras tile.

"Shall we go in?" Ky said.

Maggie turned toward the door in answer. They entered and, as they sat down on an old wooden bench, she heard a baby crying. A hunger cry, Maggie thought, as the murmur of voices took its place. Seated beside Ky, Maggie felt that bonds were forming between them. "Just think," she whispered, "people have worshiped here for over four hundred years."

"Señorita."

A whisper, and Maggie felt a light touch on her shoulder. She turned and saw the *Hedda* deckhand beckoning as he backed toward the entry. She slid from her seat and followed.

"The señor said you should have dinner at the Hotel Ceiba, and he will meet you at the plaza just before dark."

"Tell Señor Buehler we will do as he wishes." Maggie gave the boy a peso. It was too much, but her only coin.

"Gracias, Señorita." He examined the glistening coin lying flat in his palm, looked up at her with a broad grin, then proudly walked away.

Maggie hurried back to Ky. "Follow me," she whispered, then dashed out to the front corner of the courtyard from where she could see the boy trudging barefoot on the cobblestones. When he was about two hundred yards away, a gate opened, and she saw Adolf grab him by the shoulder, and jerk him behind the wall.

Just then Ky came up behind her. "What's this all about? Why the rush?"

"See that wall just past the buildings and the wooded area?"

"Uh-huh."

"Look familiar?"

"Why should it? Oh. You mean like that big hacienda we saw from the river?" Ky turned to Maggie, frowning. "You mean it looks newer than anything else?"

"Yes, but remember what Adolf said, that it belonged to someone in Mexico City." Maggie pursed her lips. "Well, I just saw Adolf there."

"Oh-oh!" Ky exclaimed. "Did he see you?"

"I'm not sure," Maggie said. "Oh, do you mean that Mrs. Williams might think Adolf and I had — Hmpf. Let's go back through the hotel. The proprietor can tell Mrs. Williams about Adolf's plans."

"You're learning," Ky said, chuckling.

* * *

That worked out just right, Maggie thought, when the hotel owner appeared at their table in the courtyard, bowed to Mrs. Williams, and escorted her group to a table in a private alcove off the dining room. *Chipachole de jaiba*, a crab chowder, was served at once.

Maggie gazed at her companions, sensing that they shared her approval of the hotel and restaurant. The walls depicted colorful village scenes. Air circulated by long bladed ceiling fans relieved the muggy heat. The place settings were cobalt blue, the glass and candelabra, crystal.

Salpicón de jaiba, a blend of shredded crab, herbs and onion, followed the soup. Then came a choice of red snapper baked in a tomato-chile-caper sauce, or seafood stuffed coconut.

They were sipping coffee after their meal when the owner announced that Adolf's cruiser had arrived.

"I don't know why Adolf's acting so strange," Mrs. Williams grumbled as they hurried outside where three boys with lanterns were waiting to take them to the *Hedda*. "He knew you wanted a tour of his hacienda, and he never let you see it."

"Perhaps he had to change plans because his sister was arriving," Ky said.

"Fiddlesticks." Mrs. Williams shot Ky a frowning glance. "Imagine letting his sister upset our plans." Sarah Williams looked back at Maggie. "You took care of the account, I presume."

"Yes, Mrs. Williams," Maggie said, determined to make sure that Adolf's treat did not appear on the woman's entertainment account.

"Mr. Buehler may have an emergency, Sarah," Ky said. "We do have to rendezvous with the ship to pick up this emerald woman. I'm determined to meet her."

"How exciting. Oh, shoot," Daitha said as she stumbled and almost fell. "Just think, we're going to rescue an emerald princess on the high seas."

Maggie couldn't even squeeze out a chuckle at the remark and, when no one spoke, supposed the others thought it trite, too. She looked ahead to the *Hedda,* and saw a man in shirt-sleeves rolled to his elbows duck behind a large object on the deck. She couldn't be sure in the darkness, but his hair looked tousled and blond. Was it Adolf? He'd never let Sarah Williams think he'd do physical labor — not in this culture where men of his stature just did not do such a thing, but it was Adolf who appeared moments later in jacket and cap to light their boarding with a flashlight and direct them to the pilothouse.

"*Ténga prisa,* hurry," Adolf snapped when Maggie dallied on shore to look at a large black object looming above the cowling on the boat deck.

"I'll throw off the lines," she offered.

"*Nein,*" Adolf barked, waving her aboard with short, choppy strokes.

That was the first time he'd been rude, she thought and, passing a tarpaulin covered mound on the afterdeck, caught a glimpse of his sweat covered forehead. The *Hedda* had barely paused to pick them up and was already turning to go downstream when she reached the salon and the steward told her to take a tray of snacks to Mrs. Williams in the pilothouse. Why the rush? Mrs. Williams was right. Something was fishy about Adolf.

Maggie paused on the steps to wrap two cookies in a napkin. The women were seated around the map table and barely glanced at her when she placed the tray before them. She reached for a cookie, then took the wrapped ones to the helmsman. Nibbling, she saw Ky motion her to a seat. Just then Adolf appeared, and she signaled to Ky that she was going below.

Why was her heart pounding? Trouble was — she really didn't have to go to the head and her heart wasn't buying that excuse to see the Ragnorak picture again and look for clues to Adolf's changed behavior. Besides, except for Kyna Johnson, she just wasn't one of their group — only an interpreter — well, to Adolf, a prospective playmate.

Scared, sure, but act bold, she thought as she reached the lower deck. Pausing to adjust to the darkness and musty smell, she felt chills shoot up her spine when footsteps sounded on the deck above. She grasped the stateroom doorknob. Locked. Quickly, she ducked into the second stateroom. Geez —

someone was watching. Now don't get into a blue funk, she told herself. That weirdy-spook picture is in the other room. She switched on the light and turned. Oops — woman's shoes on the bed, and there was a valise, too, a woman's. Clear out!

She went out and was searching for the light switch when the helmsman backed into the dim light of the passage from the master stateroom. Maggie waited quietly, thinking he would turn on a light, but he stepped back and bumped into her.

"*Gott am Himmel*," he exploded, stumbled and almost fell.

"Careful," she said softly, pushing him erect. He was a small man, so she was surprised to feel that his body was hard and muscular.

"Auf," he grunted, squeezed past her and went into the radio room.

Now what? She'd caught him red-handed. Was he spying, too?

*   *   *

Maggie returned to the pilothouse and paused to avoid crossing between Sarah Williams, seated in the second helm-seat, and the women at the low table. A moment later, Adolf summoned the helmsman to the wheel and went below. Sarah joined her friends and Maggie went to the port side to watch the arriving ship swing into a long turn. Blinded by its searchlight, she could barely see the platform and boarding ladder being lowered, and the ship's name, *Olinda*. The two vessels eased together, and she saw Adolf jump to the platform and climb to the ship's deck.

"*Fraulein.*" The helmsman beckoned Maggie to the wheel, directed her to hold the cruiser steady alongside the ship, then went below. Moments later, he appeared on the foredeck to throw a mooring line, and Maggie wondered why the deckhand was not doing it. Once the cruiser was secured, the helmsman returned, adjusted the controls to hold his craft in place and went up to the boat deck.

Maggie followed and, standing on the ladder with only her head and shoulders above the deck level, she watched the helmsman adjust a sling around the black mass she'd seen from the dock in Antigua. She heard a donkey engine chatter, saw a hook descend slowly from the night sky, the helmsman grasp it and loop the sling to it. Then he waved with a circular motion, and she heard him warn her to go below. She went down a step, heard the donkey engine again, and looked back to see the black shrouded mass lifted into the night. She gasped. Something — somebody was struggling inside the cover of that black mass.

Might the deckhand be trying to stow away on the ship? Had the helmsman helped him, why? What might be inside that black mass? If only she spoke Afrikaans she might persuade the helmsman to share what he knew. Just then she heard the donkey engine, and saw an object about the size of a bathtub lowered gently to the boat deck almost within arm's reach.

Then she saw Adolf descend the ship's boarding ladder. Close behind came a woman with platinum blond hair flowing from under an officer's cap onto her long, black cape. They'd gone below Maggie's line of vision when the donkey engine chugged again. The lines stretched taut, rolling the black box onto its side. Instinctively, she threw her arm across her face, but a cable jerked out from under the box and whipped across her forearm. As she pulled her arm back and ducked away, she saw a tall, thin man in a blood-red cape and matching wide-brimmed hat descending the ladder. He stumbled, caught himself but lost his hat into the sea. Maggie gasped. The man's head was immense — bald but for a tuft of hair above his forehead — El Ragnorak!

Chapter 8

Maggie's hands slipped on the railing, but she hung on and groped with her foot for the step below. Why wouldn't her eyes shift from that glistening bald pate and the long red cape swaying in hypnotic rhythm with each step he took. Finally, he sank from her sight, and her breath came back, pulsing, gasping.

Who was El Ragnorak to have such power over her? Get your feet on the ground, Maggie told herself. He's just another man — two legs, two arms, a body. You let yourself get caught off guard because you didn't believe a real person could be as grotesque as the face in the picture.

Confident again, she looked up, sucked in a steady breath and saw the helmsman put his foot into the cargo hook, wave a signal and rise into the black of night. Then he came into sight above the afterdeck, and she saw him lowered slowly until he vanished where she'd last seen El Ragnorak.

Think, think, Maggie urged herself. Get that Ragnorak off your mind. He tried to catch his hat but lost it, so he's human — just another man. She heard low-pitched voices and at once the floodlights went out leaving only a single lamp to illuminate the afterdeck. Why would they douse the lights unless Adolf, El Ragnorak and Catrina were determined to keep their operation secret?

She heard women's voices from the pilothouse below where lights were still bright. Oops! She was a silhouette in the hatchway to anyone on the ship. Go up? Go down? All the action was up, she thought, and rolled onto the boat deck. She heard Adolf bark an order. The helmsman snapped back. Adolf cursed and Maggie just had to see what they were doing. She wormed through the space between the lifeboat and bathtub-size black box to where she could peer down on the afterdeck. Adolf and the helmsman, both bare chested, were removing the tarpaulin cover from cargo crates. She held her breath, hoping they wouldn't look up as they piled crates on a sling then looped the sling's corners onto the cable hook. Then she saw Adolf raise his arm, point up and rotate his hand. A donkey engine woke up and she heard the clatter of rigging as she eased herself back out of their sight to watch the cargo rise, become a shadow, and swing onto the freighter.

Only moments passed before a coffin-like crate appeared over the cruiser's afterdeck and Maggie judged from their effort and caution when Adolf and the helmsman eased it into place, that it was heavy and of high value. Three more like it were swung on board, then mooring lines splashed into the sea, and the vessels drifted apart.

"Hot diggety dog — smuggling, and I caught 'em at it." Maggie mouthed the words, suppressing her excitement at catching sight of Adolf performing an operation he obviously intended to keep secret. For him to engage in physical labor, stripped to the waist and glistening with sweat, was hardly conventional, and especially damning because a crew was available to do it. Were El Ragnorak and Catrina keeping the other crew members below deck to prevent them from witnessing the cargo exchange? Was the helmsman the only one Adolf trusted? What had Adolf brought from Antigua to the freighter, and how might she find out what those four crates on the afterdeck contained? Damn. What would Adolf do to her if he caught her spying?

She scooted back to hide between the bathtub-size box and lifeboat. Too late. The helmsman appeared right beside her, pushing the cruiser free of the freighter with a pike pole as he worked his way forward along the narrow side deck. Wide eyed, she felt a ray of hope. He was facing the freighter, and might not have seen her. She made herself as small as she could, slowly sucked in a deep breath, and held it until he reached the foredeck and disappeared behind the boat deck cowling. Then she blew hard, relaxed, and scrambled on hands and knees to the hatch.

"Ekskuus."

It was the helmsman's voice and, with it, Maggie heard the thud of feet landing beside her, felt herself toppled over and her head hit the deck. Groggy, she looked down into the hatch where the helmsman had gone, and saw him bounce his finger against his lips, point up, shake his head, and touch his lips again.

"Maak die deur toe," he said softly indicating the hatch cover with a sweep of an arm, then was gone.   ·

Head throbbing, Maggie eased herself back onto the deck, wishing all those darting stars would stay put. She tried to block them out with her forearm, but could not. She still felt cold sweat on her forehead, and wished the cruiser would stop rolling in the offshore swell. She felt her stomach get queasy, and saliva filling her mouth. Dear God — getting seasick. She pushed herself up to sit on the edge of the hatch and shook her head to clear it. Then she heard the diesels roar and the shush of the sea as the cruiser got under way. Good. She turned her face to the wind and felt better.

"Oh God," Maggie murmured, overwhelmed by the predicament she'd gotten herself. Why hadn't she hidden until the helmsman got back to the pilot seat? He would talk, and how could she explain to Adolf what she'd done?

Well, she couldn't just sit there. Looking down, she saw the steward come up from the lounge with a tray of drinks.

She groped for the ladder with her foot, found it and slowly

started down. Looking back up, she slid the hatch-cover shut.
When she looked down her head spun and she saw the
pilothouse deck come up to get her. Stars flashed again. She
rolled her head, felt her nose, blinked and looked at her hand.
Bloody.

She shook her head and focused her eyes, but now her arm
hurt. Worse, she heard Adolf bellow something in Africaans
from down below.

"Ja, ja," the helmsman yelled back, suddenly kneeling
beside her. On and on he grumbled at Adolf in a throaty growl
as he helped her to her feet.

Maggie smiled in spite of her aches. The helmsman had
hustled from the helm to help her, and must be venting cooped
up profanity at Adolf. Then she heard Adolf shout in English.

"What's wrong up there?"

Maggie flashed the helmsman a smile, motioned him back
toward his seat, and yelled back. "I fell down and bloodied my
nose and nothing's wrong."

Silence below, but the helmsman looked back at her and
winked just as Ky appeared with napkins and a bottle of soda.

She handed Maggie a napkin dampened with soda. "Not
much blood," she said. There's a bit on your face — mostly
your arm." She dampened another napkin. "Tend to yourself
while I sponge off your blouse."

* * *

Freshened, hair combed, Maggie followed Ky to seats in the
pilothouse. Mrs. Williams and Daitha looked up, then went
back to their chatter. Maggie took the coffee Ky offered, closed
her eyes, and the thought that El Ragnorak was aboard came
back to haunt her.

She was aware of the women's voices, her name spoken,
then a hush. Determined to appear serene, she shook her head
and looked up. Everyone was staring at her and, in the cabin's
subdued light, she imagined El Ragnorak's visage in each

countenance. She heard Ky's voice again, concentrated on her words, and the envisioned face faded.

"Did you hear me, Maggie?" Ky repeated. "Are you all right?"

"Oh, sure." Maggie shook her head again. "I must have been daydreaming." She sipped from her cup, thinking of how to turn attention away from herself. Just then, she heard voices from the stairs behind her. "I heard talking down below," she told them. "I was trying to decide what language they were speaking,"

Sarah Williams went into a discourse on Adolf's language skills, but Maggie concentrated on the voices coming from the lower cabin.

"It is arranged then? They are here?" a woman asked in Spanish.

"Three," Adolf said, "Mrs. Williams and two others, rich and eager to buy. There is also a young one, pretty but poor."

"Get rid of her," the woman snapped.

"You don't speak English, so you need her to translate for them." Adolf changed to German, and spoke too rapidly for Maggie to understand.

So Adolf had arranged this meeting between his sister and three rich women. Was his purpose to sell emeralds, to gain favor with influential husbands through their wives, or might there be some other reason? She heard Adolf's voice in Spanish again — close, probably from the salon.

"The young one's name is Margareta Gutiérrez, the governor's daughter, and she works in the American Consulate."

"You're crazy. Irena has no children," the woman said.

"A niece, perhaps, or adopted, but to Irena and Beno, she's their daughter."

"Ah-ha, connections. I see. Influence. But you do not fool me, Adolfo. Beautiful, not just pretty, no?" The woman laughed lightly. "Well then, I must meet these charming people.

Coming?"

"They are expecting you," Adolf said. "I'll check for messages, then join you."

Maggie turned her mind to José's request to dig into Buehler's affairs. She'd never allow herself to be José's stool pigeon and betray the Buehlers or anyone else in order to further his business or romantic interests. But Adolf's strange behavior and the transfer of cargo at sea piqued her interest. Besides, she'd fallen in love with Irena's emeralds and wanted to meet the woman who had provided them.

"Buenas noches, Señora Williams," a young woman said, entering alone, and holding out her hands to the consul's wife.

"Catrina, my dear," Mrs. Williams exclaimed, shouting in English to overcome her inability to speak Spanish.

Maggie rose to offer Catrina a seat facing the other women, as the consul's wife introduced Ky and Daitha, making much more to-do over their husbands' importance than she thought Ky wanted to hear.

"Mucho gusto, Catrina," Maggie said when Mrs. Williams's introductions stopped short of herself. *"Soy Margareta Gutiérrez y Magodón."* She went on in Spanish, translating Mrs. Williams's words.

Catrina nodded her appreciation and sat down. Then Mrs. Williams fawned and fluttered on and on until Maggie drove it from her mind by thinking of her own affairs. Had Miguel installed a new lock on her apartment door? Why would Miguel, a taxi driver, be the one to change it? Strange. Everything was so confusing. She looked up when Adolf entered, took the helm and sent the helmsman below.

"Mrs. Johnson has seen the emeralds we got for Irena Gutiérrez," Adolf said to his sister in Spanish, "and would like something similar."

"I will find something," Catrina replied. "Just what does she . . .?"

Maggie saw that Adolf was occupied in taking the cruiser into the harbor, so she volunteered. "I'll ask her, but she already told me she liked the ones I borrowed from Señora Gutiérrez for the reception two days ago, the ones you got for the governor to give her on her birthday."

Ky nodded when Maggie translated.

The discussion went on briskly as they returned to Veracruz, offering Maggie a chance to observe Catrina. No wonder José was anxious to know more about the Buehlers, especially that woman. Neither he nor Irena had mentioned her, but wasn't that all the more reason to believe he had her in mind when he asked for information on Adolf's business? Maggie was sure she'd never seen anyone who could match Catrina's beauty. Was it her hair? Glistening, platinum, it hung down her back ending in an arc three or four inches below her shoulders. The subdued light in the pilothouse favored it — her complexion, too.

Daitha called Ky's attention to the emerald studs in Catrina's ears, and Maggie noticed that they were the only jewels she was wearing. Her shoes matched the color of her dress. Why would she wear heels — stiletto heels, the ones she'd seen on the stateroom bed? She must have a wardrobe on board.

Maggie looked up at Catrina across the low table, and when the woman returned her gaze with a smile, Maggie wondered if her earlier opinion of the woman may have been premature. Catrina was apparently sizing her up, too, for she threw quick glances back and forth between her and Adolf.

Just then Ky interrupted her thoughts.

"Maggie, will you make arrangements with this delightful young lady to meet us tomorrow?"

"We want to tour the shops where some of her work is sold," Daitha added, shifting her heavy body to face Maggie. "Not too late, though. We have a plane to catch tomorrow evening."

Maggie arranged the meeting for ten-thirty.

"You'll be with us, of course, Margareta," Mrs. Williams said.

Maggie smoothed her skirt, stared at her scuffed shoes, then looked up. "I'm sorry, Mrs. Williams. If my luggage has arrived, I really should unpack and get settled. If not, I'll just have to go shopping for something to wear. I've really enjoyed today, but —"

"Nonsense, child." Mrs. Williams bristled. "You look just fine the way you are. I'll hear nothing more about it."

Back to the starting line, Maggie thought. Child — Margareta — Maggie — Margareta — and now child again. She breathed deeply, determined to avoid a confrontation. "Let's see if my things have come," she said. "Perhaps I can work something out."

Maggie was watching the approach of harbor lights when she caught a glimpse of Adolf pushing a signal button. At once, the helmsman appeared. Adolf surrendered the wheel, whispered something to Mrs. Williams, and bowed to the others. "I regret I must say goodnight," he said. "My car will return you to the consulate."

Abruptly, he was gone. Moments later, lights on the wharf went out and the helmsman flicked a switch directing a searchlight toward the dock. He eased the cruiser to the jetty, then lit brighter cabin lights before hustling ashore.

"*Vámonos*, let's go," Catrina said, leading the way to the railing gate. She steadied the older women as they stepped across to the dock. "*Mañana a las diez y media. Muy buenas noches,*" she said.

Maggie watched the *Hedda* pull away and noticed that it was riding low in the stern. That cargo from the freighter must really be heavy, she thought. Could she really be sure about that while staring into the searchlight? Should she report it, and to whom? she wondered. It was a Mexican affair and she was from the USA. Better to say nothing, she decided, and never trust Adolf.

Suddenly the wharf lights came on. Now that was something, Maggie thought. The off-and-on timing just could not be coincidence, and was something to tell José. She rejoined her friends just as Adolf's long black limousine pulled up beside them, the helmsman driving.

"Sit in front, child," Mrs. Williams ordered.

Child again. Maggie shrugged the words off as she opened the rear door for Mrs. Williams. The woman would never deign to sit beside a lowly helmsman. Before climbing in, she scanned the harbor for signs of the *Hedda*. There were moving lights, but she could not be sure that any belonged to the cruiser. Way off to the left the lights of a ship marked the *Olinda*. Would Adolf meet it again? Probably not, for why would El Ragnorak have debarked when he did, rather than wait for the ship to enter the harbor?

On the ride to the consulate, Maggie's thoughts turned to Catrina. Was she really Adolf's sister? Both were blond, but seemed to have nothing else in common. Might they be married, friends, associates, or lovers?

*   *   *

Senator Johnson was coming down the stairway when Mrs. Williams and her group entered the consulate. "Well, look who's back. Trust you girls had a good time?"

"Yes, wonderful," Kyna said, then laughed and embraced her husband as the others nodded agreement. "I'm saving the run on your bank account for tomorrow."

"So you have plans for another day of it? That's just as well, because Tyler and I will be busy here through Sunday," the senator said.

Mrs. Williams motioned toward the reception room. "A buffet breakfast will be served there tomorrow morning. Good-night. Coming Daitha?"

Senator Johnson faced Ky and Maggie. "Do you suppose we could rustle up a snack?"

"This way," Maggie said, beckoning, and led them to the kitchen where a servant was wiping off the counter. Maggie helped her fix sandwiches for each and asked if her baggage had arrived.

"How awful," Ky exclaimed when the woman shook her head. "You're bushed, Maggie. Stay here tonight. Let's check the Smiths' room. They left this afternoon."

Maggie nodded and followed Ky and her husband up the stairs.

Ky opened a door. "See if this room suits you."

Maggie felt as if the weight of the world had been lifted from her shoulders. "Thank you, it's wonderful. Good night, Senator. Good night, Ky." She closed the door. My luck just changed, she thought, looking fondly about the same room where she'd met Irena and Governor Gutiérrez.

* * *

"Good morning," Maggie nodded to Daitha and Ky, who were already at the buffet table when she came down the next morning. "Sleep well?"

Stifling a yawn, Daitha nodded and gently massaged her eye with a fingertip.

"The men are being served at their meeting," Ky said, offering Maggie a cup. "The maid just took coffee up to Sarah. She was exhausted last night and may not go with us."

Just then Mrs. Williams came. A car's horn sounded, and a maid brought two thermos bottles and a basket of pastries from the kitchen. Mrs. Williams marched straight through to the back door and the others followed to Adolf's long black limousine. The three older women climbed into the back seat. Maggie sat in front between Catrina and the helmsman.

* * *

Mrs. Williams staggered to the Hotel Imperial café on the

Zócalo, laid her bundles on a table and sat down. When the other women had settled, she had Maggie order a round of drinks — scotch and soda for herself, gin and tonic for Daitha, beer for Ky and Catrina, and Coca-Cola for Maggie.

"No-no." Catrina shook her head. *"Con permiso, ya me voy.* I must leave now." Maggie translated farewells and, after shaking hands, Catrina hurried off.

"If you'll guard my things, I'll dash ahead and bring the car back to pick you up," Maggie said, placing a package on the table.

"I'll go with you," Ky said.

"No you won't, Ky, you're bushed, too." Maggie put a hand on her friend's shoulder. "Better to guard your loot."

Maggie finished her Coca-Cola, then took off in an easy trot, her heavy purse cradled in her arm. She brushed hair strands from her forehead. It didn't stay, so she shook her head to let her hair blow free. The time to meet the driver had already passed, so she stepped up her pace, red-gold hair bobbing.

Rounding a corner, she saw the limousine right where the helmsman had said he'd be waiting under a banyan tree between two buildings. She could see his head resting on his arm in the window, his officer's cap shielding his eyes. He must be asleep, she thought, and might not be too irritated at the lateness of the hour.

"El Zócalo," she directed, climbing in beside him.

He did not stir.

"Zócalo, central plaza," she repeated. "They're waiting."

Still no movement. She touched his shoulder, gave it a slight tug, and the helmsman slowly sagged toward her.

"Oh-my-God! Oh, God!" she gasped.

Chapter 9

"Wake up!" Maggie snapped, but the helmsman continued his horizontal drift. What was he doing? She heard a buzzing sound and watched a blue-bottle fly slip under the visor of his cap. His arm slipped off the window sill and she thought he'd wake up and slap the pest, but he continued to sag closer and closer. She pushed against his shoulder, but could not reverse his slide.

Get out! Maggie's hand flew to the door handle. She pushed the door open, and felt his head bump against her hip as she erupted from the car. "No you don't," she cried, and was surprised to hear the raw fear in her voice. His cap fell to the ground. She snatched it up and turned to hurl it at him. "Oh my God!" she burst out, as she saw a long fluted brown handle protruding from his left eye. She threw his cap onto his head, deliberately closed the door and heaved up her lunch.

She leaned against the car, breathed deeply to compose herself and tried to think. Was he dead? Who could have killed him? She saw people on the street minding their own business as though nothing had happened, and decided that she should act that way, too. A young woman with two children strolled past and nodded a greeting. Maggie forced herself to smile and lift a hand. Might the murderer be lying in wait for the return of parcel-laden North American shoppers?

Maggie bolted around the back of the car. Careful, don't be stupid, she told herself, pulling up short. Remember to act natural. Your red hair attracts attention so that witnesses will remember that you were at the murder site. Peering through the car window, she saw the thermos bottles and pastry basket still on the back seat. Don't panic. Think! When things go wrong, whom should Americans turn to for help? The consulate. You represent the consulate. This is your job. Some job! Maggie, Maggie, what have you gotten yourself into?

Was the helmsman really dead? She opened the rear door and set her purse beside the basket, feeling reassured by the weight of the gun inside it. Steadying her arm on the seat back, she reached over to feel the helmsman's forehead — warm. Might he be alive? She took a deep breath and placed her thumb and forefinger on his throat. No pulse. Then she saw a half-inch shaft of thin, shiny steel protruding from his eyelid. Was that fluted brown thing an ice pick? Stuck straight into his eye socket, it would be long enough to reach his brain. He must be dead.

Anyone could have stabbed him when he was asleep, even a child. Was the other eye open? She'd have to turn up his head to look. Forget it. The helmsman was a South African working for Adolf. His murder did not involve the United States Consulate. Just get away and take all the consulate property, she decided.

She made sure that the cap hid the weapon in his eye, then collected her purse, thermos bottles and basket. "Don't run, don't run," she mouthed the words, and ambled away.

How was she going to explain being so late to bitchy Sarah Williams? Maggie heard a scream behind her. "Dear God! Someone found the helmsman," she blurted, then rounded a corner and broke into a run.

Why would anyone kill a man from South Africa who'd just arrived in Mexico and not even rob him? Maybe someone from his past thought he knew too much. Or might he — she shuddered — might someone delay the limousine driver, whoever he was, so that the *Norteamericana* shoppers would be stranded at the Zócalo with all their bundles on a table.

It was dusk, a time of gathering crowds, mariachi bands jockeying for space, children screaming, thieves roaming. Her friends had spent enough on gems and loot to buy a mansion. Ky's belt pouch would advertise where her emeralds were. Mrs. Williams should have insisted that everything be delivered to the consulate, and payment withheld until it arrived. Why hadn't she thought of that herself? Catrina should have insisted on it, too. Oh God — Catrina — might she have a plot to steal back those emeralds? Catrina had left the group in plenty of time to reach the driver first. The weapon might have been a sewing awl, light in weight and handy to carry in a purse. Suddenly Maggie felt her gut jerk. She represented the consulate. She was responsible. She ran faster.

She spotted a taxi a block away and dashed for it.

"Consulado, Señorita?" a driver called from a cab going in the opposite direction.

Maggie stopped short and clambered in with her basket and bottles after the driver seesawed a turnaround in the narrow street. *"Zócalo— Toda prisa*—Hurry," she begged, clambering into the front seat.

"Bien, bien. Margareta, \no?"

"Miguel!" she burst out, recognizing the voice of José's friend. "Thank God. Hurry. The consul's wife and her guests are waiting at the Zócalo."

"Ah, you were running. Trouble?" he asked, spinning the wheel and squealing the tires as he reversed direction.

Maggie crashed against the door and the basket flew from her lap dumping its contents. "Wrong way," she snapped. "I said Zócalo."

"Shortcut." Miguel threaded the car through people flocking toward the long black limousine she'd just abandoned.

"Please hurry," Maggie pleaded, just as the taxi broke out of the throng and turned into an alley. She shot a glance at the swarthy man. Had the taxi driver's information grapevine brought him to look for her?

"Muy bien hecho, amiga mía. You did very well. You were wise to get away when you did."

Miguel must have read her thoughts. How could he know that a man lay dead in that big black limousine unless he'd seen the murder or done it himself? "Hurry," she begged, stamping her feet. "Oh, please hurry. Mrs. Williams — all of them, are in real trouble." He swung onto Avenida Independencia behind a slow trolley and slammed on the brakes. "Too slow — one block that way — run," Miguel pointed.

Maggie got out. "Wait for us — Hotel Imperial." Turning to go, she saw a woman with a fringe of platinum blond hair peeping from under a black shawl say something to a small man, then walk into the cathedral. Was she Catrina? Maggie didn't see her face, but who else in Veracruz might have platinum blond hair? The short man hurried ahead and disappeared into the Zócalo, which was pulsing with the clamor of mariachi bands, shrill-voiced children, hawking vendors.

Maggie elbowed her way through the evening throng. "Chicle." A huckster boy selling chewing gum planted himself in front of her. A small girl reached up to dangle a crude doll in front of her eyes. Maggie brushed past and caught a glimpse of Ky with her back against the hotel wall, eyes darting over the crowd. Maggie grinned. At-a-girl, she thought. Ky was hiding those coveted emeralds behind her, and would put up a fight to keep them.

"Cuidado, muchacha," Maggie warned a small girl running straight at her but looking back over her shoulder. Then she saw Mrs. Williams sipping from her glass. Daitha, seated beside her, was fanning herself jerkily with a folded newspaper. Maggie sighed with relief, but why did Ky look so worried?

Ky was staring at something behind Mrs. Williams. Maggie

looked that way, too, and saw three men emerge from the crowd. Neat and trim, in white suits, panama hats, black neckties and shoes, they looked respectable enough. The tallest one rose on his toes and craned his neck to scan the plaza, then sauntered over to stand near Ky. That man is trouble, Maggie thought and, shielding herself behind other people, worked her way closer. She saw the man wave at someone, a diversion, she was sure, to make his closing in on Ky look natural.

Maggie caught her breath. A red and white checkered tablecloth was draped over the shortest man's right hand. Was he hiding a knife — or a gun? Rounding the table, he confronted Mrs. Williams as the third man spread another checkered cloth over the packages. Oh, so smoothly they moved — no fuss, deliberate, as if they worked for the hotel. She saw Ky sidle along the hotel wall to put mariachi musicians between herself and the tall man.

Maggie wiped her wrist across her forehead and shook it free of sweat. Well, she had a gun, too, and a purse to hide it in. Scream? No. That would bring chaos, overturned tables. People would be injured, and their packages would melt into the crowd with the thieves.

She had to do something, and felt her shoulders tighten at the thought. Was her gun loaded? She knew she wouldn't shoot anyone, still, she wished she knew how to use it. She arranged the gun's muzzle so it barely stuck out the top of her handbag, then eased closer. She heard the stubby man talk quietly to Mrs. Williams, who only stuck out her chin and looked at Daitha.

"What's keeping Margaret so long?" Mrs. Williams said. "She should have been back ages ago."

"I wonder," Daitha said, paying no attention to Shorty.

Maggie cast a glance at Ky, who was wiggling a forefinger back and forth. "Sarah," Maggie said, disregarding Ky's warning, "that man's got a gun."

English — the thieves hadn't understood her, but Maggie

saw Mrs. Williams's glass slip from her hand and shatter on the flagstones. Both her hands shot up when the package table thief jerked the back of her chair, almost upsetting her.

Maggie rammed her gun into Short's back. *"Deja caer la pistola, Ladron.* Drop the gun, you thief," she barked. *"Lárgate,* beat it! I've got a forty-five. Get going, or I blow your head off."

"Scram!" came from Ky along with a grunt from the tall thug and the sound of iron chairs crashing together. Maggie saw him hurdle the chairs and break away in a limping run. She flashed a look at the package table where the thief gave a longing look at the covered packages, shrugged, then cast her a sad smile and strolled off. *"Lárgate,"* she said again, prodding Shorty's back with her gun.

What should she do? He just stood still, staring straight ahead. Then she saw his shoulders jerk, felt a moment of panic, and pulled back her gun. He spun around, and she chopped down with her purse and gun across his wrist. He howled and dropped his gun to the flagstones where it fired and spun into his foot. Hopping, he shrieked again as she stooped, scooped his gun into her purse. then stood back, her gun aimed right at him.

What would he do when he realized he wasn't badly hurt? Maggie watched him test his foot then turn toward the plaza. Suddenly he crouched.

"No lo hagas. Don't try it," Maggie snapped, raising her purse and aiming at him the way she'd seen cops do in the movies. Eyes wide, he looked back over his shoulder, then bolted, stumbled, lost his hat, and dashed off.

Maggie tried to act nonchalant as she strolled after him, picked up the panama hat and whipped it out over the crowded plaza. She heaved a deep sigh as it soared, hovered and fell oh so slowly — real time compared to all that had happened in the last few seconds. She turned back to her friends and heard Mrs. Williams croak:

"Call the police. Somebody call the police. Just imagine—robbing American citizens."

Maggie approached and took her elbow. "It's over now, Mrs. Williams, and no harm done." She motioned toward Avenida Independencia. "We'd better hurry. Taxi's waiting."

"Taxi? Where's our driver? I'll just have to speak to Adolf about this fiasco."

"Seems to me we were rather well cared for, Sarah." Ky gave Mrs. Williams a package to carry. "Come now. It's almost dark."

Maggie nodded a thank-you to Ky, plunked down on a chair and heaved a jerky sigh. She beckoned to a waiter. "*Quánto? How much?*"

He put the bill on the table. She picked it up, but a hand plucked it from her.

"*Bien hecho.* Margareta. Well done."

Maggie looked up. "Victor. Victor Dalpica. Gad, am I glad to see you!"

Victor took a cold Coca-Cola off a waiter's tray, uncapped it, poured a bit into a napkin and wiped off the bottle mouth. "What happened?" he said.

"I heard a shot just as I arrived. That man who ran off is a known scoundrel."

"He tried to rob us."

"Shall I find out who hired him?"

"You know who he is?" Maggie asked. He nodded and she shook her head. "No. There was no harm done, and I may already know." She thought of Catrina, who had left them in the Zócalo, and later had been with a man who looked a lot like Shorty. "It's best not to make a big thing of it."

"Oh, come now, Margareta, I'm a newspaper man."

"Well." Grinning, she stood up. "Just don't blow it out of proportion."

"I promise nothing. He gestured toward her friends and

handed her the Coke. "You should hurry, and don't be surprised if I make you famous. *Hasta luego.*"

"Don't you dare." Maggie lifted her bottle in a *salud.* *"Gracias, y hasta luego,"* she said, and hurried to join the others.

"Where is our limousine?" Mrs. Williams demanded as Maggie approached.

"Indisposed," Maggie said, indicating Miguel's taxi. "There's our ride." She opened the taxi door, held it while the women entered, then climbed in beside Miguel. "Thanks for waiting," she said. "I've about had it."

"I told Victor you might need help," Miguel said.

"Thanks. I sure was glad to see him." Maggie took a swig of Coke.

"That was very brave, Margaret," Mrs. Williams rasped from the rear seat. Recovering her voice, she shrilled, "Those robbers would have taken everything."

Daitha mumbled meekly, "Yes, Margaret, thank you."

"Bravo, Maggie," Ky chipped in. "How did you do it? Whatever did you say to scare them off?"

Maggie looked back. Ky must not have seen her scoop up the robber's gun. "Not much," she said, forcing a smile. "We had them outnumbered — four to three."

"Oh, you." Ky giggled.

Maggie grinned and felt all warm inside. A compliment from such a woman was really something.

Music from the plaza, shrill children's voices, vendor cries, and sounds of Saturday evening revelry had all but faded away when they reached the consulate. Another time it would have been enchanting to stay longer at the Zócalo, she thought, but not tonight.

"Please wait, Miguel," Maggie said, as he drove into the consulate parking area. "If my baggage has come, I'll take it to my apartment."

"Here's your new key." Miguel gave it to her then removed packages from the trunk. Maggie left hers in the trunk but helped carry others.

Thank God. Clothes. Maggie felt relief sweep through her at the sight of her baggage when she found it in the storeroom. She dragged it into the foyer just as Ky started to go upstairs with her packages.

"You're not leaving, Maggie?" Ky asked.

"I think I should," Maggie whispered. "I couldn't bear listening to Mrs. Williams's story when she fully recovers."

"She went straight to bed. Daitha, too. But it's early and I'm still too keyed up to turn in. Tom will be busy until late." Ky turned toward the stairway. "Wait until I put these things away. I'll go with you, help you get settled, then let's get a bite."

"Would you?" Maggie said, and couldn't help grinning her pleasure. "There's a nice little café close to the apartment."

* * *

Later, their meal finished, Maggie pushed her coffee cup toward Ky. "Just a dab. Do you and Daitha see each other often in Washington?"

Ky poured a small amount of black coffee syrup into their cups. "Our husbands were acquainted, but I first met Daitha here at the reception Thursday afternoon." She filled the cups with hot milk. "I hadn't met Sarah before, but I understand that she and Daitha have been friends for years. Philadelphia society, wealthy families, both of them." She stirred her coffee. "Why do you ask?"

"I just wondered," Maggie said. "Mr. Williams wants me to work closely with his wife, and I think it's going to be difficult. I knew she and Daitha were old friends, and I just wondered if you knew anything about them."

"Only what I've learned here."

Maggie sipped her coffee, then looked up. "I don't know

how to put this, but I'm afraid Mrs. Williams could get me into a lot of trouble."

"Oh?" Ky leaned forward. "For instance?"

"Well, I happened to meet the Treasury Department inspector for this region, and he's a stickler for detail. I'm an accountant. Mr. Williams assigned me to put the consulate accounts in order. I had about an hour with those files yesterday." Maggie threw up both hands but held tight to her spoon. "They're a rat's nest. Mrs. Williams insisted I go with you yesterday, and I was wrong to go." She put down her spoon.

"Yes and no, Maggie. This is a working trip for Tom and Mr. Tyler. As long as Daitha and I came at our own expense — at least I did, we should have been on our own. But State Department people in foreign lands can hardly afford to let the wives of visiting politicians shift for themselves. Take today, for example. You're one of the consulate staff. Just think what might have happened today if you hadn't been with us. A major news story, that's what, and my husband would never take me on another trip."

"Let's hope Mrs. Williams doesn't make a big thing of it."

Ky shook her head. "Daitha's the one. Her husband is new in the House, and he takes advantage of every opportunity to get his name in the papers. Washington will know. No doubt about it."

"Uh-oh." Maggie shrugged. "I won't let him corner me. There was nothing wrong with my going with you today because it's Saturday. I did enjoy both days with all of you, but I still think I shouldn't have gone yesterday."

"For goodness sakes, why not, Maggie? If you hadn't, Sarah would have you packing back to the States in no time." Ky put her napkin down. "Tell me. What really happened this afternoon when you went off to get the car?"

Maggie hesitated. Should she tell Ky about the helmsman's

death? No, she decided. As a U.S. Senator's wife, Ky would be obligated to report it — at least to Mr. Williams. "The limousine was right where our driver said he'd wait for us," she told Ky, "but I got a taxi because he just wasn't up to driving."

"Had he been drinking?" Ky said

"Good reason, I suppose," Maggie answered, wishing for Ky to get off the subject.

"Oh, there you go again. Another half truth." Brow furrowed, Ky peered over her glasses at Maggie. "Okay, I'll drop it. You must have a reason to evade the question. But on the plaza, I was sure I'd lost my new emerald earrings until you saved them. How did you do it?"

Maggie cleared a place on the table and put her purse on it. "In there."

Ky reached into the purse. "Oh." she exclaimed, wide-eyed. "Two. Are they loaded?"

"I have no idea." Eyes crinkling, Maggie stood up.

"Oh, you." Ky laughed. "Just a minute. There was a note in the room when we got back this evening. Apparently we're leaving early in the morning, so I won't see you again. But let's keep in touch. Here's where you can reach me." She gave Maggie her card.

"It's late, and we shouldn't be out alone," Maggie said, as they left the restaurant. "I'll walk back to the consulate with you."

"*Consulado Norteamericano*?" a taxi driver called just as they reached the street.

Maggie laughed. "That's Miguel, the man who drove us back from the plaza. He's sticking like a shadow — must appreciate the tip you gave him."

"Oh, no, Maggie." Ky chuckled. "It's the fire in your hair. You've got to be careful, you know. Men who follow you like that can be very dangerous."

Chapter 10

Maggie's eyes opened with the sound of bells — churches, how many might there be? Tintinnabulation? No, that was too nice a word to waste on the jumbled sounds — more like clangor, and ringing from far and near. Something moved on the wall across the room and she glanced that way — lizard, the mosquito patrol — shades of her childhood in Torreón. It felt good to be in her own apartment. The one room wasn't nearly as nice as her St. Louis apartment, not even a bathroom, but it was better than she'd expected, and Ky had thought it okay, too. How thoughtful of Ky to help her get settled, and how nice to have her as her first guest.

Maggie sat up, yawned, stretched and looked about, seeing the room in daylight for the first time. A corner room with balconies overlooking two streets, the light and cross ventilation more than made up for its being farthest from the bathroom. She squinted, trying to envision the accents and colors she might use to relieve the drabness of gray-beige walls and the somber darkness of the wardrobe and bureau. No hurry about that, but she'd need lamps right away, especially one for the vanity. She smiled, thinking of Ky's surprise at seeing a small wash basin with a cold water tap. The potty cabinet was under the sink, and a stack of narrow drawers supported the opposite end of the vanity.

She stretched again and glanced at her Baby Ben — ten-fifteen. How could it be so late? José would arrive at eleven.

Getting up, she pushed the package containing the dress she'd bought the day before out of her way, then thought she'd better hang it up so it wouldn't be wrinkled for work the next day. "Oh, no, wrong color," she grumbled, seeing it through its tissue wrapping. Then she saw an envelope, opened it and read:

> *Something to remember me by.*   *Daitha*
> *An appropriate outfit.   Sarah*
> *How bright were your eyes when you tried it on.   Ky*

Tenderly, Maggie removed wrapping from the dress and a handbag. Then she gathered them to her chest and threw herself back across the bed. Tears filled her eyes as she whispered, "Thank you, thank you all. I couldn't begin to afford such a wonderful dress. Oh, I just love it and love you all, too."

* * *

New dress, matching handbag, heels, gold ear hoops, hair swaying free below tortoise shell combs, Maggie swung down the stairs to the lobby. She saw José turn stiffly to her. Jeepers! His eyes just popped wide. No man had ever looked at her that way before.

"*Hermosa. Preciosa.* Gorgeous. Lovely," he exclaimed, taking two steps up to meet her. He grasped her hand and raised it to his lips. "Your baggage arrived, no? Or is the dress new? Oh, but of course, you were shopping."

"My baggage arrived, yes. The dress is new, a surprise gift from Mrs. Tyler, Mrs. Williams and Mrs. Johnson. This too, see?" She held up the purse. "Perfect match. The Washington group left on the sunrise flight." I'll write them thank-you letters this evening."

José took her hand and she stiffened, then relaxed, suddenly wanting to hold his hand, too, as they strolled to the familiar Model A coupe — black, no — dark forest green.

"I met Miguel after he dropped you off last night," José told her as he pulled the car into the street. "He was most complimentary."

"Two bits he told you about things I'm trying to forget." Maggie sniffed suspiciously, remembering the two bodies stuffed in the car's trunk only three nights before. What a trashy heap it was for a call on the governor. At least it shone with fresh polish, and she sensed that José was proud of it. Come to think of it, he should at least wear a coat and tie, and not attend a dinner wearing an open-necked shirt. He read my mind, she thought, as José parked, got out and took a white suit coat from the trunk.

"Excuse me," he said, as he rolled up the window, "I need the glass for a mirror." He knotted a tie and put on his coat. "Better?" he asked, getting back in.

"Yes. You look swell now," she said, as he pulled the car away from the curb. "Tell me, before we get to Irena's, are you spying on me?"

"Spying? Where did that come from?"

"I've taken a cab five times, all in Miguel's taxi. That's not coincidence."

"I did not know that," José said. "Were you pleased by his attention?"

"Skip it," Maggie said. "Two men died — no three in just three days. I won't stand for any more of that."

"Wait-wait-wait." José wobbled his hand, but Maggie was not about to stop.

"Who's Catrina?" she demanded. "Is she really Adolf's sister, or his wife? Are you all business partners? Is she your woman?"

"Maggie, Maggie, you've got things all wrong."

"Have I now? Tell me something else. Funny things are going on and I'm in the dark. For instance, who's El Ragnorak? — Eugh!" She braced herself against the dashboard as the car came to a squealing halt.

"Ragnorak. What about El Ragnorak?" José barked.

Maggie got into her seat again and stared at him. "You slipped up there, José. You do know about him. Tell me."

"How do you know about El Ragnorak?" José shot back. "I must know, Maggie."

Maggie saw José's chin thrust forward and stuck hers out, too. "You obviously know more about him than I do so why should I tell you a thing? Who are you? You burst into my life back in St. Louis. Two men die when I meet you here. You're an outcast at the consulate. I don't have to tell you a thing. Let's go."

"But Maggie, I . . . " José drew in a deep breath and blew hard.

"Back off, José. Irena invited us to dinner, and it's nice of you to take me. But you put me in an awkward position when you told her to ask me to snoop on the Buehlers." Maggie swung up her arm in a gesture to get going.

José shifted into gear and, shortly after, drove through an immense gate and onto a palm-lined drive.

"Slow down," Maggie begged, eyes darting from side to side. "Is this the governor's mansion?"

"That's in Jalapa," he said, as he swung into a shaded area and parked.

"This was once Irena's family home, but it's hers and Benancio's now. They own property southwest of Veracruz, another place in Mexico City, and several haciendas." José got out and went around to open her door.

Maggie paused to admire the landscaping: flagstone paths winding between flowering shrubs, and a white gazebo, almost hidden under a salmon-colored bougainvillea. Across from it and on her right there was a barn-like structure with a panel truck, blazoned with *FONTANERÍA M y M* parked in front of it.

"*Hola,* Maggie, over here." Irena's voice came to her from

the garden beside the house. "Beno's waiting for you in his office, José. Go right in."

"May I browse around before we go in?" Maggie asked, as she approached Irena. "Everything — the garden, landscaping, is just beautiful.

"Of course." Irena paused. "Well, no." She wiggled a finger at her feet and Maggie's. "Heels — perhaps another time would be better. Besides, there's much to tell you before we join the men."

Irena led Maggie through the foyer, indicating the dining room on the left with a table set for a dozen or more. "Other guests will arrive later," she said.

Short flights of marble stairs from each side of the entry met at a central railed platform about twenty feet from the entrance, then a broad single flight continued up to another landing, where it separated to curve right and left up to the balcony.

Irena took her elbow, and Maggie felt again the attraction she'd experienced when they'd first met. Arm in arm they climbed the stairs, their skirts, Maggie's linen and Irena's silk, swaying in rhythm. They sat down on white wicker love seats padded with leaf patterned ivory duck, facing each other across a low table in the alcove over the front door.

"We must give Beno and José time to settle their differences," Irena began. "We'll join them shortly, but first you deserve an explanation. I suggested that José escort you today as a ruse to make sure he would be here." Irena took off her glasses and, holding one stem, leaned forward. "You may be surprised by what I tell you," she said. "We've been planning this weekend ever since José told us a month ago that you were being assigned to the consulate here."

"I didn't know until two weeks ago," Maggie said.

"That is no surprise," Irena said. "To be frank, we have learned that José's accounts are sometimes — well, made up or altered to suit his own needs. We planned this weekend when we —"

"So you could judge me?" Maggie interrupted.

"Yes, Maggie, I suppose you might say that, but perhaps not in the way you expect. My husband has been in contact with your FBI concerning a scheme to combat German spies. José Alvarado is involved, too. Actually, it was his idea. The FBI and our government would plant a contact person in your State Department, preferably here in Veracruz." Irena leaned back, but kept her eyes fixed on Maggie.

She expects me to say something, Maggie thought, but about what— the dinner? "Are your — Oh!" Maggie's eyes widened. "Me? Do you mean me? Part of a counterespionage plan?"

Irena shrugged. "Possibly. The men are discussing it right now. José had already told us that you might be our niece, and was in Washington to make sure you would participate. We don't know why he did not, and when the telegram Beno received from José last Monday gave only your arrival time, Beno was — well, I decided to take a walk in the garden."

"Do you mean that you knew someone had been assigned to come here, but it could have been anybody?"

"Not exactly," Irena said, "only that Margaret Magodón, born in Mexico and fluent in Spanish was coming."

"So that's why nobody told me," Maggie said. "Washington people didn't know about the operation, and I never saw José while I was there. Should it make any difference if I'm the governor's niece?"

"Oh?" Irena's brow lifted. "Changing the subject, are you? Mr. Williams is a rigid man, and Beno thought that if you really were our niece, Mr. Williams would be upset to learn about it after you reported for work."

"That's just what happened, isn't it," Maggie said. "Governor Gutiérrez was right, too, because Mr. Williams was shocked."

"Prejudiced against you, I'm afraid," Irena said. "José was supposed to meet you in Mexico City and escort you directly here. He had a variety of excuses for not meeting you, but I suspect he never intended to follow my husband's instructions. At first he claimed you could not be considered because of the possible relationship, then he seemed almost relieved when he reported that you'd been killed in that terrible airplane crash. If he had checked the passenger list with the airline he'd have known your flight had been changed. As it was, he did not follow through. My husband was most upset because he expects his supporters to do as he wishes even at the expense of their own businesses. *'Chapuceada.* Botched,' Beno shouted at José Thursday evening after the reception." Irena paused at the sound of approaching footsteps. "Ah, good, here's Pía with our refreshments."

José relieved?   Maggie just didn't believe that, but something was wrong, Maggie thought, as Pía served.   José could have avoided the governor's anger by taking her to the Gutiérrez house on the night of her arrival rather than to his own apartment. Why had he told her not to let anyone know they'd met before, or that she'd spent the night in his apartment? Better be quiet and listen, she decided.

"Was the misunderstanding with José the reason you left the Williams' dinner early?" Maggie asked when Pía had gone.

Irena nodded. "Before Beno left for the capital Thursday night, he sent José back to make sure you were willing to participate. Without your approval, he was unwilling to present the anti-spy plan to his committee on Friday. José failed again."

Maggie wondered what Irena might be talking about. "Let me get this straight, Irena," she said. "He didn't mention any plan to me. He only said he had to go to Jalapa."

"I know." Irena rose, beckoning. "He stopped here to tell me to inform my husband that he refused to discuss the plan with you until you were firmly established. That's why I went to Jalapa Friday morning. I didn't dare use the telephone to tell my husband that José had failed again."

"That must have popped the governor's boiler."

"I'm trying to forget, but he settled down eventually," Irena said with a wry smile. "He then convinced other governors to attend an emergency meeting this afternoon."

"This afternoon? Sunday? But what about your guests?" Maggie rose and went to the window overlooking the driveway. "I can't believe José would ask me to do anything without the approval of my superiors. I'm new here, but not gullible. I'm not about to be tricked into doing anything my country would not support, and I refuse to take a bribe."

"Perhaps we expect too much from you," admitted Irena. "Please consider the proposal, and if you do not accept, I will support you as I would my real daughter." She extended her hand. "Come, *hija mía* . They are not patient men."

"I ordered iced tea," the governor said as they entered his office. He directed Maggie to a chair, then turned to José. "We'll have no chit-chat. Tell Maggie who you are. Show her your credentials."

"I'm a U.S. citizen," José said — "FBI."

"I don't think I should believe that," Maggie said.

Benancio cut in. "Show her."

José produced a shiny metal badge formed in the shape of a U.S. shield, and a document which confirmed his claim.

Maggie shook her head. "You can get those made lots of places."

"I told you that's what she'd say, Governor," José said.

Maggie caught José's sheepish smile when he said it with eyes downcast, and thought that she could never count on him to stand up against the governor or any man of power. She'd seen more than one good man reduced to a puppet by a domineering boss back at Douglas, and she couldn't help feeling sorry that she'd subjected José to a duel of words with the governor.

"Your instructions, José." Governor Gutiérrez slapped his desk. "Show her the letter authorizing you to engage her services."

José scowled. "How can I be sure of her after only three days when she refuses to answer questions?"

"Ojalá por eso, Would you have it any other way?" The governor banged his hand on the table. "If she were one to talk too readily, she would be of no use whatever. Show her the letter."

"Let me think a moment." José rose, cupped and rubbed his chin, then walked briskly from the room.

"Maggie, will you excuse us until José returns?" Governor Gutiérrez said, and turned to his wife to discuss the dinner guest list and how she might explain his absence.

A moment later José returned and handed Maggie the authorization.

"Good. I will summarize." Benancio Gutiérrez gulped iced tea, leaned back and twisted the tips of his mustache. Eyes fixed on the ceiling, he spoke in a low tone. "I may not know the whole story, *hija mía* , my daughter, but José can fill you in later. He chanced to meet you in St. Louis when you took another woman's job application appointment. Bravo." His eyes met Maggie's, and she caught his wink of approval.

"Your Spanish impressed him, and he recommended you to a friend in personnel at the State Department, suggesting you be assigned to Veracruz. Three weeks ago he told us that Margaret Magodón had been assigned to Veracruz and that you might be our niece. When he was in Washington last week, he examined your application again — extra training with the FBI, born in Torreón, mother's maiden name — Claudia Gutiérrez. He called us on the telephone." The governor turned to Irena. "When was that, last Sunday?"

"Monday evening," Irena said.

"You told me to bring her directly here, Governor," José cut in. "You were already traveling, Maggie," he said to her. "I did get to Mexico City in time to meet your flight, but it never arrived."

Governor Gutiérrez shook his head. "Tragic, but let's move on. José had conferred with me on several occasions about the rapid increase of exports from Veracruz to the United States and Europe, our country's manufacturing boom, and the alarming increase in the number of industrial accidents. As a result of mounting evidence that Germany has launched a major espionage effort, our president formed an anti-espionage committee of governors and selected industrial executives, which I chair. Coordination with the United States is through the FBI." The governor removed his glasses and pointed a stem at José.

Follow the dollar trail, a horse-sense maxim from her Investigative Finance course popped into Maggie's mind. *Can't find dollars, look for jewels*, was another. The governor put his glasses back on and she spoke up before he could continue. "Is José a member of your committee? If so, is he on it because precious metals and stones are easier to smuggle than cash?"

Governor Gutiérrez removed his glasses again, and Maggie wondered from the way he was looking at her if she had spoken out of turn. "What I — I mean," she stammered, "that as a jeweler, he might know of places which pay cash for smuggled jewels."

"Bravo, Maggie," the governor said. "In fact, José provided evidence indicating that a gemstone black market has cropped up — excellent work I might add, *hijo mío*." He nodded toward José.

Swell, Maggie thought, glancing at José — preening rooster. She looked back at the governor as he resumed, thinking he had José back in line again.

"Although not by treaty as yet," Governor Gutiérrez went

on, "Mexico and our friends to the north support the Allies against the Nazi-Fascist block."

Over his black rimmed glasses, he fixed dark eyes on Maggie. *"Querida mía,* This is where we hope you will help us. José seems to be reluctant to expose you to danger, but the choice should be yours. Feel free to ask questions at any time. His plan, which Irena and I support without reservation, is for you to serve as a link between José and the consulate, and between your Department of State, my state, and my country."

Maggie broke in. "Shouldn't you be working with the ambassador and Mr. Williams? Surely they —"

The governor raised his hand and cut in. "You are right as regards most matters, of course, but consider this. Your ambassador will participate, but his obligations are to United States citizens in Mexico. Mr. Williams openly supports Ireland against the British. Mrs. Williams's parents are German, and most of her friends are, too. Your consulate interpreters have roots in axis countries. Under those circumstances, do you think it possible for us to work closely with the Veracruz consul? Bear in mind that Veracruz and Tampico are in this state and are the ports of departure for almost all this country's exports in support of the allied cause in Europe."

Maggie lifted her shoulders, pursed her lips.

"So there you are, *Querida mía,*" the governor went on. "A few minutes ago, José informed me that you know something about a man of worldwide fame — El Ragnorak."

Maggie's eyes shifted from him to José and back. "I asked José who the man was, that's all. He wouldn't answer me, just demanded that I tell him everything I knew. José never told me he was FBI. When he reacted as he did, I decided to keep my mouth shut."

Benancio Gutiérrez chuckled and glanced at José. "I see your point. We're short of time, so I'll continue. José knows very little about El Ragnorak aside from his reputation as master saboteur."

Oh-oh, the governor wouldn't say that if he'd seen José's reaction when she mentioned El Ragnorak.

"During the world war," the governor went on, "the man was Germany's chief spy on the African continent. He has owned or managed many German enterprises in South America, but recently has devoted his time to his diamond and gold mining interests in Africa. He claims to be Afrikaans. He has financed many companies in Mexico. Need I say more?"

Maggie shook her head. "I'll be darned. Why didn't I know all this before I left the States?"

"You mean you wouldn't have come?" José's eyes were fixed on his right foot tracing patterns on the terrazzo floor.

"No," Maggie snapped. "I would have made a lot better use of my training time."

"I interpret that statement as your agreement to join us?" Governor Gutiérrez reached for documents on his desk.

"Let me think a moment." Maggie looked from Irena to José, and back to Irena. If she could believe what the governor had said, and she had no reason to doubt him, her information might be of great value. She swallowed, cleared her throat, and willed herself to speak clearly.

In crisp sentences, she described her activities since arriving in Mexico, beginning with an account of Adolf's first advances. Concluding, she said, "El Ragnorak arrived in Veracruz last evening. I was on the *Hedda*, Mr. Buehler's new cruiser, when we ferried El Ragnorak and Catrina Buehler from the ship, the *Olinda*, to Veracruz."

José drew in a long breath and gusted it out. "Are you sure? Does Buehler know you saw him?"

"Yes, I'm sure, and no one suspects that I saw him. It was El Ragnorak, all right. I prowled the cruiser before we met the *Olinda*, found his autographed picture in the master stateroom, and recognized him when he came down the *Olinda* ladder to the *Hedda*. But I think he did not get off at the yacht harbor. If anyone were to look for him, I believe it should be at the Buehler compound in Antigua."

"Well-well? So you already know about the place?" The governor rose. "This has been most helpful." He stooped to embrace Maggie, then sat down again, waggling a finger at Irena. "As usual, you were right to defend Maggie, my dear." He dashed off his signature on a document. "There. It's signed. José, tell our daughter what her duties will be if she agrees to join forces with us."

José's smile stretched wide his mustache. "She has me convinced. I'll give you details when we have more time, Maggie. Of course, your primary duty will be to satisfy Mr. Williams, but —"

"José." Irena's eyes flashed.

"What's wrong?" Mouth agape, José stared at Irena. Suddenly his face flushed and he stammered, "But . . . but . . . I mean . . . your job —" He breathed deeply. "You will continue as the consulate accountant under the direct supervision of Mr. Williams. Never forget, though, that keeping your job depends on that red-topped muckraker, Thompson, who'll get you fired if your accounts do not balance."

"That's two bosses. And what about Sarah Williams? She my boss, too? And you? That makes four." Maggie eyed him from under lowered lashes. How must I deal with you?"

Irena chortled. "It's not in José to tell you, but I will. Most pleasantly, I would think. You see, he will court you, openly, and I expect, over vigorous objections from Mr. and Mrs. Williams. Courting you will give José an excuse to frequent the consulate."

"Well . . ." Maggie frowned

José spoke again. "Along with it comes a hundred and fifty dollars a month extra, half your present —"

"That's — that's —" Maggie stomped her foot. "Pay me to

take up with a gigolo? Yuk! You got me down here for—"
She heard Irena squeal with laughter, glanced at the governor —
grinning, and at José — red faced. "I guess you didn't mean it
that way," she said. "I'm sorry, José. It sounds okay, but what
were you saying?"

"You will receive an additional fifty percent of your present
pay from the FBI deposited in your bank in the States so that no
one at the consulate will know."

"I'll do it, José, but I'd like the check deposited to my
account in a St. Louis bank." Now Rosa wouldn't have to take
in neighbor's laundry to support Betty, Maggie thought, and just
then Governor Benancio Gutiérrez rounded his desk and
gathered her and Irena into his arms. "Have no fear that José
will overstep his bounds, *Querida*. He is a gentleman, and will
let nothing come between him and his duties."

Maggie found herself standing, hugging Irena, and watching
as Governor Gutiérrez shoved José ahead of him toward the
door, then looked back.

"I hope with all my heart that you sign both documents."
He indicated the papers on his desk. "One is for the FBI. The
other is completed according to laws of our country. You are
already my niece. Sign it. Then Irena and I will have our
daughter."

Maggie closed her eyes and, as she pulled in a deep breath,
she felt a warm glow course within her. Then a quick glance at
José's back brought a long forgotten tune to mind — *Will you
come into my parlor, said the spider to the fly* — Let me see, she
thought, how does the rest of that tune go?

Chapter 11

Was this really happening? Eyes misting, Maggie watched Governor Benancio Gutiérrez turn into the hall and disappear.

"Will she sign, Governor?" Maggie heard José ask, then their voices faded.

She felt a deep sense of well-being when Irena wrapped her arms about her. "How can I thank you? I don't know what to say."

"Just be still, *Querida.*"

Maggie wanted to be hugged forever, but presently heard muffled voices from downstairs, Benancio's, José's, and others, and let Irena lead her to the governor's desk.

"Sit here, Maggie," Irena said, softly. "Our guests are arriving and I must go."

Maggie blinked and dried her eyes. "Should I know who they are?"

"Local business people," Irena said, lifting and rolling both hands. "Friends? Who knows? Some perhaps. In my husband's work, how can one be sure?" She glanced at a mirror on the back of the door to pat her hair into place. "Surprised, aren't you, at José's offer? Think about it, and come down when you're ready." She flashed Maggie a hurried smile and was gone.

Surprised, yes, and amazed even more by Irena's and the governor's invitation to become one of their family. How could they know and trust her enough to consider such a move?

Seated at the governor's desk, Maggie thought of the times she'd sat on her father's lap while he typed, and how shunned she'd felt when he'd lift her to the floor so he could work. She smiled, swivelling slowly as she absorbed the friendliness of the office. There were no windows. Smart, she thought, smiling wryly. More than one Mexican politician had been shot through a window. Hewn beams supported the off-white ceiling. Books on shelves set into mahogany paneled walls dignified the room with the decor of the covers and titles of the volumes. A portrait of the governor, hanging between bookcases behind his desk, caught her attention. She picked a photograph of Irena off the desk and held it up, eyes shifting from one likeness to the other. Mother? Father? Could she think of them as her parents? Would she be part of a family again after all these years?

She hugged Irena's picture to her breast, remembering how tightly knit her family had been, with her mother, father, and step-sister, Betty, until the accident more than fifteen years ago. She'd tried not to think about her father, bedridden for the next five years until he, too, had passed on. Family memories came surging back, clear and distinct, as when she and her mother would lie head to head on the Navajo rug, propped on elbows, drawing pictures. They'd camp in the mountains or at the seashore, and once in a while there would be movies in town, silent ones before talkies. Then everything had gone to pieces.

Maggie willed herself back to the present, replaced Irena's picture, and glanced at the two folders. Each promised change and, together, had struck her like a bolt of lightning. Should she sign, let herself be adopted? Best not to rush it, she decided, pushing the adoption papers aside.

She opened the one representing a pay raise to four hundred and fifty dollars a month. She'd be able to send a third of it home to Rosa and Betty. Why hadn't José told her he was FBI? It just wasn't fair of him to test her without her knowing the job was at stake. Would he be her boss if she signed? Not really.

She'd still be working for Mr. Williams and the consulate, and José would be a colleague, nothing more. She remembered thinking of him as a dashing Spaniard back in St. Louis, but that image had paled in comparison to Governor Gutiérrez.

She read José's documents again, searching for a description of the FBI job. Nothing, so she supposed it would be what José had described — to serve as a liaison agent. Could she do the job? Why not? She picked up a pen. Only after she'd signed and dated the document did she feel the responsibility the assignment entailed. Now she was a counter espionage agent, and her competence in accounting was suddenly a side talent.

Would José be pleased? He should be. After all, hadn't he gone out of his way to make sure she'd be assigned to Veracruz? She owed him, and suddenly realized that she couldn't blame him for his reluctance to promote her without a good reason.

El Ragnorak — she shook her head at the thought of the man. Apparently José and the governor were in the midst of preparing counter-measures against Nazi espionage. She smiled, thinking of their different reactions on hearing of El Ragnorak's arrival in Mexico — José's, startled — the governor's, matter of fact. Just how powerful might El Ragnorak be?

She felt her chest pound at the thought that she'd be doing her country a lot more good than if she only pushed dollars and pesos around government forms all day. She folded the document and —

"Hello, Maggie. Let me see it."

English — who? Terror that she'd not sensed before shivered her back. *"Lárgate!* Go away! Get out of here!" she barked, with a quick look at the door. Nobody. Then she saw chocolate-colored coveralls in the chair Irena had vacated. "Miguel!" she exclaimed. It couldn't be Miguel. The man had spoken English. She stared. Sure enough, it was the taxi driver.

"How did you get in?' she demanded. "Get out!"

"The bathroom. You were engrossed."

"Doesn't matter, just get out. Go, or I'll call the governor!"

"I saw you sign the form, but I must make sure. Welcome to the FBI." Miguel indicated the envelope in her hand. "I signed it already. José had to get my okay."

"What do you mean? How come you're speaking English all of a sudden?"

"My native tongue and I'll explain later. Look at the form. Did José sign? It's worthless if he didn't."

Maggie opened the envelope. "He signed," she said, placing the form on the corner of the desk.

Miguel reached for it, examined and returned it. Then he rose, got a tray of plumbing tools from the hall, and she saw *FONTANERÍA M y M* printed across the back of his brown coveralls.

"I've only got a minute," he said, putting his tool tray on the floor inside the bathroom. He opened the cabinet under the wash basin and lay on his back. "Oh-oh, here's the trouble. Is there a towel handy?"

"Hurry," she said, getting him one. "You shouldn't be here."

"Hand me the spanner wrench, will you? Know what a spanner is?"

"Sure. Helped my dad, and fixed most things around the house." Maggie got the tool and handed it to him.

"I'd better explain," Miguel said, craning his neck to look at her from under the basin. "Governor Gutiérrez doesn't know, and José's not to know I told you, but I'm José's FBI boss. Minutes ago, he told me you'd seen El Ragnorak. You sure?"

Maggie nodded vigorously. "Positive. Looks just like his picture."

"Oh? So you saw a man and a picture, both where they have reason to be. That so? What makes you think it was El Ragnorak?"

"The radio operator said he was coming aboard," Maggie snapped. "The picture was signed, Ragnorak Holtz."

"What did he look like?" Miguel lay back to tighten the drain.

"Very tall, taller than Mr. Buehler, a beanpole, but with wide shoulders. He favored his right leg." Maggie went on to describe the figure she'd seen. "And he's bald with a skeezix tuft of brown hair on the front of his immense bald head, and wore a blood-red cloak over black clothes."

"You saw through the cloak?"

"Of course not," Maggie said. "The wind blew it open when he tried to catch his hat."

"I suppose you can describe his shoes, too."

"Shiny black. And his hat was cow-dung brown. Satisfied?"

Chuckling, Miguel slid out from under the basin and held up his hand. *"Muy bien*, Maggie. You'll do. But from now on, we speak only Spanish."

Maggie grasped his hand and helped him to his feet.

Miguel picked up his tool tray and faced her. "Okay, Maggie. You uncovered El Ragnorak here when the FBI believed a man of his importance would never be sent to Mexico. Whatever contacts you —"

"Does that have any special meaning?" Maggie cut in, "like maybe the Nazis are laying the groundwork for war against us?"

Miguel gave her a hard look then a quick nod. "Sure could. Try to follow up. Keep track of the man as best you can. José's gone to Jalapa with the governor, so I'll pick you up later." He indicated the wet floor. "Clean up, will you? I've got to go."

When he had gone, Maggie cleaned the basin and wiped the floor, then went back into to the office for her purse, feeling as if she'd protected the governor's office from an intruder. She picked up Irena's picture again. At last she had someone close with whom she could share confidences that comfort, missing since the death of her mother. Softly, she whistled an all but forgotten tune, the song of the Baltimore oriole, which her parents had whistled to signal each other.

Heartened by the oriole song, she scooped up the pen and signed the adoption documents. Strange. She'd never seen a Baltimore oriole, only pictures of the beautiful birds. She whistled quietly as she descended the stairs, then lifted her hand in a two-fingered V when she saw Irena look up, and wiggled her hand as if signing.

Irena threw up her hands, clapping. "Come down, Maggie," she called. "Everybody, may I present our daughter, Margareta Gutiérrez y Magodón."

"Mucho gusto, everybody," Maggie called, waving her hand. "I'm so glad to meet you." Then she swooped down the stairs and into Irena's arms.

"Maggie-Maggie, I'm so happy," Irena murmured, then slipped her arm around Maggie's back. "You know Mr. Buehler, but have you met his sister Catrina, who just arrived from Ecuador?"

"Yes, we've met," Maggie said, shaking Catrina's hand. "Hello, Catrina." She heard Adolf's heels click together as he bowed over her hand. "How are you, Mr. Buehler?" She turned to Irena. "Catrina led us on a jewel hunt yesterday. Mrs. Williams and her guests found just what they wanted."

After introductions, Maggie asked Catrina and Adolf. "You know José Alvarado, don't you? He told me he's a silversmith. Do you know anything about his business, what he manufactures?"

"Catrina can tell you more," Adolf said abruptly. "She furnishes most of the gems for his designs."

Just then a corpulent, crimson-faced man arrived and Adolf introduced him as the manager of the Veracruz railway station. Immediately, the men got into a discussion about shipping schedules. It was a good time to pump Catrina for information,

Maggie thought, and edged her toward the living room.

"I must see José before I return to Ecuador," Catrina said. "My country is famous for its silver artisans, as is Mexico, but none can equal José Alvarado."

"Is that so?" Maggie said, hoping to keep Catrina talking about José. "I would never have expected him to be a craftsman. More like a professor."

Catrina laughed. "You insult him. You have only to look at his hands, Margareta. His fingers are long, slim and very quick — woman's hands."

"Huh-whoof, now who's insulting him?" Maggie flashed a broad grin. "Really, I think he's very much a man — *Macho — muy macho.*"

"She's right," Irena said, rejoining them. *"Con permiso,* excuse me." She raised her voice. "Please, everybody, lunch is ready in the dining room."

When guests were seated, she apologized for the governor's absence, offered a short prayer, and rang a bell to summon the servants.

There was so much to learn from Irena, Maggie thought, noting how she positioned her guests, and led discussion away from personal topics to affairs of local, state and national interest. Mindful of her new job, Maggie concentrated on their names and who was paired with whom. She noticed that both Catrina and Adolf occasionally spoke in German with the portly railroad station's manager, who appeared to be about Catrina's age.

Suddenly conversation ceased, the quiet rousing Maggie from her thoughts. Looking up, she saw Pía whispering to Irena.

"Tell him we will start at once," Irena told Pía, who nodded and left the dining room. Irena stood up. "I beg your forgiveness for asking you to continue without me. Maggie, will you take over, please? The governor beckons and I must leave you with my most sincere apologies. Thank you all for coming."

The guests rose, then resumed their seats when she had gone. Suddenly a hostess to strangers, Maggie answered questions as best she could, but made no attempt to encourage discussion. She knew that guests had come for a purpose, and had no reason to stay longer. The railway station manager and his wife ate their dessert quickly then excused themselves. Within five minutes Maggie found herself alone.

* * *

Maggie hardly knew what to think when she went out onto the driveway. The day had been so full of surprises that she longed to stretch out and mull them over. She heard the sharp toot of a car's horn, saw a parked taxi and Miguel with his arm hanging out the window.

"Hola," he said, as she approached. "Here, take the keys to the Model A Ford. It's yours to drive now. José will use another one. Follow me."

"Ugh, that gadabout morgue gives me the creeps," she said with a glance at the Model A Ford aimed straight at her. "Well, okay, but I'll have to spruce it up — give it a name like . . . like . . ."

"José calls it Francesca," Miguel told her.

"Uh-uh. Leave it to José to be shrouded by a woman. Not me. Gotta be a man — rugged — tough. I know — Clank. How you doin', Clank?" She turned back to Miguel. "It's still early. Can I use it to explore a bit?"

Miguel shrugged. "Follow me. I'll show you where it goes to bed at night."

Maggie climbed into the Model A, started the engine, and felt her moxie surge. Freedom — fancy free. With Clank, she'd poke her nose into all sorts of ruins and Nazi secrets. She'd hose out the rumble seat pit, wash away even the thought of the two corpses José had stuffed in on the night of her arrival.

Where should she go? Poke around the city? No. She could do that without a car. What about her job — spying? Where was El Ragnorak? Might he be at Adolf's hacienda in Antigua? What would she do if El Ragnorak caught her snooping? Well, so what? Dangerous and foolhardy as it might be, she'd try to pick up El Ragnorak's trail.

Maggie followed Miguel to the parking garage, then stopped at her apartment to change into the outfit she'd worn on her trip from the States and get her camera. Back in the car, she found a map José must have drawn. It showed the coastal area north of Veracruz. Five penciled lines off the Antigua road indicated unpaved lanes to the gulf. The third and fifth had tiny circles at the gulf end — probably fishermen's dwellings. Or had José marked them for some other reason? Might the one farthest north be a trail leading to the stilt-mounted shack at the mouth of the Antigua River which Daitha and Mrs. Williams had talked about? Might it be close enough to the river for her to observe Adolf's hacienda on the opposite bank?

She drove north past the railroad switch yards, crossed the tracks, and took the coastal road. Just past a field where a man plowed rain-soaked soil behind a single yoked ox, she turned into the third break in the ceiba forest and drove down an unpaved trail toward the Gulf of Mexico. Cresting a low dune, she smelled the sea, and saw a thin blue strip of the gulf. She veered left to get a better view and crunched to a stop in a thicket.

"Sorry, Clank," she muttered, "I didn't intend to make a palm tree mower of you, but I've just got to see the gulf." She got out and looked up at coconut palms waving majestically overhead. Propped against Clank, she closed her eyes and pulled in a deep breath — fresh salt air from the sea. She listened to palm fronds stirring in the breeze, the rustle mellowed by the shush-like roll of the gentle surf.

Drawn by the sound, Maggie headed for the beach, but

stopped. Not yet, she thought, turning back to make sure Clank wasn't stuck. She circled the car— no damage, but the left front wheel was hidden by the thicket. She grasped a vine, pulled, and back she went when it gave way suddenly, plopping her down in the fern groundcover. She felt a mass of vines and plants pile over her legs, lay back and let out a whoop. Good thing she'd changed her clothes before going out with a guy like Clank.

Free, she could do as she pleased, botch whatever she felt like doing with nobody around to tell her off. She looked up — lovely, would she ever again see clouds so perfectly framed — a fringe of ferns, scattered palms waving their fronds gently above clusters of coconuts hugging their trunks. Soaring seagulls and clouds were bedded against the deep gulf blue of the sky.

Too bad she couldn't lie there and enjoy it, she thought, as she untangled herself and stood up. Could she back Clank away from the mess? Probably, if she avoided the plants the car had uprooted. She picked up a young palm. It looked okay, and she wondered if she might transplant it to the consulate grounds, the Gutiérrez estate, or a pot on her balcony. Looking about, she found two more, and stuffed all three into the rumble seat space before heading for the shore.

Maggie walked a winding path through ferns, beach shrubs, and over a low sand ridge. Pausing, she leaned against the trunk of a palm on the edge of the beach to watch a man cast his net into the surf. Off to the south, a freighter, low in the water, headed in a direction she thought might be toward Cuba. Farther out, and northeast, a wisp of smoke marked another ship just over the horizon.

Absently, she pinched the fiddlehead from the tip of a fern frond, put it between her lips. The taste, something like that of a fresh asparagus tip, reminded her of the scolding she'd received when she'd cut short the growth of fresh fronds in her mother's garden. How wonderful to nip off another and another, and nibble free of constraint. She felt the breeze off the sea ruffle her hair, luxuriated in it and the gentle movement of the palm trunk against her back.

A sudden shrill of gulls lifted her gaze to the source of their frenzy — the fisherman, hauling in his catch. Just beyond — No! The *Hedda.* It was approaching slowly, and was close, just outside the lazy surf. Adolf, with field glasses directed straight at her, was leaning against the skiff on the boat deck. She saw him lower the glasses, wave and heard him call her name.

She lifted an arm in indifferent response, then swung around the palm trunk, ducked behind bushes and went over the bank. Peering back from between branches, she saw him pick up a megaphone, and this time his shout was louder.

What might Adolf be looking for? She ran to Clank, got in and drove away. If she waited to talk to him, he'd be curious about why she was alone on a remote beach. He must have recognized her cranberry and lemon outfit. Why hadn't she thought to wear something less conspicuous?

She'd come back to this place again, she decided, but now she'd have to hurry to get to Antigua before dusk. Might she be in time to observe Adolf docking the *Hedda* at the hacienda and see who was with him?

Maggie drove slowly, the rustle of coco palm fronds coming to her through the open windows. There's my excuse if someone should question what I'm doing here, she thought. Collecting plant specimens, that's what.

She came to the Rio Antigua bridge, crossed it but turned back. At its center, she paused to look east and west. There were no structures bordering the stream, but dense foliage, dark in the approaching dusk, lined the riverbanks. According to José's map, the village would be downriver on the north bank, just past the bend about a half-kilometer away. Adolf's hacienda would be just beyond. She turned east onto the trail along the south riverbank.

"Buenas tardes, Señor," she called to a man picking fruit in a pawpaw grove. "How much for a small papaya?"

He approached. *"Muy buenas tardes, Señorita.* The papayas are very good. Are you going to Veracruz? Would you take a crate to the Hotel Imperial?"

"Como no." She nodded. "Sure. Why not? But before I go I want to drive to the end of this trail. Is there a place where I can take a picture of Antigua from this side of the river?"

He squatted beside the car and, using a short stick, drew a map in the mud showing the river channel and the trail close to it. Finally he stabbed his pointer into the ground and stood up. "Right there," he said. "That's a good place to take a picture."

"Gracias. I must go before it's too dark. Would you put the papayas on the seat cushion in back?"

He made room beside the palms, trotted off to get the crate, then put it on the rumble seat cushion. "The hotel will pay me to tomorrow," he said, backing away and waving. *"Muchas gracias."*

"De nada. Think nothing of it." She started the car.

He slapped the hood with a loud bang. *"Un momentito,"* he said, dashing off. A moment later, he returned with a papaya longer than his forearm and put it on the seat beside her. "For you," he said, and waved her off.

"Muchas gracias. I'll take the papayas to the hotel tonight." Maggie caught a movement beside the clearing, and saw two little children standing hand in hand. "Are they your children?" she asked. "What are their names?"

"Grandchildren. This one is Primo, and this is Segunda."

Maggie wiggled her fingers at them. "It's late now, but sometime I'll come back and take you for a ride in the car. Would you like that?" Both nodded and, waving again, she drove down the trail.

She followed his directions past a ferry dock and hid Clank

in a dense thicket. Then she took a jungle path until it emerged on the riverbank.

Peering across the river, she saw two large men and a short woman standing on Adolf's landing about a hundred yards upstream from her. Instead of responding when the woman waved, she walked slowly upstream, then ducked into the forest. "Damn." She'd let her cranberry skirt and lemon blouse give her away again.

She found a place where she could peer downstream through the undergrowth, and settled down to wait for the *Hedda*. It was still light on the open river, but nearly dark under the forest cover. "Hope there's enough light," she murmured, as she adjusted her camera to focus on the far bank. She heard the sound of the *Hedda's* diesels and, moments later, the *Hedda* appeared.

Maggie watched a tree branch drift slowly east. Hmm, high tide and changing, so the cruiser would stay close to the far bank and dock with its bow upstream. As the *Hedda* passed her, she saw two tall men on the afterdeck, Adolf and, if it weren't for the blond hair escaping from under Adolf's cap, another man who looked just like him. She snapped a picture, got another, and swung her view left to take in the entire cruiser. A smaller man wearing nothing but pants appeared on the foredeck — the deck hand. Adolf's partner was facing the far shore talking loudly enough for her to hear his guttural tones, but not what he said. She waited until the deck hand faced her way, then stepped from the shadows and waved. He responded with a quick jerk of his left arm.

She was sure the deck hand had recognized her cranberry-lemon outfit, but why had he not waved openly? Was he in some sort of trouble? Might he know something about El Ragnorak, the newcomer, and what went on behind the hacienda walls? Of the original *Hedda* crew, the helmsman had been murdered, another had escaped onto the *Olinda*. Was he hoping to escape, too?

From behind a massive ceiba tree she watched him grasp the bowline, jump ashore and moor the bow as a man from the shore moored the stern. Adolf and his lookalike debarked and, after handshakes, everyone disappeared behind the compound wall.

Who might the newcomer be? Might the proprietor of the Hotel Ceiba know? There was sure to be gossip among the village folk about the goings-on behind those walls, so she determined to make friends among them.

She was about to go back to her car when a husky blond man, sleeves rolled up over cantaloupe-sized biceps, emerged from the cabin. Two men dressed in gray business suits came out behind him.

Maggie pursed her lips in a silent whistle. Veracruz men didn't wear gray suits, so these two must be newcomers. Had the *Hedda* met another ship at sea? Might they be replacements for the murdered helmsman and the man who'd escaped?

Voices carried to her, but she could understand nothing. The gray-suited men shook hands with the burly crewman, then disappeared through the hacienda gate. When they had gone, the big man rubbed his hands together in a gesture of satisfaction, nimbly boarded the *Hedda*, and disappeared into the cabin.

Maggie turned away again, but a bellow of rage brought her attention back to the hacienda dock. The burly giant appeared on the afterdeck brandishing a pistol and scanning the river.

Where was the deck hand? Shielded behind a tree, Maggie searched the opposite shore. Nothing. From the corner of her eye she caught a movement on the water — a floating branch moving faster than other debris and coming her way. It had passed midstream, and was in a straight line between her and the hacienda dock when she heard a shot. Looking back at the *Hedda,* she saw a man on the boat deck aiming right at her. Three flashes burst from his pistol. The river churned, and she felt muddy water spray about her as three sharp retorts sounded as one.

Maggie couldn't help ducking, but popped her head back out when she heard shouting. She saw the two men in gray on the dock again, rifles ready, searching, searching. She still hadn't seen the deck hand, so he must be hiding in floating foliage. Adolf was back with others — seven men, all shooting, and she saw a floating branch burst apart and a dark head duck under the surface right at the river bend.

"Dear God!" Maggie gasped, stuffing her camera into her purse as she backed away. "Hope he made it." She ran along a path by the river, stumbled, picked herself up, and ran past a clearing with a thatched shed, a ramp leading into the river, and a small boat resting on it. She snatched loose the mooring line and held it tight as she pushed the boat into the water. Should she board? Was there time? No oars.

She heard the *Hedda's* diesels burst alive, looked for it upstream, but the river bend hid it. The cruiser must be turning around to come in pursuit of the deck hand, but where was he? Then she saw his face, eyes wide with horror. He was close, but drifting past as she aimed the boat and waded knee deep. Gripping the bowline tight, she pushed with all her might.

Chapter 12

Slower and slower the boat drifted toward the deckhand. "Go on — go on!" she wheedled, whipping the bow line to urge the boat on. "Dear God, hope it keeps going," she murmured, wading deeper and holding the tip of the rope as she reached as far as she could. She slipped, teetered and lost sight of him as she regained her balance. Where was he? About to plunge after him, she saw a hand rise above the boat's stern, grab, slip off.

"Reach! Try again!!" Maggie hissed. "Right there. You can do it." Then she saw an arm rise, a hand grasp the stern, and lost her grip on the line when he jerked the boat. She snatched the line from the water, set her feet and pulled gently.

"Hang on. Don't let go," she begged, tugging harder.

The diesels sounded louder — the *Hedda* was closer, but she dared not look as she grasped the boat's bow. She pulled it as far as she could onto the ramp and into semidarkness under spreading ceiba boughs.

"Quick! Come on! Oh no," Maggie hissed as a bright light caught the corner of her eye. *"Hedda* searchlights. They'll see us."

She saw the deck hand try to rise, fall back, then inch himself onto the ramp. She reached out to help, but felt her stomach wrench when foliage all about them suddenly blossomed under the searchlight beam. She dropped and lay flat in the boat's shadow, and saw that the deck hand was hidden, too. Had she been seen? Maybe, but willed herself to squirm back to grasp his wrist and pull as far as the boat could hide them.

Louder, closer, came the diesel's sound, but then the searchlight beam swung upriver, and Maggie grabbed the deck hand's belt and lifted him to hands and knees.

"Vámonos, ya! Let's go, right now!" Maggie snapped, and pulled as he tried to crawl. No use. He slumped again. She grasped his belt, lifted him bottom up and suspended as baggage, then lugged him off the ramp. He scrambled to help, arms flailing, a foot pumping. The other, dragging, got caught on a root, and they sprawled into underbrush as the searchlight beam returned and hovered on the clearing about them.

"Don't move," Maggie hissed, but the deckhand elbowed past her through the undergrowth. Maggie copied him and followed, worming, squirming, elbows pushing. Why did the light beam stay still unless they'd been seen? Her purse! Dear Lord! It was out on the ramp right where she'd dropped it, black, and looking like a dead cat with the strap its twisted legs.

She tried to pull air past a lump in her throat as she watched the cruiser come downstream. She heard the diesels go quiet then surge again as it reversed direction and backed slowly upriver.

"Not that way," she heard a man shout. "Look farther down — the broken branch, leafy part hanging into the river."

Then came shouts, and the light beam swung that way. She dashed out, snatched up her purse and dove back to cover as two rifle shots smothered the diesel's pulsing. She heard a cheer from the *Hedda* and, peering back, saw two men swing the dinghy off the cruiser's boat deck.

Maggie just had to get her breath. She plopped down onto soggy forest soil with her back against a tree, and looked at the deck hand stretched out close by. Just who might he be, and why had he gambled his life to escape? Why was she helping him? He might tell her about El Ragnorak and the Buehler hacienda, but was that worth risking her safety? Sure, she wanted to know, but he needed help and that was reason enough.

The deckhand stirred, pulled up a leg, pushed up onto an elbow and slowly sat up. She couldn't see much in the murky light, but could tell that his right pant leg was in tatters and his skin looked mangled, a bloody mess just above his knee.

"We've got to go," she said. "Can you walk? I'll help. I have a car and will take you to Veracruz. Do you have any money?"

No answer.

Maggie heard a roar like breaking surf, steady and coming closer. Suddenly branches thrashed and torrents pelted the forest cover. She saw a flash of light, low in the forest — the searchlight, not lightning. The cruiser's diesels, hushed by the storm, had given them no warning.

"*Vámonos,* let's go," she insisted, scrambling to her feet. He was already struggling to rise and Maggie pulled him to his feet. "Hang onto my shoulder," she told him, as she reached across his back to grasp his belt. Staggering, stumbling, they sloshed through the dripping, drenching jungle to her car.

She opened the door and sat him on the running board. "You're bleeding too much," she said. "Sit there while I bandage your leg." She snatched a polishing rag from the door pocket, turned and saw him tear off the bottom of his pant leg, wring out the river water, and fold it into a pad. "Here, tie it on with this. Hurry, they're close."

He took it. "Out you go, cocopalmito," she said and she pulled the palms from the rumble seat. "Geez you're heavy," she muttered, lifting the papaya crate out, too. She tilted the seat cushion up against the back rest, turned, and found him beside her. Standing on one leg, he reached for the cowling, grasped the rumble seat handle and jumped with his good leg. She lifted, pushed, and up and over he tumbled into the rumble seat. "Scoot way down," she whispered. "I'll hide you under the palms."

Roots first, she shoved in a palm, lifted the papaya crate up and on top of him. She saw a glow of light from where they had just come as she piled the other palm saplings into the car and stuffed the roots down. Her hand brushed his leg, slippery with blood and she jerked it out. He needed treatment, and soon.

"Eat a papaya," she said, and clambered into the car.

"Gracias, Señorita," he said softly.

Just then Maggie heard shouting from the direction of the river and, through rain and mist, saw lights bobbing— flashlights — searchers.

"Good boy, Clank," she murmured when the engine fired. "Let's get out of here."

She backed onto the trail. Without lights, she eased ahead through the murky forest. Suddenly the car stopped and she had to back away from a tree. She found the trail again, and drove about fifty yards before turning on the headlights. Only then did she pull in a deep breath, hold it an instant, then gust it out. Her hands shook, and she couldn't control her chattering teeth. She clapped her hands and rubbed her wrists, trying to calm herself, and finally shouted out a song she detested:

Oh my darling, oh my darling, oh my darling Clementine
You are lost and gone forever, dreadful sorry, Clementine.

She felt her chest relax and her hands steady. She waved at an old man in the clearing where the trail branched. It had stopped raining she noticed when he waved back. She honked an *ah-OO-gas* reply and went on with her song.

Drove she ducklings, to the water, every morning just at nine
But alas she was no swimmer, and I lost my Clementine.

She stomped on the brake as bright headlights appeared in the road ahead. Proceeding slowly, she noticed that her hands were steady. Not such a bad song at that, she thought as she stopped at the paw-paw grove where she'd gotten the crate of papayas. A large car blocked the trail, and the driver's door was open.

What would she say if someone questioned her? She sang quietly, calm now, and confident that she could cope with whatever might be going on. Stay in the car, she told herself. Her skirt and blouse — damp, muddy, and blood smeared, would invite questions and the inspection of her cargo. Singing yet more softly, she got her comb from her purse and began to untangle her snarled hair.

She saw the farmer approach from the grove with another man, who must be the driver. A tall blond man emerged from the car's rear door and went across to meet them. "Oh-no," she muttered. "Adolf Buehler. How did he get here so soon?"

She leaned out the window. "Mr. Buehler," she called in English. "It's me, Maggie Magodón. Am I ever glad to see you! Will you tell your driver to close his door so I can get through?" She inched Clank forward.

He held up a hand to stop her and went on talking to the farmer. Finally, he approached her. "Did you get some good pictures, Miss Magodón?"

"Much too dark and you know it. I did find views I want to get, so I'll be back."

He came to her window and looked inside. "It's too dangerous for a woman to be in the country alone, especially after dark. Come. My driver will return your Ford —"

"Mr. Buehler," she broke in, "I'm in a hurry to deliver papayas to the chef at the Hotel Imperial. Please tell your driver to close his door."

"Does José know you're driving his car?" Adolf said, then shifted his position so he could see the load in the rumble seat.

Apparently he saw nothing suspicious, for he looked in her window again. "What will José think when he sees the damaged fender and broken headlight?"

"Stupid question, Adolf. He'll agree with what you're thinking — women shouldn't be allowed to drive. *Oiga amigo*," she called to the farmer. "Will you push those car doors closed, please?" She eased the car forward as the farmer complied. "See you in Veracruz, Adolf," she called back. *"Gracias y hasta luego,"* she said to the farmer. *"Buenos noches,* Catrina," she shouted, noticing a platinum blond woman in the back seat as she squeezed Clank past the long black limousine.

Maggie turned left onto the Veracruz road and poked along at thirty miles per hour. Except for treating the deck hand's injury, there was no reason to hurry. Adolf's limousine could overtake any Model A Ford.

She heard the noise of tires on wet pavement above the purr of Clank's engine. Might the boy hear her if she shouted? Eyes glued to the road, she called down into the cab, *"Amigo,* can you hear me?"

No answer, but she tried again.

"Amigo, what do I call you? What's's your name?"

"Trece Conejo."

She was surprised by how well she could hear him. "Is that what they called you on the cruiser?"

"No, Señorita. I am from Chichicastenango in Guatemala. They called me Chichi."

"I won't tell anybody, and I'll call you *Jóven,* young man," she said. "Now we talk no more."

She drove on in silence, her thoughts on her injured passenger. *Trece Conejo — Trece,* thirteen, in Spanish. Might the boy named Tracy she'd known in high school have been the thirteenth child in a family? And *Conejo,* rabbit, hadn't there been a famous Mexican warrior named Thirteen Rabbit during the days of the Conquistadores? What a fine name it was in

Mexico, and how awful for a boy in the States.

Adolf's limousine caught and roared past her, and Maggie drove faster. Thirteen Rabbit needed attention, so she went directly to the garage, where two quick *ah-OO-gas* opened the door. Miguel waved as she drove in. Miguel closed the door behind her, and indicated a place to put the car.

"Miguel." She shook her head and beckoned. "Come here." He came to her window, and she whispered, "Is anybody else here?"

"No. Only the two watchdogs." He turned to two brown short-haired monsters and pointed toward a fenced area. "*Quédense por allá,*" he demanded. The dogs obeyed.

"Good, they're scary," Maggie said, watching them go. She thumbed over her shoulder. "I just helped a boy escape from Buehler's hacienda. He's been shot — needs help."

By the time she got out of the car Miguel had already unloaded the palms, and was unloading the papayas.

"Let me talk to him first, Miguel," Maggie said, and waited until Miguel took the palms away before talking to Trece. "This man is Miguel. He will help us. Tell him your name if you wish, but you don't have to tell him anything. We're in a garage in Veracruz. I'll help you get out now." She looked down into the rumble seat and saw him staring back at her, but he did not move.

"Take your time." Maggie motioned behind her for Miguel to stay away. "We'll find pants and a shirt for you, and you can clean up, get something to eat, too." She chuckled. "Boys are always hungry. After you eat, you can go whenever you want. Please come now, Jóven. I must take the papayas to the hotel, and someone might see you if you are still in the car."

"*Bueno.* I will come," Trece said.

Maggie beckoned to Miguel. "He's really stuffed in. Will you get these seat cushions out of his way?"

Miguel removed them. "There's a platform lift by the stairs.

I'll take him up to my apartment. Can you bring the papayas?"

"Only the one on the front seat. The crate goes to the Hotel Imperial." Maggie carried the large papaya to the lift, then helped Miguel take Trece to the apartment. Returning to the car, she arranged the rumble seat to look as it had before, and had turned the car around when Miguel returned to open the garage door.

"How badly hurt?" she asked.

"Not serious. A bullet grazed his leg. He lost a lot of blood and he was badly beaten. I'll know more by the time you get back." He opened the garage door and Maggie drove out.

Centuries old, and fronting the Zócalo, the Hotel Imperial's only access was from the plaza. Maggie parked on Avenida Independencia, and beckoned to a boy selling Chicle chewing gum. "Please ask one of the Hotel Imperial waiters to come get the crate of papayas in back."

The boy looked at the crate. "Twenty centavos."

Maggie shook her head. "Ten."

He hefted the crate, came back to the window. "Thirty, and I take it in."

Maggie pursed her lips. "Ten now. Take it and I'll give you twenty more when you come back." He nodded and she gave him ten.

He put two fingers in his mouth, whistled, and two other boys appeared. He told them where to take the crate, then leaned against the car until they returned.

"Gracias, y buenas noches," Maggie said, paying him.

The boys saluted and dashed off.

When Maggie pulled onto the street, she saw in the mirror that a long black limousine followed her. Lucky she dropped Thirteen Rabbit off, she thought. Grinning, she started to hum *Clementine*. Why, of all the songs she knew, had one she'd always disliked popped into her mind?

The long black car followed her right into the garage, and

went to a space evidently designated for it. The driver got out and Maggie felt no surprise to see that it was Adolf's driver when he approached.

Miguel reached her first. Maggie did not get out but held the door slightly ajar.

"Buenas noches," Miguel greeted her as if she'd been away all day. "Did you dig up the palm trees yourself? That must have been hard work." He turned to the driver. "What do you think of these *Norteamericana* women who dig up trees all by themselves?"

The driver looked past Maggie into the car, swept palm fronds aside to see into the rumble seat, then grunted and walked, stiff-legged, out of the garage.

Miguel locked the door behind him and came back to Maggie with a twisted smile on his lips. "German," he said, nodding after the man. "Speaks no Spanish. He doesn't trust you, Señorita."

"At least he didn't see how muddy I am," Maggie said, getting out. "How's our friend?"

"Callado. He's a mute," Miguel told her. "You'll get no information from that boy. Risked your life for nothing, *Señorita.*"

Chapter 13

Maggie scowled, trying to hold back the laugh bubbling within her. Of course Trece could talk. No good, she just had to smile, and hid it from Miguel by bending over to wipe her muddy hands on her skirt. How could he say she'd wasted her time when she'd saved the boy's life? Still, she felt a tickling satisfaction from Thirteen Rabbit's refusal to say a word to Miguel, although he had spoken freely to her

"He's hurt, hungry, and scared, Miguel," she said, looking up. "You can't expect him to trust anybody after what he's been through, especially in a gloomy, ghostly place like this." She tried to change the subject by pointing at the car's damaged front end. "My fault. I'll pay for that."

"Ghostly?" Miguel shook his head. "Maybe so in the garage, but he's in my apartment where it's bright and cheerful."

"But he's in a strange country, and —"

"Slipped up there," Miguel cut in. "So he can talk. Where's he from?"

Maggie closed her eyes and hung her head. He'd tricked her and she'd blabbed. "Gotta watch that, don't I?" she said. "He's from Guatemala. That's all I know, but he has too much hair for a Veracruzano. Got any scissors?"

"I'll get them," Miguel said as he stooped to examine the damage. "He's eating now — roast goat, rice, beans, coffee. I've eaten. There's plenty for you, too, if you're hungry." .

"Why not. How does he feel? His leg was a mess."

Miguel straightened and slapped the fender. "Enrique will repair it. The car's not José's, but he borrows it when he's in the mood to mingle with commoners. Don't let the car he drives mislead you." He pointed. "Those two cars just beyond Adolf's limousine belong to José, a Lincoln and a Cadillac. One of these days he'll be whipping you about in his Chrysler roadster."

"Then why — ?"

"He fancies himself as a gallant cavalier. You should see him at bullfights."

"Why there especially?"

"Toreador — fights bulls — dresses to kill. He puts on quite a show — even wears a red ostrich plume in his hat. He bows to the bulls real formal like, swoops off the hat and tickles their noses with the plumes. You should hear the crowds roar, especially the señoritas." Chuckling, Miguel cast her a sideways glance. "And you would be one of the ladies screaming for his attention."

Maggie snorted. "Enough about José. How badly hurt is the boy?"

"He'll be okay. Tough — hardly winced when I cleaned his wound with alcohol. I dusted sulfa into it, then stitched it up. Better come now if you want to talk to him. He'll conk out before long."

"You give him a shot? I'm surprised he'd let you."

"In the coffee, and he likes coffee."

"Can he stay here tonight?"

"*Sí.* He'll sleep in the watchman's room, you in my apartment."

"No," Maggie snapped, facing him.

"I won't be here, and I can't risk leaving him alone in my shop."

Maggie waited for him to suggest something else. Two nights in José's bunk, one at the consulate, another in hers, and now the fourth in five nights? "You can't expect me to —"

"You have two other choices," he said finally. "Lose him or bed him in —"

"Okay-okay. You win. Boy or not, no way will I share my room. Do you have a robe I can borrow until my things get dry?"

He nodded, then backed toward the steps to the upper floor. "Beans are still warm. Come on. You can eat while you talk to him."

She unloaded the palms, moved the car, then dallied, wondering if Miguel's comments about José had been a warning. Was he really wealthy, or did he have other financial support? Was he a silversmith, or a torero? Bullfighter, ugh — What a surprise. She didn't know much about bullfighters — only what she'd seen in movies and they were always with gorgeous women. Who might his be? There'd been no pictures of women in his apartment, and while there she'd thought he might be leading a double life. Was he really favored by Mexico City women, known for their classic beauty? She plucked her wet blouse to free it from her body and looked down at her skirt. She'd worn the outfit during the break-in at the consulate only five nights before. "Well," she snorted. José would never see her in it again.

She glanced at José's luxury cars parked in what must be a converted warehouse. Above, and seemingly distant in the dim light, a row of night-black clerestory windows extended along each side of the central ceiling channel. There must be thirty or more cars, trucks, taxis, and three of the brown *FONTANERÍA* plumbing vans. It was too dark to read two signs over doors at the far end — office and repair shop, she guessed, and fixed the layout in her mind before going up to the apartment.

Miguel indicated a robe, scissors, and pans on the stove. "Help yourself. I'll change the sheets while you eat."

"I'll cut his hair first." Maggie glanced at Trece. "Yes I will," she said, meeting the challenge in his eyes. "They'll catch you if you don't look like a Veracruzano. You'll sleep in the watchman's room."

She saw him look at his coffee cup, reach, get it and fall asleep with it on his lap. She cut his hair quickly, then helped Miguel settle him on a mat in the watchman's room. Miguel took a chocolate-brown garment off a shelf and laid it over him.

"A trifle large, but he can wear that while he's here," Miguel said. "Might disguise him for a while."

Upstairs again, Maggie changed into the robe then dished a hot meal for herself from the stove. Miguel poured coffee, and they sat across from each other at the table.

"I've never tasted goat before," Maggie said. "It's good, at least the way you fixed it."

"Gracias." Steam drifted from Miguel's cup as he stirred his coffee and spoke quietly. He told her about his boyhood, his family and where they had lived. He suggested ways by which she might dovetail her FBI responsibilities into those at the consulate, and eventually got back to the reason Maggie was in his garage. "Why did you bring the boy here? What do you know about him?"

"Not much." Maggie put down her cup. "He was the deck hand on Mr. Buehler's new cruiser. I first saw him on Friday when Mr. Buehler took Mrs. Williams and her group to Antigua for dinner last Friday."

"You went, too? Why?"

Maggie shrugged. "Interpreter. Mrs. Williams — I had no choice. Anyhow, the *Hedda* had four crewmen. I know one of them is dead and I think two others are, too. Could be that this boy is the only one left alive and I want to know why they tried to kill him."

Maggie knew from Miguel's gaze, shifting back and forth from her to his cup, that he liked what he was hearing. "After I left the governor's this afternoon, I drove out to the beach where I got the palms. "I saw the *Hedda* going north, slowly, with Mr. Buehler and a man who looks like him scanning the shoreline with field glasses. I was curious, so I went on to Antigua, and got there in time to watch from across the river when his cruiser docked at his hacienda. I saw the deck hand on the foredeck and waved. By the way, his name's Trece Conejo. He signaled back, sort of hiding it, and must have sneaked away while I was watching those foreign-looking men get off. The next thing I knew, he was the middle of the river and they were shooting at him."

"Men? What makes you think they were foreigners?"

"Their suits — gray or blue-gray. Locals would be in white. Americans wouldn't wear their coats." That must have impressed him, Maggie thought, when Miguel nodded, his lips pursed.

"Risked your neck to save a rabbit? Why?"

"Because he needed help. Why else?"

"You might have been shot."

"So?" He's just teasing, Maggie decided when the corners of his eyes crinkled. "Anyhow, he was on the cruiser when we picked up El Ragnorak, and why would they shoot him unless he knew too much? Just think, Miguel. One crewman murdered. Two escaped, but dollars to doughnuts they got caught and are dead, too. I'd give a peck of gold for what Trece must know."

"Hmm." Elbow on the table, chin cradled in his hand, Miguel chewed his lower lip. "No wonder you took a chance. Judging by the way Adolf's driver checked the car out there in the garage, none of them trust you."

"You can say that again. Adolf looked in the rumble seat just as I left Antigua, but it was almost dark and the palms fooled him."

Miguel grinned. "You hid the boy well. Think José might know anything about the newcomers?"

"Doubt it. I sure never expected to get involved in all this. Say, do you suppose those foreigners had anything to do with the burglary at the consulate last Wednesday?"

"Burglary?" Miguel reached for the coffee pot.

"Yeah. That's why I screamed. You and José showed up just in time."

"You mean they weren't mugging you?"

"They didn't know I was there. I saw a packet come flying out the window and —"

"How big?"

"Pound of butter — two, maybe three. Ask José. He put it in his safe that night so he could return it to the consulate the next day."

"Oh, of course. Now, back to the boy. You'll get whatever he knows?"

"Try and stop me," Maggie said, wondering if the way he'd said *of course*
meant that he'd get at José for not reporting the burglary.

Miguel chuckled. "Get details, but keep it all secret — no notes — no talk."

"Listen to that — wonderful!" Maggie exclaimed as a sudden downpour drummed the roof. "It took a rain like that to get down through the leaves and help us escape by washing away the trail of blood between the riverbank and the car."

"Don't gloat," Miguel shook his head. "I've got to drive all night — Mexico City — fly to Panama tomorrow. The garage manager gets here at six."

"Just a minute." Maggie leaned forward. "You say you're my boss. Why should I believe you're even FBI?"

Miguel stood up. "Come into the office." He took a long nail from a tiny drawer in a roll-top desk, inserted its point into a small hole on the right rear corner of the desk top and pressed the head.

Maggie heard a faint click as the desk's end panel popped open, exposing a shallow space about a foot wide and eighteen inches high. Miguel took out a folder, laid it open, and pointed at a document.

"That's all the proof I can give you at the moment," he said, "but you should recognize the signatures. Satisfied?"

"Well. Okay. Sure. But why are you here? Looks fishy to me for the Central America FBI spy honcho to be a taxi driver in Veracruz."

"Fair enough." Miguel grinned. "I wondered why you hadn't challenged me before this." He stooped to replace the documents. "Needless to say, you'll forget this little safe. By the way," he tore a sheet from a notepad and handed it to her, "I've okayed three men for the watchman job and favor the name on top. Tell Enrique to be sure to have a man tomorrow."

"Sure." Miguel seemed taller and quite dignified when he stood erect and looked into her eyes. "You a taxi driver? Plumber? Are you really?"

Miguel nodded. "I have the skills. Understand, Maggie, I was once a fulltime FBI agent, but not now, and neither is José. By all appearances, you'll be borrowing — renting, if you choose — from *garage Enrique*, but the U.S. government owns the car."

"So I just say something like, 'I've got a deal with the garage. Okay?"

"Right. The business is legitimate. It gives me a cover, a sort of flexible identity — and money. Your case is an example. I vigorously opposed a woman for the work we expect from you. José insisted that you had the best qualifications. I came to Veracruz to check you out, expecting to turn you down. I even sent José on a wild goose chase to divert him from meeting your plane in Mexico City. Can you imagine any way I might have judged you quickly if you had started here as the long lost pampered niece of the governor, and now under the wings of the domineering consul's wife?"

"Makes sense," Maggie said, and both laughed as they returned to the kitchen.

"The business gives me a chance to see who comes, goes, and visits whom," Miguel went on. "It provides access to the taxi driver's information grapevine. We'd lost track of El Ragnorak in South Africa. Then I got a grapevine tip that he might be headed this way on his cruiser. He wasn't aboard when the cruiser refueled in Recife, Brazil, so we thought the tip was false. Now we know where he is, thanks to you. I must go."

Maggie lifted her shoulders and pulled in a deep breath as a surge of pride coursed through her. Pride — pride in herself and in being associated with such a man.

* * *

A steady rain greeted Maggie when she swung open the garage door. Miguel drove out, swung left, and she watched his car tracks wash away as the siffling of tires on wet pavement faded.

She closed and barred the door, then peeked into the watchman's room. Trece was facing the wall and did not stir.

Returning to the apartment, she cleared the table and washed the dishes, but her mind was on the small man she knew as Miguel. The Canal Zone had been his boyhood home, he'd said. His father, U.S. Army General Franklin Macott, had been the commanding officer. Miguel had been in no rush to leave while the rain drummed the roof, and had sipped coffee while answering questions. Strange. He'd said he owned the building but that title was held by Enrique Salazar. Raul Enrique managed the garage and repair shop named *Garage Enrique*. Miguel must have reason for generating such confusion, she decided, and wondered what the names of his similar businesses in Mexico City, the Canal Zone, Colon, and Panama City might be.

"Whew!" How could Miguel contend with all that, the FBI, and still make his home on his tiny island in the Pearle Archipelago near Panama City? She'd been especially interested to hear how he'd met his wife during his Marine Corps duty, and learn of his three children, the oldest already a college graduate. When she'd called him Michael Macott, he shook his head. Miguel, he'd insisted, and said that his last name varied with the needs of his work. She shrugged. Might she ever need an alias? At the moment, she couldn't imagine why. Still, one never knew.

Alias? — just what Thirteen Rabbit needed. He'd been known only as Chichi. She dried her hands and sat down with another cup of coffee.

"Got it!" Maggie burst out suddenly. "You're gone forever, Chichi."

She picked the telephone receiver off its cradle and glanced at her watch — not yet ten o'clock .

"El Examen, por favor," she said into the mouthpiece. Victor Dalpica was not in, but she reached him at the Naval Academy.

"Victor? Victor Dalpica? This is Margareta Magodón."

"Muy buenas noches, Señorita Maggie. This is a pleasant surprise."

"You'll be . . ." Maggie hesitated. "I could use a favor."

"Of course. How may I help you?"

"I hear there was trouble at Antigua this evening — someone shot a man swimming in the river."

"Why would they shoot him? Was he a thief?"

"If you say so, Victor. And do you suppose a body might have been sighted in the sea off the mouth of the river? An unidentified body?"

"If you say so, Maggie. By a fisherman perhaps, and badly mutilated?"

"If you say so, Victor. And are not the sharks close to shore at this time of year?"

"If you say so." Victor paused. "It might be appropriate for *El Examen* to publish a shark warning at this time. Don't you think so?"

"If you say so, Victor. And many, many times I thank you."
She heard him chuckle, then a click as he rang off.

Chapter 14

Maggie was getting used to waking up on a strange pallet. She'd been in Mexico five nights, slept on four different beds, but never before one like this. She rolled over to savor its comfort. Where might she be sleeping this night? Might she return? What would she — Rabbit!

Was Thirteen Rabbit awake? She scooted into the bathroom and dressed in clothes still damp. Making sure she could get back into the apartment, she stepped out to gray morning light on the upper landing. Looking up through clerestory windows, she saw a gray cloud suddenly turn golden, colored by the dawning sun. The garage brightened, too, and she scampered down to the watchman's room. She knocked. No answer. She knocked again, then opened the door. Thirteen Rabbit was gone.

She spun about with an eerie feeling that she was not alone but saw nobody. Doors, large and small, were both barred on the inside so he must be somewhere near. She took a deep breath, felt better and poked along the center aisle, her rubber-soled saddle shoes making no sound on the concrete floor. A scratching sound came from Clank's direction and, turning, she saw a frazzled branch slide out from under it.

"*Buenos días, Señorita.* That branch scraped the road right under my ear all the way from Antigua," Thirteen Rabbit said as he squirmed out from under the car. "You saved me. I'll fix it." Still on his back, he waggled his thumb at the car's damaged front end.

"*Buenos días*, Trece. Are you sure you can?" He looked disgusted and gave her a 'stupid question' bob with his head. Fat chance he can, she thought. A boy from deep in the Guatemala mountains would hardly have an opportunity to learn the skills needed to repair the damage. Still, garage work would provide convenient cover for him until she found out whatever he knew about El Ragnorak.

"*Hola por allá,*" a man approaching from the office called.

"*Buenos días.* You must be Raul Enrique?" she said, extending her hand. She glanced at Trece as he stood up and saw *GARAGE ENRIQUE,* printed in large gold letters across the back of his chocolate-colored coveralls, and that he favored his leg only a little. "I'm Señorita Gutiérrez y Magodón. Miguel said to —"

"*Sí. Lo se,* I know. *Buenos días, Señorita.* He told me you will use the Ford now." Enrique shook Maggie's hand, and turned to Trece. "Are you the new watchman?"

"He's Trece Conejo," Maggie said, as the two men shook hands. "I ran into a tree and Trece said he would fix it. Show him, Trece."

Maggie looked for the dogs while the men examined the car, but she couldn't see them. Come to think of it, she hadn't seen them after delivering the papayas the night before, so Miguel must have done something with them. He'd laid out the garage uniform for Thirteen Rabbit, too, and wasn't that hint enough to just let the young man have the watchman job? She'd check on him every day, of course. She owed that much to Miguel.

"Trece can do many things, Señor Enrique," she said.

"Is Miguel upstairs?" the garage man asked. "*Borracho?* Is he drunk?"

Maggie shook her head. "He went to Mexico City last night. Maybe he left a message for you. I'll go look."

"Don't bother yourself. I know what he wants." Scowling,

Enrique turned to Trece. "Watchman, *bien,* okay. What else did he say you would do — wash cars, polish, sweep, drive a taxi?"

Jeez, we've got a man, not a boy, Maggie thought when Thirteen Rabbit's lips curled into a twisted smile as he faced Enrique and eyed him a moment before speaking.

"I repair cars, trucks — small ones, big ones, engines — petrol, diesel. I can fix that," he indicated the damaged fender, "tires, too — anything."

Made a good impression, Maggie decided when Enrique's brow lifted.

"Is that so?" he said. "One week — four pesos a day — seven if you're still here after a week. Tell the *jefe* I sent you. He'll show you what to do." Enrique waved toward the repair shop, shook hands, then returned to his office.

"He'll be there in a few minutes," Maggie called after Enrique. "Come, Trece." She hurried to the steps, ran up and turned to make sure he was following. Poor guy, she thought, watching him approach with set jaw and careful steps. He was not limping, and only by comparison to his agility and quickness when she'd seen him on the cruiser, did she perceive the pain he suffered. He must know that the appearance of injury invited suspicion. Uh-oh, his bent-kneed loping walk might mark him as mountain bred, and a stranger to Veracruz.

Maggie warmed rice and beans for their breakfast, then sat across the table from him. He sat silent, only nibbled. Did he feel caged? Was he itching to get away? Still, he'd volunteered to repair the car, but perhaps that was no more than a gesture of thanks.

Then it struck her. He's on Miguel's turf. He thinks I'm Miguel's woman and, even worse, accepting favors during Miguel's absence. No wonder he'd clammed up.

"I am not Miguel's woman," she said, slowly shaking her head.

No answer, not even a frown.

Right track, she thought. He'd probably survived the *Hedda* and hacienda by remaining quiet. She'd have to gain his trust.

"I am not his woman," she said again, looking into his eyes. "He lives here, but is often away. The garage is his, too. I brought you here because I knew he would help you. I stayed all night to make sure you were safe, only because he had to go to Mexico City last night. I am *Norteamericana,* and work at the *Consulado de los Estados Unidos.* We will help you and we want you to help us."

He leaned forward to take in a heaping mouthful of beans.

Maggie grinned. "We know El Ragnorak is in Antigua." Getting there, she thought, as his eyes widened. "We think he is very bad, and hope that you will work here and help us find out what El Ragnorak is doing at the hacienda. But I will help you return to your home when you want to go."

She poured coffee to give him a moment to consider her meaning, hoping that Miguel or José would back her if he chose to leave Veracruz. If not, she'd see to it herself.

She filled his plate again, then asked, "Why did you risk your life to escape from Señor Buehler's hacienda?"

His gaze shifted to the exit door and she went on. "I found the helmsman from South Africa, *muerto* — dead. Did you know? Were you afraid they would kill you, too?" Maggie willed herself not to look away when he stared back at her, eyes blazing.

"Asesino," Trece growled. "Crew — all dead."

Maggie gulped. Back off, she told herself. He might know more than she cared to pursue. She swallowed again then went on, "I saw one of the crew escape onto the *Olinda.*"

Thirteen Rabbit shook his head. *"Sí, Señorita.* The diesel engineer got away, but they caught him again. The radio man, too. I saw them tied and beaten. I ran the *Hedda* engines early Saturday morning. They were still alive when El Ragnorak threw them to the sharks.

Maggie shuddered, squeezed a tight blink to throw off a vision of that fiend heaving whip-torn bodies into gaping jaws. She shook her head. "El Ragnorak!" she repeated, and saw Trace's head bobbing, eyelids squeezed tight.

"Were Señor Buehler and his sister on board?" Maggie asked.

Thirteen Rabbit opened his eyes, took a bite, then shook his head.

Maggie dreaded hearing more, but pressed on. "Are you sure El Ra —"

"More Germans came," he broke in. "Some speak our tongue, but none would talk to me."

"Would any of them know you? I mean — would it be dangerous for you to work here?"

Thirteen Rabbit took a deep breath and shook his head. "Only one would know me, and today he goes to Tampico."

"Have you been inside the hacienda?"

"Sí," he said, nodding.

Maggie went into Miguel's office and returned with paper and pencil. "Can you draw me a plan of the hacienda?" she asked, "something like this." She sketched a sample, showing a river, boundary walls and the location of roads and structures within them.

"Sí. I can do that."

"Do it when you have time. One more thing, Trece. Would Señor Buehler recognize you?"

"I don't think so, but he is not bad, *Señorita.* He and the white-haired woman argued with El Ragnorak. They never came back to the hacienda after that. I'm not afraid of him."

"Do you have any money?" When he shook his head, she handed him five pesos and went on. "Pay me back later, Trece. I must go to work now, but I'll be back before dark."

She watched him walk slowly to the repair shop. Got to hurry — clean up Miguel's apartment, she thought, and got busy.

Later, as Maggie unlocked the door to her apartment, she heard Helen's voice behind her.

"Night on the town?"

"Good morning, Helen," Maggie said, as she pushed her door open.

"You look a wreck. Mr. Williams tried to reach you all day yesterday."

Maggie faced her. About to retort, she thought better of it and said sweetly, "Beautiful day for a brisk early walk. You should try it sometime. Great for your complexion."

"Well." Helen bristled. "Just remember I warned you. But it won't do you any —"

Maggie shut the door behind her

*　*　*

When Maggie entered the consulate a half-hour later, she found it difficult to believe that it was only her second work day, and the beginning of her first full week at the consulate. Thank goodness the interpreter had switched back her clean desk and she wouldn't have to put up with tobacco odors in the drawers. She scribbled a thank-you note and, as she put it on the interpreter's desk, heard voices from behind Mr. Williams's office door. He must like the quiet before the staff arrived to do his dictation, so she decided to go up to the alcove over the foyer where she'd been working on the entertainment accounts. The records were still where Mrs. Williams had shoved them.

At ten-thirty she leaned back and stretched, glad that Mrs. Williams had not appeared. Many transactions lacked supporting documents, and she hoped the consul's wife had kept them. Grasping her list, she rose and went down to Mr. Williams's office.

"Mr. Williams just asked me to call you," Helen told her, motioning for her to enter.

What might he want? Maggie wondered as she entered.

"You sent for me, Mr. Williams?"

"Yes," he said, continuing to sort papers on his desk

Maggie waited — and waited. Why wouldn't he tell her why he'd called her? Finally she said, "I've been working on the entertainment account as you suggested, Mr. Williams, but can't find supporting documents for many of last fiscal year's transactions." She paused. He stared at the documents. She went on. "Might Mrs. Williams have any canceled checks, purchase orders, receipts? Do I have your permission to ask her?"

The consul leaned back, picked up a pencil and tapped the eraser on his desk. "I would never allow such a thing. You may be sure that everything is in proper order. Nothing has changed since last year when Mrs. Williams personally attended to that account. We had no trouble closing the fiscal year at an early date. Helen will know."

"Thank you. I'll ask her." Maggie turned to leave.

"Miss Magodón."

"Yes Mr. Williams?" She paused at the door. Now what? she wondered. Was he about to pry into what she'd done yesterday?

"Mrs. Williams can hardly praise you enough for your help over the weekend. She's delighted to have you on our staff. Thank you."

"Thank you — thank you very much, Mr. Williams," she blurted, and wondered if he'd summoned her only to convey his wife's approval. Hmm. Hardly — kindness just didn't come from any man who scowled out a compliment. So why had he asked Helen to call her?

"He likes to keep tabs on his entire staff," Helen answered when Maggie asked. "If something's missing, it's probably in one of those cabinets."

Maggie looked through the files and asked each of the office staff to search, too. When only few missing items showed up, she wondered how her predecessor had balanced the accounts if the system had not changed. Had it cost him his job?

She glimpsed a newspaper heading on the interpreter's desk, *Thief Killed in Rio Antigua*. "Attaway, Victor," she murmured, and read on. A fisherman had reported seeing a mutilated body outside the river mouth. She took in a deep breath, exhaled through pursed lips, and murmured, "Thank you, Victor Dalpica. So long, Chichi. Welcome, Thirteen Rabbit."

* * *

Maggie concentrated on the consulate accounts during the following weeks, often working into the night to make up for the time lost to Mrs. Williams's demands for a companion, interpreter or bridge partner. Detest but respect her, she decided, thinking that through her she'd become acquainted with the English-speaking community. Grudgingly, she had to admire the woman's success in maintaining respect for the consulate and for the many things she'd learned from her.

Her introduction to the more important business people of the city and state resulted from her occasional presence at parties and celebrations with Adolf Buehler. Gracious, although somewhat stilted, Adolf was an attentive escort. How he beamed when she was referred to as his woman, and how scandalized the comments caused her to feel.

Such occasions never failed to irritate José, and she felt herself drawn ever closer to him because of it. He courted her openly, often dropping in at the consulate during the day. She enjoyed weekend jaunts to historic sites, museums, and local fiestas with him and, especially, sessions in his shop where he had samples of filigree silver pieces crafted by her mother, who'd been a gifted artisan. Reminded of those wondrous hours helping her mother, she welcomed the ever-increasing warmth between herself and José as she honed her own skills.

José never referred to El Ragnorak, nor had she heard from Miguel since his abrupt departure on that rainy night in July.

Only with Thirteen Rabbit did she speak of El Ragnorak, and then only when she needed Clank and he drove for her. He told her of *Hedda* sightings in Tuxpan and Tampico, the country's oil-producing region several miles to the north, but said he'd heard nothing of El Ragnorak. Was the man active in Mexico? What had become of him?

* * *

The rains of summer slackened, and months passed into October. On a Wednesday, Maggie got a folder from a cabinet and returned to her desk

"Aren't you ready, child? We always leave at one-thirty on Wednesday."

Maggie spun around and saw Mrs. Williams pulling on long, white gloves at the door to her husband's office.

"I'm sorry, Mrs. Williams," Maggie said. "We're into the fourth month of the fiscal year, and Mr. Williams insists that last year's accounts be in order before the end of this week."

"Margaret, come here," Mrs. Williams said with a jerk of her shoulders.

Deliberately, Maggie replaced the file in the cabinet, turned the key, and approached Sarah Williams. "Yes, Mrs. Williams?"

Sarah Williams swung wide the door. "My husband will talk to you. When he's through, come right out to the parking area."

The consul was dictating to Helen when Maggie entered. He looked up, nodded quickly to acknowledge her entrance, and continued to dictate. Finally he leaned back, tapped his pencil on the desk, then reached across his chest to rub the eraser behind his left ear.

"During previous meetings, Miss Gutiérrez — Miss Magodón — confound it, whatever you call yourself," he threw the pencil onto the desk, "I made it abundantly clear to you that Mrs. Williams's activities, in which she leads the American community in social functions, and maintains cultural contact with our Mexican hosts, is of primary importance for the continued success of our mission in this city, state and country. She works tirelessly to enhance our friendly position, with remarkable success, I must say." He reached for his pencil, tapped his desk again, and went on. "Do you not recall my instructions?"

"You told me to fin —"

The consul did not wait for an answer. "You have no experience in the subtleties of foreign customs. I gave you explicit instructions to follow closely the example Mrs. Williams sets for you."

He swivelled to face his secretary. "Now, Helen, will you read me back my last paragraph, please."

Maggie stretched her fingers to stop them from curling into fists and stomped out, sure that the consul had dismissed her from his mind. She'd hurry — no use letting that three- chinned bitch build up a head of steam waiting for her. Then she saw a man at her desk jerking on the center drawer.

"Hold it, mister," she snapped. "Private things in there."

The man straightened, swung around, and Maggie felt furious with him. It was Nolan Thompson, the United States Treasury examiner.

"Well-well, Miss Magodón," he said, "sit down, please, and we'll get started on —"

"I'm afraid you'll have to get in line, Mr. Thompson." Maggie unlocked the desk to get her purse. "You rank no higher than boss number three this afternoon."

"Now see here. Mr. Williams promised me all your time this afternoon."

"What makes you think Mr. Williams has any say around here?" Maggie unlocked the file cabinets. "Help yourself, Nolan Thompson. I'm off with her highness for an afternoon of bridge and peacock dropping *canapés*. Good-bye!"

Maggie wheeled away, pulled in a deep breath, blew it out and turned back. "I'm sorry, Mr. Thompson. I have no choice. I'll be back later to burn candles over those accounts, but I'm warning you, I'll be hungry. If you want any work out of me, you'd better be ready to offer something better than canapes." She raised her fist, pumped it, and marched out.

Chapter 15

Maggie reached the parking area just as Mrs. Williams went into her house. "Honk when she comes out," Maggie told the driver, who was waiting in the consulate's Chrysler sedan. She plucked a gardenia, held it up to smell the aroma, and sat down on a bench nestled into shrubbery surrounding the pergola.

Presently she heard footsteps, chairs scuffing and Mr. Williams's voice behind her.

"I expected you last month, Thompson, but as it is, your timing is perfect."

"Emergency in Ecuador," the Treasury man said. "Here, have a light."

Maggie heard a match strike, smelled cigarette smoke, then the consul came on again.

"Pleasant out here, and we won't be interrupted. What's Ecuador's problem?"

Maggie got up to leave. God forbid that she'd let herself get caught eavesdropping on the consul's discussion with the Treasury representative.

"Personnel matter," Nolan said. " The ambassador showed me your request yesterday. You still insist on replacing Miss Magodón?"

"Well." Mr. Williams paused. "Yes and no. Her situation is delicate, although she has made certain contributions to our program."

Was that a compliment from the consul? Maggie pursed her

lips as a cloud of smoke drifted through the shrubbery. Not really, Maggie thought, and sat down again, careful to make no sound. She leaned back to watch a smoke ring drift out from under the pergola roof and break up, thinking that it was just an I'm-a-good-guy statement to establish his own credibility.

"How so?" Nolan asked.

"She's effective with the local community."

"That's reason to keep her," Nolan said. "That's a State Department matter, not Treasury. I'm not involved unless I find fault in the accounts."

"Oh, no," Maggie mouthed. He's here to give me the boot.

"I'd be obliged, Thompson. No question she's bungled the books, missing financial documents, flagrant vi —"

"And you hate her guts," Nolan cut in.

"Yea, Nolan!" Maggie breathed. Maybe he wasn't so bad at that. She recalled a remark José had made — Nolan had no sympathy for lily-livered diplomats who let their affairs get out of hand. She listened as Nolan went on.

"Reason enough if her work's below par."

"It's her personality," the consul said. "She's feisty and —"

""Understood, Al. I just encountered her."

"Encounter, was it? Hmpf! She has the entire staff upset — one run-in after another, challenges everybody, pokes her nose into affairs that have nothing to do with her job."

"So?"

One word — that's all Nolan said — score one for me, Willumsey boy. No finance inspector would fault her for prying into dark corners. After all, wasn't that at the heart of an accountant's job?

"Sarah's schedule is so tight," the consul said. "You've met my wife?"

"Haven't yet had the pleasure. Capable woman, I hear. Go on."

Sarah, Sarah, stay on your potty or whatever you're doing,

Maggie prayed. I gotta hear more of this.

"Confound it, Thompson, the woman doesn't recognize how important it is for Sarah to support all the consulate functions. She maintains the social integrity of the American community impeccably, but Miss Magodón does not volunteer. She carries none of the responsibilities unless she's forced."

Maggie sucked in her cheeks. Even Nolan wouldn't bite on that one. How could he condone what that mucky-muck and his hoity-toity squaw were making her do right now? And did he understand what the consul meant by his wife's defense of social integrity?

"I met Magodón and reviewed her record before she was hired," Nolan said. "I did not recommend her to State. In fact, I turned her down flat and was surprised to learn she was here. I just got a taste of her temper when she stormed out like a she-tiger that lost her cubs. Her temperament may be a moot subject, Al. The woman I originally recommended for this post is already working in the embassy."

Visions of a cat licking its chops struck her as Mr. Williams cleared his throat.

"The matter must be handled with the utmost finesse," Mr. Williams said. "Are you aware that she signs her name *'Margareta Gutiérrez y Magodón*? Furthermore —"

"Come again," Nolan said. "I recall only Margaret Magodón."

Maggie heard chairs being pushed back. They're leaving — gotta get to the car, she thought as Mr. Williams spoke again.

"The devil take her. Governor Gutiérrez and his wife adopted her. It was all over the society pages."

"Damn. Then it is delicate," Nolan agreed. "Cause friction with the locals?"

"Nothing yet. But here in the consulate, it's like sharing the bathtub with a shark. Just this morning . . ."

A door bang ended his tale, leaving Maggie to ponder her

shark-like qualities. How could Mr. Williams be so vindictive? And Nolan was scarcely better. Play bridge after hearing that? Geez.

So Nolan had come as a hatchet man primed to fire her, and was simply a gofer for a coward. So what? She was ready and felt confident that the Treasury man would not fault her work. But was he reasonable? Might he trump up a detail to support the consul's charges? She plucked a fresh gardenia for Mrs. Williams, strolled to the car and blasted the horn to waken the driver.

* * *

Dusk had darkened the windows when Maggie returned to the consulate.
Good, nobody here, she thought, but her heart sank when she saw light streaming from her office and Nolan at her desk. Tired and not yet ready to face him, she sat down where she could see him, slipped off her shoes, and waited for him to look up. Minutes passed, and she thought he might be sleeping. Then he moved.

"Everything in order?" she asked.

Nolan's head jerked around. "Just get back?" He scooted over to make room. "Pull up a chair."

Maggie swung her head slowly from side to side, her thumb keeping time with jabs at the door.

"You're late." Nolan sputtered. "Mrs. Williams bustled through more than an hour ago."

"Got here soon as I could," Maggie said, her thumb still motioning at the door. "Had to walk. It didn't pay to win all the prize money. Queenie got mad, scooped it up, said I was only a substitute and didn't deserve it. Then she huffed off, and left me with no taxi fare."

"Sit down," Nolan ordered.

"I am sitting down, but I'll not sit over there until after we eat." She slumped farther down. "I had a sunrise breakfast and no lunch. Thirteen hours. After we eat, I'll work all night if you're up to it."

Jaws clenched, Nolan took off his glasses, whipped out a handkerchief, polished vigorously, then put them back on. Meticulously then, he packed papers into his briefcase.

"Thank you, Mr. Thompson." Maggie stood up. "Give me a second. There's a little restaurant close by. I'll freshen up and be right back."

She returned moments later, got two envelopes from a desk drawer and put them in her purse. Her stomach growled. "Hear that?"

"Yeah. Scolding me, is it?" Nolan said, smiling. "My stomach hasn't complained yet, but it's about to."

Maggie felt herself smiling. "Well, then," she said, "let's just see if we can keep them quiet."

                              * * *

"A bit hot for October isn't — Damn!" Nolan burst out, and swung wildly at a bat.

He's embarrassed — tongue-tied — cursed a bat just for something to say, Maggie thought, casting a sideways glance at him. "Sure is," she said, "but we can get nights like this at any time of year. I hear you just came from Ecuador. What's it like there?"

"Cool in the Andes," Nolan said, and walked on in silence.

` She'd expected him to review her work since her arrival, and was surprised when he told Mr. Williams that he hadn't known she was in Veracruz. Might her presence be troubling him? Or was he debating how to tell her she'd be fired? Probably neither, she thought, for financial examiners would not deal with such matters. She recalled how shocked he'd looked when she'd entered the Washington University interview room months ago after he'd painted the town with Fred Dilgaard before waking up in her bed the next morning. Might he be afraid she'd hold it over his head, blackmail him to keep her job?

"Damn!" He swung his arm at a bat.

Just that morning she'd heard him boast that he'd flat out turned down her application. Was he having second thoughts after examining her work?

"Damn!"

There he goes again, mildly explosive this time, she thought. Might he be a confirmed bachelor and resent having to dine alone with a woman? No. She could tell by the way he looked at her that he found her attractive. Besides, too many men back at Douglas had convinced her that she was attractive to most men. Well, no chance she'd come on to him. His fraternity brother Fred Dilgaard was well over thirty, and Nolan must be at least five years older than Fred.

"Dammit — damn!"

This time she heard the bat flick his hat. Why was he wearing one? Perhaps he wondered what had happened when he was drunk that night in St. Louis and was afraid she knew what he'd done and he did not.

"Dammit, Miss Magodón, I should have — "

She couldn't help chuckling. "Oh, shush. Mighty important bats to get five damns out of you. Here's where we'll eat."

* * *

Time dragged. They sat in silence waiting to be served. Obviously Nolan was troubled, and Maggie regretted teasing him about the bats. She remembered how red his face looked and how he'd stared at her in the Washington University interview room just before booting her out. Yet when her job had come through, she'd dismissed the snub. If that were now the reason for his strange behavior, she'd just get it out in the open.

Her chance came when the waiter brought the wine list.

"An aperitif?" Nolan asked.

"Iced tea, please."

"You sure? A glass of wine might relax you after a long day."

"Just iced tea," she said. "Occasionally I'll take a little wine or beer, but not now."

"Iced tea for both of us," he ordered.

"*Un momentito, por favor*," Maggie said to the waiter who had not understood Nolan. "Don't let me crimp your ways, Nolan. I know you drink. After all, you were thoroughly pickled when my sister and your buddy Fred Dilgaard dumped you off in my apartment." When he clenched his teeth and bowed his head, she felt sorry for him, and added quickly, "Don't worry. Nothing happened. I slept at a friend's place across the hall. So what will it be?" She saw his eyes close and his chest heave in a long breath, and couldn't help bursting into laughter. "You look like a little boy who's just been forgiven for stealing a cookie."

Nolan laughed, too. "Scotch and soda, please."

After Maggie ordered, Nolan broke open a pack of cigarettes. He lit one, tipped back his head to blow a smoke ring, then leaned toward her. "Mr. Williams and —"

"Please, Nolan, not yet," Maggie said, and bit into a tortilla chip. "My stomach's got to have its way first or it'll growl at you."

He grinned. "Okay. Eat first."

* * *

"Steak was a trifle peppery, but good," Maggie said, stirring hot milk into black coffee syrup. Nolan said nothing. Uh-oh, he's hyping himself to preach at me, she thought, and decided to beat him to it. "You came to Veracruz intending to fire me. Didn't you?"

Nolan's cigarette slipped from his fingers. "Why uh — ah." He leaned over to pick his smoke off the floor. "What brought that up?"

"You're here three weeks ahead of schedule. The consulate

accounts are a shambles. Mr. Williams needs a scapegoat to get himself off the hook. Queenie's been dipping into the government till. You don't know what to say to me or how to say it. That reason enough?"

"I notice that you've set up ledgers and balance sheets for this fiscal year." He took notes from his pocket and laid them on the table. "Here we are. You have last year's books ready to close. Williams is greatly upset. He claims that documents have vanished, including many supporting recent transactions."

"Not even one since July Fourth, but he's right about last fiscal year," Maggie said. "Only one thing needs doing before I close last year's books, and I want to do it while you're here."

"While I'm here? Why?"

"Because someone who outranks Mr. Williams has to okay them." Maggie reached down to pull her purse from between her feet. "Read this." She took out an envelope and handed it to him.

He opened it and read.

Memorandum

From: Margaret Gutiérrez y Magodón
To: Mr. Albert Williams, U.S. Consul, Veracruz. Mexico
Subject: 1940-41 Fiscal year closing

A review of the consulate account at Banco Nacional reveals charges spread over the year for which supporting documents cannot be found. You will recall that I have, both verbally and in writing, asked you and others in the office to provide them, and that you prevented me from questioning Mrs. Williams. None have appeared. Considering that the debits date back a full twelve months prior to last July first, it is assumed that the missing papers will not show up.

Expenditures lacking support documentation total $38,268.67
U.S. dollars, distributed over several accounts. This is a
staggering deficit considering the small size of the consulate
budget. The largest single entry, $6,548.21 U.S., was paid to the
Santiago Steamship Line in March, 1941. I am unable to locate
either the canceled check or a receipt for the transaction.

Currently, the consulate account at Banco Nacional is
overdrawn. I have been able to access Mrs. Williams's personal
account, also at Banco Nacional. It shows a balance of
$69,712.07

I suggest that Mrs. Williams make out a check on her Banco
Nacional account payable to the consulate for $38,268.67, so
that we may deposit it at once. I would then be able to close
fiscal year 1940-41.

Nolan stared at the page. "You gave him the original?" he
asked without looking up.
"Sure did — in person, a week ago. I hid a third copy. You
may keep that one."
Nolan frowned and shook his head. "Your memorandum
insinuates a great deal, but lacks detail and proof." He removed
his glasses, polished vigorously, and put them back on.
"Of course it does. You saw the files with all the supporting
documents I could locate. I could never get Mr. Williams to
look at any details. Besides," Maggie indicated the memo, "that
thing doesn't tell Mr. Williams anything he doesn't already
know."
"Why did you write it then?"
"Isn't it obvious? I'm fighting for my job and my
reputation. The memo gets things out on the table. It's
conciliatory and only implies wrongdoing. It gives Mr.
Williams a graceful way for his wife to avoid charges of using

U.S. government funds for her own profit. That's embezzlement, and he'd be caught up in it, too."

Nolan reached for a smoking cigarette stub in the ashtray and ground it out. "I saw no mention in the memo of evidence to support your contention."

Arms folded, Maggie leaned toward him. "That's the point. You know I wouldn't write it without back-up material, and so does he. No evidence to give them details to quibble about. Here's an example: Her Highness shops with bigwig wives. They buy, charging purchases to the consulate entertainment account. That, by the way, is budgeted way out of proportion to the total budget. Shoppers pay Queenie later and, I'm kind when I say this, she just can't seem to remember to reimburse the entertainment account." Maggie took a sip of coffee. "It's really stupid. The bank records show that she never missed depositing into her account."

"Irregular system, but a convenient way for visiting dignitaries to shop without carrying local currency," Nolan said. "The government loses nothing as long as she reimburses the account."

Maggie put down her cup. "Right, except that Mrs. Williams tells people that she pays all entertainment expenses out of her own pocket. Until July, she had the reimbursement checks made out to 'USA-Sarah Williams,' and deposited them to her own bank account. See the rub?"

Nolan lit a cigarette and eyed her through a cloud of smoke.

Does he think he's impressing me with those stupid cigarettes? Maggie wondered. No. Probably just his way to stall for time to think.

"Legal? Hell!" he burst out. "Considerable sums — slipshod accounting —
government money. No wonder Sarah wouldn't let you have the receipts."

"Last year, Nolan, not now," Maggie said. "She tried once

right after I arrived. I stopped it but didn't catch on to her scheme right away." Maggie stared into his eyes. "So there you are, Nolan Thompson. It's all in your lap now. If this doesn't get cleared up while you're here, I'll come at them with raking claws and slashing fangs rather than take the rap for Mr. Williams's ah — well, I'll call it sloppiness."

Nolan took a short drag. "Did that example you mentioned put you onto this, Maggie?"

"Uh-huh. I went shopping with Mrs. Williams, Congressman Tyler's wife, Daitha, and Senator Johnson's wife, Kyna. Sarah insisted that they charge everything to the consulate, but I made sure they did not. Later, it dawned on me that charging purchases to the consulate caused confusion. Then I got the feeling I was being set up as a patsy. I hadn't been here a single day during the last fiscal year, but I was already being framed to take the blame for last year's shortage." Maggie paused to watch Nolan blow a long chain of rings.

"I went to the bank," she went on, "and the manager gave me all the information I needed." Head cocked, Maggie winked and shrugged. "He was most cooperative. You see, I spent four hours alone with him in the bank vault."

"Did he —?" Nolan's jaw sagged as he snuffed out his cigarette. He removed his glasses again, snatched up his napkin and wiped his face.

Maggie burst out laughing. "He was a perfect gentleman — really. He got me everything I needed: dates, parties involved, the whole shebang. You see, he told me that he'd never met Mrs. Williams, but when he confronted Mr. Williams, they negotiated a settlement for last year in which the bank agreed to a loss rather than lose the consulate business. Stakes are higher this year, and the bank's afraid the consulate will try to negotiate again. The compromise check Mrs. Williams wrote last year was for much less, just a little over eleven thousand."

Nolan put his glasses back on. "So? You haven't answered

my question. If Al knew all about his wife's shenanigans, why did you write the memo?"

"I was sure those missing records were gone forever. To protect myself, I had to expose the mess before it continued into this fiscal year. I don't know how well off Mr. Williams is, but Queenie's worth millions. He's meticulous in many ways, but not with dollars. He leaves money matters to Queenie."

Nolan poured coffee syrup and hot milk into his cup, held his glasses over the steam, polished, and put them back on. "This memo in the wrong hands could tumble —"

Reading his thought, Maggie was quick to interrupt. "I tried to leave it open enough so you could go either way with it, Mr. Thompson. He knows I have proof, so he doesn't have much choice — close fiscal '41 or resign."

"You've been calling me Nolan. No reason not to."

Maggie nodded and smiled. "Okay, Nolan. You'd have canned me if your eagle eye had found that I couldn't justify the books. Wouldn't you now?"

"Maggie, Maggie." Nolan raised his hand. "It's all clear now. Let's just say you've said good-bye to fiscal '41." He put his napkin on the table and pushed back his chair.

"Wait a minute, Nolan. The chocolate ice cream here is quite good." She signaled for the waiter.

He grinned, and pulled his chair back to the table. "Tell you what. Don't show up tomorrow. My flight leaves for Mexico City at eleven-forty. That leaves enough time for Al to wheedle a check from his wife. I'll deposit it myself. If I take that flight, you'll know FY 40-41 is closed and you can start training your boss."

"Or worming my way out of Queenie's mud hole." Nolan roared, and she thought he might be human after all. "She'll be furious, but I'm all set to woo myself back into her good graces."

Chapter 16

Maggie tried to tune out the rapping on her door, but it just got louder. *"Sí, sí, estoy despierta,* I'm awake," she shouted, burying her head under the pillow.

"Señorita, está por abaja el Señor Alvarado."

She shook her head to rid the cobwebs, then rolled out of bed. *"Bueno.* Tell the señor fifteen minutes. "Squinting through blurred eyes, she saw the time. Nine. That late? "Ten minutes," she shouted as she threw on a robe then raced down the hall to the bathroom.

She made it in ten, and strolled into the waiting room knuckling her eyes. Black skirt swinging against her calves, she wore a sleeved black bolero over a beige blouse, and her hair was tucked into a snood under a flat, wide-brimmed black hat.

"Good morning, José," she said.

"Bellísima, Margareta. New outfit? You look wonderful." They shook hands. "But are you okay?"

"Sure." She nodded, wanting more than just his hand, but brightening with his touch. "Worked late, that's all."

"With Nolan Thompson?" When she nodded, his face clouded. Shifting his weight from foot to foot, he sputtered, "Whatever did you — He's mad as hell. I looked for you at the consulate, heard he was there and decided to say hello. He came storming out of a shout-down in the consul's office, then stomped out with his briefcase arm hanging stiff like it does when he's pissed off. I called, but he just scowled at me and went out. They said you weren't coming in." Frowning, José paused. "Does that — did he — are you —"

Maggie laughed. "Fired? No. You know where he went?"

"With a face that red, I didn't want to know."

"Bad news," she said. "Well, maybe not. I'll bet he's mad because Mr. Williams wouldn't dare wake Queenie this early. Nolan needs for her to write a check so we can close fiscal year '40." José was eyeing her with a questioning frown and wasn't interested in Nolan, she decided, and it made her feel good.

"Are you in trouble?" José asked.

"I don't think so, but I might be. I won't know until I meet Nolan at the

airfield before the Mexico City flight takes off. Coffee at the *Café de la Parroquia?"*

"My pleasure." José gestured toward the door. "After you. But I must stop at my shop for a moment."

"I don't have much time." Maggie paused. "Well, okay, if you'll call Enrique and have him send Trece and the Model A to pick me up at eleven."

*   *   *

"May I see that filigree necklace?" Maggie asked, indicating a display when they entered José's showroom. He nodded, and she examined it while he went to his office. She was reaching for another when he returned.

"That can wait, Maggie. You're in a hurry, remember?"

"Sure," she said, and preceded him out the door.

The *Café de la Parroquia* filled the end of a block, and was open to the sidewalk on one side and both ends. Pillars supported the high ceiling and folding iron gates offered night-time security from the street. They took seats and ordered pastries and coffee.

"Are you ready for that run up to Puebla?" José asked. "Last weekend you backed out at the last minute. Let's leave this afternoon."

"Uh-uh, José. I was busy last week and had to work. Besides, I never agreed to go. Today I have to see Nolan at the airfield before he takes off, then I'm driving to Jalapa to visit Irena."

José shrugged and dug into his pocket. "Maybe this will change your mind." He reached for her hand then closed her fingers around a small package.

"What's this?" Maggie said, feeling warm, tender and prickly all over, knowing that from José it would be something special. "Oh, José —"

"Made especially for you."

"Oh, you shouldn't, but thank you. I'm dying to see what it is."

Carefully, she untied the silver ribbon and removed the golden wrapping. "Wait, José," she said when he picked up the ribbon and stood up. "I'm not in that big a hurry."

"Your hat could use another *galón*," he said, wrapping the ribbon around the crown.

Maggie held still, eyeing the blue velvet box resting on its gold wrapping paper. She felt a thrill run up her spine when he touched her hat, and closed her eyes. So many ways he found to please her, and she savored the anticipation of opening the box.

"Too short," he said, sitting down at last. "Go on, Maggie, it's yours to open."

She lifted the cover and took out silver ear hoops, lace patterned, hollow, and tapering from pencil size around to slender tips.

"Oh you shouldn't, José." She held one up to examine it. "They're exquisite." She slipped one in her ear and shook her head. "And it's so light I can hardly feel it. But I can't keep them."

José picked up the other one. "And there's my trademark on back near the top. Looks like a little spot. See?"

She examined it, nodded, squinted. "Mmm. I see."

"Now look at the spot through this hand lens — twenty power." He put the lens in her hand. "Now what do you see?"

"The spot's a tiny 'A'."

"What else?" José leaned back, grinning.

"I don't — Oh, a teeny-weeny 'J' in the A's triangle."

"That's it. Everything we make has that trademark, but only the pieces I make myself have the little 'J'. No one else can make it that small."

"Will you show me how sometime?" She held out the earring and glass.

He took the lens. "Please wear them, Maggie. I made them for you, and with your new outfit, you are truly *Mejicana*."

Maggie hesitated, blinked to clear her eyes and felt herself melt under his gaze. She just couldn't deny him and put on the other earring.

"They're lovely, José. Thank you. I've never had anything so beautiful." She shook her head to feel their lightness. "They feel so good, too. I'm so sorry about missing Puebla." She glanced at her watch and rose quickly. "Oops, I'm late," she said, leaned over and whispered into his ear. "Thank you. You're such a dear friend."

He stood up, indicated a taxi waiting at the curb and called after her. "Enrique sent a taxi for you."

She waved her arm in response but did not pause. Taxi? She'd asked for Thirteen Rabbit and Clank. Take a taxi to Jalapa — Uh-uh!

That José! What was he up to? She ran past the waiting taxi, another three blocks, and stormed into Enrique's office.

"*Buenos días,* Señ— "

"I know the Ford's ready." Maggie banged her purse on his desk. "Where's Trece?"

"I caught him stealing, and Señor Alvarado needs the car."

"I said, where's Trece. Remember what Miguel told you?

Señor Alvarado has no right to the Ford. Where is he?"

"Señor Alvarado is coming to get him."

"So. You have him. I'm here to get him. Bring him here."

Enrique rose. He won't budge unless he believes I'm Miguel's mistress, Maggie thought as he unlocked the door to a room behind the office and went in. Presently, Thirteen Rabbit came out, grinning and rolling up the sleeves of a white shirt.

Maggie couldn't help smiling at the sight of baggy pants gathered at the waist, the cuffs doubled up. She beckoned and took off running. Looking back, she saw Rabbit grab keys and papers off Enrique's desk and follow.

"I'll drive. Open the big door then hop in," she barked, as she ran to Clank. Passing, he gave her the key and papers, and had the door open in time for her to drive through.

"Maggie, stop! Move over. I'll drive."

"Geez — José!" Maggie swung right and felt her stomach seesaw when she caught a glimpse of José waving from across the street before a succession of three large trucks blocked him from view.

"Vámonos, vámonos, let's go."

Trece's voice — and there he was. It had better be Trece's hand on the windowsill. He'd be on the running board and she'd have to turn left so José wouldn't see him from behind. Easy-easy, slow, don't throw him off, she cautioned as she rounded the next corner, then pulled in a deep breath when Thirteen Rabbit squirmed in through the window.

So far so good. Rabbit was safe for the moment, but she couldn't take him to the airfield because José was sure to follow her there — damn him! She gripped the wheel to beat down the fury churning her thinking. Just when everything seemed right, he'd double crossed her. She'd won Nolan's support and José's admiration, she'd thought. Love her? Ha! Gorgeous earrings — together in Puebla — out of touch — away while Thirteen

Rabbit got whisked off to kingdom come. She shot Rabbit a quick glance and forced a smile in response to his bright eyes and broad grin.

"Gracias, Señorita," he said quietly. "You saved my life again."

"De nada, don't mention it, Trece," she said, trying to emulate his calmness, then feeling surprise at her composure. Forget José Alvarado, she determined. Your job — meet Nolan at the airstrip. Just then Thirteen Rabbit spoke up and she caught the pride in his inflection.

"These are the drawings I made of the hacienda in Antigua," he said, tapping the papers on the seat between them. "Señor Enrique found them in my old uniform after he gave me a new one. That's when he locked me up."

"Olé!" Maggie exclaimed, and suddenly the world seemed bright again. "You can't stay in Veracruz, so I'll take you to the mountains." She turned down a side street and stopped near a small cantina. "Here's ten pesos." She put his drawings in her purse and took out a bill. "I must go to the airfield. Get yourself some clothes and something to eat and I'll meet you here in just one hour — and bring two cold Coca-Colas with you."

"Bueno, Señorita," he said, and was gone.

* * *

Maggie approached the airfield just as a DC-3 landed. She parked, left her hat on the driver's seat and locked the car. Might Nolan be waiting? José, too? She circulated among the 11:40 a.m. flight passengers and Godspeeders. No luck. Queenie couldn't have outsmarted Nolan. Or could she?

She heard an announcer call names of priority passengers and watched one after another walk out to board the DC-3. *"Last one, Rendón,"* came a call, and Maggie turned away. Queenie had won again. Nolan hadn't closed FY '40 books..

Chapter 17

"No, I have a higher priority," a man shouted, and just then Maggie heard the squeal of braking tires.

"Thompson has highest priority," she shouted, "He's here."

The taxi door opened and Nolan's panama hat flipped off as he clambered out. Reaching back he pulled out a briefcase and grip. The driver got another from the trunk. Nolan reached for it but the driver pulled it away.

"Run, Nolan. Catch your plane," Maggie yelled as she dashed toward him and the taxi. "I'll pay and bring your hat and grip." She saw Nolan dash off, and called to the driver in Spanish, "I'll pay his fare and take his luggage."

Maggie got Nolan's hat and grip, wheeled and ran smack into a guard. "Nolan," she yelled when the guard detained her, "what about FY-40?"

He turned at the top of the boarding ladder, raised his hand with thumb and forefinger circled and shouted something just as an engine roared to life. She couldn't hear a word, but saw his arm pump three times before a steward pulled him into the cabin.

Maggie sucked in a deep breath and let it out in a whoosh. Nolan had brsten Queenie after all, and she'd have the weekend to visit in Jalapa.

Hat and her purse in one hand, grip in the other, Maggie watched the airplane taxi out to the runway. Now to pick up Thirteen Rabbit, she thought, putting Nolan's hat on her head and turning back to her car.

Strange. She'd run after Nolan with that grip, but now it seemed to weigh a ton. She put it down and looked out to Clank about fifty yards away. A man approached the car, pulled a key from his pocket and grasped the door handle.

"José," Maggie screamed. "José Alvarado, don't you dare touch that car!"

José turned the key.

"Stop, José," Maggie shouted. "Don't sit on my hat." José always backed into a car and sat down without looking. Had he seen her hat? Once in the driver's seat, he'd never get out and she'd lose contact with Thirteen Rabbit.

"Stop! *Párese ya!*" she yelled, but he opened the door. She had to stop him, however, whatever it took, She dropped Nolan's grip, flopped across it and screamed, "Jos — Josaieee," fading out his name as Nolan's panama hat tipped off her head to rest bottom up, right under her face.

"Maggie, what happened?" José shouted. "You hurt? Wait, don't move!"

Swell! Maggie thought. Got him away from the car. He tricked me — tricked him back. She heard feet running. Don't look up — got to go through with this. Don't laugh, and don't feel sorry. Think of something, like — like the hat. José's — she'd puke in it. But Nolan's — fine weave, woven from rushes in the moist dawn air in Jipijapa, Ecuador, and blocked in Panama. How proud —

"What happened? You okay?"

José was right above her. "Tripped," she moaned, and groped behind herself for something to hold on to.

José helped her up. "You hurt? Where?'

"I'm okay, but I gotta sit down." She flexed her left leg, winced, reached for her purse, groaned and grabbed him to keep her balance. With José's support, she headed for the car. "Oh," she moaned, after going about ten yards, "Nolan's hat and grip are back where I fell. Will you get them?"

"We'll get you settled first," he said.

"I'll never hear the end of it if someone steals them," Maggie said, pulling her arm from his grasp. "I'll be okay. Please get them." She limped a few steps, careful not to favor the wrong leg. "See, I'll be fine."

"You sure?" José said, and when she nodded, went back for Nolan's hat and grip.

She hobbled to the car, climbed in and locked the door just as José arrived.

"Your key," he said. "Slide over. I'll put the bag in the rumble seat then drive you back to town."

Maggie rolled her window down a crack and shook her head. "I'm going to Jalapa, and if I let you have my key, how could I ever get it back?" She got a compact from her purse, applied lipstick and adjusted her snood. "Do me a favor. Nolan's one of your old chums. Drop his stuff off at the consulate, will you?" She started the engine.

"Come on, Maggie. I came in a taxi and need a ride back."

"Look over there, José — taxis — three," she said, shifting into gear. "Why did you come? Even after I told you I was going to Irena's, you had Enrique send a taxi."

No answer. Maggie watched José trudge to a taxi, climb in with Nolan's gear and drive away without so much as a wave of his hand.

What have I done? she thought, her foot still on the clutch pedal. She bit her lips to stop them from quivering. My only friend, and I just sent him packing. He'd come running when she called, the concern and tenderness in his voice proof that he cared. "Okay," she said aloud, "so I feel like a crumb brushed off the table. I just could not welsh on Thirteen Rabbit."

Maggie released the clutch and drove toward Jalapa. Then, when sure José was not following, circled back to meet Thirteen Rabbit.

* * *

Where was Thirteen Rabbit?   Maggie drove slowly.
There'd been a cantina when she let him off, and now she saw
three. How could she — The passenger door opened suddenly
and Rabbit scrambled in with two Coca-Colas and her change.
He popped the cap off a bottle with his teeth, grinned when
Maggie flinched, handed her the bottle, and opened the other.

Irena preferred to go to Jalapa by way of Antigua, Maggie
remembered. She drove that way, but pulled to the side after a
short distance.

"You drive, Trece," she told him. They exchanged seats,
and she took a swig of her Coke. "Do you know the road to
Jalapa?"

"*No, Señorita.*"

"See if you can find a map." She pointed at the door pocket
beside him. "There's a map in there. Let's look at it."

He found one showing roads in Veracruz state, and another
of Jalapa. She put a finger on the location of the governor's
mansion.

"That's where we're going, Trece, right there, the
governor's house."

"*El Gobernador?*" Wide-eyed, mouth agape, he stared at
her. "*Ooh, no, Señorita.* I can't go there."

"*Sí,* Trece, the governor's house, my father's house, and I
want to talk to my mother."

"*Su madre?*"

"*Sí.*" Maggie explained her relationship to the governor.
"They have an hacienda in the mountains," she went on.
"Perhaps you can work there. You can't go back to the garage.
Why did Señor Enrique lock you up? Was it because of your
sketches of the hacienda?"

"*Sí.* He took them out of my pocket when I changed to a
clean uniform."

Maggie indicated the baggy pants he was wearing. "Whose

are those?"

"They were not made for me," he said.

"Señor Enrique's?" When he gave no answer, she asked, "What time did that happen, Trece? How long were you in that room?"

"When he came to work — daylight."

Four — five hours ago, so José had known when he first saw her that morning. Rabbit went on and she wanted to listen.

"Señor Enrique took my uniform off the hook while I was changing. When I came from the room he was looking at my sketches. The telephone rang, and he said —"

"To the man on the telephone?"

Trece nodded. "He told him I had a plan of the Buehler hacienda. When he stopped talking, he pushed me back into the dark room and locked the door."

Maggie pursed her lips. "Do you know who he was talking to?"

"No." Trece shook his head. "Only that he said he would send a taxi."

José, Maggie thought. She was silent a moment, then asked, "You know who Señor Alvarado is, don't you — the man who sometimes uses this car?"

Thirteen Rabbit nodded.

"When did you first see him? Was it before you started working at the garage?"

"Sí, Señorita. I was trying to escape from the hacienda and heard two men talking when I hid in the bushes near the hacienda's back gate. One was Señor Alvarado. The other was tall and ugly, the man they call El Ragnorak."

Maggie clamped her mouth shut. She wanted to scream, tell this nobody beside her he was lying — making up a story to save his own skin. How dare he accuse José? She stared into the jungle beside the trail, but saw nothing.

"Señorita."

She was vaguely aware of the young man beside her, Thirteen Rabbit, who had just riddled her already shattered day. Leave me be, kiddo, or I'll take you back, she thought, but managed to hold her tongue.

"*Señorita,*" he repeated, "have you looked at my sketches?"

"Sketches? Oh, *si.*" She stretched out her fingers to relieve her tension. Settle down, she told herself. He'd risked his life to do just what she'd asked him to do, and how could she fault him for that? She took a deep breath, a gulp of Coca-Cola, and took out his drawings. "We'll look at them now," she said, spreading a sheet showing the outside walls of the compound

"There are four gates." He freed a hand from the wheel to indicate their locations. "Two large warehouses are just inside the one by the river dock." He pointed again. "And this is the gate near the church where I brought you the message from Señor Buehler. The big house is between those two gates."

Maggie forced herself to concentrate. "Where did Señor Alvarado meet El Ragnorak?"

"There's another gate here by a restaurant." He pointed. "But the first time I saw him was over here, a long way from the other gates." He slid his finger across the page then grabbed the wheel again. "A paved road inside the wall runs about a half-kilometer to it from the warehouses. We were hiding in the bushes when a truck came from the dock."

"We? Was someone with you?"

"*Si.* It was the night El Ragnorak came. The *Hedda* radio operator was begging the guard to let us through when El Ragnorak came in the truck with the cargo we unloaded from the *Hedda*. He told the radio man to go back to the restaurant and just then Señor Alvarado came.

Maggie broke in. "It was dark and you said you were hiding, so why do you think it was Señor Alvarado?"

"I heard his voice. And here," he indicated the restaurant between two parallel walls. "This is the dining hall for people who work on the hacienda. We were too late to get something to eat, but we heard voices coming from an upstairs window. I climbed a tree and saw El Ragnorak give Señor Alvarado a lot of money. That's when the guards caught the radio man. I was up in the tree."

Maggie found no flaw in his tale, except she thought his identification of José Alvarado must have been wrong. That had happened on Friday, the fifth of July, the night of El Ragnorak's arrival. José had gone to Jalapa with the governor the previous evening and had not returned until late Saturday. Reassured, she said, "Then what happened?"

"I thought the engineer had escaped, but he and the radio man were in our room when I went back, covered with blood, and screaming for help. I called for help but no one came. Late that night El Ragnorak came with two men. I tried to get one of their guns but something hit me on the head. When I woke up I was locked in another room."

Wide-eyed, Maggie stared at him and mumbled, "The radio operator and the engineer? Both gone?"

"*Sí.* Sometime I go back."

Maggie took in his profile, the protruding brow in an otherwise smooth rounded face, the set of his jaw. He was no longer a boy, but a man with a purpose, and it dawned on her suddenly that they had a common goal.

"Those men were your friends," she murmured softly. "You never saw them again, did you?"

His eyes were narrow slits as he faced her. "Yes, I saw them. They were still alive at dawn the next morning. We were at sea. I heard El Ragnorak tell a man to slash a pig so it would bleed, then tow it on a rope to bring the sharks. Then El Ragnorak came to the engine room and said my friends wanted me on deck. I thought he was lying so I pretended to be busy. I grabbed my big hammer, but he hit me on the head with his pistol, and two men dragged me from the engine room onto the deck. He was not lying. My friends were so bloody I could hardly tell them apart. He told me to push them into the sea. 'No, they are my friends,' I said. Then he said the sharks were my friends, too, and wanted me to be the one to give them their lunch."

"How awful!" Maggie squeezed her eyes shut, breathed deeply, and turned her head slowly from side to side. She fought back the bile rising within her, hoping he would stop talking.

He went on. "My friends were dying or dead. I looked into black holes— El Ragnorak's eyes and the gun in his hand, and knew I could not fight him from the belly of a shark. So I pushed my friends into the sea and went below to the diesels. The diesels are my friends, and they spoke to me. 'El Rag-nor-ak, El Rag-nor-ak, over and over, all through the day, and I knew that I must kill him. I live to fight El Ragnorak."

Maggie shuddered, picturing the scene, the gruesome face, and the afterdeck of the cruiser. "Bravo," she exclaimed in a low tone. Moments later, he inhaled deeply and blew out a sudden gust.

Maggie thought he was finished, but he went on.

"They kept me to run the diesels. More Germans came: three engineers, one to run the diesels, a radio operator and a ship captain. I heard them say that a railroad locomotive engineer was coming from Germany."

"And you would have been next to die," Maggie said, thinking of the helmsman she'd found murdered the next day. She hoped José had not been the man Rabbit had seen with El Ragnorak, but she dared not rule out the possibility. Hadn't he killed two men on the consulate grounds the night of her arrival? That had been okay at the time, she thought, because he'd been protecting her. She bit her lip. Or had he killed them to get the packet he'd stored in his safe while unaware that she was watching? Wasn't he a torero, a bullfighter, one who killed for money? Might El Ragnorak have paid José for disposing of the helmsman?

She folded the sketch. "Here's Antigua. Show me the road coming away from the fourth hacienda gate."

He rubbed his neck, rolled his shoulders, but said nothing.

She allowed him time for a mood change. "Can we look for the road now?"

She saw the corner of his eyes crinkle. "There is no road, Señorita."

"Impossible. If trucks use the road inside the hacienda and go out the gate, they have to go somewhere."

"*Sí*. But it was low tide then." His cheek's gave a quick twitch. "Now it's high tide so it's gone."

Maggie forced herself to laugh. "You mean that it's only the beach? Okay. On to Jalapa, Trece. Sometime I'll find it when the tide is low." As she put the drawings in her purse, she felt José's heavy gun. "Wait." she exclaimed. "Can you shoot a pistol?"

"Me?" He stared.

He must think she was a moron. What mountain boy from Guatemala couldn't handle a gun? "Show me."

He nodded, said, "Of course," and found a place to pull off the road.

She got it out and handed it to him.

He examined it carefully. "You might have killed somebody, *Señorita*. See this?" He turned on the safety. "It should always be like this."

* * *

They drove through scattered showers, past fields of sugar cane, patches of corn and other crops. The winding road climbed slowly to Jalapa, nearly a mile above sea level. She let Trece find his way while she considered the possible alliance of José and El Ragnorak. His description of the hacienda was much better than she'd expected, and she was especially interested in the road that was not a road, but a track through a swamp connected to a sand spit between the swamp and the sea. This area would almost always be deserted, and tire tracks would vanish with each high tide.

What better location could a smuggler find than the site of the Buehler hacienda? The large, fast cruiser was there to off-load cargo from ships at sea. The hacienda had warehouses, a deep river dock, and was connected by an obscure *"sometimes"* road to inland highway and rail.

Mrs. Williams had referred to the hacienda as belonging to Adolf. Did he really own it, or rent it? Or did it belong to the Santiago Steamship Line? Governor Gutiérrez had said that El Ragnorak had a number of investments in Mexico and South America. Perhaps the hacienda belonged to him. Did Miguel or José know? She shuddered at the thought that José might actually be a Ragnorak colleague— a traitor. Somehow, she could not believe it, even if the details of Rabbit's account were accurate. Right or wrong, Thirteen Rabbit's knowledge of the hacienda grounds should prove useful in the future, and she suspected that he knew much more than he had divulged.

Thirteen Rabbit had been driving at a reasonable speed, but suddenly she was thrown almost against him as the car skidded around a bend. He's fit to commit murder and who could blame him, she thought, noting his set jaw and flashing eyes.

"We have plenty of time," she cautioned.

He slowed the car and glanced her way. "I am not a big man, Señorita, but I am very strong. People are wrong to think I am only a boy. Two more months and I will be twenty." He pointed out the window. "Look. *Pico Orizaba.*" A gap in the clouds revealed the snow- capped peak towering in the west. "My father took my mother high onto the volcano Tajumulco, so I would be born with the strength of Volcan. *Volcan Orizaba* is even greater. I will seek the power of the mountain, then El Ragnorak will be mine."

Chapter 18

Thirteen Rabbit pulled the car off the road and gazed across a broad valley to the mass of Volcán Orizaba. Maggie realized that the mountain was a source of life, of power to him, and no wonder. To a back-mountain boy, it must seem like a god. Perhaps he had reason, for as she gazed, she felt the doubts and confusion within her mellow and take focus as awe of the mountain's majesty overwhelmed her.

The young man glanced at her, his lips set and protruding, brow arched, tight lines at his eye corners. Through narrowed lids, she envisioned a growing maturity wrenching away the last vestiges of his boyhood. She hunched her shoulders to embrace the substance of his words into her own resolve.

He's setting his goals, she mused, forcing her gaze back to the mountain. It was distracting, too. She had to think, not revere nature, and turned her eyes down to the floorboard.

To what extreme might Thirteen Rabbit go to avenge his friends' death? Might he target people other than El Ragnorak? Might providing him refuge endanger herself and others? Wondering, she shook her head, and the gentle bobbing of the earrings against her neck brought thoughts of the man who had crafted them. She leaned back and closed her eyes to bring back his look of devotion when he had given them to her. I made them especially for you, he'd said, and she knew she'd cherish the moment for the rest of her life.

Wouldn't it be lovely to view Orizaba with José beside her

instead of — Forget it! After what he'd done that very day, forget José. Besides, romance had no place in her life right now, and José had probably tried to protect her from dangers inherent to counterespionage work by denying her the use of the Model A. She couldn't believe José was in league with El Ragnorak as the young man had implied. How could she be sure? What if Rabbit were right, and El Ragnorak had paid José a lot of money? Come on, Mags, she scolded herself. Wipe the boy-girl stuff out of your mind. After all, José was FBI, so he might have to operate in a clandestine manner at any time. Wasn't she doing the same thing? Might José want to make sure that Thirteen Rabbit would never expose him? Oh — of course he would— either way — a Ragnorak colleague or FBI. Wasn't she FBI, too? Wouldn't it make sense for José to confide in her— cooperate, work with her as a team?

"Trece," she said. There was no response and she tapped his shoulder. "Trece, do you think Señor Alvarado would recognize you if he saw you someplace outside of Enrique's garage?"

Thirteen Rabbit kept his gaze on the mountain. *"No, Señorita.* I worked on engines in the machine room, and he never came in there. Sometimes I saw him in the office talking with Señor Enrique and I opened the garage doors when he brought a car back late at night."

"He must have seen you then."

"Si, but I was nothing — only a *cholo,* and the garage is dim at night.

"Did he ever see you on the *Hedda?"*

"He never came to the *Hedda."*

Maggie motioned him to drive on, and presently she jabbed her finger at a narrow road branching to their right. "Turn there," she said. "Look for a place to hide the rumble seat cushions. You'll have to ride back there again because all the servants in my parents' house know Señor Alvarado. They might tell him you came with me. I have to stop there for a few minutes, then go on to meet my father. When you see him, tell Governor Gutiérrez what you can do and I'm sure he'll find work for you on his hacienda.

*   *   *

"This is a beautiful town," Maggie called out as she drove through Jalapa. "Flowers everywhere, and I've seen bandstands in the middle of three plazas."

"There are many hills," came Rabbit's voice from behind her.

"That house, Trece. It must be two hundred years old. And this street is —"

"You took my eyes, Señorita. Now you shake out my teeth and the bolts of the car."

"Sorry — cobblestones. You okay back there?"

"How much farther?"

"Fifty meters."

"Then I'm okay," he called.

"Be very still now, Trece," she said. "Don't say anything, no matter what you hear. And don't move and rock the car while I arrange to meet the governor."

"Muy buenas tardes, Señorita," a guard said as he approached her window when Maggie reached the gate, "I saw the car and expected Señor Alvarado. You are Señorita Gutiérrez, no?"

"Si. Buenas tardes y mucho gusto. You are Carlos?" When he nodded, she went on. "Where can I find doña Irena?"

He looked over his spectacles and pointed a forefinger toward the building entrance. "Pía comes."

Maggie parked, got out, and hugged Pía. *"La Señora?* Is she here?"

"Just now she is saying good-bye to a group of ladies," Pía said as they entered the building. "She expected you to arrive in time to meet them. Perhaps it is not too late. This way, please."

Maggie hung back. "How did you know I was coming, Pía?"

"Don José told doña Irena you expected to meet him here."

Maggie shook her head. "Is he coming?"

Pía smiled. "She told him it would not be convenient."

"*Gracias por eso,* thank goodness!" Maggie said with a laugh. "Don Benancio? Can I reach him on the telephone?"

Just then Irena rushed into the hall and pulled Maggie into her arms. "I heard what Pía told you. José called. He said to expect you and that he would be along later. Not this time, I insisted." She glanced sideways at Maggie. "Is that all right? I thought you'd have come with him if you'd wanted him here."

"What a relief," Maggie said. "Yes, I need private time and advice from you and Benancio."

"Pía," Irena beckoned. "Please bring iced tea to the terrace."

"Wait, Pía." Maggie turned back to Irena. "Before we do that, I should get gas and the car needs —"

"One of the men can tend to that," Irena cut in.

"Thank you, but I must explain what needs to be done." Maggie rubbed her chin. "I know he's terribly busy, but do you think — is there any chance Benancio could meet me at the warehouse?"

"I'll come with you. Pía, my hat, the red one with a wide brim like Maggie's." Irena indicated Maggie's black hat. "Won't it be fun to take a jaunt in that rickety old car José likes so much, especially overdressed as we are? One moment. I'll make sure Beno will meet us."

Minutes later, Maggie and Irena set out for the *almacén Gutiérrez y Montoya* in the old Ford. Two guards followed in Irena's long black limousine.

Maggie could hardly wait to introduce her stowaway, but Irena spoke first. "Beno may be late. When I explained that you had something very important to discuss, he agreed to meet us as soon as he could get away." Head cocked, she stared across at Maggie. "Now what's your secret? Why meet at the warehouse where there's only a bench to sit on? At home we would —"

Maggie's chuckle cut her short. "Does the name Trece Conejo mean anything to you?"

"Of course. Everybody knows the name."

"Trece." Maggie called in a loud voice. "Say hello to Señora Gutiérrez."

"Buenas tardes, Señora. Mucho gusto," came a voice from behind them.

Irena slid quickly to the outside edge of her seat and looked at the seat back. "Trece Conejo. What a wonderful name. *Buenas,* Trece. Why did my daughter stuff you into that small space?"

"She helped me escape from El Ragnorak."

"Oh, Maggie. You smuggled him out of Veracruz? You? What a story! Is that why José is so upset with you?"

Maggie sniffed. "I'm afraid there's more to it than that. I suspect he thinks —" She thumbed over her shoulder. "It's about him. He's from the mountains and wants to go back. But I might need him sometime because he knows a lot about the Buehler hacienda. I think it's El Ragnorak's headquarters now. Trece escaped from there and escaped again today. José had Enrique lock him in a garage room. He's worked on coffee plantations in Guatemala, and is good at repairing engines, too."

"I see. And you hope Beno will have something for him to do, no?"

"Yes, but José is looking for him and must not know I brought him here."

Irena indicated a broad open door ahead. "Go in there and swing to the left." She turned her head to speak to Thirteen Rabbit. "I'll get out by the front office. Did you hear me, Trece?"

"Sí, Señora."

"Muy Bien. Señorita Maggie will let you out the back door of the warehouse. Keep to the right, go to the office in the front of the building and say you are looking for work. Do you understand?"

"Sí, Señora."

* * *

"This will be your room," Irena said, after they returned to the governor's mansion. She stretched out on a chaise longue, then asked, "Just what is it about José?"

Perched on the edge of the bed, Maggie began with Nolan's review of consulate accounts, her own exposure of Mrs. Williams's scheme to cheat the government, and the closing of the consulate's books for the previous fiscal year. When she mentioned the meeting with José that morning, tears filled her eyes. She removed an earring and showed it to Irena.

"Hmm, exquisite!" Irena exclaimed as she examined it.

"He made them just for me. I love them, but I can't keep them."

"You must love him to be so upset, *querida*."

"Irena, no!" Maggie rose abruptly and went to look out the window. "Well, maybe I thought so this morning. Then I found out he was just buttering me up so I wouldn't interfere in his business."

"Tell me about it, Maggie. He sounded upset like a man in love when he called this afternoon."

"Upset, yeah! Know why? I caught him red-handed. That's why." Maggie sat down again and poured out her doubts about José, omitting details of the *Hedda* crew murders, but emphasizing her concern over José's possible connection with El Ragnorak.

"Remember when he claimed he knew nothing about El Ragnorak's arrival in Veracruz?"

"I remember," Irena said, nodding.

"Well." Maggie paused, then spoke in modulated tones. "Thirteen Rabbit insists that he saw El Ragnorak pay José a lot of money two nights before José made that statement. I just don't know what to make of it."

"Your Rabbit must be mistaken," Irena said. "As I recall, José was here in Jalapa that day and the next." She stood up. "But even if he did meet El Ragnorak, it may have been for business reasons. The man deals in gems and precious metals, as does José. José may have been shocked because you had identified El Ragnorak and he had known him only as a trader. Beno will know if José stayed in Jalapa that night. Come. Let's have that iced tea now."

"I feel better already," Maggie said, rising, "and I want your advice on something else. Mrs. Williams is upset with me because — ah — I had to stop her from doing something our government just will not allow the wife of a consul to do. Now I have to find a way to get back into her good graces." Pausing at the head of the stairs, she asked, "Do you have any suggestions? I think she'd like to get acquainted with the women of Veracruz. It's her turn to have bridge club on Monday, and I wondered —"

"What a wonderful idea," Irena cut in, hands clasped at her chest. "Leave it to me. My club just might raid the consulate on Monday demanding a friendly game of bridge."

Maggie burst into laughter. "Sounds swell," she said, and descended to the step on which Irena waited. "I wonder." She laughed again. "If they enjoy it, I'd appreciate any suggestions on how to thank Mrs. Williams for throwing such a grand surprise party."

"Now aren't you a sly one?" Irena looked down then cast a sideways glance at Maggie. "I can't imagine your needing help with such a trick. Excuse me a moment while I look into dinner plans, then we'll discuss our invasion on the terrace."

* * *

Maggie wandered a path between hibiscus, gardenia, frangipani, and other flowering shrubs she did not know. She had paused to look across a broad valley to mountains in the west when she heard Irena call.

"Be right there," she answered, waving. "I'm admiring your gardens." She saw Irena ease herself down into a chair and remembered that Irena had immediately stretched out on the chaise longue as soon as they returned from the warehouse. She must be exhausted after entertaining her gaggle of politically minded women — never an easy task. The telephone call from José in the middle of her garden tour must have tried her patience, too. Her own visit had been contingent on a successful meeting with Nolan Thompson, making the uncertainty of her arrival time, or even if she would come at all, a complication which could not be easily fit into a busy schedule. Then, when she'd arrived late with her tale of woe — Oh. She shook her head in disgust. How insensitive she'd been — how self-indulgent. Irena had made a game of it, had joked about their jaunt in the old car, had even helped her protect Thirteen Rabbit for no reason other than to lessen Maggie's own disillusionment over José's conduct.

Irena was such a gem. She looked so serene in her moment of quiet that Maggie hesitated to join her. She found a perfectly shaped gardenia and plucked it, taking care not to touch the white petals.

What a welcoming smile, Maggie thought as she approached Irena with the flower held up so she could smell its fragrance.

"Ah, heavenly," Irena purred, closing her eyes as Maggie passed the gardenia back and forth in front of her. Then she sat still as Maggie tucked it into her hair over the right temple. "Have you ever noticed," she said with eyes still closed, "how flowers are more fragrant and beautiful when offered by friendly hands?"

"How nicely you put it," Maggie said. "Thank you. Gardenias happen to be my favorites, and your grounds are enchanting." Maggie gazed over the gardens, but her thoughts were on Irena's meaning — from friendly hands, loving hands, missing from her own life since the accident which had claimed her mother. Suddenly she understood the impulse which had prompted her to sign the papers binding her to the lives of Irena and Benancio. She saw Irena's eyes crinkle and look up, so was not surprised when she felt firm hands rest for a moment on her shoulders.

"I'm impressed by your young man," the governor said as he moved around her to embrace his wife. He pulled up a chair and sat between them, then went on. "Irena and I have discussed what we might do when you finally visited us here. A jaunt to Hacienda Perla on the slopes of Pico Orizaba is high on the list. I've arranged to have Trece start to work there. If it suits you, he'll drive us to Perla tomorrow morning."

* * *

Irena was such a wise woman, Maggie thought, as she got ready for bed that night. Benancio was wise, too, of course. They'd talked on the screened veranda, sounds of the city faint and remote, and the incessant chirring of the cicadas mellowing the languor of the tropic night. She spoke Spanish with Irena and Benancio as she had as a child with her mother. Her father had insisted she speak English with him. Might that be why she was not quite ready to think of Benancio as her father? Still, he was her real uncle, and when he used a gesture or phrase like her mother's, she found herself accepting him, and called him Beno.

She put the earrings on the nightstand and snuggled into bed with Irena's words in mind. Had José's hands been friendly or loving when he'd given her the earrings? She recalled how she'd felt warmed by his touch. Then, on hearing Thirteen Rabbit's account, she had been furious and sure José's had been selfish hands — even greedy. Irena had not let her drop José from their conversation and had finally convinced her that there were many possible explanations for what he had done. Act as if nothing has changed, Benancio had said. José is strong, proud, essential qualities of magnificent men. To show distrust toward such a man is to belittle him. If you do, you'll lower yourself in his eyes, and never get close enough to get the truth from him. With that thought, she decided to accept him as he was, and drifted off to sleep.

Maggie got up at dawn, dressed, and put on the earrings. Where had José spent the night? Had he returned to Veracruz? She went downstairs, heard voices from the kitchen and entered.

"Muy buenos días, Señorita."

Man's voice — Thirteen Rabbit — Maggie gulped back a greeting that would have indicated that she knew him.

"I repaired the Ford. Is it yours?" he said.

"Ah, sí, buenos días," she said, glad that Rabbit had the presence of mind to act as a stranger.

"Perhaps it needs more work. You should look it over," he said.

Maggie picked two hot bread rolls off a tray, and headed for the door. Outside, she pretended to look under Clank, then got in. *"Buenos días, Trece.* Seat cushions, you drive," she said, and he got into the driver's seat.

"I came to thank you," he said. "Plans have changed. The Perla truck driver is sick, so I must drive it. Which way to the seat cushions?"

"That way," Maggie pointed.

"I should tell you," he said, "Señor Alvarado brought his big black car to the *almacén* last night and the woman who came to the *Hedda* at the same time as El Ragnorak was with him."

Maggie felt her body lurch. Another arrow — Thirteen Rabbit's — had struck José's character.

She looked out the window, and pulled in a deep breath. Was he warning her? He must think José was part of the

Ragnorak circle and not to be trusted. If true, might José be the most treacherous of them all?

"The platinum blonde?" she asked finally. "What time was that?"

"I didn't count, but the church chimes rang many times right after that."

"Did they see you?" she asked. "What were you doing there?"

"I'm sure they didn't see me. I had no place to go so I slept in the car."

"In this car?"

He nodded, then followed her hand signals until they found the cushions.

Returning, Maggie felt Rabbit's eyes flick to her, and wondered if he might have something more to tell her. Why wouldn't he just open up? She recalled different times when he'd answered questions curtly, then lapsed into silence. At other times, when she'd posed her questions in an uncertain manner, he'd become more conversant. There wasn't much time left.

"Trece, I don't know how to find out more about El Ragnorak and what's happening at Señor Buehler's hacienda. Is there anything more you can tell me before you leave for the mountains?"

"He's not there now — Tampico."

"Tampico? El Ragnorak? How do you know?"

"My friend told me."

"A friend at the hacienda?"

Thirteen Rabbit nodded. "*Mostacho rojo,* red moustache. I call him Mostacho."

"No, Trece." she exclaimed. "He shot at you, remember? I saw his gun flash. A bullet hit you while you were in the river. Another bullet almost hit me."

"*Con perdón,* Señorita. He missed me on purpose. I looked

back, thinking I was safe. Then I saw the guard at the gate aiming a rifle. I ducked but got hit."

"Are you sure?"

Sí, Señorita. Sometimes he drove Señor Buehler's big black car and I had a chance to talk to him at the garage. He used to be the helmsman on the other cruiser, the *Riesa.* His brother was helmsman on the *Hedda,* and when he was murdered, Mostacho took his place on the *Hedda.*"

Maggie's head snapped around. "His brother? Why didn't you tell me sooner? Just yesterday you said they killed the engineer and radio man."

Thirteen Rabbit shrugged. "You didn't ask me. Now I am free. I go to Pico Orizaba. I will return and Mostacho will tell me where to find *Cola hoya del Puerco.*"

"Who? Oh, I see. You call El Ragnorak that because of that pigtail of hair on his forehead?"

"No, Señorita, Ano de Puerco."

"Oh." Maggie chuckled at the name — pig's ass. "I see."

Eyes bright, Thirteen Rabbit flashed her a glance.

"Where can I find Mostacho?" she asked.

Thirteen Rabbit pulled up outside the coffee warehouse. "The woman at the cantina in the hacienda wall is sister to Mostacho's wife. She is his friend, but her man is not. Perhaps she will help you." Arched brows asked if she were through with him and, when she nodded, he got out and gestured with his hand. *"Gracias, Señorita.* There's the truck I will drive." He dashed to a canvas-covered stake bed truck and climbed into the driver's seat.

She watched the truck pull away with an arm waving good-bye, then drove back to the governor's mansion.

Maggie pulled the door open and out tumbled the houseboy and a travel grip. Travel? Surely not to the hacienda. She rushed to the foyer, stopped and sighed when she saw Irena and the governor in a tight embrace.

"Bad news. Another oil tanker torpedoed." Governor Gutiérrez pulled Maggie close. . The president called an emergency meeting. Hacienda Perla must wait."

"Ooh no!" Maggie groaned. "So that's why El Ragnorak went to Tampico."

Governor Gutiérrez spun her about. "He did? How do you know?"

Geez, did he ever look fierce, but Maggie came right back at him. "The *Hedda* helmsman told Trece the night before he left Antigua on the cruiser."

"Follow up on that, Maggie. Find out all you can," Governor Gutiérrez barked, then turned to his wife. "Mexico City, *Querida.* Are you packed?"

"No, Beno. I promised —"

"No, Irena. I'll help you pack," Maggie said, and pulled her to the stairway.

Chapter 19

Motorcycle engines roared. Maggie watched the governor's cavalcade roll through the gate with José waving from the trailing limousine. He must be trying to tell me something, she thought. He'd come in a taxi just in time to be thrust, protesting, into the car by the governor himself. As a key member of the national and state security councils, José's presence would be crucial to the success of the meetings, and Maggie wondered if Governor Gutiérrez, her father, might have delayed his departure knowing that José would appear. "Bet he did, and partly for me," she murmured. "He knew I wasn't ready to deal with José, and might have wanted to check on José's loyalty, too. Father — dad — just the words sound good."

Maggie had so wanted to have time with her adopted parents. Now she'd miss the trip to the plantation on the slopes of Pico Orizaba. She supposed she could find it, but following a new lead on El Ragnorak and planning Monday's bridge party just wouldn't leave her enough time.

She returned to her room, put on a visored cap and burst out laughing when she happened to see herself in the mirror. Cap and earrings didn't exactly go together. Oh well, the visor would help when driving eastward into the sun, and the earrings just felt good.

* * *

Visor skewed to shield her eyes from the morning sun, Maggie followed a pick-up truck down a winding road. A grinning boy swayed from side to side, bare feet hanging from the open gate. He waved and, with the other hand, clutched two chickens, legs bound together and beating their wings to get free.

What a picture, she thought — flapping wings, legs brown and swaying, angelic face — and just then the truck swung off the road and up a steep side trail as if heaven bound.

Driving on, Maggie's thoughts turned to the events of the day before. José, once her hero, had been sullied by Thirteen Rabbit's account and had acted like a boor. On the other hand, Nolan Thomson, whom she'd considered to be a fuddy-duddy fuss-budget, had recognized her competence and cleared the way for her to set up a viable office system. What next? She sighed. Whenever things seemed clear, riddles kept popping up. Would she have a vindictive Sarah Williams to contend with?

Now another tanker had been torpedoed. Might it change her assignment? FBI, Miguel, José, what had they accomplished since her early days in Veracruz? She had heard nothing from Miguel, but supposed that José had reported to him. What had she herself accomplished for the FBI? Not much.

The *Hedda* had been sighted at Tuxpan and, farther north, at Tampico, about three hundred miles from Veracruz. Brownsville, Texas, was only another three hundred from Tampico, so might not the cruiser range along the Texas coast, too? With its speed and elaborate radio equipment, was it a roving communications base for directing sabotage operations in the Americas ringing the Caribbean and Gulf of Mexico?

Jeepers! Ragnorak was on it! What a coup it would be to corner his helmsman, Thirteen Rabbit's friend Mostacho. He'd know so much of vital importance. Find him, get him on our side, Maggie determined, and do it before he suffered the same fate as his brother. Mustering details of Thirteen Rabbit's hacienda map from her memory, she headed for Antigua.

Maggie drove slowly down the cobblestone street, past the

old church, the Cortez ruin, and the mooring tree plaza. Then she turned around and, driving back, saw a two-story structure protruding from the wall. Thirteen Rabbit might never have seen this side, but it probably housed the cantina where the woman who knew Mostacho worked.

She parked close to a wide double gate with a pedestrian door framed into the left section. It opened, and out stepped a blond guard wearing a dark green uniform. She saw him lean his rifle against the wall then slouch beside it.

"Wish me luck, Clank ol' boy," she whispered, as she took off her visored cap. She adjusted her snood, put on her wide-brimmed hat, then looked in the mirror. Better a tourist, she decided, and put the cap back on. Then she got out and indicated the block-like, two-story structure. "Is that a cantina where I can get coffee?" she asked the guard in Spanish.

He shook his head and motioned her around the corner.

Probably doesn't speak Spanish, much less English, she thought, rounding the corner and glancing up at the front windows — barred horizontal slots. She'd have to be a ten footer to see inside. The building must have been a guardhouse at one time, and possibly still was. Heart pounding, she approached the entry. Should she go in? A woman, especially one dressed as a woman of class, just did not go into strange cantinas alone.

Maggie tensed her shoulders, and went up steps to an iron-barred gate set into the thick stone wall. She pushed it open, made sure she could get back out, then shoved at the heavy interior door. It groaned open to gloom and the smell of garlic and stale tobacco smoke.

Maggie entered slowly, backed against the door to close it and, as her eyes adjusted, surveyed the large room. There was a stage on her right, set up for a band. Past it, a mural — fiesta on the plaza — covered the wall at the end of the room. She lifted her gaze to a balcony above it — chairs, a place to listen to music, watch a performance, or relax after dancing. She felt tension drain from her shoulders, let out a deep breath, and looked further. Daylight outside the windows across from the entrance reflected across gleaming copper-topped tables.

She heard a toilet flush, so there was someone near. A door in the mural swung open and a man, indistinct in the dimness, emerged and joined two men she hadn't seen who were sitting at a table by the window.

Maggie sat down in a leather barrel chair where she could view the entire room. She saw a match flare at another table, revealing a full black mustache and eyes in a round florid face fixed on her. Smoke trailed from his nostrils, then the match burned out, leaving the man's head silhouetted against the window. Three men, eyes ogling, silent, unmoving — what might they think of a woman wandering alone into such a place?

Maggie faced the three men. *"Buenos, Señores. Café? Una comida?* Can I get coffee and a meal?" she said.

The silhouette shouted, "Zita." When there was no response, he jabbed a finger toward a door close to the entry.

Maggie got up, pushed it open and went into a long kitchen. *"Buenos días, Señora,"* she said, "am I too early for lunch?" No answer. A cupboard filled the wall on her left, and a tiled counter ran the entire length of the kitchen across from her. Above it, too high for any mortal to see out, five slits of windows about six inches high and three feet wide, allowed murky light to enter. A central air shaft right beside her provided most of the light. It was separated from the kitchen by a framework of iron bars which reminded her of a bear cage she'd seen in a zoo. Interior walls were white, and there was a wooden ice box, a coal-oil stove with an oven, and a massive masonry oven. The room hooked right at its end, and she heard voices from around the corner. She went that way, and saw a tall thin woman passing steaming plates through a slot in a barred barrier to three men in a room beyond.

"Perdóname, are you Zita?" Maggie asked.

The woman rushed back past her to take a pan from the oven and put it on the counter.

"Mmm." Maggie inhaled deeply. "Smells heavenly. Are you Zita?" she repeated. "Am I too early for lunch?"

The woman took out three more iron trays and closed the oven. "These are ready," she said, and put one on a plate.

Magpie looked over the pans. "Chiles rellenos — smell delicious. What are those?" she said.

"Pepitarias, jaibas rellenas, chipachongos."

"Breaded monkey meat? Or do you really use pork?"

Zita smiled. "Half are pork, other half monkey."

"I'll take two chiles rellenos and —" Maggie paused, the others were hors d'oeuvre size, "two each of those and coffee."

Zita nodded and got plates from a rack. "Go sit down."

"One more thing, Zita," Maggie whispered. "I must talk to a man with a big red mustache. Do you know where I can find him?"

Zita frowned, shook her head.

"I thought —" Maggie paused. "The boy from Guatemala is safe in the mountains. He told me —"

"Ah, entonces." Zita nodded, pointed an index finger straight down and tapped the counter. "Monday. Four-thirty. Right here," she said in a low tone.

"I'll be here," Maggie said, and returned to the main room. The three men fell silent again until Zita served their meals, then their chatter resumed. Just then two other men entered from the street, one in white shirt and pants, the other with black pants, white shirt and a black mourning armband. They took a table next to Maggie's and, when Zita served her, craned their necks to see what she'd ordered.

"What's that?" the man in white asked, pointing.

"Chipachongo," Maggie said.

"That's what I thought," Armband snickered and sat down.

"A gringa would never eat monkey," his friend said, bursting into laughter. "You speak English," he said to his friend in mourning. "Why don't you tell her?"

"Why not? She's facing you. I'll wait until she's eaten some before I tell her, then she'll spew the monkey all over you." He tipped back in his chair and roared.

The three at the other table joined in.

Maggie put on a tenuous grin, pretending to be bewildered. She'd gain friends if she went along with their fun. On the other hand, if she pretended not to understand and, later, they heard her speak their language, they'd distrust her forever. Better to make friends, she decided.

She caught the eye of Armband and spoke in English. "Am I gringa because of the color of my hair?" Talk ceased, but expectant eyes focused on Armband, waiting for him to answer.

He met her gaze and finally nodded.

Maggie went on. "Or my clothes? Oh, I know. I'm gringa because of this." She swooped off the visored cap and waved it over her head.

He smiled, but still did not answer.

She gazed over them, stood up, and said in Spanish, "My friend knows I speak your language. He came in and saw red hair with a cap and visor gee-hawed to one side, so he decided to have some fun. Señores, I am Mexican, too, born in Torreón. Your language is my language. Your monkeys are mine, too. I have four *chipachongos*, two monkey, two pork. I ah . . ."

No one said a word, and what more could she say? She looked at each and went on. "I am Margareta Gutiérrez y Magodón. I work for the consul of the United States in Veracruz. If you ever have trouble with the gringos, come to me."

She shook hands with them all and the mustached man held onto her hand. "You are friend of Señor Buehler, no?"

"*Si*," she answered. "And I have visited Antigua with him."

She studied each face, trying to fix them in her mind so she might recognize them in the future. The mustached man unlocked the door leading out to the hacienda, his two companions went out and he locked it behind them. He must be the proprietor of the cantina, and was probably one of Adolf Buehler's trusted allies.

Interesting, she thought. The cantina was locked to people on hacienda grounds, but not to anybody coming in from the street. What might that mean?

She ate the last of her meal, paid, and went out to her car.

So far, so good, Maggie thought, climbing into the driver's seat. She hoped Zita would have Mostacho here on Monday, but there wasn't much she could do to assure it. Her own presence might be more difficult to arrange, for how was she to escape from Mrs. Williams's bridge group that same afternoon? If only Irena were available to make sure that her club members would come and mix with Mrs. Williams's regulars. If the two groups mingled well, she'd be able to ease away without being noticed.

She smiled, thinking about the monkey meat banter only a few minutes ago. It had caused patrons to talk to her, tease her, and had resulted in a pleasant encounter. Why not serve monkey hors d'oeuvres to the bridge group, too? And why shouldn't she send out her own invitations to Veracruz bridge playing women? There'd be two tables, eight women in Mrs. Williams's group, including herself, and as many more local ladies. She might as well invite an extra woman or two. That way she wouldn't be forced to play bridge, and could leave for Antigua in time to meet Mostacho. "Why not?" she muttered, and got out of the car to return to the cantina.

Inside again, Maggie approached the proprietor as he put three beers on a couple's table and sat down with them. *"Perdóname,"* she said quietly, taking the fourth chair. The proprietor introduced her, and told the couple how they had teased her about the monkey meat. At length, he asked, *"Cerveza?* May I get you a beer?"

"No, thank you, but perhaps you can help me." Maggie leaned forward. "There's a women's bridge party at the United States Consulate on Monday afternoon. I wonder if Zita could make lunch for the bridge players — the same things I ordered?"

He laughed. "Monkey, too?"

"Sí. People joked about it here. Why not at the consulate?"

"Bueno." He frowned. "But here they were men. With ladies? Gringa ladies?" He shrugged and grinned. "Tell Zita what you need."

Maggie went into the kitchen, told Zita what she needed, and was met by a frown. Suddenly a wide grin spread across her face. "But why ask me?" she said. "Many women in Veracruz want to cook for the United States Consulate."

Maggie tapped her foot and pointed straight down. "On Monday," she whispered, "at four-thirty I will be here to return all your cooking pans and trays." Louder, she said, "I want just what I had today, enough for twenty people, and nothing that looks like gringo food."

Maggie began to describe everything she wanted.

"Los hago, I make them," Zita said.

Maggie dug into her purse for a notepad.

"Hágolos," Zita repeated, urging Maggie to the door.

So Zita couldn't read, Maggie thought as she returned to her car.

* * *

Siesta time, with the road and Veracruz streets nearly free of traffic, made for a quick ride back to Enrique's garage. Maggie honked her horn. The door opened, and she noticed a young man she'd not seen before waiting by the door to close it. *"Gracias,"* she said, as she drove in. "Oh-mi-God, Enrique!" She exclaimed, spying the man in the office at the far end of the garage. He'd been murdering mad yesterday, so she'd have to patch things up. But how?"

She parked, got out and strode to the office. *"Señor Enrique,"* she began, trying to sound bold. "I'm so sorry about yesterday. I had a very important meeting at the airfield, and needed the driver to run an errand." She held out her hand.

He swivelled in his chair to face her but did not stand up. "Señor Alvarado told me —"

"Señor Enrique," Maggie cut in, fist on hip with her elbow sticking way out, "Miguel hired the mechanic to help me, not Señor Alvarado." Then she softened her voice, her hand still extended. "I think the mechanic will not return. He's gone. If you give me his wages, I will send the money to him. Then may we forget him and be friends again?"

Slowly Enrique stood up. *"Bueno, Señorita,"* he said, then paid her money from a drawer and took her hand.

* * *

Five minutes later, the weekend watchman let her into the consulate. When she reached her desk, she found four messages in her in-basket from Mr. Williams, one from his wife, and one from José. She sat down, put her purse in a drawer, and read the first note from Mr. Williams when she heard the door knocker. It was Saturday. The office was closed. She wanted to be left alone, but answered it. A man handed her a telegram. She signed for it, gave him a coin, and closed the door. It was addressed to her from Kyna Johnson, telling her that Kyna planned to arrive in Veracruz the next day.

"Yowee," Maggie shrieked, and threw the message as high as she could. It fluttered against the balcony, then drifted down. She caught it, struck up a jig, and clattered back to her desk.

How could she get everything done before Kyna arrived? Was Senator Johnson coming, too? Why? She reached for the telephone.

"Victor Dalpica, please." Maggie tapped her foot and

drummed her fingers while she waited. Why was he taking so long?

"Maggie," he finally answered. "Nice to hear from you. How are you?"

"Fine, Victor. I won't hold you, but would you tell me how to get in touch with your mother. I talked with her back at the July Fourth reception, and I remember that she plays bridge. I'm in charge of arrangements for Mrs. Williams's bridge parties, and I'd like to invite her and some of her friends."

"Where can she reach you? She's home now, and I'll have her call you right back." He paused. "And, Maggie."

"Yes."

"My fiancée likes to play, too, and one of her best friends is visiting from Mexico City. How many do you need?"

"A bunch — at least nine to play bridge. I only want your mother to suggest the names and give me the telephone numbers of women who might like to come. I'm at the consulate." She gave Victor her number. "I don't want her to take on the burden of calling people. Besides, invitations should come directly from the consulate, especially as it's a spur of the moment affair in honor of visiting dignitaries."

"Important people, you said?"

"Well, Irena will be busy in Mexico City, but the wife of a United States senator will be here." Maggie heard him chuckle, and could just picture his grin and the whiteness of his teeth.

"Count on her, Maggie. She'll call you. *Hasta luego.*"

Chapter 20

Efficiency was definitely a trait Maggie associated with Victor, and she remembered thinking the same of his mother the one time they had met. She would have preferred to call his mother herself, but Victor seemed to be in a hurry and hung up before she got the telephone number. She was still trying to interpret the scrawled handwriting on Mr. Williams's first message when Señora Daria Dalpica called.

"How delightful to hear from you," the woman said. "Victor could give me no details, but what's this about a visitor, a dignitary, I believe he said?"

"That's right, Senator Johnson's wife. You met her at the Fourth of July reception."

Inescapable social chatter faltered, a signal to Maggie that it was time to get to the point. "I remember you mentioned to Mrs. Williams that you'd do whatever you could to help the women from our countries get acquainted."

"So I did, and I've done nothing because so many of our people are away during the hot, muggy summer. I've heard nothing from Mrs. Williams and supposed she felt much the same way."

Maggie grimaced into the speaker, certain that Señora Dalpica was aware that planning such a get-together would hardly enter Mrs. Williams's mind. "I'm the one making the plans for Monday," she said, "and Mrs. Williams seldom asks me for any details. Her group of eight meets every Monday, and

I hoped you might suggest the names of enough for two tables."
Maggie picked up a pencil. "I know it's terribly short notice and
might interfere with siesta, but I hope a few might be able to
come. If you'll give me their —"

"No-no. I'll take care of it," Daria said. "You see, we have
a tennis club group. You know how it is — tennis on a hot
summer day, they choose to play bridge. Eight or nine, you
say?"

"Wonderful, and there will be something for those who
don't play bridge."

"One of our reporters speaks English, takes wonderful
photographs, and plays excellent bridge. I'll see to it that she
brings her equipment and dresses appropriately."

Maggie chuckled. "I hadn't given publicity a thought. But
of course, yours is a news family, and Mrs. Williams — well,
she just —" The other woman's chuckle cut short Maggie's
words and she burst into laughter.

"We know how to smooth the feathers of diplomats and
their wives, Maggie. And how else may I help you?"

"Your coming will make the party. And thank you so much,
doña Daria. About one-thirty on Monday? — better say one
o'clock."

Maggie remembered to get the telephone number before
hanging up, then looked over her messages. "The boss comes
first," she muttered, picking up the four from Mr. Williams. His
wife had signed her note: *Mrs. Williams,* rather than "*Sarah*",
indicating that she'd been in a tizzy when she wrote it. If she
were still steaming and they w0ere confronted at the same time,
her fortissimo might accompany her husband's overture.
Maggie stuffed the messages into her purse without bothering to
read them.

She heard voices and laughter as she approached the
consul's residence. They're entertaining, she thought, and
decided to leave a message with the houseboy and return to her

office.

"Un momentito," the boy said. "I think Mr. Williams is expecting you." He went into the other room.

"Maggie here? That's just dandy!"

Nolan's voice, but what might have brought him back to Veracruz the day after rushing off to Mexico City?

Mrs. Williams bustled out to meet her, followed by her husband and Nolan. "Come right in, Margareta, and meet our guests," Mrs. Williams said. "We were just discussing how you —" She gasped, backed into Nolan, lurched forward, and wheeled back into the living room.

Had Nolan pinched her bottom? What a turnabout! Never before had Mrs. Williams greeted her with more than a scowl. No wonder — guests. She must suddenly have remembered that the person she'd just welcomed was responsible for gutting her bank account the day before. Maggie glanced at Nolan. No, he couldn't have pinched her. He was beaming right back at her, and twirling his glasses by the stem.

Mr. Williams led her past Nolan and into the living room. "Here she is," he announced, "the bookkeeper I was telling you about."

She'd never seen him with a toothy grin before, much less talk through it. Was this really her boss talking?

"Oh, we did have thorny moments leading to the eventual compromise, but without her help, I just don't know."

What a double-tongued liar the consul was. She froze a smile on her lips as Mrs. Williams introduced her to three men from the embassy and their wives. She'd met one of the men, a career diplomat stationed at the embassy, but had paid him little attention. Just what was Mr. Williams trying to do, sell her to the embassy? He hadn't been able to trick Nolan into getting rid of her. Now he must be trying to promote her up and away. The consul had never even shaken hands with her before, and now — ugh.

Mention of Adolf turned her to Mrs. Williams. "Adolf will take us in his new cruiser to see where Cortez first landed in Mexico more than four hundred years ago," Mrs. Williams told the group. "He'll treat us to lunch at his enormous hacienda, and Margareta will be our interpreter. Her father is the governor, you know, and she . . ."

Maggie retreated to join Nolan, who was alone in the foyer and smoking a cigarette. She could still hear Mrs. Williams, but paid no attention. "What's going on, Nolan?" she asked. "Al just heard that the ambassador will be here Monday, and it scared the shit out of him."

"Why's he coming? That why you came back so soon?"

"Partly. I showed him the account system you set up for this fiscal year. He liked it — wants to talk to you about it. He's upset about the war in Europe. You heard about the torpedoed tanker?"

Maggie nodded. "First thing this morning."

I don't know exactly what's in the ambassador's mind," Nolan said. "The sinking must have something to do with his coming, because he had no such plan yesterday. I'd guess he wants to be sure Al Williams is clear on just how our government can help Mexico keep its major port open."

"Might that involve the consulate in counter-intelligence operations?"

"Possibly, but it won't affect you unless it gives you a larger budget to work with," Nolan said. "By the way, where did you pick up cost accounting? At the university?"

"I was a foreign language major, not accounting. My experience was at Douglas Aircraft for six years— mostly cost accounting."

"I didn't see that on your application."

Maggie suppressed a smile. "You never looked at the application," she said. "You'd have seen that I'd taken the CPA exam. Incidentally, I passed. She laughed openly when Nolan snatched out a handkerchief to polish his glasses.

Just then Mrs. Williams came into the foyer. "You'll plan for another table for the Monday club, won't you, Margareta?"

"Certainly, Mrs. Williams. I believe the *Hedda* is in Tampico, but —"

Sarah Williams stretched her double chin. "No it's not. Adolf promised the *Hedda*."

"What time did he suggest?" Maggie asked, thinking to arrange for the *Riesa*.

"Luncheon will be shortly after one, I believe."

"Okay." Maggie tucked her purse under her arm. "Then everybody should be here, ready to go, at eleven sharp. See you tomorrow." She excused herself and returned to her office.

Why did everything happen at once, and just when she'd picked up a new Ragnorak trail. Or might the ambassador know of her part time appointment with the FBI and be willing to relieve her of consulate duties? Smiling at the thought, she picked up the telephone ear piece and gave Señora Dalpica's number to the operator.

"Yes, Maggie," Señora Dalpica said when she came on the line.

"I thought you'd like to know. Our little party is growing. The United States ambassador will be here with other men from the embassy on Monday, and their wives will be playing bridge with us."

"My-oh-my."

That sure tweaked her fancy, Maggie thought and went on. "Mrs. Williams's group is already up to twelve and, unless I'm mistaken, the rumor will spread to other North American women. Some don't play bridge."

"Reunión de mujeres?"

"Sí. A good old-fashioned hen party. Invite as many as you like. Tell them invitations are from the consulate. Use my name if you need one. If things go well, it will be Mrs. Williams who

invited everybody, of course."

"She doesn't know about it?" Señora Dalpica said. "Am I right?"

"No — yes, you're right," Maggie added quickly.

There was a period of silence. Finally Señora Dalpica said, "Won't she be very angry?"

Maggie chuckled. "Furious. But I'm depending on *El Examen* and its photographs to make it the highlight of her year."

"Oh, Qué guasón! You really are a rascal. We'll be there."

"And, doña Daria, *chipachongas will be —*"

"Really? You mean monkey?"

"Some, but pork, too. I hope to have fun with them."

"Your mother must have been a scamp."

"She was don Benancio's sister."

"Aaah, sí. No wonder you drive Mrs. Williams crazy. *Hasta luego."*

Maggie hung up. Love that woman, she mused, leaning back and kicking off her shoes. She yawned, but her mind raced with plans for the party. How many tables? She decided on two bridge areas with a removable screen between them. There'd have to be chit-chat space. Where should the hors d'oeuvres table be placed?

Hors d'oeuvres — she'd have to double the order. No — triple, at least, and have Mr. Williams's staff prepare tidbits acceptable to picky American tastes.

"Put your shoes on and let's get a bite."

"Nolan!" Maggie exclaimed, swinging around to face him. "I'd love it. Lots to do but there's no more I can do here tonight. I thought you'd be at the Williamses for dinner."

"I don't fit. Too much State talk for me. Any ideas? The Central Plaza?"

"Okay. The Zócalo is fine. But are you sure you want vendors dangling dancing dolls and doodads over your plate?"

"There's marimba music."

Maggie scrunched her nose. "It never lets up. Have you been to Café de La Parroquia?"

* * *

Sunday, eleven o'clock had come and gone. The consulate driver should have returned from the airport with Kyna Johnson at least a half-hour ago. The *Hedda* arrived as promised, and moored with an ocean-going tug between it and the Malecón seawall. Maggie crossed to peer into the pilothouse window and saw Mostacho and a man in uniform who looked like the guard at Hacienda Buehler.

Maggie helped Mrs. Williams board then told her that Kyna was expected to arrive. "I'm going to wait here for her," Maggie said. "One of the men from the embassy speaks excellent Spanish and he —"

Sarah Williams stamped her foot. "Just who do you think you are to send an invitation to the wife of a United States senator?" She waved toward the pilothouse. "Go up there this instant and tell that man to get going this minute."

Maggie sat down on the tug's railing and said in a low tone, "That's the point, Mrs. Williams. She is a senator's wife."

What had become of the charming woman of the previous evening? To remind Mrs. Williams now that both she and her husband had known of the invitation would only make her more furious. Oh, no, she thought, as the vice consul from the embassy came up behind Mrs. Williams. Whatever he said was sure to fan the flame.

"Did I hear you say senator's wife, Sarah?"

"Yes," Maggie cut in. "Mrs. Johnson."

"Johnson? Kyna Johnson?" He winked at Maggie over Sarah Williams's head. Maggie nodded and he said, "Sarah. How thoughtful of you! Such a grand surprise!" He turned and called back into the cabin. "Guess what, everybody. Sarah had a surprise up her sleeve. We're waiting for Kyna Johnson." He flashed a grin at Maggie, then followed Mrs. Williams back into the cabin.

Maggie thanked him with her lips. Career diplomat — a pro doing his stuff.

Within a minute, the consulate car arrived. Maggie dashed out to meet it, hugged Kyna, and directed the driver to take her baggage to the consulate room which the Johnsons had occupied on their last visit. "You come alone, Kyna?"

"Only from Mexico City. Tom will arrive tomorrow with the ambassador."

"I'm counting on you to go to Antigua with us." Maggie lowered her voice. "I'm under orders, and things are a bit tense."

Kyna grinned. "So what's new? Thanks for the warning."

Maggie shouted to the helmsman to get underway. A tug seaman cast off the bow line and Maggie, the stern line.

Nolan, grinning, polished his glasses and waved as she entered the midship salon with Kyna. He was seated on the far bar stool. The six members of the embassy group filled the L-shaped settee, and Mrs. Williams, facing the bar, sat on the closest stool.

"Don't get up, anybody." Kyna motioned for them to keep their seats. She gave Mrs. Williams a quick hug, and shook Nolan's hand. "Nice to meet you, Nolan," she said. "Your mother's a great friend." She glanced at Maggie, who was signaling toward the pilothouse ladder. "Excuse us. There's a matter I must discuss with Maggie."

Mostacho fit Thirteen Rabbit's description perfectly — blond hair, red mustache. The guard, seated in the second helm seat, had a pistol in his hand and, even worse, a rifle hung within reach. Maggie tried to disregard him, but felt clammy under his weasel eyes as she took the far lounge seat. Kyna sat down across the table from her, and she wondered how much of their conversation the two men might understand. The guard probably spoke Afrikaans, possibly German, and was more likely to speak English than Spanish.

"Guard," she asked in Spanish, "have you worked for Señor Buehler a long time?" When he turned up his hands, she repeated the question in English.

"Two - ah, two mons. Fader - auf." He threw wide his hands.

Fader? What did he mean? His own father — Adolf's? "Helmsman," she said to Mostacho in Spanish, "Mrs. Williams told me you worked on the other cruiser, the *Riesa*. Do you like the *Hedda* better?"

He nodded and, when the guard growled at him, snapped back with a heated retort in Afrikaans. Oh-oh. Mostacho's a prisoner. The thought flashed to her that the storm trooper-like creature wasn't about to let Mostacho out of his sight, and in no way was on board for the security of Adolf's guests. Guarded, he'd have no chance to talk to her tomorrow. Just as with Rabbit, escape was his only chance. Maybe Zita could warn him to be ready, or she'd do it herself if she could get him alone.

"Guard," she said in English, "Mr. Buehler often invites us to use this cruiser, and he usually has his steward serve refreshments right here in the pilothouse. Shall I call the others to come?"

He scowled, looked flustered for a moment, then shook his head.

So. She'd found out one thing. He might not speak English, but he surely caught the gist of what she'd said. "Helmsman." She reverted to Spanish. "You must know a lot about this coast, the river mouths, and the hidden inlets. There must be lots of places where smugglers can hide, and where it's too shallow for patrol boats to follow them."

She saw the guard frown and stare right at her, but as she chatted on, she noted that he slumped slightly in his seat, his fist relaxed, and his chest rose and fell more evenly. She waited until he looked away from her and toward the shoreline, to touch Kyna's knee and signaled for her to remain seated. She sauntered to a place where the guard was on a straight line between herself and Mostacho. If he faced one, his back would be to the other.

A cluster of flotsam appeared ahead of them. "Some day, helmsman . . ." She jumbled rapidly in Spanish. "I want you to tell me about the coast of Mexico — like when I hold the guard's attention so you run us into that black thing up ahead — and make a big noise to scare everybody and on the boat deck you help me tie down the lifeboat while I tell you the Guatemala boy is safe and wants me to help you escape and I tell you how we'll do it."

The guard cast her a suspicious glance and waved both hands back and forth across his chest to quiet her.

Maggie said to him in English, "You don't speak our language so I have to ask the helmsman about the scenery in Spanish. My friend from North America wants to know everything about Mexico." She faced Kyna. "Don't you, Kyna?"

"Yes," Kyna said, "and we want to know about you, too, guard, about your family and children."

Straight ahead, the flotsam was getting close. "See what I mean, guard?" Maggie said, pushing away from the pilothouse window. "I'll go up to the boat deck while you talk to her." Looking past him, she saw Mostacho reach up to a lever on the ceiling. The former helmsman had explained it as the release lever to free the lifeboat from its cradle.

She mounted the ladder, slid open the hatch cover and felt the *Hedda* quiver just as she climbed out. The diesels died and the bow pitched down. She careened against the lifeboat, staggered and fell as it rocked off its cradle. The *Hedda* wallowed to a stop as Mostacho erupted out of the hatchway.

Chapter 21

Maggie rolled over, kicked the hatch cover, heard a shriek as it slammed shut and her foot tripped Mostacho. Finger smashed in the hatch, she thought — maybe the guard's. She saw Mostacho sprawl onto his face, scramble up, and another guard leveling a rifle at him only ten feet away.

"Don't shoot!" Maggie screamed in English then Spanish. "Nein! Nein! The lifeboat broke loose. We need it to see if there's any damage."

Mostacho, motionless over the lifeboat's stern, began talking in Afrikaans, she thought, getting only the gist of his harang with the guard, whose arm was hooked over the boat-deck railing to steady his aim. The *Hedda,* broadside to the swell of the sea, tilted to port as it climbed a wave. Cresting, it suddenly rocked to starboard, throwing the guard off balance. He dropped the rifle to grab the railing and whipped out a handgun. "What happened? Speak English," he barked, aiming straight at Maggie.

"Yikes!" Maggie stared into the black muzzle hole. "I . . . I . . . I . . ." She paddled her hand sideways. "P . . . Put that down! He doesn't speak English." She saw the gun tip down. "Whew!" She sucked in a long breath. "That's better. We rammed something and the lifeboat shook loose."

The guard leaned far out over the water. "Nothing," he said in English, then shouted an order Maggie did not understand. "The engineer will check for leaks. Secure the boat," he said, again in English.

"The guard lost his rifle but has a pistol," Maggie told Mostacho, who was still bent over the dinghy's stern. He's out there on that little side deck. You can look. Do you know the voice — who he is? Does he speak Spanish?"

Mostacho nodded. *"Sí, lo conosco.* I know him. *Nada —* no Spanish."

"Good. Here's how I'll help you escape." In short bursts, she explained her plan while helping him secure the dinghy in its cradle.

Mostacho cocked his head toward the open gulf. "Don't look now, horizon, smoke, ship. *La Cola de Puerco's* personal helmsman is on it." He secured the lifeboat and Maggie slid the hatch cover open. Mostacho spoke. "When the helmsman comes, El Puerco will send me to my friends — *engordar los tiburones* — fatten the sharks."

Maggie could believe that. She faced the guard. "He says for the engineer to signal him when it is safe to go on. Monday, four-thirty," she reminded Mostacho in Spanish. "Thank you," Maggie said to the guard as she shook his hand, then looked down the hatch. Kyna was clinging to the ladder and the pilothouse guard was tugging to get her off.

"Look out below," Maggie shouted, and just then heard a dull thud. Looking down, she saw the guard lying on the deck and Kyna struggling to get off him. "Kyna, you hurt?" she yelped, and scrambled down to help.

"No, but let's don't do that again." Kyna reached back to rub her bottom. "That man banged his head on the floor then I sat on it, knocked out, I guess — oh, no. He's getting — look out!"

Maggie wheeled, saw Nolan burst up from below and kick the guard's pistol from his hand. She ducked and felt the pistol flick her hair as it whizzed past. The guard, still sitting on the deck, grabbed Nolan's leg and wrestled to pull him down.

Hopping, Nolan managed to stay erect.

It seemed to Maggie that everything happened at once. She saw Mostacho come off the ladder and kick the guard's jaw, releasing Nolan, then hurdle the guard to get the rifle. Kyna got to it first. Then came a scream, and wheeling, she saw Nolan twisting the guard's arm into a hammerlock as he propelled him to the down ladder. Kyna darted by with the rifle, Mostacho in pursuit. Just then Maggie spied the pistol, snatched it off the floor and spun around. Kyna, fire in her eyes, had the rifle by the barrel, raised and ready to strike. Mostacho had Kyna cornered and was inching forward.

"Quédase, Mostacho!" Maggie hissed, and gestured him toward the helm seat when he glanced back at her. *"Siéntese ya,* Sit down," she said quietly, making sure he could see her finger on the trigger. "I can't let you have the gun. If you try to escape now, there will be shooting, and people will be hurt."

Was he listening? Would he settle down — trust her? Did he know that a guard was peering in through the pilothouse window? He was desperate to escape, but there might be several guards on board, and the time just wasn't right.

Mostacho glared at her, and Maggie stared right back. "Listen to me, Mostacho. Your passengers are *Norteamericanos* — *muy importantes,* and are guests of Señor Buehler. They know nothing of *El Puerco,* and if you try to escape now, they will help the guards. But if you take the *Hedda* to Antigua as if there had been no trouble, they will say you're very good, and will be glad to help you."

No response. Maggie waited, waited, and he finally sat down in the helmseat.

"Everything okay?" the vice consul asked, coming up from below.

"You missed all the excitement," Kyna said. She was seated again, and Maggie saw no sign of the rifle.

Maggie crossed her arms to hide the pistol under her armpit

and backed to where Mostacho and the vice consul were in her line of sight.

"Nolan took a guard below," the diplomat said. "He told us there was a misunderstanding, a minor scuffle, but didn't know what caused it. Anything I can report to put the gang below at ease?"

"Just that Maggie saved the day," Kyna put in.

"Hardly," Maggie said and shook her head. "Kyna's the one who kept things from getting bloody."

"There was a lot of talk below — loud, too, so we had no idea anything was wrong until the engines stopped," the vice consul said.

"The cruiser hit something below the surface and the helmsman did exactly the right thing," Maggie told him. "He cut the engines and released the lifeboat. The guard objected when the helmsman went up to get the lifeboat ready."

"*Héroe verdadero! Bien hecho, Capitán.* Well done," the embassy man said, crossing the pilothouse to shake hands with Mostacho and slap him on the back. "That fits one guard's account — Nolan's, too." He circled his thumb and forefinger, jerked it Maggie's way and went below.

Mostacho grinned. "*Gracias, Señorita,*" he said, then brought the diesels to life.

Maggie got her purse from beside Kyna and slipped the pistol inside. "Never know when you might need those things," she said, grinning. "I know how to use it now. Last time you were here I carried one around without the safety turned on." She sat down at the map table kitty-corner from Kyna, heaved a deep sigh and slumped down. Her ruse to acquaint Mostacho with her plan had almost ended in disaster. Thank goodness, it had worked. She smiled at Kyna, who must have guessed that the fracas had been staged. "Gotta talk to the helmsman," she blurted, and went to stand beside him.

Maggie made sure the speaking tube to the engine room was

closed, then went over her escape plan with him.

"I heard you call the helmsman by name during all the excitement," Kyna said, as Maggie returned to her seat.

"Did I really? I don't know his name, so I suppose I called him mustache because he has such a big one." Maggie found herself wanting to confide in someone, but decided not to burden Kyna with her story.

"That Green Dragon with the guns gave me the heebies," Kyna said. "I noticed two other guards as we boarded. The last time I was here I didn't see any. What's going on?"

"I can only guess and hope I'm wrong," Maggie said. "I'm sure of one thing, though. If a radio message arrived right now telling the crew that we were at war with the Axis, golly-gee — I'd be thinking escape."

Kyna clasped her hands. "What are you getting at?"

"Mind you, I might be wrong," Maggie said in a low tone. "Remember, in July, when we went to Antigua? This cruiser had a four-man crew at the time. Now only one of them is still alive, and I helped him escape to the mountains two days ago. Everyone thinks he's dead, too. These guards are all German or sympathetic to the Nazis. This helmsman is the brother of the former helmsman who got murdered the last time you were here."

"Murdered? What do you mean?"

"Remember the robbery attempt at the Zócalo? I went to get Adolf's limousine and came back in a taxi? I'd found the driver dead. Anyhow," Maggie lifted a finger toward Mostacho, "he's scared, and I've promised to help him escape. We put on the hubbub minutes ago just so I could get a chance to explain the escape plan."

Eyes wide, Kyna formed an "oh" with her lips and took a deep breath. "Need help, count me in," she murmured.

* * *

At last she'd get a chance to look inside Adolf's hacienda,

Maggie thought, as Mostacho took them slowly up the Rio Antigua, but the cruiser went past it to the Mooring Tree Plaza, where Adolf, dressed as the don of the Hacienda, met them at the riverbank. His hat was flat-topped, black, and broad of brim. He wore a frilled white shirt under a black bolero embroidered in gold, red and green. His cummerbund was scarlet, as were the stripes trimming slim black leggings.

"My God," exclaimed Maggie. "He's even wearing boots and spurs."

"Don't see any horses," said Nolan, who was standing behind her. "Who the hell is that — the Buehler guy Sarah talks about?"

Maggie giggled. "In person."

"Welcome to Hacienda Buehler," Adolf called, and Maggie heard spurs jangle when he clicked his heels. As his guests reached the shore, he bowed to touch his lips to each woman's hand, and shook hands with each man. Gathering his guests under spreading boughs of the Cortez mooring tree, he explained over the chatter of hawking vendors, that the hacienda chef was indisposed, and that the proprietor of the Hotel Ceiba had insisted on hosting them for dinner.

"Still has a case on you, doesn't he?" Kyna whispered. "He can't take his eyes off you just like back in July."

"Just woman hungry — any woman," Maggie whispered.

"There's another with adoring eyes behind you," Kyna said into Maggie's ear. Then she spoke over her shoulder, "Some tree, isn't it, Nolan?"

"Hmpf, Nolan grunted. "Looks like a sleeping elephant waving his legs at the seagulls."

"About the right gray color, too," Maggie said. "Oh my." She nudged Kyna. "Speaking of color, look at Sarah — crimson!"

"I came ashore just behind her," Nolan said. She was sputtering at that pampas cowboy for not going directly to the hacienda."

Kyna nodded. "I heard her boasting about the shop she'd helped him set up featuring Catrina's jewelry."

Maggie turned to face her. "Here in Antigua?" This was a new twist. Might Sarah Williams really be a business partner with Adolf and Catrina? "Are you sure, Kana?"

"Uh-huh." Kyna gave her a questioning glance. "Haven't you heard? In Washington circles, Sarah's well known for access to Catrina's gems and Alvarada's designs."

"Oh, yes," Maggie replied quickly to avoid comment until she had time to consider Kyna's words. She glanced from Kyna to Nolan. "I'm going to the cantina down the road to give Zita a message. There's time before lunch. Want to come?"

Both nodded, and they walked north toward the Cortez ruin. Maggie let Kyna answer Nolan's questions while she organized her thoughts. Was it true what Kyna had said: go through Sarah Williams to get Alvarado jewelry? If true, why had Mrs. Williams given her an ultimatum never to see José again during the Fourth of July reception? Might she and José be secret partners? Kyna might be mistaken, of course. Oh-my-God. Was Kyna here to take part in the deal? What was involved — potentially, lots of money — bypassing customs — Treasury Department — Nolan? She glanced their way— Kyna, animated, ears sparkling, pierced since her July visit — Nolan, bewitched. She shook her head. *Mind your own business, Mags.*

Easier said than done. What was she to make of Kyna's remark about Sarah's helping Adolf? Bit by bit, snatches of information from strange quarters gave Thirteen Rabbit's linking of José and El Ragnorak the ring of truth. If José had business ties to El Ragnorak, did that mean Sarah was involved with him, too, and through her, the entire Veracruz consulate?

Hold on, she told herself. Commerce, trade, business, nothing wrong with that. Supposing there were linkages, were they wrong or just suspect because of the probability of United States participation in the war raging in Europe?

Kyna's voice caught her attention. "Nolan's taking pictures. Said he'd meet us on the way back."

Maggie stopped and faced Kyna. "I'd feel better going into the cantina with a man along."

Kyna shrugged, called, then beckoned when Nolan looked their way.

"I need only a minute with the cantina cook to change my order and make a partial payment," Maggie told Kyna. "It may take longer if he's with us, but —"

Interrupting, Kyna laughed. "You mean he'll insist on documents —like a purchase order?"

"Something like that. But he's okay. Handled that guard on the *Hedda* like he knew what to do."

"More than that. You don't know much about him, do you? He's vice president of a major mining firm, has a first-mate rating on Great Lakes ore ships, and took his current job because the country needed his skills in a time of crisis."

Maggie shortened her steps. "How come you know all this?"

Kyna took Maggie's elbow to urge her on. "Nolan's coming. He'll catch up and I don't want to miss that cowboy's dinner. Nolan's mother is a Gillingham — red hair just like his. My husband was on the Gillingham Mining Corporation board of directors when his mother took over as chief executive officer, and was instrumental in getting Nolan into government service." She paused. "This where we're going?"

"Uh-huh. Looks like a jail but it's attractive inside," Maggie said.

While they waited for Nolan, Maggie thought how nice it was to hear complimentary words about him. He'd been easy to work with and, except for Kyna's visit, had been linked with all the good things that had happened to her since — well, since

José's's gift of the earrings. She smiled. Kyna was going to drool over those earrings, specially designed Alvarado earrings, and wasn't Kyna in for a surprise when she heard of her friendship with José?

Grinning, Nolan gestured at a bullfight poster as he approached. "What do you know? Joe, my old buddy's still going strong. Bet he's real good, too."

"Dashing!" Kyna put in. "What does it say, Maggie?"

Maggie felt a thrill run up her back. That was strange because the thought of José fighting bulls was so repugnant. "Saturday, sixth of December," she translated. "Mexico City Bull Ring, and José Alvarado is to be the featured toreador. Weren't you fraternity brothers at the University of Minnesota, Nolan?"

"I forgot you knew. Right. I was getting my master's degree. He was intercollegiate fencing champion. Amazing fellow. Say, do you suppose they'd have an extra poster here?"

"I'll ask," Maggie replied, then followed Kyna into the cantina when Nolan opened the door.

Bullfight posters were such a staple of cantina decor that Maggie had paid them no attention the day before. Now she felt José's eyes watching her from every direction. She approached the cantina owner seated at the table where he'd been the day before, and introduced Kyna and Nolan.

"*Cerveza?*" the owner offered after the customary handshakes.

Nolan nodded, yes, he would like a beer, and Maggie thought it was probably one of a dozen or so Spanish words he understood. She declined for herself and Kyna, and asked if she might see Zita. "By the way," she said, "Señor Thompson is a close friend of José's Alvarado. Do you know where he can get one of the bullfight posters?"

The owner lifted both hands. "How fortunate. I'll get one." He turned toward the counter.

"He's getting you one, a beer, too," Maggie said.

"How about two?" Nolan piped up.

"Three," Kyna said.

"Tres carteles, solamente una Cerveza," Maggie called out, then went into the kitchen with Kyna.

Maggie introduced Kyna, then concluded her business with Zita.

"Delightful woman," Kyna said, as they returned to the dining room.

"Zita? Sure is." Maggie nodded. "Didn't bother her a bit when I more than tripled the order. I'd thought I'd have to come pick it up, but she said she'd send everything on the *Hedda* in the morning."

"Why did she wham the meat cleaver into the chopping block?"

Maggie laughed. "Fierce, wasn't she? Emphasis, that's all. Bring back those pans by four-thirty tomorrow — or else." She saw Nolan at a table with two other men. "Ready to go?" she asked. "Quite a stack of posters you got."

"Yup. One for each of the gang, and a couple to spare." Nolan rolled them up, tucked them under his arm and waved to the two men. "Good-bye and thank you," he called.

"That man speaks pretty good English," Nolan said when they were outside. "He told me Joe lives in Veracruz, and works out with bulls three times a week right here on this hacienda."

"Did you know that his parents came from Alvarado, a town just south of Veracruz?"

"He was thoroughly Americanized, Maggie."

"What about me? My mother was Mexican. I was born in Mexico, and Spanish was my first language. I feel very much at home here. Am I — oh, skip it. Kyna," she said quickly, "do you think the embassy wives would like to see some Alvarado jewelry designs? Alvarado Silversmiths is only about four blocks from the consulate."

Chapter 22

Perhaps Kyna was right, Maggie thought the next morning as she checked Clank's rumble compartment to make sure the cushions had been removed. Last evening they'd eaten at the *Café de la Parroquia*. Afterward, Kyna had asked who she was working for. Mr. Williams, of course, she'd answered. Then Kyna had said just one word — really— with raised brow, and *"think about it, you stupid fool,"* written all over her face.

"Got gas, Clank?" she said to no one in particular as she got into the Model A and checked the gauge — full.

They'd dropped the subject then. Now she could hardly wait to pick Kyna up at the consulate, take her to the *Parroquia* for breakfast, and get an explanation for that remark.

"Chorizo, huevos revueltos," Maggie ordered when they were seated at the café. "That's scrambled eggs and sausage," she told Kyna. "How about papaya and coffee?"

"Mismo," Kyna said, grinning. "See, I'll get this language yet."

"You're doing fine." Maggie laughed. "How about jewelry designs, a tour of Alvarado Silversmiths? Any takers on the idea?"

"Oh, yes. Including a few I met at Sarah's house last night, there will be eight or ten. We're meeting at nine at the consulate. Will you join us?"

"I can't — expect a madhouse all day long, but I'll let the shop know you're coming."

"You made their day, Maggie. One of the husbands suggested a tour of Ulua Fortress. That's when I mentioned Alvarado's. José you call him? How well do you know him?"

"Quite well." Maggie looked down to her lap and opened her purse. "Maybe too well." She took out the earrings and handed them to Kyna. "He gave these to me."

"Good gracious!"

Maggie waited while Kyna examined the earrings. "I thought you would like them," she said finally.

"Like them?" Another pause. "He gave them to you? Maggie, these are works of art — priceless! Make me drool like the emeralds did the last time I was here, but these are something else. I guess you do know this José Alvarado. Is he serious, Maggie? You sure?"

"I don't know, Kyna. Such a gift would seem to say so. He's quite gregarious, but a loner, and lives in a world of secrets. It's as though he's trying to buy my loyalty so I won't divulge his secrets when I don't even know what they might be." Kyna had a way of probing into deep feelings and Maggie was relieved to get away from talk of José when the waiter served their breakfast.

While she ate, Maggie considered how to open the *who's my boss* topic when Kyna beat her to it.

"Nolan cornered me after you went home last night," Kyna said. "He told me Mr. Williams had promised him your time for Thursday afternoon but you played bridge instead. I know it's not for me to say anything, but I wondered why."

"Because Mr. Williams told me to, and he's my boss," Maggie said, and signaled the waiter for more coffee. "It just wasn't fair for Kyna to ask why she'd obeyed her boss, and Maggie felt resentment welling within her as Kyna went on.

"I'm only one of millions of taxpayers, Maggie. Do you think I, or anyone else, think my tax money should pay for you to play bridge with the girls?"

Maggie gusted out her breath. "Of course not. I object every time Mrs. Williams summons me, but what can I do when Mr. Williams orders me to obey his wife?"

Kyna smiled. "You might try asking him to give you signed instructions typed on Department of State letterhead. There's another point, too," Kyna said. "You're still the only Spanish speaking member of the consular staff, aren't you?"

Maggie nodded. "The only U.S. citizen, yes."

"Well then," Kyna said, pushing back her chair, "that makes you the communications link between the United States and this area. You're more than that, because you're the taxpayer's money watchdog with power to keep Mr. Williams in line. He's afraid of you — scared stiff — caught between a wife who's prone to taking liberties and whom he can't control, and a watchdog with bared teeth. Nolan told me how you forced Mr. Williams to get his wife in line when he'd not been able to do it before."

"I had to protect myself," Maggie said.

"Better than that," Kyna said. "You defied Mr. Williams, your superior in rank, by doing what you were hired to do. Never forget, Maggie, work in the public sector differs from the same sort of work in private business because you're responsible to every taxpayer." "I see what you mean. I would have slept better if you'd told me that last night," Maggie said. "Of course you mean citizens and not just taxpayers."

Kyna smiled. "Yes, and guests of the country, too. Frankly, Maggie, if I'd said more last night, it would have been to tell you to do the kind of thing you'd already done."

* * *

Maggie unlocked the files. "I'll be busy all afternoon," she told Carlos after he returned from conducting the silver tour. "Get acquainted with the various accounts. Any questions will have to wait until tomorrow."

She went out to the foyer and sat down on a sofa, hoping to

snatch a moment to relax. Three blasts from a ship's horn signaled its departure and she heard the Seth-Thomas ticking on the wall behind her, but why bother to look. It must be one o'clock or close to it. She gazed into the reception room. Three bridge tables, just what Queenie had requested, but she knew there were as many more in a screened area. After what Kyna had said at breakfast, she just knew this would be her last stint as Queenie Quiverchin's bridge pigeon.

Then her thoughts wandered back to the Fourth of July reception, elegant dresses, sparkling jewels. This wouldn't be like that, but there would be cocktail dresses and plenty of sparkle, too. As to herself, she'd changed to the beige linen dress given to her by Kyna, Daitha and Mrs. Williams, and she wore the silver earrings José had given her.

Kyna had loved the earrings. Had she returned from José's showroom with something more splendid? She was upstairs now, the embassy wives, too. This was to be a hen party. The ambassador and his staff, Mr. Williams, Senator Johnson, and Nolan were cloistered in the conference room. They might hear the sound of women's voices, but it should not disturb them unless doors were left open. Maggie got up, closed the doors to the office area, and returned to the foyer just as two members of Mrs. Williams's bridge club arrived. After seating them at a bridge table, she sent a servant to summon Mrs. Williams.

Bolstered by Kyna's breakfast pep talk, Maggie felt an unexpected confidence that she'd be able to shrug off Mrs. Williams's sputter, and was prepared to either laud her for hosting a grand bridge party, or suffer one of her verbal whippings if it turned into a disaster. If only Señora Dalpica would arrive early with a photographer. She and Mrs. Williams were both influential, both powerful. *Dear God, please don't let Mrs. Williams explode.*

Maggie noticed a label — *chipachonga*, but no platter. She hurried into the pantry to get it, caught her image in the wall mirror, combed her hair, touched up her lips, and felt her confidence surge. Kyna's voice reached her from the ballroom.

"There's a plant on the veranda with the most gorgeous blooms I've ever seen," Kyna said. "Let me show you?"

Maggie peeked out and felt like staring forever at Kyna's companion. She was tall and about fifty-five. Stunning, dignified, poised and, even from where she stood, Maggie felt her charm.

She joined them, and Kyna introduced her to the ambassador's wife, who took both of Maggie's hands in hers.

"How nice to meet you, Maggie," she said. "Irena has told me so much about you, and speaks of you as her newborn adult daughter, and a great joy."

Maggie felt her face redden, and repressed an urge to wrap her arms about the woman. She couldn't find words, and just listened.

"I heard about your dramatic arrival after Irena and Benancio had given you up as a victim of that tragic air crash. What a moment that must have been for them to find you here."

"And what a surprise it was for me to learn that I had living relatives in Mexico — such dear ones, too," Maggie said.

"Maggie hadn't even started to work yet when she took a few of us on a two-day shopping tour," Kyna said. "She's simply the best guide, interpreter and body guard imaginable."

"Body guard?" The ambassador's wife raised a brow. "You don't mean it, of course."

"Yes I do." Kyna's eyes flashed. "Three men with pistols mugged —"

"Margareta."

It was Sarah Williams's voice, and it rose with each syllable. "Excuse me," Maggie said, backing away.

"Love your earrings," Kyna put in.

"Love yours, too — Alvarado earrings, I can tell," Maggie said. "I love this dress, too, and thank you again." Maggie wheeled and rushed to the foyer where Mrs. Williams was waiting with her toe tapping the floor. "I'm entertaining a few Veracruz ladies this afternoon, too, Mrs. Williams," Maggie said before Mrs. Williams got started.

"You have no right to invite anybody, child."

"Maggie." Nolan interrupted from the office area. "The ambassador wants a demonstration."

"Maggie, can you spare a minute?" Kyna called from behind the ballroom screens.

Mrs. Williams's toe continued to tap the terrazzo floor as Maggie raised her finger and jabbed. " That's Mrs. Johnson, and the ambassador's wife is with her."

"Mrs. Williams," Kyna called, appearing from behind a screen, "would you explain something, please. You know all about these plants, and we need your opinion."

Mrs. Williams bustled off in that direction, and Maggie went into the conference room where Senator Johnson had seized the time gap to brief the group on the latest news of the war in Europe. "I have a crowd out there," she whispered to Nolan, "and Mrs. Williams needs an introduction. Be right back."

Fists on hips, Mrs. Williams intercepted her just outside the office. "Margareta, this is the last straw. Now you —"

"Look who's here," Maggie cut in, "Daria Dalpica. Señora Dalpica," she called, beckoning over Mrs. Williams's shoulder. "Do you see who's with her, Mrs. Williams? One's a photographer, and the other is a society reporter."

The consul's wife turned that way. "Well, I'll just have to see what they want," she sputtered, and hurried to greet her guests.

Just then Kyna and the ambassador's wife appeared from behind a screen, and Maggie chewed her cheek wondering what might happen as they approached Sarah Williams and Daria Dalpica. Maggie saw Kyna cast her a glance and wink, and shot back a quick lift of her chin. "Whew. So much for Sarah Williams," she muttered.

"Got a place I can stash some of this?" the photographer asked.

"Sure," Maggie said, taken back by the outfit the young woman was wearing. Her dress was fuchsia-colored with the hemline just above her knee caps like the one Helen was wearing. "I'm glad you speak English," Maggie said.

"Born in Los Angeles, and this is my mom, used to be a reporter on the *Los Angeles Times.*"

Maggie took them into the office and introduced them to Helen. "Would you see to something, Helen?" Maggie said. "With all the dignitaries around, Mr. and Mrs. Williams are anxious to get some good photographs and interviews. You're —"

"Show me where to stash my stuff," the photographer interrupted.

"And Helen," Maggie said, disregarding the interruption and backing toward the conference room, "do you play bridge? Doesn't matter. Join the party. Have some fun."

It was two-fifteen when Maggie entered the conference room, and she wondered how long she would have to stay? Not past two-thirty, she hoped. Were Zita's baking pans clean yet? How many? Would there be enough room in Clank's rumble pit? She'd have to leave for Antigua by three-thirty at the latest. She watched Nolan distribute copies of a report she'd prepared. Senator Johnson ended his briefing, then it was her turn, and Maggie wondered if Nolan really believed the flattering comments he made about her in his introduction.

"Go to it, Maggie," he said, taking his seat. "Everybody has a copy of your examples."

Maggie stepped to the front of the room and, one by one, met the eyes of each man while slowly leafing through a copy of the report. "When I came to work here," she began, "I found that the entire annual budget was divided into twelve equal parts, one for each month. The system is quite common, and has certain advantages, a principal one being that it provides a device to monitor spending and avoid going broke before the end of the year — fiscal year, of course. It's easy to keep books under that system, but not easy to stay honest. Its rigidity forces conscientious managers to play it safe by copying the previous —"

"That's not dishonest," someone interrupted.

"You're right," Maggie shot back, "but suppose we look at example C2 on page twelve of the handout Mr. Thompson distributed. It lists thirty-three unbudgeted expenditures of two hundred fifty dollars or more by this consulate during FY1940. Now consider figure two in that example, and note that August, October and March have none of those thirty-three. May had eight, the most of any month, indicating that someone was aware of the closeness of the fiscal year's ending."

Maggie paused to allow snickers to die, then went on. "Managers are praised for handling emergencies with resources already available. Conversely, if they request supplemental or emergency funding, they —"

"Gravestone in hell," a low voice cut in, and the room rocked with laughter.

"Precisely, and thank you," Maggie said between her own outbursts of laughter. "So the cunning manager learns to hide behind confusion by setting aside small reserves here and there. Think about all the paperwork and time it takes to dream up imaginary situations and accounts which are nothing more than hiding places for discretionary money which an effective manager must have to do his job. If not used, hidden money tends to be stripped away at the end of the fiscal year. Sometimes, I suppose, it finds use by walking home in a pants pocket, lady's' purse, elaborate entertainment or —" Maggie shrugged. She heard a snicker and quipped, "Don't misunderstand me. I'm not proposing a way to set up secret money pockets."

Laughter again.

"Consider this," she went on. "Those out of sight piggy banks are characteristic of the system I inherited, and I'm sure Mr. Williams inherited many from his predecessor, too. Other examples in the handout indicate a way to give a manager more discretion in the use of funds, and are modified from an accounting system I used at Douglas Aircraft Company in St. Louis."

Maggie went on to explain her examples, then yielded to Nolan, who announced a short break.

Maggie heard voices — gladsome, spirited tones that attract men. Better to invite them, get pictures, and make sure the consul gets the credit. She caught Mr. Williams's eye, wiggled her fingers in front of her mouth, then jabbed toward the large ballroom. She saw him nod, then dashed out.

Three o'clock — running late, she'd have to hurry. Maggie scurried through the back hall to the kitchen and beckoned a servant. "Are the cantina pans all clean?" Assured that they were, she told the woman to put them in the Model A Ford's rumble seat compartment. "It's open," she said, then asked another woman to help her remove the screens from around the hors d'oeuvre tables. She went into the party room and saw coiffed hair, scads of jewels, and heard the babble of voices, laughter, occasional squeals, and suddenly Kyna was beside her.

"I'm dummy," Kyna said, helping Maggie fold up a screen. "Sarah and Daria have us way down."

"Who's your partner?" Maggie asked.

"I can't pronounce her name — railroad wife."

"Know who you mean. Nice woman," Maggie said. They put another screen away, then Maggie pulled the covering cloth from a table laden with hors d'oeuvres, and Kyna uncovered another. "Help yourselves, everybody," she called in English

then in Spanish. "There's something for gringo tastes —
Mexican, too, and a punch bowl on the end table."

Flashbulbs flared.   Maggie saw Helen with the
photographer, both laughing.   What a difference the
photographer had made in Helen. The men emerged from the
office, but held back, watching, until the ambassador stepped
forward.

Maggie stood aside for a moment, pulled in a deep breath
and let it out slowly. Mrs. Williams just had to be pleased with
the way her bridge party had turned out, and now she'd be
boasting about how she'd brought the American and Mexican
women of Veracruz together. They were mixing, chattering,
when Maggie sampled an hors d'oeuvre.

"What's that you're eating?" one of the embassy wives
asked.

"Chipachonga," Maggie said, smiling.

Kyna approached. "I think I'll try one, too. Mmm, two
kinds of chipa . . . chipa . . . whatever you call it. Which do you
have?"

Maggie indicated a tray. Kyna selected one and took a bite.
"Mmm, tasty. Are these the ones you said were made from
monkey meat?"

"Monkey!" the embassy woman exclaimed.   "Well, I
never."

"Not that one, Kyna. This is the monkey meat tray. Try
one?"

"I dare you," one of the North American women urged.

Laughing, a Mexican woman put one on her plate. Kyna
tasted one, nodded, and ate it all. Women squealed. Guests
surrounded the hors d'oeuvre table, and Maggie drew Kyna
aside. "I have to take the pans back to Zita now. Do you mind
staying? I don't know how I'd have managed this crowd
without you."

"I'm enjoying it immensely." Kyna touched her arm. "Such

nice people, and you were right. There must be at least sixty here and every one of them will be in the society pages. Oops, got company. The ambassador's headed this way."

"Why now when I've just got to leave? Help, Kyna. Get him a tray — anything." Maggie turned to face him.

"I understand you arranged all this. Wonderful idea. May I call you Maggie?"

"Of course you may. I hope your meetings are going well." How was she to get out of this?

"Quite well, thank you. I've asked Mr. Williams to include you in the remainder of the day's meeting, but might we have a word in private first?"

Maggie closed her eyes a moment, then fixed them on his. "Something extremely important has come up, and there's no way I can avoid tending to it. I'll be with you as soon as I can."

"Don't be long," he said, and turned to the hors d'oeuvres table.

"You'll lose your job if you defy him, Maggie," Kyna whispered

"I have no choice, Kyna. My job or a man's life." Maggie darted into the kitchen, took the back stairway to the Johnsons' room where she changed clothes, then raced out to the Model A Ford, swung open the door and gasped. José Alvarado was in the driver's seat, hands gripping the steering wheel.

"Well, hello, Maggie. Hardly dressed for your party, are you? We've got a few things to iron out, and we're going to do it right now."

Chapter 23

"Get out!" Maggie hissed. How dare José just sit and jut his chin out at her? "Of all the contemptible —" She blew the words out. "I can't believe you'd — ooh." Fists clenched, shoulders tensed, she felt her chest quivering and forced herself to pull in a deep calming breath. Poor Mostacho. She had to get going, had to risk taking José. "I'll drive. Move over!"

"Talk back to your boss?"

"You're not my boss," she snapped. At least he was talking. She thumbed over her shoulder. "Back there — the ambassador just told me to hurry back. He is my boss, and much more important than you are. Get out!"

"Miguel contacted me," José said, lifting his legs over the gear lever. "New orders. We've gotta talk."

Maggie slid into the seat, started the car, and screeched the tires as she swung onto *Avenida General Figueroa.* She braked to avoid a nun at *Avenida Aristas,* and stopped in front of José's shop. "Get out," she barked.

"We've gotta talk." José did not move.

Maggie gunned Clank forward. After his attempt to trap Thirteen Rabbit, she dared not trust José to sit by while she helped Mostacho escape. She skirted the monument circle. "What's the quickest way to the Antigua road?" she asked.

"Slow down! You scraped that donkey. Hear it?" José braced himself against the dashboard. "Go straight ahead, right on *Cuahtemoc* and cross the tracks."

It must be four already and she wasn't even out of town. She caught a glimpse of José with one hand on the dashboard and the other against the ceiling. "Hang on," she said, approaching the railroad crossing, then bounced the Ford across. Leveling out, she saw that José had relaxed. "What did Miguel say?"

José motioned her left onto the Antigua road. "He's taking you off the case."

"I can't conjure up a single reason to believe you," she snapped.

"Well! If you're going to act that way, take me back."

Maggie gritted her teeth. Already late, she couldn't take him back. Minutes passed. She saw that he was sketching in a notebook, a sign that he was cooling off. Maybe he'd be reasonable now. She slowed down to maneuver through a series of potholes but hit one anyway, jouncing the car. The earrings he'd made bobbed against her neck with a caressing touch that brought a smile to her lips. José's gift — how tenderly he'd given them. She swung her head to embrace the sensation and shifted her eyes his way. Forget it, Mags! It had been a bribe, she told herself, and you'd better not forget it. "Yikes." She jerked the wheel to avoid a bush, throwing José against the door.

"*Cuidado!*" José yelped. "Stop. I'll drive."

"*Mí culpa.*" She glanced at him — fierce, and pictured how he might look if he'd known what she'd been thinking. She suppressed a smile, but couldn't keep her eyes from crinkling.

Quit dreaming, be careful, Mags. José was exciting, a real man, *mucho hombre,* but something about him just didn't add up. Thirteen Rabbit, Kyna, Nolan, and even Miguel had infused her mind with doubts about him. His presence at the cantina might ensure Mostacho's release, but dare she count on him to help her? No. She'd have to ditch him — trick him away from the car. Would he ever forgive her? Maybe. Ditch him, but don't get him angry. Humor him. Keep him talking

"What got you into bullfighting?" she asked.

"Depression, Maggie. All through high school I fought the bulls over the border in El Paso, Texas. I was good enough to get a sponsor and fought throughout the Americas and for more than two years in Spain — all the famous arenas. Between fights, and for two more years, I studied in Antwerp, Brussels, and in museums. I polished my fencing skills with masters in Europe until I had enough money for a university with a fencing team. I still fight the bulls, only exhibitions now, and not the best bulls. But the people remember the name, and I can still tease the bulls, even the tender-hearted ones, and rouse them so they look very fierce."

"Thank you for telling me," Maggie said. "Guess I was wrong. I had the impression that you grew up with a silver spoon in your mouth and had financial backing from a wealthy El Paso family."

He stared straight ahead but said nothing and, from his stiffness, she got the impression that his life had been a struggle he was reluctant to talk about. She drove in silence until she pulled into Antigua and stopped in front of the Hotel Ceiba. "We're here," she said. "Do you mind asking in the hotel where I should take the baking pans? Better yet, see if they'll send someone out to get them?"

"Oh, okay," José said as if waking from a dream, and went into the hotel.

Got rid of him, Maggie thought, shifting into gear. Just then she saw Adolf jump ashore from the *Riesa*, wave, and come running toward her. Pretending not to see him, she gunned Clank toward the cantina. She had no reason to see Adolf.

"Sorry to leave you behind, José," Maggie muttered, as she passed the Cortez ruin and the hermitage. No, she wasn't really sorry. He deserved much worse.

The hacienda wall loomed on her right, and it struck her that the glass fragments protruding from the wall cap might deter a thief from entering, but would never discourage a man facing death from an escape attempt. Guards — she shivered. Professional killers — they might be everywhere, and armed with knives, pistols and rifles. Ahead, the roadway looked like a channel between the hacienda wall and dense jungle.

Zita had told her to park in the recess where the cantina jutted out from the hacienda wall, and to signal her arrival by banging on a pan. Maggie backed into the niche so that the hood of the car was beside the narrow door set into the heavy plank gate. She got out and stood under the narrow horizontal windows, listened, and heard the tune Zita had said would be her all's well signal. The road was deserted, as Zita had said it would be in the late afternoon, except for a black dog, trotting briskly as if it knew exactly where it wanted to go. The dog crossed the road and disappeared into a small gap in the wall of foliage directly across from the hacienda gate. Hmm, animal trail through the jungle — an escape route? She crossed to it, stooped and entered. A branch snapped as she pushed past, but she put it back in place before returning to the car. One minute to go. Everything had to happen quickly, so she took Zita's pans from the rumble compartment, and piled all but a warped one onto the car's engine hood.

"Dear God. Four-thirty," Maggie murmured, "I hope Zita hears me bang this thing." She swung the warped pan and winced at its clanging as it whammed against the rock wall.

There came a crashing sound through the window— metallic, laced with curses and Zita's screams to get out of her kitchen.

Maggie banged the pan again, this time against the gateway door. "Open up," she shouted in Spanish, then English. "I have pans for Zita."

She heard Zita order someone to open the gate. "They don't understand Spanish or English, Zita," she yelled. "I'll try to speak German. *Aufmachen die Tür,*" she yelled. The people-door opened a crack, and Maggie stared into blue eyes set in a pink-cheeked fuzzy face. Just a boy in uniform, she thought as he gestured for her to go to the front entrance. She shook her head, held up the pan and pointed through the gap toward the kitchen. Wham! Lucky— her finger jerked out just before the door slammed shut.

Maggie kicked the door, battered her pan against it and shouted, *"Aufmachen sie weber,"* whatever that meant. She kept on banging, and finally the door swung in. Oh no. Two guards now. One was Mostacho's watchdog from the *Hedda* — scary. He'd be especially careful.

"Hello, mizz," he said.

"Oh, hello," she blurted, taken aback by his seeming friendliness. He must have seen her stop Mostacho from grabbing the rifle from Kyna while Nolan was dragging him out of the *Hedda* pilothouse. Besides, wasn't she Adolf's friend? "Am I glad you speak some English," she said, forcing a smile as she entered. Then she saw a man crumpled against the cantina wall, face down, shirt torn and bloody — Mostacho. She wagged a thumb toward him. "Is that the man who caused all the trouble on the *Hedda* yesterday? Is he sleeping — drunk? Can you make him carry Zita's pans into the kitchen?" She beckoned. "They're in the car."

"My cooking pans — *ya mismo me las me traigo*," Zita screamed from the kitchen door.

Maggie saw Mostacho start to rise. No-no, she thought. He didn't dare act too eager lest he give their plan away. Watchdog prodded him with his rifle. Maggie grabbed his elbow and pulled him up and out to the car. Both guards followed. Maggie loaded Mostacho with baking pans and shoved him through the gate. Watchdog followed, but she blocked Fuzzyface from going, too. Then she thumbed at herself and at him and motioned to the pile of pans.

He shook his head, stood still.

Maggie shoved a pan at his stomach. He grabbed at it with one hand, she snatched his rifle from the other and leaned it against the wall. "Wait. Take more and I'll bring what's left," she snapped. Whether he understood or not, he stood docilely while she piled his arms full, then picked up all that were left.

"Luck and the Lord be with me," Maggie murmured, following the fuzzy- faced guard with the last three pans, the largest, bulkiest, and flimsiest. "Dear God, help Mostacho do his part."

The aroma of steaming pinto beans and white cheese tortilla sauce wafted toward her at the kitchen door. Zita had said she'd put a crock of cornmeal mush in a basket with a high arcing handle beside the door, and there it was. Pots steamed on the cast iron stove: white sauce, boiling with a gluck-gluck sound, beans simmering — three gallons, at least. She scrunched her nose and nodded quickly to Zita, who widened her eyes in return.

Maggie drew in a long breath. Zita had done her part — set the stage. Now it was Mostacho's turn, and her own. Mostacho stood rigid, arms loaded with pans and stared at Zita, who was between him and the door to the dining room. Sure he was on the verge of bolting for that door when Maggie called, "Mo — " She caught herself. "Guard, tell that man to put those pans on the counter and come get these."

Watchdog growled an order. Nothing happened, so he jammed the muzzle of his rifle under Mostacho's armpit.

Mostacho erupted. Swinging about, he threw all his pans into the air, a corner gashing Watchdog's face as it rose to him. He grabbed for the rifle, missed, but knocked it to the floor among falling pans, then bulled past Watchdog.

Fuzzy dropped his pans and, reaching for his pistol, backed into Maggie.

Maggie saw the gun come out of its holster and rammed the corners of a pan into the back of Fuzzyface's hand.

Fuzzy screamed as Mostacho bowled him to the floor and brushed past Maggie, spinning her about.

We're back to the plan, she thought as she spun full circle with pans extended to sweep the stove clean. Boiling white sauce poured onto Fuzzy as the bean pot slid across the stove top toward Watchdog.

He saw it coming and shot out his hand to stop it, but the pot tipped over at the edge of the stove, and his hand plunged into boiling pinto beans. Howling, he jerked out his hand, sending the pot spinning toward the dining room door, and spreading beans over the floor. Zita dodged it and let out a gleeful shriek. The door opened and a third guard burst in, skidded and sat in hot beans as a fourth piled onto him and rolled onto clanging pans. Pandemonium — swell, Maggie thought. She wheeled — no Mostacho, and she saw that the mush basket was gone, too. She dashed after him. Fighting men, the guards would not be long licking their wounds. Then she heard Zita shouting, "Out, get out—" words without end.

Maggie rushed to the gate, grabbed the handle and pulled. No use. Mostacho had wedged it tight, but had dropped the mush basket. She grasped the handle, swung it up and around — around again, and let it fly over the wall toward where she thought the gap in the jungle foliage might be.

The noise from the kitchen suddenly ceased, then Watchdog's howl warned her that the guards were coming. Desperate to get out the gate before anyone came, she jerked it again. It opened. She dashed through, glanced at Clank and saw the rumble seat lid closing.

"Guards," she shouted, sprinting across the road. Pointing at the mush trail and gap in the foliage with her left hand, she swung her right arm in circles, waving for them to follow. "In there," she screamed, started to go in, then backed out. "He took the guard's rifle. Be careful."

Watchdog, his hand tucked into his shirt, led two guards

into the gap and Fuzzyface brought up the rear.

They hadn't been burned too badly, then, Maggie decided, and burst into laughter at the sight of Fuzzy's white sauce bottom. Unless they recaptured Mostacho, the guards would probably suffer more from the disgrace of losing their quarry than from their burns.

Maggie approached her car just as patrons emptied the cantina and crowded the scene. Asked what had happened, Maggie said, "Who knows? Perhaps the guards are looking for a thief." As she climbed into Clank and started the engine, she heard her words repeated again and again,

"Straight ahead," Maggie heard a hushed voice say just as a the sound of gunshots reached her. "Oh, no," she murmured. "They shot that poor black dog." Well, they had to kill something, she supposed, thinking of the story the guards might tell — chased him into the jungle — gun fight — got him — left him to rot in the bog and the rifle went down, too.

"Go right when the road angles left," Mostacho said from the rumble pit, "then drive straight through the hanging banyan tree roots."

Maggie followed his directions, then stopped and let him out of the rumble pit. "Are you hurt badly?" she asked.

"We must hurry," he said, disregarding her concern, and climbing into the passenger seat.

"Do you think they will look for us here?" Maggie was sure that they'd made a clean getaway.

"You must hurry, *Señorita*. The tide is rising. At first I did not like your plan and almost spoiled it. I am sorry. Thank you."

"De nada, It turned out well, *"* she said, and thought she might be on Thirteen Rabbit's road that wasn't really a road. Mostacho directed her to a lagoon where his wife had instructed a fisherman to pick him up.

"I'm building a boat," he told her as he got out, "one for the sea, and I need the Guatemala boy to run the engine. Where is he?"

"I'll tell him. Where can I find you?"

"I'll send a messenger to tell you," he said. "This trail will take you out to the road. Good-bye. You have time before the tide. Thank you." He waved and was gone.

Details of Mostacho's escape raced through Maggie's mind as she drove to the mooring tree plaza. José would be furious if he were still there. She should rush back to meet the ambassador, but José knew the shortcuts and might get her there sooner. Suddenly thirsty, she parked, flexed her legs, then ran to the Hotel Ceiba courtyard to order a Coca-Cola.

"You missed all the excitement."

Expecting an angry José, she was startled by his pleasant tone of voice. "Did I?" she said. "What happened? Got to run. Want something? Get it quick and come." She ran out and got into the passenger seat. "You drive," she said when he followed. "So what happened?"

"Cantina up the road." He started the engine. "You'd been there and gone when Adolf and I arrived. "One of the hacienda employees walked off the job and took a couple of guns with him."

"Do you know the man?"

"Only from seeing him on Adolf's cruiser. No big deal. Adolf was about to let him go anyhow. There was a chase, and that was that."

"I heard gunshots after I dropped off the pans," Maggie said, sipping her Coke. She was not surprised by José's answer and, especially, not by his reaction to word of Mostacho's death, but she felt deeply disappointed. José must know that it was a killing to hide secrets. Might that have been his reason for killing two men on the night of her arrival in Veracruz? She had stuck to her belief that he had killed to protect her. Now she wasn't so sure, and the thought that the packet he put in his safe was the real cause haunted her.

"Please hurry," she said. "Will you drop me off at the back gate then take the car back to Enrique's?"

"Can do. Are you busy this evening?"

"What about joining us at the Zócalo tonight? Nolan will be there, the ambassador, too, I think. But I . . ."

"But you what?"

"Never mind." She had been about to tell him that she would be leaving the group early, but it occurred to her that she'd never had a chance to observe José interacting with people other than at organized social functions. She was sure of one thing. He would never understand why she would choose to risk losing her job just to return baking pans to a cantina cook.

Chapter 24

" Maggie tiptoed into the conference room and had settled into a back-row seat when she felt a tap on her shoulder with a whispered message to meet in the hall. She rose and turned just in time to see a man wearing a Palm Beach suit go out the door.

Uh-oh. Only the ambassador might be wearing Palm Beach, and she was late returning. She hurried out the door he was holding open. "I'm sorry I took —"

"Don't bother to cook up an excuse," the ambassador said. "We're a trifle late. The Imperial. Wild goose chase, but I gave my word. We'll walk."

He hadn't fired her then — not yet at least. He'd already started for the rear door and she set off to keep up with him. He'd said, "We're late," "We", not "you," and it struck her that every man or woman she'd ever known would have harped on her lateness and rubbed it in. She liked him for the difference, then felt a twinge of disappointment when he barged out the back door ahead of her and let it slam in her face as he strode down the driveway.

"Shouldn't I change before we go?" she said, scampering to catch up. "It'll only take—"

"No time for that," he said, and went out the gate. He zigzagged between children playing on the street, shoved a burro's head down to cross in front of it and strode on.

"Perdón," Maggie said to the driver, and circled behind his cart to catch up and maintained a pace slightly behind the

ambassador. He made a beeline through the Zócalo, shunned vendors, and entered the crowded lobby of the Hotel Imperial. Chatter faded, and heads turned their way as he led Maggie back to the elevator kiosk. Euph, middle-aged man, fastidious, taking a pretty maid up to a hotel bedroom.

What thoughts lay hidden behind those scandal-hungry looks, backstairs glances, furtive smiles? Maggie wondered, as she escaped into the stained-glass elevator kiosk with the ambassador. The platform lifted them slowly out of stained-glass privacy, and showcased them in the open brass-barred elevator cage. What matter that her escort was the United States ambassador to Mexico, fastidious in his Palm Beach suit, crimson tie, panama hat? She must look like a hotsy-totsy — strawberry blonde, large silver ear hoops, and rumpled white maid's uniform. At least it wasn't low-cut and scarlet. She glanced down at gaping faces, mouths open, then forced herself to look up and pay attention as the ambassador spoke.

"So this is the Hotel Imperial — magnificent — built in 1794, I'm told — a Veracruz landmark, and famous the world over for its stained-glass dome."

How could he be so callous?   Why had the ambassador humiliated her by dragging her through the plaza, then parading her across the lobby and up to a bedroom? Why had she allowed him to do it? Well, he was the ambassador, and she'd delayed him, so she'd better try to forget it. "It is a grand old hotel, isn't it," she said, thinking it might be a first-class relic but not hotel. Just how sumptuous could it be when the lobby was less than ten yards long and six wide, and the opening up to the dome was no larger? The hotel just didn't compare in grandeur to the Sheraton in St. Louis. Mags, Mags! You're wrong, and you know it.

The cage topped at the second balcony encircling the central opening. They got out, turned right, and paused at the railing to look up at the dome.

"Oh, the stained-glass scene really is something!" Maggie exclaimed, thinking she'd judged too soon. "Look how the evening sky mellows all those shades of blue and green. There's rose, gold, and amber, too. The sections of stained glass blend so nicely, and make the dome's tropical scene quite realistic."

"More rooms back there." The ambassador motioned past the elevator and stairwell. "They say that only luxury rooms open onto the balcony."

She looked down to the lobby and faces still upturned. Oh, they're looking at the stained-glass dome, and never noticed me, she realized. Feeling better, she saw that each upper-floor bedroom opened onto the balcony circling the open shaft to the dome. The railing was of patterned wrought iron, painted in antique brass and capped by a walnut rail. Guest room double doors were about five feet wide, and crested by arched cornices.

"Go left and I'll go right," the ambassador said, swinging away from the railing. "Holler if you see the Hernan Cortez room."

Hmm. He still sounded brusque, but almost civil again. Maybe he wasn't furious, and had just been impatient because she'd been so late. Well, she'd still better watch her step. Maggie rounded a balcony corner, and saw a name from Mexico's history on a plaque beside each door: *Napoleon Bonaparte, Carlota Amelia Grau,* and others. Hmm, surprising — rooms named for women.

"Found it. Come on around," the ambassador called.

"The names of the rooms take one back in time, don't they," she said as she approached him. He knocked, and she whispered, "Mind telling me why we're here?"

"*Sigue,*" she heard someone answer from within.

Sounded like Miguel's voice, she thought. Why was he here?

The ambassador pushed the door open, then stood back so she could enter first. She hesitated. The room was dark, but she went in when she saw a small man silhouetted in the window against the gray of evening.

"Good evening," the ambassador said as he entered. "That you, Price?"

"Evening, ambassador, and a pleasant evening to you, too, Maggie."

So it was Miguel, and speaking English. "Hello, Miguel," Maggie said. "I hoped to see you soon." She heard the ambassador throw a switch beside the door, but the room remained dark.

"Any way to get some light in here?"

Maggie heard a series of clicks, a sign that the ambassador was still impatient. Why no handshakes, for the men, at least? Might the ambassador resent being summoned? What might Miguel want from him?

When her eyes had adjusted to the darkness, Maggie saw Miguel indicate chairs around a knee-high table and they all sat down.

"There's no power in this room," Miguel said. "We wont need it."

"You put me at a disadvantage, Price," the ambassador said. "I knew Maggie was assembling odds and ends of data for the FBI, but not that you two were acquainted." He faced Maggie. "Just how did you meet?"

"I . . . We . . ." Maggie paused. The ambassador might know of Miguel's taxi driver disguise, but she wasn't about to reveal it. Talk about disadvantage, she still had no inkling of why she'd been brought to the room. "If you don't mind, sir, I think I should say nothing until someone tells me why I'm here. What I mean is that if I'm being accused of some terrible crime, I can't defend myself without knowing what I'm supposed to have done." She heard Miguel chuckle.

The ambassador glanced at him, then back to Maggie. "You mean to say you don't know about the FBI plan to send you to

Tampico?"

"What plan?" Maggie said. "I don't know what you're talking about." Had José planted a rumor to prevent her from going?

"That's beside the point," the ambassador said, because I gave the FBI a flat no. Two reasons. First, it's a man's job. Second, during our session this afternoon while you were playing hooky, we decided to transfer you to the embassy in Mexico City."

"Played hooky?" Maggie said. "Isn't that's a low blow? Mr. Williams is my boss, and has never invited me to attend a meeting. Quite the contrary, he orders me to go shopping with Mrs. Williams, plan her parties, and play bridge with her club. Then you pop up and transfer me without asking me."

"Confound it, Maggie. You gave me a lame excuse, and took off with that silver hustler when I was about to explain what we had in mind."

Be careful, Maggie told herself, and pulled in a deep breath. She willed herself to answer calmly. "I'm very sorry about that, sir, but I had no choice."

"Care to explain?"

"It was a most successful errand," Maggie said, folding her arms and leaning back.

The ambassador squirmed around to face her directly. "That's not enough, Maggie."

"Mr. Ambassador," Miguel cut in, "Does the name El Ragnorak ring a bell with you?"

"Of course. Dangerous man."

"If he were to show up in Mexico, would you be alarmed?"

"Ye gods, Price. We discarded that rumor months ago. That come up again?"

Miguel tapped the table in front of Maggie. "Tell him."

Confident that Miguel would direct her with questions, Maggie held her account of El Ragnorak's arrival to a few short sentences.

"So that's how the rumor got its start." The ambassador slapped his knee. "You had no other witnesses. You can't be sure you saw this Ragnorak creature if you got only a glimpse at night. Makes no difference. I don't see this has any bearing on Maggie's assignment, Price. No matter how —"

"Go on, Maggie," Miguel interrupted. "You saved a man's life. Get to that. Tell the ambassador where he is now."

How clever this Miguel, asking her to report to himself in a such a way that the ambassador would get the impression that she and Miguel functioned well as a team. "Sure, but I'd better explain who he was." She faced the ambassador. "He was the young deck hand in the four-man crew of the cabin cruiser, *Hedda,* which landed El Ragnorak in Mexico. All four witnessed his arrival and are now believed to be dead." She described Thirteen Rabbit's escape, and how he had worked in the garage, been discovered, rescued again, then taken to Jalapa.

"Okay. I'll concede that this Ragnorak may have arrived, but what's the point?" the ambassador said. "This darkness is ridiculous. Can't you do —"

A flashlight shone suddenly from under Miguel's chair, easing the murkiness so that Maggie could see the ambassador sitting erect in his Palm Beach suit with arms folded. Sensing his limited patience, she said, "I don't object to being transferred, but I have things to finish here. I'm just telling you what I know. Miguel asked me to find out everything I could about El Ragnorak. I believe Adolf Buehler's hacienda is now El Ragnorak's headquarters, and that the *Hedda*, the cruiser we assumed to belong to the steamship company, is his principal mode of transportation. He had just left Tampico when the last tanker was torpedoed."

"See any airplanes — a landing strip?"

"The property borders the Gulf of Mexico with a beach a small plane can use, and the Antigua River can accommodate a sea plane."

"Why do you think he headquarters there?"

Good, the ambassador was listening. "Adolf hasn't been on the hacienda in months, except for short periods during special events which keep him in good graces with our consulate. That makes me think —"

"Whoa there!" the ambassador cut in. "Are you suggesting a connection between Ragnorak and our office?"

"No, sir," Maggie replied, "unless indirectly through the friendship of Mrs. Williams with Mr. Buehler. I suspect that there's some sort of relationship between El Ragnorak and Adolf Buehler and his sister."

"Hmm. We'll talk more about that later." The ambassador turned to Miguel. "Okay by you, Price?"

"Better than for me to relay it," Miguel said. "Proceed, Maggie."

Bravo, Miguel, Maggie thought. He wasn't about to let the ambassador cut the meeting short without getting what he wanted.

"Back to El Ragnorak then," Maggie said. "After El Ragnorak killed the helmsman who brought the *Hedda* from South Africa, he took the *Riesa's* helmsman from Mr. Buehler, and has kept him under armed guard ever since. I have reason to believe that he does not know that the two helmsmen were brothers. The one off the *Riesa* knows the Mexico coastline like a book. He's been everywhere with El Ragnorak for months and could give us oodles of information. For instance, he's the one who told me El Ragnorak had been in the Tampico area when the tanker was torpedoed. Pig's asshole, that's what they call the man, is here now to pick up a new helmsman who just arrived from South Africa. Tonight, he's sailing for Tampico again, and planned to dump the *Riesa* helmsman in the gulf to silence him forever. But he escaped. Four guards chased him, shot him, and left his body in the bog."

"Ye gods! Is that true, Price?"

"It just happened," Maggie cut in. "Miguel didn't know about it. A man I work with told me."

"I suppose we should check this out, Price. I'll assign one of our —"

"Sir, I —"

"Not so loud, Maggie," Miguel cut in. "Mr. Ambassador, I'm going to insist that the young lady say her piece." He paused, and when the ambassador raised no objection, said to Maggie, "I happened to see you and a companion dash from the consulate this afternoon. I also know he returned with you. Was he the one who told you about the helmsman's escape?"

"Yes."

"Did he witness any part of it?"

"Yes."

"Did you?"

"We were separated for nearly half an hour."

"I repeat. Did you see what happened?"

"More than he did."

"Should we believe him?"

"Publicly, yes, believe him."

"So that's the way it is," Miguel said. "Mr. Ambassador, I've seen Maggie operate before. Maggie, be more careful with your answers. No harm done because we're on the same side. It's apparent from what you said that you know more about the escape attempt than your companion does. Right?"

"I wasn't hiding anything. I just have to tell about it in my own way. Yes, I planned it. Kyna knew what I was up to — "

"Kyna, Kyna Johnson?" The ambassador chuckled. "That's Kyna for you."

"She helped by taking control of the bridge party. You," she tapped the table in front of him, "and the other guy nearly ruined it. I generated a row in a cantina so the helmsman could duck out and hide in the Model A's rumble pit, then drove him away."

"Ye gods!" The ambassador jumped to his feet. "Have I got this straight? Ragnorak's helmsman? What a witness! You know where he is?"

"I can reach him. I think I should . . ." She looked up at the ambassador, then at Miguel. "I want to catch El Ragnorak more than anything in the world. I want to go to Tampico to track him down, but have never mentioned that to anybody. There are records to search here and in Mexico City, first. Please leave Miguel and me alone for a few minutes to iron out a few details. Then I'll explain what I'd like to do if I work at the embassy."

"Five minutes," Miguel said.

"Very well, I'll consider it. Hmm! What am I saying? Unbelievable! Hmm! Don't be long."

Miguel went to the door with the ambassador, then returned and handed Maggie an envelope. "It contains travel authorization forms and a copy of the rental document for the Model A Ford." He opened the window and turned back to Maggie. "The ambassador assumes that I requested this meeting to discuss your going to Tampico. I did not. It was to impress him with the severity of Ragnorak's operations. You've made remarkable progress, Maggie. I take it you want to continue?"

"More than anything," she said. "You know, there might be real advantages to working out of Mexico City, but not if I'm tied down to day-in-day-out routine."

"That's all I need to know." Miguel leaned out, scanned all about then sat on the sill with a leg outside. "Your job is to lead us to the rat and you know who I mean. I will not give you instructions, and what I tell you now should be taken as guidance only. Are you comfortable with that?"

"Swell. As long as I have a way to contact you. But —"

"I'll get to that," he cut in. "I'll support whatever you need from the ambassador, but bear in mind that he'll need your cooperation. If he doesn't get it, he'll cut you off and I won't be able to stop him. Other than that, this is all I can say. You've demonstrated good instincts, so I give you a free hand to pick your colleagues, go wherever you need to go, do as you see fit. I suggest that you forget José. To him you're a woman, not a colleague, so help him only if he asks. Ragnorak is your assignment, not his." He paused and checked outside the window again. "One thing more," he said. "Contact me through Irena and definitely not José."

Chapter 25

"Bats!" Maggie exclaimed when one of the creatures flicked her hair as it flew into the room. She slammed shut the window to prevent more from entering. "Forget the bat," she muttered. "Forget José, too. Wise, maybe, but not so —hmm — and how come Irena's my contact with Miguel?" She opened the door. "Kyna!"

"I heard you mumbling, and what's this about Miguel?" Kyna pushed the switch. Light flooded the room and Maggie burst out laughing. "I thought you might need these." What's so funny?" She held out a package.

"My dress," Maggie sputtered through her laughter. "You're an angel from heaven. Shoes, too, I hope." She got the flashlight from under the chair and held it up. "It's just that we only had this for light during our meeting. How did you find me?"

"The ambassador. He told me the most scrumptious maid he ever did see would have to change in the dark. Who's Miguel?"

"Handy-man — plumber." He must have pulled the light fuse to put the ambassador at a disadvantage. Maggie thought it best not to tell Kyna who Miguel really was. "Is the ambassador in the lobby?"

Kyna nodded. "He and Nolan are side-by-side getting their shoes polished." Better hurry. Those are impatient men, and so am I. I'm on pins and nee —"

"Everything was wonderful at the cantina," Maggie said, holding a finger to her lips. Kyna had heard her through the door and there was no telling who might be in the next room. "Oh, and the cook. I'm not fond of pinto beans, but they couldn't have been better — scalding hot, too. Lucky she had plenty because the pot tipped over onto the floor — slick — and three men slid all over the place and crashed when they tried to race through the kitchen. And the cheese sauce — mmm. It spilled too — oh so slippery."

"Must have been fun," Kyna said, laughing. "Let's go, Maggie."

Maggie followed Kyna to the elevator. As they descended, she whispered, "If José mentions that a thief was shot and killed while running away from the cantina, you'll go along with his story, won't you?"

"Even if it's not true? Oh, you. Just what does José — what do you mean?"

"He wasn't upset by the shooting, which makes me wonder, what side is he on? Tell you more later, and I want to know about the bridge, especially her highness." Maggie opened the kiosk door and found herself face to face with the ambassador and Nolan.

"Back up you go, Maggie," the ambassador said. "You have a proposal for me?"

Maggie backed into the elevator. Nolan stepped forward, too, but the ambassador beckoned him out.

"Excuse us, Nolan," he said. Maggie and I have a State Department matter to iron out."

"Nolan, we're intruding," Kyna said, taking Nolan's arm and urging him aside. "Let's get a table on the plaza."

"I never expected a transfer to the embassy," Maggie said as the elevator rose. "What a surprise. Miguel has no objection as long as I'm able to continue with his assignment."

"I gather that Nolan does not know of your FBI connection.

Am I right?"

"No one knows except you, another agent and the governor and his wife."

They returned to the Hernan Cortez room where Maggie turned on the light and sat down at the table. The ambassador closed the door and sat across from her.

"I've decided to assign one of my military — "

"Please, sir," Maggie interrupted, then said in a low tone, "The main condition for my working at the embassy is that nobody know I have ties to the FBI."

"Surely you don't think Nolan would —"

"Excuse me," Maggie cut in. "I mean nobody. As for Nolan, he wouldn't approve. He's outspoken and can't help himself. His protest would spill the beans. My life depends on it. There are other conditions, too. I must report directly to you on everything related to my FBI work. I won't abuse the privilege by running in and out of your office. To do so would attract attention and cause gossip."

"Off base, Maggie. Don't push me."

"I don't mean to. Actually, if I don't fit into the embassy's normal routine, I'll attract suspicion." Maggie paused. How might she get him to allow her to work without close supervision? With military attachés on his staff, he'd be sure to assign anything having to do with the threat of war to them. "I knew nothing about a transfer to the embassy until I heard you and Miguel discuss it. Why the transfer? What will I do there? Nobody has told me a thing. Miguel didn't seem to know either. My assignment from him is to be alert for any sign of subversive activity and keep track of El Ragnorak. If I have enough freedom to continue that, he'll support the move."

"We have limited responsibility for counterespionage activities in Mexico, Maggie, but it does include cooperation with the FBI."

"Of course you know better than I do about that. But if El

Ragnorak is the Nazi's ace saboteur, as people seem to believe, doesn't it make sense to assume he's in Mexico to supervise Nazi espionage in this entire hemisphere?"

The ambassador nodded.

"Isn't it also logical for him to work out of Mexico, close to the States, but shielded from the intense surveillance he'd get at a stateside location?"

"I've considered that." The ambassador leaned forward. "This is getting us nowhere. Just what do you and Price propose?"

Maggie took a deep breath. "A tryout month. A period in which I can go back and forth between the embassy and Veracruz or any other consular offices in Mexico." Maggie paused, but the ambassador said nothing and she continued. "A while ago you mentioned that you knew that I was collecting export and import data for the FBI. May I show it to you?"

"Tomorrow, perhaps. What's the nature of this information?"

"We don't hear much about the war here, but I've noticed in the newspaper that Mexico and the States are negotiating a trade agreement. I've been listing manufacturers of different products, where they get their materials, particularly imports and export destinations, redlining those that tend to be sympathetic to the fascist bloc. Mexican raw materials might be in great demand in the States should we be drawn into the war, so I thought I'd list sources — stuff like that."

"I see." Elbow on his knee he cupped his chin. "Have you seen the agenda for our current meeting?

"No, sir. Nolan's obsession, I assume — standardizing procedures?"

"Oh, yes, Thompson's hang-up. Actually, no. Our agenda focuses on trade, including the topics you just listed. Come to the meetings tomorrow, and bring samples."

"Ah . . ." Maggie hesitated.

The ambassador slapped his knee and burst into laughter. "Oh, yes. Al Williams. Can you be in the office at seven tomorrow?"

Maggie nodded.

"I'll take a look at your data," he said. "If it's what you claim, we'll corner Al when he comes in and transfer you to the embassy staff on the spot."

"With freedom to track El Ragnorak?"

"Yep. Within reasonable limits, it will be your first priority,"

"I'd like to keep two late-afternoon appointments tomorrow," Maggie said. "One is to talk to girls at the Veracruz Middle School on growing up to take their place among the women of the world."

"Hmm, great subject. What's the other?"

"Business people. There's a group which meets at about six o'clock Tuesday evenings in one of the Santiago Steamship Company warehouses. I lead a discussion on doing business with the States. Some export/import, but mostly we get into finding markets for local products, equipment sources, U.S. laws pertaining to foreign trade — stuff like that."

"Is that an invitation?" the ambassador asked. "Want me to come?"

What a blunder that would be. Maggie swung her head slowly from side to side. "Did you know that Governor Gutierrez is my uncle, my mother's brother, and my father by adoption?"

"I had dismissed that as a rumor. Well, in that case I won't flaunt protocol." He stood up. "This has been most interesting. It's settled then. We'll see how it goes for a month or so. How about I see you at the embassy on Monday a week from today?"

"I'll be there." Maggie rolled her spare shoes and the flashlight into the maid's dress and headed for the door.

"Get word back to Price, will you, Maggie? Tell him to stop

by next time he's in Mexico City." He switched off the light and followed Maggie to the elevator.

* * *

Maggie just did not understand why José preferred the Hotel Imperial's sidewalk café on the teeming clangorous Zócalo as a haunt for relaxing. She said as much when she joined Kyna and Nolan at their table. "It's like a bee's nest here," she added.

"That's easy," Nolan said. "Change from the hum-drum hush of a jewelry shop."

José's shop was anything but placid, Maggie thought, but did not comment. José should have arrived by now. She found herself standing up to look for him and, disappointed, sat back down.

"Did you hear me, Maggie?"

Maggie faced Kyna. "Guess not. Daydreaming, I suppose."

"You look relaxed — picture of contentment."

"She's anticipating her new job," Nolan said, "and basking with relief to be off Sarah's bridge detail."

How little Nolan knew. Maggie sat up straighter. "It's been one of those rare days when everything turned out just right." She caught a glimpse of José striding toward them, and reached out her hand. "And to top it off, I'm with all the friends who mean the most to me. Pull up a chair, José."

He took her hand, then shook hands with Nolan and Kyna before sitting down. He and Nolan disposed of chatter about seeing each other again, then he said to Maggie. "Miguel told me you're being transferred to Mexico City. When are you leaving?"

"Next weekend. I'm taking *Clank.*"

"Oh, yes, the Model A. I have to go, too." He pulled his chair closer. "Go together? We might leave Friday afternoon, stop at my shop in Puebla, then leave early on Saturday for Mexico City."

"Swell," Maggie said. I'm meeting Irena's family that

afternoon."

* * *

"Beginning of a glorious morning," Maggie murmured, as she left her apartment the next morning. She watched golden fingers climb the eastern sky only to be eclipsed by the rising sun. She waved at the crew of a seagoing tug, dropped her briefcase on a park bench, and sat down. Far to the right of the breakwater, she saw the low, black lines of a freighter. A sailor cast off the tug moorings, steam hissed and she let her gaze follow the tug as it slipped quietly out to meet the freighter.

"Pan, Señorita. Bien fresco?"

"Sí, gracias, Señora, y una banana también." She paid for the banana and bread roll and enjoyed the dawning as she ate them. Morning and evening strolls on the Malecon had become a daily routine since the summer rains. What might she find in Mexico City to take their place?

New job with new associates— she'd be transferred within an hour. Get ready, get going or it might not happen, she told herself, bolting to her feet.

An hour later, she'd stacked her journals on the desk in the alcove above the consulate entrance. "There now, Quiver-chin," Maggie muttered, "have a good tizzy if you must, but the ambassador's gonna put your cubbyhole to work for a change." She gave the alcove a final check then headed for the kitchen.

"Good morning, Maggie," she heard the ambassador say just as she started up the stairs with a tray.

"Good morning — beautiful day," she said. "How about coffee and juice? The data you asked for is upstairs in the alcove over the front door. How do you like your eggs?"

"Over-easy. No hurry," he said, and followed her.

"You'll be too busy later. Besides, cook's waiting for your pleasure. Bacon, ham, sausage?"

"You mean all three?"

"Why not. There'll be toast, guava and strawberry jam. and

papaya."

"What service." The ambassador settled into the desk chair. "You type, I presume. I'd like to get your transfer out of the way as soon as Williams comes in."

"May I suggest —" Maggie picked up a notepad and pencil. "If you dictate the memo, I'll type it while the cook gets your breakfast." She tore the top sheet off the pad and put it on the stack of folders. "That's a list of topics on which I collected data for Miguel. There's a separate file for each item on the list."

"Aren't you a bundle of energy this morning. Okay. Good idea. Sit and take a letter." The ambassador closed his eyes, tipped back his chair and, glasses hanging from steepled fingers, dictated the memorandum transferring Maggie to the embassy.

"Mr. Williams is in his office," Maggie told him when she returned with the completed memorandum. "Helen said he wanted to see me right away, but ah . . . Perhaps you'd prefer that I wait."

The ambassador flashed her a grin, checked and signed the document, and stuffed it in an envelope. "Looks fine. I'll settle your transfer with Al, then meet you back here." He rose, started for the stairs and turned back. "Good breakfast. By the way, is there someone here to take your place?"

"A new man started yesterday. Oh-oh." Maggie let out a whooshing whistle. "I'm not sure Mr. Williams remembers that he okayed hiring him. I'll be at my desk in the office getting him started, but call me when you're ready."

She followed him down the stairs and, hardly had the ambassador closed the door behind him, when Maggie heard loud voices from inside the consul's office. She glanced at Helen, who was typing furiously, obviously trying to disregard the ruckus behind her. The noise quieted suddenly and Maggie concentrated on her work with Carlos. Presently the ambassador called her name. Indicating Mr. Williams's office, he shook his head, then beckoned for her to follow him.

"Changed my mind," he said, looking back from halfway up the stairs. "Bring coffee — you too."

What might he mean? That she should not go in to see Mr. Williams? Had he canceled her transfer? What did he mean by — coffee — you too? Was he always hard to understand? Maybe he was just explosive and unpredictable by nature, as yesterday when he dragged her to the hotel.

Maggie told the cook to send coffee to the alcove, then hurried upstairs where the ambassador was sitting by the window overlooking the municipal docks. He indicated a document on a low table and motioned her to a chair.

"That's the draft of the trade agreement between the U.S. and Mexico I told you about yesterday," he said, and grinned as a maid placed coffee and cups on the table. He sipped from his cup, then leaned back. "Yep, changed my mind — called off today's meeting, and asked Al to arrange for our return to the capital on the eleven-forty flight. Right there is the reason I canceled the meeting." He indicated Maggie's journals. "Your file titles are somewhat slangy but, once I got their meaning, I saw that they reflect precisely the sort of stuff we pressed Williams to get for us during yesterday's meeting." He sipped coffee then went on. "Most of Mexico's foreign trade goes through Veracruz, so I'd hoped Al would jump at setting up a system to collect shipping data. Yesterday he was reluctant, so our agenda today was to establish the scope of the project and outline procedure." He put down his cup. "By the way, what prompted you to do it?"

"Two things," Maggie said. "Six months ago I followed the news about the war in Europe and thought it was just that — a European war. Since then, events seem to have aimed us straight into it."

She noticed his pursed lips, that he was nodding slowly, and leaning on the chair's arm rest. He must be thinking much the same thing, she decided, and went on. "The second reason was that documents on exports or through shipments to the States had a lot of information which might be useful if we were at war. Getting the same data for all cargoes passing through Veracruz was easy to arrange but, so far, I've had no way to secure it from anyplace else."

"Did Al Williams ever discuss this with you?"

"He ah"— Maggie chuckled. "I'd rather not answer that."

"We'll let it go then, Maggie. Excuse me a moment."

The ambassador sat erect as one of his staff approached. While they discussed arrangements for the return to Mexico City, Maggie skimmed the English and Spanish versions of the trade agreement. Legalese, both of them, but the Spanish wording did not mean quite what the English version did. When the embassy man left, she cleared her throat.

"Sir," she said, "may I make a suggestion?"

The ambassador whipped his head around to face her. "Well?"

More than a frown — a scowl creased his forehead, and she took a deep breath. "Are the men working on this agreement here today?"

He nodded. "Two, yes, but there are others."

"Do they speak Spanish?"

The ambassador leaned forward. "Both are lawyers, one is fluent in Spanish. What are you driving at, Maggie?"

"I'm sure they know what they're doing, but I think that if they were to stay another day and attend the trade meeting this evening, they might want to make a few changes."

He shook his head. "Flight's already arranged, but I'll listen if you've got a good reason."

"It starts out all friendly like, claiming to provide advantages for both countries. Then it states that the U.S. will step in and assume Britain's mercantilist position. I believe the English version is intended to be reassuring. The Spanish wording could trigger a trade war."

Maggie saw him suck in his left cheek and chew on it. He was listening. "Of course I haven't had time to read it all, so maybe it's okay," she said. "The men at the meeting will be Mexican manufacturers, marketers, shippers, those who run the businesses, and they won't be lawyers. It will be conducted by Adolf Buehler, a German born in Argentina, and now the representative in Mexico for the Santiago Steamship Line — Chilean. He has every reason in this world to prevent the United States from cornering trade advantage in Mexico. Expert opposition to that agreement will —"

"Got it, Maggie. Sold." The ambassador slapped the table and stood up. "How about this? My guys will study your journals today, attend your trade meeting this evening, then bring your journals to the City tomorrow. You'll get them back when you report to the embassy next week."

* * *

What enthusiastic girls, Maggie thought, as she left the middle school after her talk. They'd been so bright-eyed and eager that she hated to end the meeting. Still thinking of them, she reached the Malecon with a few minutes to spare before meeting the embassy men. She sat down on a bench just as the vendor she'd seen that morning approached her.

"Pan, Señorita. Bien fresco."

Maggie smiled. *"Sí, gracias. Tiene Coca-Cola fría?"*

"Sí, bastante fría."

Maggie paid for the cold Coke and bread roll with a bill and felt a small folded paper about an inch square among the change. She palmed the note, put the Coke bottle on the bench, and took a bite of bread. Gazing over the harbor, she opened her purse, reached in to unfold the tiny message, then glanced down. *Seven — launch here — please come — Mostacho.*

She could almost hear her heart pounding as she picked up the Coke. Sipping, she saw the woman near the steps leading

down to the water. The woman waved jerkily as if at a flying
bug, then pointed at the steps.

Maggie nodded slowly, then watched from the corner of her
eye as the vendor lifted her head and shouted, *"Pan —
panecillos frescos."*

A small boy scuffed bare footed in front of her, eyes on her
bottle. Poor kid, Maggie thought, took a sip, then offered it to
him

"We're here, Miss Magodon," she heard a man say from
behind her.

"Right on time," Maggie said, and got up to take them to the
meeting.

* * *

Ten minutes later, Maggie introduced the two embassy men
to Adolf Buehler. "They're from the United States Embassy in
Mexico City," she said in English, "and are here to get ideas
from your group to include in a trade agreement between the
United States and Mexico. This gentleman who's shaking your
hand speaks Spanish. I brought them to the meeting so that the
men here can make sure the agreement is fair."

"Most interesting," Adolf said.

Maggie turned away and called out in Spanish, "We have
guests tonight from the United States Embassy. They would like
you to tell them what you think should be included in a trade
agreement between Mexico and the United States."

The room fell silent, then the men began to drift toward the
newcomers. One asked a question. Another complained bitterly
in English against existing United States trade restrictions
against Mexico.

That got them started, Maggie thought, and began to arrange
chairs into a circle. Two local men helped her, then she sat
down on a seat by the door. She'd done what she'd come to do,
and turned her thoughts to the note from Mostacho. She'd meet
him if he showed up — wouldn't miss it for the world. What

might be so important that he would risk exposure by coming to get her? Through the clerestory window she watched the sky darken. Finally it was time to go, and she slipped out.

Arms folded, Maggie tried to appear as if on a casual evening stroll. Approaching the Malecon, she heard frenzied insects blitzing the corner streetlight. As the crescendo grew to a steady *zzzz*, she felt her spine *zizz* right back, and forced herself to walk deliberately to the seawall steps. Shoulders tensed, she started down, heard an engine cough, sputter, and catch as a small craft emerged from the seawall shadow.

"Noches, Señorita," a man whispered.

It was Mostacho. Maggie waited for a small launch to glide close, then boarded.

Mostacho took the launch out into the harbor, then struck a match to the running lights. *"Gracias, Señorita,"* he said. "I prayed for you to come."

"You should have sent somebody to get me," Maggie said, sliding closer to him so she could hear over the engine's thrum. "How may I help you?"

"Tell me where Chichi is, *Señorita*, the Guatemalan boy."

"I can't do that," she said," and heard his groan above the engine noise. She sighed, reluctant to endanger Thirteen Rabbit. "What should I tell him?"

"I need him to repair my diesel engine."

"Why him? There must be other diesel engine mechanics."

"Verdad, Señorita. That is true, but then the asshole will know I'm —"

"You're right," Maggie interrupted. "Most are German, and would report seeing you. Where is the boat? Can I see it?" He didn't answer and, from the slowly changing position of the city's lights, she decided that he must be circling while he considered what to do. "You're right to keep your boat a secret," she said. "It must be hard to hide the boat and the noise of building it. If the boy comes to Veracruz, they'll kill him if they catch him. Should he risk his life for your engine?"

"Not for my engine, *Señorita*, but for the boat to hunt the asshole. I ask you the same question. Why did you risk your life to help Chichi escape, and me? You helped me, too."

"I did not risk my life."

"*Señorita,* you do not know El Ragnorak. You were near when Chichi escaped and even closer when you helped me. "*Sí,. Señorita,* you risked your life for us. *Chichi* will risk his to repair the engine as I will risk mine to have a boat which will take us to El Ragnorak. I beg you. Tell me where to find him."

I've got to see that boat, Maggie thought. What right did she have to keep the two men apart? None, really. Besides, Thirteen Rabbit was her only contact with Mostacho and his knowledge of El Ragnorak. Mostacho had every reason to trust her, and she was sure that he considered her to be an ally. Keep him talking. Find out what he intends to do with his — "Uh-oh. Wait," she said, as Mostacho turned his launch back toward the Malecon. "I need your help, too, Mostacho."

The launch kept on turning.

Chapter 26

"I'll tell him your engine is ready, and will bring him to you if he wants to come. But I want you to tell me all the places where El Ragnorak went since he came to Mexico, how long he stayed, and what he did. Everything you can tell us about El Ragnorak will be very important if my country and Mexico are drawn into the war in Europe."

The man responded with a low growl as he swung the boat back to his former course. "The asshole is already at war for the Nazis — big plans. I don't know what they are, but I will tell you everything I know."

"Did you keep a log? Who was on your crew?"

"There is a log, but it is locked in the asshole's safe on the *Hedda*. Now I will show you my boat."

Maggie saw his profile against the city lights as Mostacho took a southerly direction — no mustache, and there was something different about the way he talked. Perhaps he just spoke with more confidence. "You shaved," she said. "What do I call you now?"

"My hair is now black. My wife calls me Oso."

"Oso, bear — black bear." Maggie chuckled. "She picked a name that fits you, but Oso died yesterday. I'll call you Mosto. I like you, and it's my favorite pasta." She saw his huge shoulders shrug.

"Hmpf, I am not pasta."

Maggie let out a quick giggle. "No, you are not pasta, and

not a mustache, either. I will call you Oso, too."
* * *

Three days later, dressed in a white blouse, black skirt, and saddle shoes, Maggie drove into the alley beside José's shop. She wore a broad-brimmed black hat, gold studs in her ears, and her hair in a snood. "Moving day at last," she muttered as she *ah-oo-gahed* the horn twice, then sat back to wait. Had José remembered their change to a morning departure? And what might she have forgotten to do?

Maggie couldn't help smiling. Mr. and Mrs. Williams had been courteous, and Sarah hadn't addressed her as *child* since hearing of her transfer. She'd finished cleaning her apartment just that morning before taking a few items to the consulate so she'd have something to wear on occasions when she returned. Carlos had two easily answered questions for her, and appeared to be comfortable in his new job. She thought of Mostacho, now Oso, and the craft he'd designed to look like a coastal trawler, but with a lay-back mast and hull built for speed. She plucked the list of places where he'd taken El Ragnorak from her purse, and grinned, thinking of how he'd bristled when she'd hinted at going with him and Thirteen Rabbit on the Ragnorak hunt.

"What's that you're looking at?"

Startled by José's voice right outside her half-open window, she shoved the note back into her purse.

"Tell me after we get started," he said. "How about the key to the rumble seat? My key doesn't seem to work."

Maggie saw three boys behind him, one with a grip, and each of the others lugging a large valise. "I had the lock changed," she said. "I told you there would be room for one small package. The rumble space is full. It looks like rain and I'm not about to risk getting all my things wet. She heard him try to unlock the rumble compartment again, then tap her window.

"Take all that junk back inside — every bit of it, then we'll go."

"Come on, Maggie," José shouted. "These are sample cases, and I'll need them in Puebla and Mexico City. There'll be room if I take out the seat cushions." Maggie shook her head. "They're out already," she yelled back Whatever those cases might contain, José would never transport anything of real value tied on the on top of a Model A Ford's rumble trunk where it might get wet. She backed out of the alley, then stopped when she looked at the mirror and saw him wave the boys back into the warehouse with their burdens, then come running.

"My apologies, Maggie," José said when he climbed in beside her.

But she saw no penitence in the glare he leveled at her, and she glowered right back. "You gotta be mad, José, if you think you can shrivel me with rapier stares you use to cower those imbecile bulls you murder. I was looking forward to a glorious day, and you're not going to ruin it. What's the best way, and about how far is it to Puebla?"

José pointed right. "Under two hundred miles, even if we take a side jaunt to see the Moorish tower Cortez built in Tepeaca in 1520."

"Interesting, but not today," Maggie said. Why was José intent on changing all her plans?

She drove southward then westward beside the *Rio Atoyac* through coastal lowlands before rising into a foothills area known for its fruit, cotton and tobacco.

"I'd like to go back to Cordoba sometime, and especially come here to Fortín de las Flores," Maggie remarked a while later. Rain started to fall and she turned on the windshield wipers. "All these flowers must be glorious when the sun shines, and isn't it a good name for the town. I suppose there's a fort. Have you seen it?"

"No. It's small." José squirmed in his seat. "Better let me drive now."

"No thanks. I'm fine." There he was, trying to get the key again. "I know about the twisty-turny road and steep grade up ahead. Oh-oh, fog." Maggie shifted gears to follow a slow truck up a grade. They had nearly reached Orizaba when the rain changed to a misty drizzle.

"*Chipi-chipi,* that's what they call rain like this," José said. "Lots of it here."

They skirted south of *Citlaltepetl,* Maggie's thoughts flitting now and then to Thirteen Rabbit, now working at the *Hacienda Perla* on the eastern slope of the great mountain. She wished she could confide in José, at least speak of subjects other than scenery, historic places and his heritage.

Trust him? She thought of times when she'd basked in his attention, only to be thrown aside. Finally, she'd come to understand that everything had to center on José. Subdued by the thought, Maggie drove in silence, shifting to low gear to creep up the twisting pot-holed road across the *cumbre de Acultzingo* to a high plateau, clear skies and a better road to Puebla.

Maggie slowed to pass an ox-drawn cart. "Look!" she exclaimed, veering off the road.

"*Cuidado*! Take care," José barked, reaching for the wheel. "Damn. That was close."

"Let go." Maggie elbowed him away and drove up a dirt path to stop high above the road. "Just look — three snow-capped peaks. Do you know their names? Is one of them Popo . . . Oh, you know."

"*Popocatépetl.* Yeah, farthest left. Next is *Iztaccíhuatl.* Both are west of Puebla, and the other, *Malinda,* is east." José got out of the car, then glanced back in. "Look back, Maggie, *Citlaltépetl,* too."

"Freezing!" Maggie exclaimed as she got out, hugging

herself with one arm and the other hand controlling her hair. "I never," she gasped. "José, did you ever —" She broke off, wanting him not to answer, just stay still. Tall, muscular, a foot lifted onto a black lava boulder, he was part of the expanse just as his ancestors must have been for more than four centuries. Here lies his heritage, she thought, backing slowly to the car. She took a basket from it then, without a sound, returned to place it on a flat rock. Wishing she might share his thoughts, she waited, and finally he turned to face her.

"Puebla's down there, Maggie," he said, extending his arm. "Just think. From here we can see three of the seven highest peaks in North America."

Why did she feel let down by his words when they were just what she would have expected from a man as macho as José? Was there no romance in his blood? "Amazing, isn't it?" she said, her mood shattered. "Mrs. Williams's cook made sandwiches for us. Let's sit where we can see ol' Popo and eat lunch." She was about to sit on a broad, flat rock when he grasped both her elbows and moved her to the end of the rock. "What's that all about — where I sit?"

"No wind here."

"Yeah, swell," she said, and smiled when he sat where their eyes would meet every time he looked up. "Popo's really grand. About how far away is it?"

"About thirty-five miles," he said, but did not look up—just munched.

Maggie finished her sandwich, gave José another and took one for herself. Still he didn't look at her. "Something's troubling you, José. We're good friends now, and it might help to tell me about it.

"I suppose you'll keep hounding me, so I might as well." He glanced her way then rested his eyes on the far volcanoes. "I'm thinking about quitting the FBI."

He couldn't do that. He'd been too proud of his service to

both his native land and adopted country. "For goodness sake why, José? Come on. That's not all."

"You're right." There was a brief silence before he went on. "Two weeks, then — torero no more."

He was still skirting the issue. Afraid he would clam up if she pressed too hard, Maggie said, "And you're going to miss the bulls?"

"Hardly." He gave her a wry smile. "You see, fighting bulls paid for my education, and got the family business out of debt. Then I signed a ten-year contract, ending in the Mexico City Arena on the first weekend in December."

"Won't that take a huge load off your back?" At least his eyes flashed as he stared back at her.

"You miss the point," he said. "To win consistently at anything, you've gotta be razor sharp. I don't practice enough. Sure, there's money in it — " He rubbed a thumb across his fingertips, then clapped — "and a final price."

She saw him turn to look across the broad valley, but knew from his fixed stare that he saw nothing.

"What do I do? What will they do?" he said. "Fight the bulls for five more years and I am free, they tell me. No, I say. One last time I'll make you a grand profit, I tell them, so they will pit me against the world's most ferocious bull." He got up. "Come, Maggie. I'll drive now."

Something in the way he moved told her that he'd never sell himself for another five years and that, somehow, he'd beat that bull. Did she dare believe him? Nope. She'd learned her lesson. "No, José," she said. "It'll take a better sob-story than that to get the key from me. Will you put this away? The rumble isn't locked now." She handed him the lunch basket then climbed into the driver's seat.

She thought he might have loosened up a bit as they got back on the road. His head was turning from side to side to take in the view. "You're really looking forward to stopping in

Puebla, aren't you, José?" she said.

"Yes, and I wish we'd have more time there because there's so much to show you."

"I know about its history, but is there something of special importance to your family?" Maggie caught his quick glance, the gleam in his eyes, and was glad she'd asked the question.

"The people — their vigor," he said, leaning forward and indicating the landscape ahead. "How's that for grandeur? I hadn't thought much about it before, but the area blazes with the vitality which drove Spain and France from Mexico. The people may appear to be deliberate but, caramba! They are tough! It's not only the people. The wealth of Mexico flows through this corridor with Puebla the hub. Many sources combine to provide an abundant richness which the Nazis are trying to bleed to support their operations. Just think, Maggie, bases on the Veracruz coast and Carribean Islands are ideally situated as havens from which Nazi submarines might control shipping on the Gulf of Mexico, the Carribean Sea and out into the Atlantic."

My goodness, was José ever worked up. No wonder the FBI would want someone with José's background to ferret out and destroy the traffic lanes and cash sources the Nazis needed to support espionage operations. To be effective, he'd have to maintain a position in the gem dealer circuit. Might the mysterious packet he'd hidden in his safe, and the payment from El Ragnorak which Thirteen Rabbit had told her about, have something to do with maintaining that role? Well, maybe, just maybe, and how did Catrina and Adolf fit into the puzzle?

"Do you know how to get to the *Hotel del Portal*?" Maggie asked as they entered the city. "Irena reserved rooms for us there."

"Sure. I'll get off at my showroom. The hotel's a block farther on. I'll stop by for you in an hour."

* * *

José shortened his steps as they followed narrow streets to the house of the Serdan brothers. Maggie glanced back and saw that his eyes were wide and his lips parted. He flashed her an expectant look, and she sensed that he was just dying to tell her about the house.

"I know the Serdan brothers are famous," Maggie said. "Its age and what else is special about the house?"

"The Serdans were my father's cousins," he said, as they sat down on a stone bench beside the entry. My father was with them when they launched the revolution from this house against the dictator Diaz in 1910."

Maggie beckoned a shoeshine boy and indicated José's shoes.

"Months before the fighting started, my father took his family to safety across the Rio Grande. Then he came back to help his cousins. Most of the family were killed in the battle, and my father died of his wounds three years later. Now this house is the museum of the revolution."

Maggie touched the boy's shoulder to remind him to polish as José talked on. "May we go inside?" she asked when he paused.

"Of course," he said. He got up and gave the boy a coin, but just then the doors closed. "We'll come back another time. There is so much to see. Let's go to the Cathedral of the Immaculate Conception. It's famous for its tilework."

"How about the library?" Maggie asked. "My dad said he spent a lot of time there while he was in Puebla. He told me it has thousands of sixteenth- and seventeenth-century volumes."

"It's on the way, and I can hardly wait for you see it," José said, and led her onto *Avenida 5 Oriente,* and the library's entrance. They entered a vast room with water-filled flasks suspended from the high ceiling for fire protection, and worn red tile floors. Reading tables were inlaid with onyx, and were surrounded by carved cedar bookshelves.

Maggie pulled a volume off a shelf, sat down at a table, and idly leafed through a few pages.

"It's getting late, Maggie." José beckoned. "We should go."

"Look. Isn't that *Popo?*" Maggie exclaimed, peering westward as they emerged from the library. She dashed across the street to get a better view.

"Breathtaking!" Maggie exclaimed when he joined her. "Glorious sunset, too, and what a background it is for the mountain." She felt José take her hand and, liking it, she squeezed his in return. "Not in Mexico, José," she murmured, and pulled her hand away.

José grinned and stepped aside to let a group of mariachi musicians go by. "The dining room opens at seven," he said. "Suppose we meet there at seven-thirty."

* * *

"Surprise, surprise! Irena, you shouldn't have," Maggie exclaimed, when she found a package in her room. Irena must have had it delivered. Maggie dropped her handbag on the bed and unwrapped the bundle. "Gee! Oh, Irena, a *china poblana!*" She stood before the mirror and held up the wide-necked white blouse. "Kinda wild, Irena, and I love — oh, the embroidery — scrumptious!" She glanced back at the opened package and put down the blouse. "Skirt embroidered, too — perfect match." She held the white skirt against her waist. "Thank you, thank you, Irena," she said into the empty room. "I've looked and looked for a *china poblana* just like it."

Hugging the outfit, she went to the window to gaze over the darkening city. She saw a black limousine stop across the street, and a man cross in front of its headlights — José. He got in, and the car pulled away. Who might have picked him up? She sat on the edge of the bed to consider what to do. Would he return in time to meet her for dinner? Was he even registered in the same hotel? Why was it that whenever she felt herself warming to him he'd plunge her into ice water? Should she demand an explanation? No, nothing wrong, really, unless he didn't show up for dinner.

*   *   *

Red-gold hair flowing from tortoise shell combs, silver ear hoops, dressed in her *china poblana,* Maggie scanned the lobby as she descended the stairs. Where was José?

"Qué belleza! Beautiful!"

José's voice— close. Maggie felt him take her elbow even before she turned to see him, smiling, eyes admiring.

"Thank you, José." How gratifying his compliment, when she'd wondered if he'd even show up. Maggie leaned back to see better his slim black leggings, white silk shirt, red cummerbund, and the black hat in his hand. "You're what I call snazzy yourself, José," she said.

"Come, Maggie. The *chiles en nogada* are excellent here, and you must try the *mole poblano.*"

"Irena suggested a few specialties of the house, too," Maggie said as they entered the dining room, but she let José make all the choices when the waiter took their order.

"Aren't you the peppy one tonight," Maggie said as the waiter served their soup. "You've been worked up ever since we got to Puebla. It's the altitude, I suppose, together with the fact that it's your favorite city."

She couldn't help smiling when José's eyes lit up. His personal touches and descriptions of his ancestors' experiences gave her a feeling close to living them herself.

"Too bad it isn't Saturday," José said over coffee after they'd eaten. "There's dancing in the plaza every evening, but on Saturdays it's a major event with a feast at midnight."

Maggie pushed her coffee aside. "If that's an invitation, let's go."

*   *   *

"Señor Alvarado," a man called when they reached the

Zócalo.

"Excuse us, Maggie. This is my Puebla store manager," José said as the man approached. He introduced Maggie then and, while the two men talked, Maggie watched the dancers.

Recognizing a dance as one she'd learned from Rosa Valdez, Maggie began to dance, forgetting José until he spoke.

"How professional, Maggie. Where did you learn the dances of our people?"

She danced over to him. "You forget, José. Rosa Valdez, our housekeeper in St. Louis, was from Veracruz. Excuse us," she said to José's manager, then pulled José into the fiesta.

"I'll see you later at the hotel," José called to his manager, and swung into step with Maggie.

Why haven't we done this before? she thought, admiring his graceful movement. How great he looked, too, especially with that wide-brimmed black hat with its silver galon around its crown hanging down his back.

They danced until the cathedral chimes strok eleven, when Maggie called a halt. José walked with her to the hotel lobby where his manager was waiting.

As Maggie approached her room, she saw a man in the hall ahead of her stop and knock on her door. Tall with blond hair — Adolf Buehler.

Chapter 27

The man looked like Adolf in the dimly lit hallway, so she tiptoed close enough to be sure. "Mr. Buehler," she said.

He wheeled. "Oh — ah, Mizz Magodon. I uh — If you will let me have your key, I will be pleased to unlock your door for you."

"No, Adolf." Maggie glared, and rocked her thumb toward the elevator.

"I thought we might —"

"Wanna hear how loud I can scream, Adolf? Now you just beat your shiny black boots down that hall or I'll shriek 'til everybody in this hotel comes running." Back and forth, Maggie rocked her thumb. Why didn't he go? Adolf just stood there, eyes raking her, and she glared right back. She didn't dare say a thing for fear he'd believe she'd bargain. Think tough, she told herself, squeezing her lids to narrow slits.

He shifted his weight to his other leg.

Wait him out. Don't get him angry. Maggie kept her thumb rocking.

Finally, a sneer crossed his face. He mumbled something in German, lifted his chin and stalked down the hall.

Maggie gusted out a breath, unlocked her door and stomped into her room. Grinning at the thought that she'd made Adolf eat dirt, she tossed her purse onto the bed and headed for the bathroom. Uh-oh. Something was wrong. The *china poblana* box was closed, and she'd left it open. She'd sat on the bed with her travel bag opening toward her. Now it opened toward the room entrance. Adolf had searched her room. He must have seen her coming down the hall and turned back to knock at her door. Rejected Romeo, my eye. She hadn't stared him down. He'd made a stupid boob of her, and must have been laughing up his sleeve as he faked a downcast retreat.

She heaved a deep sigh and sat down by the window. What could he have been looking for, and how did he know she was staying at the *Hotel del Portal*, or even that she was in Puebla? José hadn't known which hotel she'd be staying in until she'd told him herself just as they entered the city. Oh, yes, Adolf must have been the one who'd picked him up in the long car when she'd looked out the window just after she registered. Dear Lord. She'd been betrayed by José, burgled by Adolf. Was there no one she could trust?

Maggie knuckled tears from her eyes. She shook her head, and thought of how her dad would greet her tears. Buck up, he'd say, and she'd grit her teeth, poke him in the stomach, and they'd both laugh.

She forced a grin, landed a flurry of punches on the pillow and felt better. Cinderella days — belle of the ball — governor's daughter, hmpf, those days were over. No more party planning, social secretary stuff, flunky to the boss's wife. She had a job to do — an important one. She was on her own.

Now she couldn't help grinning. Confident again, she made sure the door was secure, put her pistol under her pillow, and went to bed.

Chimes tolled six o'clock. Wide awake, Maggie got up and dressed, wishing she'd arranged with José for an early breakfast. She decided not to wait, and went down to the lobby where the desk clerk was on the telephone.

"Señorita." The clerk beckoned with the telephone receiver. "Señor Alvarado."

After disposing of wake-up pleasantries, José got down to

business.

"This is my plan for the day, Maggie. Come to the *Hotel Aristos* at about — hold on a minute."

Sure, she'd hold on, listen, then tell him what she'd do.

"Meet me at nine-thirty," he said, coming back on the line. "We'll have breakfast here. After that, I have some business to take care of, but will be ready to go up to Mexico City at about two o'clock."

"That will be fine, José," Maggie said. "You just go ahead. I'm at breakfast now. I'll be busy until ten, then will leave for the City."

"You can't do that, Maggie. After all —"

His voice died with the hang up-click, and she went into the dining room. She ordered fruit and eggs, *huevos rancheros*, and snacks for the drive to the City: *buñuelos,* which reminded her of donuts, and a mixture of red and purple *capotes,* sweet potato morsels cooked in brown sugar.

While eating, she thought of all the sights Puebla offered. To visit its historic churches and museums would take days. She smiled, thinking of her father's stories about the May 5, 1862 battle when, outnumbered and poorly armed, Mexicans had defeated thousands of French troops at the forts of *Loreto* and *Guadalupe.* After finishing her breakfast, she checked out of the hotel, then drove out to see the forts.

She drove around each but, short of time, returned to the hotel at five minutes to ten. When she opened the door to get out, she saw José standing at the curb with Adolf Buehler and got right back in. Talking to Adolf would prolong their departure and she was in no mood to spar with the man.

Presently a long limousine paused, blocking them from her view, then moved on leaving Adolf but not José.

Had he left a message at the desk? She saw Adolf walk away, checked her watch — ten o'clock, then entered the hotel. No message, the desk clerk told her, and just then she heard

Adolf's voice.

"Good morning, Mizz Magodon. I hope you awoke refreshed."

Yes, thank you," she said. "And you?"

"Very good, thank you." He extended a hand to take her arm but she backed away. "There's a cocktail lounge, *muy elegante,* around the corner. May I escort you. José will meet us there for lunch."

"Thank you, but I'm leaving for Mexico City this very minute."

"But José. What will — "

"Just tell him good-bye, thank you," she cut in, then wheeled and marched out of the hotel.

He'd looked surprised that she'd leave without José, she thought, as she climbed into Clank. Hmm, come to think of it, Monday evening at the Zócalo, José had mentioned that he already had plans to go to Mexico City when he suggested that they go together. He and Adolf must have arranged to meet in Puebla before that. Still, she couldn't help feeling that he'd purposely deceived her. Only last Monday she'd found herself warming to him again, even thinking of life as Mrs. José Alvarado. Something always seemed to come up to spoil her plans: a matter related to her FBI work or the prospect of war — damn Hitler. Time after time, José had caused her to doubt him. Would she ever trust him? Did she really care?

* * *

The outskirts of Mexico City seemed to go on forever, but finally Maggie found herself on *Avenida Lazaro.* She threaded northward through pedestrians and vendors to *Avenida Madero,* and an area which must have once been the most prestigious residential section of the city.

Both the street and back alley gates to our property are blue, Irena had said.

Maggie drove slowly, found a blue gate, then drove around to a walled service alley, and stopped outside a high, blue, double gate and honked. It opened, and she drove into a cobblestone courtyard. "Horses and carriages belong in here," she muttered, getting out and taking in her surroundings.

"Señorita Gutierrez."

She looked up, and saw a man leaning out of a window above the entry passage. *"Buenas tardes,"* she said. "You were expecting me?"

"Si, fiesta, and all are busy. You'll find them in there." He waved toward double doors on the opposite side of the courtyard.

"Swanky!" she burst out. "No, not a bit ostentatious, simply gorgeous, heavenly," she murmured, amazed by the profusion of color and the fragrance of flowers when she entered a patio inside the doors. How refreshing was the smell of flowers after the long drive through the city and its odors. She saw blossoms everywhere, on bushes and potted plants on the patio and balconies. Bougainvillea covered the walls. Palm trees rose above the rooftops from each patio corner.

"Maggie!"

"Irena!" She saw Irena waving from a balcony, and dashed to steps curving up in a corner of the patio, and met Irena as she came down. "I'm so glad to see you. Your house is gorgeous, and I have so much to talk to you about."

Irena gave her a second hug. "Then let's talk," she said. "Come to your room where we won't be disturbed. And I've just got to tell you all the nice things Daria Dalpica said about the party. Your ears must have been burning."

"She called you? It's hard to believe the bridge party was only last Monday, and so much has happened since we were in Jalapa just a week ago."

"This is your room." Irena opened a door and followed Maggie into a small sitting room. "It was my room when I was a girl, but we made it into a small apartment." She sat down on a lounge chair.

"I just love it." Maggie sat on a chair facing Irena. "It's just perfect."

They talked on, eventually getting to Maggie's new job, then to Thirteen Rabbit. "Do you know where he is? Is there any way I can see him?"

"You'll have to ask Beno. He's at the capital, and won't be home until —"

Just then they heard a knock and the governor's voice.

"May I come in?" He burst in without waiting.

Maggie popped up, Irena, too, and they all hugged.

"I picked Juan up at the airport," he said, sitting down. "He's Irena's brother, Maggie, Juan Montoya." Facing his wife, he said, "He came early so he wouldn't miss the birthday party."

Maggie saw him wink at Irena. "Is it your birthday?" she asked. "Your ring is a blue topaz, isn't it — November birth stone, your earrings, too? I wish I'd known." What a coincidence, she thought. Her own birthday was tomorrow, but nobody knew that.

"You're here. What more could I want." Irena turned to her husband. "Maggie wants to talk to Trece."

"But I have to explain everything to you first," Maggie said. "It's sort of complicated and I —"

Governor Gutierrez stood up and lifted a hand to cut her off. "There's a chance he's here in the city. I'll get on the telephone."

He left the room and Irena got back to discussing the bridge party. "Daria was surprised that you served *chipachonga.*" She burst into laughter, and said, "I'd never have dared to do that."

"Do you remember Kyna, Senator Johnson's wife?" Maggie saw Irena nod, and went on. "She was the first to taste it."

"Now that I know her, I'm not surprised. By the way, she's in the city and I spoke with her last evening — sings your— "

"Trece drove a truck in from Perla today," Governor Gutierrez interrupted, coming back in. "I told the warehouse to send him over here tonight." He took his seat. "Now, Maggie, why do you need Trece?"

"While I was taking Trece to Jalapa," Maggie said, "he told me that a man he called Mostacho, was El Ragnorak's helmsman for months on his sorties up and down the gulf coast." She went on to explain how she'd snatched Mostacho from death, and described the boat he was building. "It's nearly finished, but Mostacho needs Trece to get his diesel engine started." She paused, glanced at each, then added, "My life would be in danger if you mention this to anybody except Miguel or the ambassador. Especially, don't tell José."

The governor leaned forward. "Why not? He's FBI."

"My FBI assignment is to track El Ragnorak," Maggie said. "Miguel wants José off the case because of a possible conflict of interest."

"I think Miguel's right about that, Beno," Irena said. "Go on, Maggie."

"*Un momento.*" The governor lifted his hand to cut her off. "José — conflict of interest, and he's FBI? Why, Maggie?"

"Maybe it's only because he's close to the Buehlers, but let me finish. Oso, we don't call him Mostacho any more, is South African. Oso, a Mexican sailor and Trece are determined to destroy El Ragnorak to avenge the torture and death of their friends." She pulled in a deep breath. "You see, I want to contract Oso to use his boat to find out what El Ragnorak will do if we're caught in a world war."

"Dear Lord," Irena breathed.

The governor stared at the ceiling, rubbed his chin.

He needs a shave, Maggie thought, hearing his stubble bristle. "I'll cut my hair and dye it black," she said, chuckling, and snapped a glance at Benancio when he burst out laughing. Then she glanced at Irena, who was looking at her with a wry smile and shaking head.

"We'll talk again after Trece shows up," the governor said. "Expect we all have plenty to do before guests arrive." He hustled out.

Irena took both Maggie's hands in hers and looked into her eyes. "If you were my son I would be so proud of you, but this is so unexpected. I'm not sure how I feel, but I suppose I'm prouder because you're not." She pulled Maggie close.

"Oh, Irena, I'm so lucky to have you," Maggie said. She heard Irena sniff. They drew apart, and Maggie got Irena a handkerchief from her purse. "I'd better unload the car and clean up."

"We had some of your things sent up from the Veracruz house." Irena indicated the armoire. "The party's not formal, just a light dinner with friends, — perhaps a cocktail dress." She looked back before leaving the room. "Short black hair —eegh," she muttered, shaking her head.

"You must be Maggie," a man said in English when she reached the patio. "I'm Juan Montoya, your uncle, on paper at least."

Maggie couldn't help laughing as she shook his hand. "You look more real than like paper to me and you speak like a Californian. I'm so glad to meet you. You're from Ecuador, I'm told."

"That's right, Quito, but I attended university in California. You were in a hurry. Anything I can do?"

"Well, I can manage," she said, nodding in spite of her denial. "I've got to move my things to my room." She paused, then said, "Irena put me in your apartment. I shouldn't be in there."

"Yes, you should. It was always Irena's room, and I'm back where I grew up. Let's go. I'll give you a hand."

Each carried a load, then Juan brought up the rest while Maggie put things in order.

When she'd dressed for the party, Maggie stepped onto her balcony, watched a man light torches, then found herself staring in wonder at the colors in the west, a background for the palms rising above the patio walls. Their fronds, silhouetted against the sky's glory, stirred gently with a rustling sound which softened the drone of the city outside the walls. Transfixed, she watched clouds redden, the reds deepen, and layers of gold blend with the redness. A seam opened — gold above, red below, and widened to a narrow peephole revealing an azure sky in its depths. She watched it close slowly, the sky darkening, and embraced again the flagrance and torchlit colors of the patio.

Maggie heard voices, greetings, and shook her head, thinking she must have been watching the sunset for at least a half-hour. She hurried down to the patio, then followed the sound of voices to the foyer, where she lingered in the shadowed hall, touched by the warmth with which Irena, Benancio and Juan received neighbors and family friends. She smiled. Their welcoming words were contagious, and she felt the glow of being one of them. So what would it matter if she wouldn't know a soul among them.

She supposed there were perhaps a dozen guests milling about, greeting each other, when she heard the doorknocker sound, and saw Benancio pull the door open. He stepped back suddenly, and she thought he might have been caught off guard. Then he extended his hand.

"How are you, Adolf? Welcome, Catrina," he said into the darkness.

Chapter 28

Maggie thought she'd choke as Catrina skittered into the foyer. Oh-mi-gosh. All that glitter — Benancio caught off guard? Hardly. Jewels, formal dress, Catrina's hair was even laced with sparkling gems. A hush fell over the foyer as attention swung to the newcomers. After her encounters with him in Puebla, how could Adolf have the gall to come? Or had Catrina forced him?

Maggie tiptoed to Irena's side to squeeze her hand and was watching Catrina circle the foyer when Adolf spoke.

"José Alvarado sends his regrets and begs your forgiveness for not presenting this to you in person." Adolf held out a package and Catrina returned to his side .

Planned performance, Maggie thought. So José was responsible for their intrusion, and Catrina had been quick to use the situation to worm her way into the governor's private party.

"How nice of you," Irena said, stepping up beside her husband.

Stop being catty and act more like Irena, Maggie told herself. She heard the telephone ring in the hall behind her and answered. It was the gateman, who reported the arrival of a truck driver who said the governor had sent for him.

Maggie hung up just as Irena joined her. "Thirteen Rabbit is here," she said. "Okay if I go out?"

"Hurry." Irena waved her off. "If he is, stay there until Beno can break away."

"Hola, Trece, Mostacho escaped and is working on his boat," Maggie called out as she approached Thirteen Rabbit, who was waiting beside the truck.

"Es Verdad?" he yelped, pounding a fist into his hand then grasping hers to pump it. *"Perdóname, Señorita. Buenas noches.* How did it happen?"

Did that ever break Rabbit out of his stolid self, Maggie thought. "Chichi is dead, Trece lives," she said. "Mostacho is dead, now he is Oso, and he will tell you all about it if you want to fix his engine and help him build his boat."

Thirteen Rabbit rubbed his hands together, threw back his shoulders and looked her squarely in the eyes. "I promised to work for the governor, and he might not —"

"He'll be here in a moment and you can ask him," Maggie interrupted. "When I told him you might want to go, he called the warehouse and told them to send you here. We'll wait in the — Here he comes."

"Buenas noches, Trece," the governor called as he came into the courtyard. He shook Thirteen Rabbit's hand then led them to the gatehouse waiting room. "My daughter says your friend is building a boat," he said when they were seated. "You want to help him, no?"

"Sí, Gobernador. With your permission I go, but there are two irrigation pumps in the truck and they are needed tomorrow at the Hacienda Perla."

"I'll have to show him where to find Mostacho — oops, Oso," Maggie said, then turned to Thirteen Rabbit. "I'll follow you to the hacienda, then take you to Veracruz."

"Slow down," the governor cut in, laughing. "My wife and I are concerned for the safety of our daughter." He gestured toward Maggie. "Trece, did you know that she hopes to use the boat your friend is building to help defend our country against the Nazis?"

Thirteen Rabbit shook his head. "Mostacho will use it to

avenge the death of our friends."

"Oso," Maggie reminded him of the name change. "We want the same thing, Trece, because El Ragnorak is the Nazi *jefe*. I need you and Oso to help me trap him."

Thirteen Rabbit rubbed the side of his nose and glanced at her with narrowed eyes, but said nothing.

He doesn't like the idea of having a woman along. Neither will Oso, Maggie thought, and found herself even more determined to go on with her plans.

"The watchman will show you where you can sleep tonight," the governor said, and stood up. He slapped Trece on the back and went to the door. "Try not to be long, Maggie. Take good care of my daughter, Trece."

"Yo, Señor? Me, protect her when she has saved my life two times?"

Maggie heard her father chuckle as he closed the door. Both he and Irena must be aware of the risks confronting her, and she wondered if they would sanction her plans quite so readily if they were her blood parents.

"It's a long way, Señorita. Maybe two days?"

Maggie shook her head. "One. We'll start early — five o'clock — be out of the city before sunrise. *Está bien así?*"

"Cierto, o podemos —"

"Maggie!" Kyna Johnson's voice cut Trece off.

Maggie popped off the bench. "Kyna!" They embraced, then Maggie introduced Trece! "This is Trece Conejo. He was the cruiser deckhand when we went to Antigua last July."

Kyna extended her hand. *"Cómo está,"* she said, then in English, "See, I know a little Spanish. Of course I remember him. Isn't he the one who told you the *Hedda* helmsman was in danger?"

"Mucho gusto," the young man said, shaking her hand.

"He's the one." Maggie nodded, then spoke to Thirteen Rabbit. "Señora Johnson helped Oso escape from the

Hacienda."

"Es verdad?" Thirteen Rabbit's eyes gleamed.

"Are you busy tomorrow?" Kyna asked.

Maggie cocked her head, eyed Thirteen Rabbit, then looked back at
Kyna. "Irena didn't tell you what I'm planning then. I suppose
you wouldn't want to leave here at five tomorrow to take Trece
to Veracruz?"

"Morning? Kyna paused. "In your clanker?"

"Uh-huh." She thinks I'm out of my mind, Maggie decided
when Kyna's head swung slowly from side to side.

"Aren't you something else," Kyna muttered. "Well — oh
pshaw. Tom went gallivanting around South America with
Nolan Thompson, so why shouldn't I just play it cozy with all
the charms of the place where he left me."

"Stay here tonight," Maggie said. "Trece can take you to
get what you need, then check over Clank and be ready to leave
here at five in the morning."

*   *   *

The patio was chilly and deserted when Maggie hurried
through and slipped into the parlor.

"Maggie, over here."

"Sorry I took so long," Maggie whispered when she turned
back and saw Irena sitting just inside the door.

Irena rose and led her back into the patio. "Is Kyna going
too?"

"Yes. Trece drove her to —" Maggie paused. Why had
Irena pulled her back into the patio? "Is something wrong?
Would it be better if I don't go?"

Irena indicated chairs and they sat down. "I just need a
moment to collect myself so I won't explode at those Buehler
creatures. Perhaps if I blow a little steam — eeghsh! You see,
José promised to come today, and we expected him to stay here
tonight. When Adolf and Catrina appeared, I had the most

dreadful time being polite."

"I never would have guessed. I'd just come in when the phone rang."

"I know. I told Beno to come out first and that I'd come as soon as he returned to our guests. I used the call as an excuse to escape." Irena took a deep breath. "I so looked forward to tonight as a happy family occasion with Juan and old family friends. But now . . ." She pulled in another breath and whooshed it out. "But now I'm afraid you're going to see into a dark family closet."

About to speak, Maggie leaned forward, but Irena lifted her hand.

"There's nothing really bad, Maggie, and please, let me get this off my mind. You see, Juan and I had an older brother. He was killed in the war and his wife died during the flu epidemic a short time later. Their two children then came to live with us, a girl about your age, and a boy somewhat older. Perhaps you've wondered why José has been a close family friend and Catrina — well, overly familiar. Loreta — that was her name — fell in love with José and expected to marry him."

Irena paused, then went on. "Once, when Raul was visiting Juan in Ecuador, he happened to go into Catrina's shop. That started it all."

"Raul was Loreta's brother, your nephew?" Maggie asked.

Irena nodded. "He was infatuated — blind. He visited Catrina in Ecuador, and she came twice to see him." Head swinging slowly from side to side, Irena lowered her gaze and paused. Then she shook her head and went on. "They planned to marry in spite of our opposition. As Beno said, 'She had no eyes for him, and still sees women through the eyes of a man.' When she was here, she examined everything as if taking inventory of Raul's inheritance. We were sure she wanted only the family possessions, name and political connections a marriage to Raul would bring her."

Why had she heard none of this before? Maggie wondered as Irena went on.

"At about that time Catrina's brother became the shipping company agent in Veracruz, and offered Loreta and Raul passage to Ecuador as his guests. Raul was determined to visit Catrina, and Loreta insisted on going, too. They planned to stay with their uncle Juan and their cousins in Quito. We never saw them again."

"I'm so sorry," Maggie said, reaching out to take Irena's hands.

Irena lifted her head. "Thank you for being so patient. I'm fine now and will go upstairs to freshen up. I saw Kyna get in your Ford with Trece. I suppose he took her to get a travel outfit for tomorrow?"

Maggie nodded. "Wants to outdo her wandering husband."

"No one noticed you during Catrina's histrionics, Maggie, so you might wait here for Kyna. Take her to the room beside yours, then let's meet at the top of the stairs and join the others together."

* * *

Maggie saw Irena signal her husband as, three abreast, they entered the living room with Kyna. Benancio held high his hand and raised his voice.

"Irena joins me in thanking you for coming to welcome my niece, now our daughter, on such short notice. Among you are those who witnessed the arrival of a package and heard rumors about a birthday. Irena, will you come here, please?"

"Isn't she beautiful?" Maggie whispered to Kyna. Irena's distress of a short time before was on her mind and she marveled at how quickly Irena had composed herself. How radiant she was now as she joined her husband with a broad smile.

"Please accept this gift," the governor said, "a small but worthy token of love and appreciation."

"Thank you, Beno," Irena said and planted a kiss on his lips. "You know I'm an emerald girl, and my Saint's Day is May twenty-seventh, Santa Carolina Day, in the emerald birth stone month of May. Whatever is in this package, I cannot accept it." She offered the package back to her husband.

He hunched his shoulders and, both hands protesting, scowled while grinning, and refused to take it. Maggie heard twitters and a humph sound from a portly man close to her. He's trying to give the impression he knows what they're doing, when he's in the dark just as much as I am, she thought. Then she heard Irena's voice again.

"Many of you know José Alvarado. He asked Catrina and Adolf to bring another birthday gift." She beckoned them forward. "Did he send a birthday message with you, too?"

Adolf took Catrina by the arm. "I will explain everything," he said, strutting forward and pulling his sister.

"Oh, no. Don't let her get started," Maggie murmured.

As if she'd read Maggie's mind, Irena spoke up. "We do have a November birthday. My brother, Juan's. He was born in November." She glanced at her husband. He was grinning, and she burst out with a short laugh. "This has gone far enough. Maggie, Margareta, we know it's your birthday. Come here."

How did they know? She'd told nobody. Maggie heard Kyna urge her, felt hands on her hips, pushing. "I never meant it to be secret," she said, eyes moistening, Then she found herself wrapped in the arms of Irena and Benancio, with Kyna, Catrina and Adolf off to her left.

"Beno and I want you to have this, Maggie." Irena handed her the small package.

"Thank you," Maggie said, wishing she could open the present with only the two of them present. She removed the wrapping paper and lifted the lid of a green velvet box revealing a gold necklace with a large emerald pendant. She flung her arms around Irena, then Benancio. "They're beautiful. Thank you so much," she murmured, then held the necklace high for all to see.

"Doña Kyna," the governor said. "It's your turn. Adolf, will you translate, please?"

"Muchas gracias, Don Benancio," Kyna said, then spoke English. "That's the extent of my Spanish." She explained that Daitha Tyler and other wives of United States visitors to Veracruz had asked her to commission José Alvarado and Catrina Buehler to furnish a gift of appreciation to be presented to Maggie on her birthday. "Catrina, will you do the honors?"

Adolf translated what Kyna had said while Catrina opened another velvet box.

Maggie's eyes bulged at the sight of emerald earrings, large crystal pendants reminding her of the ones borrowed from Irena during the July reception. While Adolf expounded, Catrina cooed in a voice so low Maggie could hardly hear her while she removed José's gift of silver hoops from Maggie's ears.

"Only José could make these," she said, and he will make some for me, too. And you are his emerald girl, and mine, and with these emeralds none can resist you."

Maggie looked into Catrina's eyes, shivered and, swayed by the whispered tone of her voice, thought that if José ever looked at her that way she'd melt. She forced herself to block out Catrina and listen to Adolf's translation.

"Mr. and Mrs. Williams and the Veracruz consulate staff contributed," he announced in a stentorian voice. "The Veracruz bridge club and many business people assisted, too."

Maggie was sure Governor Gutierrez found Adolf's pomposity amusing and was trying not to laugh when he cleared his throat, coughed and turned away.

Apparently Adolf caught the hint, for he paused before going on in a moderated tone, "Now this beautiful señorita, Margareta Gutierrez y Magodon,, brings her charm to your city and we in Veracruz hope that she will return to us soon."

Sarah Williams and the bridge club — had they really chipped in? Nobody spoke, and Maggie sensed that they were waiting for her.

"Thank you, Kyna, Adolf, and Catrina. Oh yes, Catrina, the silver earrings," Maggie added, and held out her hand. Catrina returned them and Maggie went on. "Thank you, everybody. You've made me feel so welcome, and I hope to get better acquainted with each of you in the days to come."

Guests had come to welcome Maggie and, that done, said their good-byes. Catrina and Adolf were the last to leave, Catrina the quieter, and Adolf the more verbose. When they had gone, Maggie scrunched her shoulders, gritted her teeth, and shook her head.

"You did well to tolerate the Buehler pair, Maggie," Juan said.

So he'd noticed. Maggie nodded. "Thank you, Juan. Have you run across them in Ecuador?"

"Only Catrina and her sister. There are four of them. The youngest went to Germany with his mother when a boy, and they never returned. Catrina's sister is the oldest, lives in Quito, and is very influential. I understand that Catrina has expanded her operations in Mexico, and lusts for power here to surpass that of her sister in Ecuador."

Chapter 29

Maggie's Baby Ben glowed four-fifteen. It would ring at four-thirty, so she decided to get dressed and let Kyna sleep a few minutes longer.

"What are you wearing?" Kyna asked through a yawn when Maggie awakened her. "Happy Birthday."

"Good morning and thank you. Just a simple china poblana, loafers and my St. Louis Cardinals baseball cap."

Kyna stifled another yawn. "Great minds run in something or other, but it's too early to know what." She went into the bathroom and looked back. "Same for me, only I'll wear a Washington Senators cap. That's Tom's team, and I'd lose him if I wore any other."

Maggie grinned. "I'm taking a blouse and skirt for flying back tomorrow."

"Me, too. See, great minds. I arranged seat priority for our return before I left the embassy last night."

She tapped on Maggie's door a few minutes later and, together, they tiptoed the dimly lit staircase and hallway to the dining room.

"Good morning. Wake up well?" Governor Gutierrez rose from the table and indicated chairs. "Help yourself to papaya and coffee. Pia's fixing *buñuelos,* and will bring eggs and sausage if you care to wait."

Maggie responded with a hug and kiss.

"Good morning," Kyna said. "You're up early. Did I hear

bun or something. That's all for me."

"*Buñuelos* are like doughnuts without holes," Maggie said when they were seated. "When Pia brings them I'll take some out to Thirteen Rabbit."

"She already did, and for his rider, too," the governor said. "Our company drivers always have an armed guard who doubles as a mechanic. Maggie, I have a question about José." He wiped a napkin across his chin and stood up. "We understood that he would drive from Veracruz with you to attend the Security Council session yesterday afternoon. He missed it. Last night Adolf told me you drove from Puebla alone. I have a meeting at the capitol and no time now. When you return tomorrow, I want a memo on his actions Friday and yesterday." He bent over Maggie for a quick embrace, shook Kyna's hand, and hurried off.

Maggie nibbled on a *buñuelo* as she mulled the governor's request. "I wish Beno'd told me why he wants a report on José," she said. "If I knew, writing it would be so much easier."

"Time's up, Maggie." Kyna stood up. "We'll have hours for talk. I'd say the way he asked for a report is an example of why your illustrious father is just that. Come on. Jackets? Will we need them?" she asked when Maggie handed her one.

Maggie nodded. "We're nearly a mile and a half above sea level and will be higher. It's cold outside and there's no heater in the car."

Trece waved and started the truck engine when they reached the courtyard. They climbed into Clank and followed the truck onto the street.

With the dawning light and sparse Sunday traffic, they reached the city's outskirts sooner than Maggie expected. "Look, Kyna." Maggie indicated terraced slopes and snow-capped peaks on her left. "Did you bring your camera?"

"Misty valleys on this side. I wish I had it, but Tom's camera was stolen so mine went with him. Kyna watched the scenery a few moments, then went on. "I've been thinking about what your father said this morning. He doesn't trust José, does he? Any idea why, other than a natural concern for your welfare?" She chuckled. "Or should I say your future?"

"My future, you mean with José?" Maggie felt her shoulders tighten. "I should say not." Kyna'd only been kidding, and she should have gone along with it. Softening her reply, she said, "I think Beno wants to be sure José upholds his Security Council obligations."

"Come on, kiddo. Surely he's concerned for your future as well as for Mexico's."

"It would be entirely out of character for my father to let my future interfere with his responsibility for the security of his country. "I'll admit to occasional romantic dreams involving José, but my father would hardly expect an unbiased report from me if he thought I was interested in José."

"Want my real opinion?" Maggie nodded, and Kyna went on. "I think he's using a subtle approach to teach you a lesson. You see —"

"No, Kyna. He asked me to write a report."

Kyna laughed. "Don't you see what he meant to do? Think about it. If he'd told you exactly what he wanted, your report would reflect your personal viewpoint on those items. The way he worded his request suggests that he has doubts about José but isn't sure why. He hopes you come up with something he hasn't considered."

Maggie drove in silence for a time, then said, "I don't believe so, Kyna. I see what you mean and you may be right. He probably knows many valid reasons for José to miss the Security Council meetings and needs no help from me. Like a professor, he gave me an assignment, so it's possible that there's something improbable I should know but wouldn't believe unless I figured it out for myself." Maggie felt Kyna studying her and wished she'd drop the subject, but Kyna dug in.

"So how are you going to put together a report when you have no evidence and won't be able to get any today?"

"I'll just put something together."

"Your father is not a man to accept guesses, Maggie."

"You're right, but he's hungry for ideas, so that's what I'll try to give him."

"Speaking of hungry." Kyna grasped a basket off the floor. "How about a bun — bun — bump your elbow or whatever you call it?"

Maggie laughed. "Buñuelo. Swell."

* * *

"Try to pronounce that." Maggie pointed at a sign which read, Ixhuatlancillo? It's just an area, and we're now in the state of Veracruz."

Irena had told her that the Hacienda Perla was close to the main road, but it took more than an hour to maneuver the branching byways along the east slope of Pico Orizaba. At last, they wound through a coffee plantation to a beige-colored stone wall capped with red tile, and the *Hacienda Perla* gate.

"Bienvenida, Señorita," a man shouted as they entered.

"Hola, amigo mio," Maggie called back, and drove on. "This hacienda is part of Irena's family legacy," Maggie told Kyna. "Except for the lack of gorgeous sunsets, it's her favorite place in the whole world." She followed the truck into a large graveled yard ringed with buildings, low and beige, with red tile roofs. She saw Thirteen Rabbit's arm point from the truck at a small structure with a sign above the entrance tabbing it as the office.

"It's like a tiny village, isn't it?" Kyna said as they parked and got out. She indicated a two-story box-like structure surrounded by a wide porch off toward higher ground. "That must be their house, and aren't the grounds lovely with all the flowering trees and shrubs?"

"I left the keys in the car so you can load it, Trece," Maggie called when she saw him approaching. "They want to keep it like a village," she said, turning back to Kyna. "Irena says that's part of its charm. Their house was built on the site of the original, which burned about twenty years ago. I've never been here before and suppose we could see it, but time's getting short. I won't be able to find Oso after dark."

A stout man of about sixty introduced himself as the hacienda superintendent and greeted them in English as they entered the office. "Your father sent me a list of provisions which Trece is loading into your car. Ah, here is my wife with your lunch. We wish you could stay longer, but your father says you must hurry." He helped his wife put enchiladas on the table while he talked.

"I just gave Trece his pay. Don Benancio told me Trece will remain on the payroll at one-quarter pay while he works with you. Where shall I send it?"

"In my care at the consulate in Veracruz. Does Trece know this?"

The superintendent shook his head. "Better you tell him yourself."

"*Vámonos,* let's go," Thirteen Rabbit bellowed from the entry. "Are there more enchiladas?"

* * *

Maggie tooted three *ah-oo-gahs,* waved, and drove off after Thirteen Rabbit declined Maggie's suggestion that he ride in front. Instead, he chose a perch of tarpaulin covered sacks of beans and rice forming a crude rumble seat.

"Trece must have forgotten something," Maggie said as they approached the exit gate where a group of men were waving for them to stop. She heard Trece speaking as she pulled up, but did not understand.

"*Qué hay* — what's going on?" Maggie asked, leaning across Kyna.

"*Nada, Señorita* — nothing," a man said with a wide grin.

"We just came to say good-bye to our friend."

More of Trece's friends arrived, and Maggie felt the car rock under their weight as they swarmed over the car to shake Trece's hand. Finally she heard him shout for her to get going, and a chorus of farewells as she rolled Clank slowly forward. "We've got quite a load — dragging — riding the rear axle," she muttered. She reached up to adjust the rearview mirror, and erupted into laughter.

"What's funny?"

Still laughing, Maggie thumbed over her shoulder.

Kyna swivelled, looked back and exploded. "Oink-oink, she squealed. "You wanted a menagerie — got thirteen rabbits." She laughed harder. "Rabbits wanted a buddy — got themselves a pig!"

Infected by Kyna's hilarity, Maggie squealed through her laughter, "How d'yu like that, Kyna? Rabbit chose a pig's company instead of riding up front with us."

There came a rapid tapping on the rear window. Maggie glanced at the mirror, and saw Thirteen Rabbit jabbing a finger left. She cut the car into a sharp turn. Pig yowled. The car careened, skidded and she wrestled it onto the narrow brush-lined trail to Cordoba.

"Stop," Kyna yelled, pivoting to look back.

Maggie slowed, spun the wheel to turn again and whooshed her bottled breath. She flicked a glance to the mirror — gaping jaws, tusks— the pig's head dwarfed Rabbit's.

"Pig's on top," Kyna shrieked.

Maggie glanced again, saw Rabbit struggling, grinning, waving her on, and porker — jaws wide, its squeals banshee-like to her ears. Ahead, a herder dove for the bushes. His goats scattered, all except a lone ram guarding the middle of the road. Maggie eased Clank past in sudden quiet.

"Monster's eating green weeds out of a black sack," Kyna reported, "and Rabbit's trying to tie the sack over its head. My stars. If he had to bring a pig, why such a huge one. Whee-ooo!" She arranged herself back in the seat and looked at Maggie. "You just sit there as if nothing happened."

"Exciting, but nothing really did happen," Maggie said. "But now I know why Clank's overloaded and acting like a sick cow."

Kyna hadn't really stopped laughing yet. "A cow, too?" she shrieked. "Nothing happened? Okay, we didn't butt that goat or dump our pig, so what was there about those few seconds to make us laugh so hard unless something happened? Oh well, what's the next stop, check in at the consulate?"

Maggie shook her head. "Oso first — we need daylight, and I don't want an encounter with Sarah."

"How come? She'd be delighted to see you."

"Kyna, no — not unless it's to scrub her floors. Only a week ago I made her pay back tens of thousands of government dollars she'd embezzled."

Kyna shrugged. "That's chicken feed to Sarah. It's like if you took an office pen home, would you think you were embezzling?"

"Eugh! How can you say that?" Maggie shook her head. Kyna was just another rich woman justifying the faults of her circle. "There's not a smidgeon of similarity," she said. "Those dollars belong to the people, Kyna, and she had no right to them. Besides, why would I want to see her after the way she's been dumping on me all these months?" Aware that Kyna was frowning at her, she kept her eyes on the road. How in heaven's name could Kyna take Sarah Williams's side?

"Didn't you tell me the ambassador thought Al Williams was doing a good job as the consul?" Kyna asked.

"That's what he said, but —"

Kyna cut in. "You claim that Al did nothing without Sarah's approval, and that means Al was only a paper boss and Sarah was your real one. The consul and his wife have to work as a team. Williamses are good at that, and Sarah's the one who makes it work."

"But Kyna —"

"Let me finish, Maggie. Al Williams is a handsome nothing, a nincompoop, and that's exactly the kind of man Sarah needs. She's utterly without tact, but gets her way with challenges and threats. Most people knuckle under, like Al's secretary, Helen, who checks everything Al tells her to do with Sarah. Others quit the way your predecessors did. But you didn't. You did what had to be done and learned a lot. If you think she's an old meany, just think of her as a woman version of a man who teaches his kids to swim by throwing them in the river, and they do swim because they don't dare cry for help. Did Nolan tell you about the trouble he had getting back the money she embezzled?"

"So you admit that she stole it." Maggie shook her head. "No, he didn't say a word about it." She'd wondered how Nolan got the reimbursement check from Mrs. Williams. Now, by the way Kyna wriggled forward and turned to face her, she knew Kyna couldn't wait to tell her.

"Well, Nolan told me Al was the problem, not Sarah. He said Al threatened to report him to the Treasury secretary if he even hinted to Sarah that she owed all that money. They got into a real shouting session, and Al actually tried to throw him out of the building. Nolan's smaller, but much tougher, and got Al pinned down on the floor in no time."

"No kidding. Wish I'd seen that." Maggie thought of José's description of Nolan's red, hot face and straight-armed march from the consulate following the ruckus in Mr. Williams's office.

"Al finally calmed down and sat there lily-livered while Nolan went to see Sarah. She wrote a check at once. Nolan said she even told him to thank you for discovering the mistake."

"Horse feathers." Maggie felt months of built-up disgust for the woman well up within her. "That Sarah's just a cheap conniving crook."

"I won't argue that," Kyna said and sat back in her seat. "Sarah wouldn't want me to tell you this, but it wouldn't be fair to her if I didn't."

"I really don't care, Kyna."

"Well, you should. When we went shopping back in July, it was Sarah who suggested that we get you something to show our appreciation for all you were doing for us. That was before you foiled the robbery. Daitha agreed, and I suggested that we give you the dress I'd seen you try on. It cost next to nothing compared to the thousands we'd have lost if you hadn't skedaddled those thieves. 'Not enough,' Sarah said after you'd sent them packing. You'd saved our belongings and our pride, as well as the consulate's reputation and prestige. She wouldn't have it any other way, and insisted on getting you a very special gift."

"I was just doing my job."

"You did more than that, Maggie. Remember, I'd asked about your emerald earrings, and you said you'd borrowed them. Anyway, Sarah thought they were just right for you, and said she'd arrange with Adolf to get us a bargain. She had your birth date from the files, so we decided to give you the dress then, and get the earrings for your birthday."

"Just the dress was too much, and it's still the nicest one I've ever had." Maggie reached over to squeeze Kyna's hand. "Now I feel cheap — the things I've thought about Sarah. I'm glad you told me, and I will thank her and write to Daitha, too."

"That's not all of it, Maggie. She — Watch out!"

Maggie slammed the brakes, blaring forth squeals from the pig.

"*Qué pasa?*" Thirteen Rabbit shouted.

Maggie skidded the car to a stop barely short of a burro's nose. "Whew, close. Okay, burro-burro, I'll let you have the right of way. Pack saddle's empty," she said to Kyna, "so someone must have turned it loose to find its way home."

Kyna pulled in a deep breath. "Careful. Don't bump the poor beast," she said as Maggie eased the car around the creature. "Where was I? Oh — Last week I was with Sarah when Adolf showed her the birthday earrings. Dear Lord, what a tizzy Sarah threw. Adolf was really put out, but agreed to replace them." She yawned. "I don't see how you stay awake — hardly keep my eyes open."

A glance in the mirror revealed Thirteen Rabbit pillowed onto pig. Maggie reached for the enchilada basket, and saw that Kyna was slouched against the corner, eyes closed. Drowsy herself, she ate two enchiladas, sipped coffee from the thermos, and considered Kyna's words about Sarah Williams and what she should do about it.   When she approached Veracruz, she honked to awaken her riders.

"Where are we?" Kyna asked, tapping her lips to suppress a yawn.

"Nearly there," Maggie answered as she turned onto a road to Boca del Rio. "Count the bridges we cross, even little ones. We turn just past the seventh."

"There's one," Kyna said a moment later.

"That was two." Maggie waved at another.

"Three. That was easy," Kyna said, and leaned forward so she could see better. "There's the seventh, Mags," she said after about five minutes.

"Swell." Maggie turned right. "We stay on this weedy trail until we reach a clearing with a big log on the right side. The far end of the log juts into the river, and we'll use it as a pier while we load the boat."

"Mostacho's boat? We there already?"

"Oso's," Maggie reminded Kyna. "No, a rowboat. See, there's the log." She backed carefully through hip-high grass until Clank stopped against the log with a gentle *thump*. "We'll unload here, then rent a boat at a place around that bend." She pointed, and just then Thirteen Rabbit appeared beside Maggie's window.

"*Está narcotizada la puerca con la hierba mala* — pig ate too much dope weed. We must lift her out." He disappeared into a thicket with a machete and came back with three short poles and a long one.

"Care for an enchilada and coffee?" Maggie asked Kyna. "Rabbit seems to know what to do, so we may as well have a bite now. He can eat while we get the rowboat."

They watched Thirteen Rabbit make a tripod, then place the long pole across it so that it served as both fulcrum and pivot for the long pole. He pulled the pole's short end down and attached it to a rope harness around pig, then beckoned.

"*Listo, Señorita*—ready," he called. "You two pull down." He indicated a rope dangling from the high end of the long pole. "When pig is out of the car, move sideways until she is over the log, then let her down."

"That pig must weigh at least four hundred pounds," Kyna moaned when they finally levered pig up and swung it to the far side of the log. She looked at Rabbit, who was removing the last of the car's load. "He didn't even help us. Now I suppose he'll expect us to load pig into the boat."

"Smart — used us to provide the brawn," Maggie said. "Let's go. The car's empty."

* * *

They heard Thirteen Rabbit coaxing, pleading, before they saw him when they rowed back. Then they saw him, rope over his shoulder — tugging — pig on her side — moving only inches each time Rabbit lunged toward the river. He'd pulled it into shallow water by the time Kyna and Maggie squished the boat's stern into the riverbank mud.

"Stay in the boat while I load it," he said as he placed dry branches in the boat's bottom. "Beans, rice, ammunition, must not get wet."

"Municiones?" Maggie asked as he picked up a long box.

"Sí, for the rifles, three in this box — pistols, dynamite, too."

Maggie caught a glimpse of gunmetal blue hidden in the weeds, a fourth rifle tucked beside the log. Should she tell Kyna what was in the box? Not now, she decided. Kyna was engrossed in watching flamingos and a lone white egret standing one legged in the shallows upriver. She heard Thirteen Rabbit murmur something about waiting for pig to shake off the green weed dope, and swung around to face him.

"There's no time, Trece. Pull pig close and tie her to the stern with her head above water. I know where to go, so I'll sit in the stern and steer with this paddle."

Thirteen Rabbit grinned. "It will be hard to steer if we tow pig."

"Hard to row, too, and slow," Maggie shot back.

Thirteen Rabbit nodded. *"Sí, bueno para los cocodrilos.* I will row in the middle seat and be ready to shoot the crocodiles." Eyes flashing he bent over to pick up the rifle and looked back sideways at Maggie. "Maybe we can trade our pork for good leather and crocodile meat. *Sí, muy bueno."*

"What in heaven's name was all that about?" Kyna asked from her seat on the fore thwart.

"Just a bit of concern because we'll have to tow pig," Maggie said. "Harder to row, but easier than loading her." Why let Kyna focus her thoughts on a most unlikely meat transaction? Of course if it should come about, Kyna would have to row even harder towing both pig and crocodile.

Chapter 30

Maggie just had to chuckle. Kyna must have hugged every one of Oso's family at least twice before Gitana led her to the rowboat for their return to the rental dock. With seven children between eight and twenty it had taken more time than Maggie wanted to spare. Now they were on their way with Gitana and her two oldest in the small launch towing them before going on to their vending stints on the Malecon. She'd seen Thirteen Rabbit sidle over from his diesels so as not to be left out. Recalling how he'd hung around for repeat hugs, she burst out laughing.

Kyna looked back from the fore thwart. "Care to share it?"

"Just tickled by the impression you made — got them started when you went over to help Gitana butcher the crocodile. When Rabbit told them you shot it, that did it. You're part of their family forever."

"Sure — my trophy — shot three times, maybe more. Then all those rabbits snatched the rifle and pulled the trigger just once. Pig got the croc to follow us so it deserves the credit — not me, for sure."

"They've got you, Kyna. You can't escape the credit until you learn to speak Spanish. Turn around. Gitana's waving us off so pull in the tow line."

* * *

"What do you think of Oso's boat?" Maggie asked as they drove to the consulate.

"I think you've lost your mind. That's an ocean out there, Maggie, not a lake. Even ships get swamped." Kyna shook her head. "Are you sure Irena and the governor know you're actually planning to live on that scow?"

"You saw the rifles we picked up at the hacienda, didn't you? Beno sent them. I call that support. Besides, he's footing the bill for fuel until we trap Ragnorak."

"Dear Jesus." Kyna was silent a moment. "When do you leave?"

"I'm not sure. Two weeks, I hope. Oso'll send a message to the embassy to let me know."

Kyna shook her head. "No good, Maggie. Can't stay hush-hush if it goes through the embassy."

"Code — my pet rabbit had three bunnies means I meet Oso in Boca del Rio at sunup three days later."

Kyna snorted. "Red flag, Maggie — too obvious — come-ye-come ye, all ye snoops."

Maggie couldn't help laughing. "Just kidding. Actually, all's set except the day. Gitana peddles bread at the consulate. She'll tell Carlos, who will then call me at the embassy. I'll work out a code with him.

Dusk was falling when they reached the consulate. Mr. Williams had been summoned to Mexico City by the ambassador. Sarah had gone, too, the watchman told them, and nobody was there except him and the Williamses' housekeeper.

"Any choice on where we eat? I'd rather not rustle something in the kitchen."

"Let me think." Kyna frowned. "Bunch of rabbits, one pig, one egret, flock of flamingos, goats, burros, one crocodile and I saw hundreds of parakeets at Oso's camp — there you are. What about that parrot place where we ate last week?"

"Parroquia," Maggie grinned. "That's the word for a parish or neighborhood. A parrot is a *papagayo.* Another possibility is the cantina in Antigua. It's more driving, but it

would save my going there at dawn tomorrow to return two of Zita's pans left over from last week's bridge."

"Of course," Kyna exclaimed. "That's where you got the monkey meat, and won't that place be appropriate for a finale to menagerie day."

* * *

"Up with the seagulls," Maggie murmured as she closed the consulate door behind her. She turned toward the harbor wondering if she would ever take this stroll again? She crossed the street onto the Malecon waterfront park and set off with long strides.

What might she make of what Zita had told her last night about El Ragnorak's comings and goings? Zita hadn't known much, had never seen the man, and only knew of his arrival and departure from people who came into the cantina. Maggie smiled, thinking of how Zita had bristled when asked how she got her information. "Of course I know about them," she'd snapped. "Men come — stay ten days, two weeks — I cook them our best meals, then they want French, Polish, German, gringo food like those four *Norteamericanos* out there."

Maggie'd hurried back to the dining room, but the men had gone. Kyna had told her they were delightful men, just passing through.

"Pan, pan fresco, buñuelos," Maggie heard Gitana cry. She wheeled and approached the vendor's cart. *"Muy buenos dias, Gitana."* She bought bananas and buñuelos, chatted a few moments, then ambled to the consulate.

She made coffee, and was starting to eat in her former office when the telephone rang. It was a message for Kyna. Her husband's flight from Panama was scheduled to arrive in Mexico City at eleven o'clock, and she should be ready to leave with him for the States at eleven forty-five.

"Okay unless she calls you back," Maggie told the embassy clerk. She'd started up the stairs to waken Kyna when Carlos arrived. "Good morning, Carlos. Emergency — Senator Johnson's wife is with me and must meet the senator in Mexico City at eleven. We have reservations from here on the eleven-forty. Can you get us on the early flight?"

He picked up the telephone.

"Thank you, Carlos, and will you drive us to the airfield then return the Model A Ford to Enrique's garage?" Mounting the stairs, she yelled, "Wake up, Kyna, *ya mismo,* right now, *tout suite, chop-chop.* Earlier flight leaves in half an hour. We've got to get on it."

The bedroom door opened. "Ready in two minutes," Kyna barked.

* * *

"Goodness gracious, all that rush to wait for a late plane," Kyna said. "Now we'll be lucky to be on time. Lucky we went to the cantina last night instead of this morning."

"That was fun, wasn't it? I wish we had more time. Things seem to happen when you and I bum around."

"I'll say." Kyna laughed. "You missed the fun last night when that young American put on his torero act. He was —"

"What did he look like?" Maggie cut in. "I asked on the way back last night but you'd fallen asleep."

"Sort of Spanish, a lot like your friend José."

The plane roared down the runway and Maggie waited until they were airborne. "This is important, Kyna. You said there were four. When they left the cantina, did they use the same door we did?"

Kyna shook her head. "No, middle of the room, straight back."

Maggie dug in her purse for a note-pad. "Did a burly man, ruddy face, big black moustache, take them out that way?"

Kyna twisted around to stare at Maggie. "You saw him?"

"He's the cantina owner, Zita's husband, and a Nazi supporter." Maggie scribbled on her notepad. "Go on, what did the young man tell you? Speak softly." She saw Kyna's face cloud over. "I don't mean to alarm you, Kyna. It's just that you may have hit pay dirt on a large chunk of a giant puzzle. What was he talking about?"

Kyna frowned. "Well, let me think. I'd heard the oldest man, the one with gray hair, say a torero would be their instructor next week. There was more talk but I wasn't paying attention. Suddenly the young one jumped up and snatched one of those red checkered tablecloths off a table. He pointed at a poster and shouted, 'There's our coach and we'll see him fight a bull in two weeks.' Then he pranced around, feinting and dodging, while he flapped the tablecloth. I clapped — shouted '*Olé*,' too, and he came over and asked if I spoke English."

Maggie could just picture Kyna's picking up the spirit of the occasion. "Sure you didn't put on a torera act? What did you say?"

Kyna leaned forward and looked up sideways at Maggie. "Almost did. How did you know? "I guess I said something like it was nice to hear something I understood for a change."

"What did the others look like?"

"Well, the José look-alike was about your age, then there was a mid-thirties man with sandy-colored hair, an early forties — the kind who spends hours looking at a mirror. Oh, yes. He had eyes for you, and kept glancing at the kitchen door from the time you went in to see Zita until they left."

"The fifties one, what about him?" Maggie asked.

"Dark blue — but maybe his eyes were dark because of deep eye sockets. He had heavy brows, snow-white like his hair, and I guess early fifties because his face had no wrinkles." Kyna went on to describe their voices, how they laughed, and even how they walked as they were herded from the cantina.

Maggie made a note that it seemed strange that four so far apart in age should just pass through together. "Thank you so much," she said, putting the pad in her purse. "I would never have noticed so much about those men."

Kyna shrugged. "Pshaw, Mags. If I know you, you'd have soaked up a lot more if you'd seen the torero act."

"I hate to say good-bye," Maggie said as the plane taxied to the terminal. "You've helped me so much. I'd wondered what to report to Beno. Now I have it right here." She tapped her purse.

Kyna gave her a sideways glance. "I know nothing about the man — didn't even mention his name."

"The poster — torero, but that's for me to work out. We're here. Don't keep Tom waiting, Kyna. Go ahead." Maggie rose and held back in the aisle to let Kyna go first.

"Señorita," a man behind Maggie said.

She glanced back and saw a man reaching into Kyna's seat pocket. *"Muchas gracias, Señor,"* she said when he handed her Kyna's Washington Senators cap. Descending the ladder, she tried to put it over her own — too small, so she snugged Kyna's into hers and pulled hers down on top. She saw Kyna round the end of the wing and dash toward the terminal. Straight ahead, Senator Johnson was coming down the ladder of another plane which had just landed.

"Kyna, this way. I saw Tom," she shouted, then hurried out past the wing's end, called again, and saw Kyna turn back.

"So I'm suddenly married to a strawberry blonde."

Maggie recognized the senator's voice, and felt herself gathered in by a powerful arm. Then Kyna flew in and his other arm circled her. She saw his lips find Kyna's, and felt a bolt of jealousy as the senator released her and took Kyna's Washington Senators cap from her head. Then her own cap came down low on her forehead. She felt an arm swoop her against a hard body, a firm hand tip back her head, and carnal lips meet hers.

She clung tight in response to her craving, then she smelled smoke in his clothing and her spirits plunged. This man's hair would be red, not black — Nolan Thompson.

She heard Kyna call to keep in touch. "Shall do," she answered, then pushed Nolan away. She looked up into waffling eyes, saw them pie, cross, then focus on something above her. His hair and face were flaming red — ripe — and it crossed her mind that it might not be too bad to kiss a tomato.

"My goodness, Nolan," she murmured. "You sure took me by surprise."

"Me, too," he gasped, then took off after Tom and Kyna.

What a surprise Nolan had turned out to be, Maggie thought as she went through the terminal. He would never match the flair of José, but dependable? Yeah.

"Over here, Maggie."

Maggie spotted a waving arm beside an open car as she emerged from the terminal, and recognized a vice consul from the embassy. "I hoped you'd still be here," she said, approaching him. "You must be the one who checked Kyna's luggage through to Washington."

"Right." They shook hands. "I'm your cicerone for the afternoon, show you about, introduce you to who's who around the place. The ambassador wants you at a two o'clock briefing and in his office for a few minutes later. I'll be at your beck and call as long as you need me. We have plenty of time. Lunch?"

"Love to." Fancy talk, cicerone. Who was he trying to impress? She got in the car ahead of him. "I'll have to change first," she said, and directed the driver to the Gutierrez residence.

*   *   *

For Maggie, their lunch dragged and, after a traffic delay, they arrived barely in time. They sat against the wall just before the ambassador entered the room with another man and took chairs at the end of a long conference table.

"Is that the consul general?" Maggie whispered.

"Uh-huh." Her companion nodded. "He usually runs the meetings, but the ambassador likes to introduce new staff and visitors."

Just then the ambassador stood up. "Before we get started — Maggie, stand up please."

She did, then he motioned for her to be seated.

"Maggie, Margaret Magodon, is a U.S. citizen," he announced. "She was born in Torreon, Mexico, hence, Mexico can claim her citizenship, too. Spanish and English are her native tongues, and she's fluent in other romance languages as well. Reads German, too. She's a certified public accountant, and has six years of private sector accounting experience with a major aircraft manufacturing firm. Welcome, Maggie."

"When we were in Veracruz she was *Señorita Gutierrez,*" a voice piped up from behind Maggie.

The ambassador rose again. "Quite right. She's also known as *"Margareta Gutierrez y Magodon."*

Maggie shook her head, wishing he would stop, but he went on.

"Governor Gutierrez of Veracruz state is her uncle, now her father by adoption." He started to sit, but popped back up. "Oh yes. She'll be working with me on various tasks somewhat outside the normal functions of this office. However, she'll be glad to help whenever I can spare her time." He sat down and the consul general rose.

Maggie heard subdued murmurs, then quiet, and let herself heave a sigh of relief at no longer being the center of attention. The consul general called on the military attachés for reports on the war in Europe and, from the following discussion, she learned that war updates were posted daily on the embassy bulletin board. Didn't El Ragnorak, with top-notch radio equipment aboard the *Hedda* and at the Hacienda have the same information? Coded radio messages from Nazi headquarters would also tie his operations to overall Nazi strategy.

Ragnorak must be licking his chops over the news that German armies had laid siege to Leningrad and Sevastopol, and had been stalled just short of Moscow by the Russian winter, and not by Russian military resistance. The reports painted a grim picture, the only encouraging note being that the British were holding their own in the battle of Tobruk against General Rommel's Afrika Tank Korps.

A nudge on her elbow interrupted her thoughts, and she took a sketch her escort gave her. It showed the names and nicknames of staff members seated around the table, including titles and responsibilities. As she listened to the briefings, she made notes on their expressions and reactions. I know something about every one and can call them by name, she thought, as the meeting came to an end.

Her guide showed her the layout of the embassy building after the meeting, then stopped at the ambassador's door. "Do you enjoy bullfights?" he asked,

"I don't know." Maggie shrugged. Why bullfights at a time like this? "I haven't been to one since I was a child, and don't remember much except that it was terribly exciting." She couldn't hold back a chuckle. "What my mother said to my dad when she found out was classic. Why do you ask?"

"Just that Mr. Thompson said you knew a bullfighter, and a few of the guys plan to go to one in a couple of weeks."

Maggie nodded. "José Alvarado. They were fraternity brothers in college." Was this man about to ask for a date? He seemed nice, but far too prissy, and there were lots of things she'd rather do than watch a man heckle a bull. She felt no attraction to the vice consul. Still, it was to be José's last bullfight, and Irena had said he put on a spectacular show. If she went as one of the guys, it wouldn't really be a date. "I'll think about it," she said. "José's the main attraction next week Saturday and Sunday at the Grand Bull Arena, his last before retiring, so it might be interesting to see his act."

"Act? I heard they can be gory. Talk to you later about it." He opened the ambassador's door. "I'll leave you with Jennifer now. Jen, meet Maggie."

"Thanks for the tour," Maggie called after him. "Hello, Jen." She shook hands with the woman, who appeared to be about her own age, pretty, with lustrous black hair, and blue eyes crinkling at the corners.

"Muy buenas tardes.   Cómo está usted, Señorita Magodon?" Jenny said.

American classroom Spanish, Maggie thought, but at least the receptionist wasn't afraid to speak the language. *"Bien, bien,"* Maggie said, then dispensed with get acquainted talk in English.

"A desk will be ready for you in the main office tomorrow," Jenny told her, "but the ambassador said you needed a private place to work on his projects." She opened a door on their left. "This is his study room, burrow, library or, whenever he's really intent, it's his hunker room."

"Meaning hunker down and get at it."

"Well." Jenny shrugged. "Get it done is more like it. You know what that means, don't you?"

"Curiosity pests, I suppose," Maggie said, "but I can cope."

It's soundproofed for security conferences, so you might get a gentle boot occasionally." The telephone cut Jenny short and she left.

Maggie found the files the trade agreement team had borrowed, then turned her attention to a map on a broad drafting table. She sucked in a whistling breath. What a map it was of the coastline just north of Veracruz. She'd never have dreamed such detail existed. A cabinet beside the table yielded others, all with a U. S. Navy stamp. Might she take them with her? How pleased Oso would be!

She tore herself away from the maps to pull a memorandum pad from a drawer and start her report to Governor Gutiérrez. How could she possibly list incriminating evidence against José so soon after her passionate response to the embrace she'd believed was his? She just couldn't believe that José would collaborate with a Nazi against his own country. Just the thought of tattling on him made her feel like a traitor.

Traitor — double agent — Oh-mi-God, Maggie thought. Speak of the devil. What am I doing? I'm American. I work for the government — the FBI and so does José. Sure, I'm Mexican, too, but does that give me the right to report on — spy on José for an official of another government, even if he is my father? She started to type.

Dear Beno, my beloved father:

This note will be very difficult for me to write. As you read it, I hope you understand why I must back away from writing the report concerning José Alvarado which you requested yesterday morning. Perhaps I should not even write this note and explain my reasons during dinner this evening. If I did, it might be hard for me to come up with the right wording.

I had started to write the report when I paused to consider the responsibilities of parties involved, and the relationships between them.

I hope you understand, my dear father, that circumstances of family and citizenship make it impossible for me to write the report you requested without setting myself up as a traitor. However, you may be sure that I will let you know at once if I become aware of any act on his part which poses a threat to our two countries.

Your loving daughter,

Maggie

Maggie glanced at her watch — late. She stuffed the note in her purse and went to the woman's room.

The ambassador was waiting when she returned. "I repeat my welcome, Maggie," he said, tapping the map table. "At work already, I see. Find everything you need?"

She nodded and shook his hand, thinking that he and others on the staff had picked up on the frequent handshake custom.

"A couple of questions. Those maps are just what I need. Is there a way I might get copies of the ones showing the gulf coast and northeast border with the States?"

"I'm sure. Check with the attachés. What else?"

"If there's no objection, I'll stay at my family's house, the old Montoya place, at least for the time being."

"None whatsoever." He edged toward the door, then turned back. "Say, sit down, Maggie. Let me bounce something off you."

Maggie sat at her desk and he on the draftsman's stool with a foot on the floor and the other hanging from a bent knee.

"My wife and Kyna have been bending my ear about the bridge party you pulled off in Veracruz the other day. How'd you do it?"

"That was Sarah Williams's party — her regular bridge group."

"Come now, Maggie. They were part of it, and I saw it. What's the secret?"

"I saw a picture of a man in uniform and a little boy on Jenny's desk." Maggie caught the ambassador's grimace and deep frown, and said quickly, "I'm not changing the subject, just taking a different tack."

"Lost her husband and son to a bomb in London while she was at work at the U.S. Embassy there. She's trying to get her life back together. You haven't answered my question."

Head bowed, Maggie gave it a quick shake. "I'm so sorry. I'll talk to Jenny about social events. Is it okay if I call your wife?"

"You bet," he said, spinning off the stool and heading for the door. "Don't fail me, Maggie."

Maggie watched him go. He hadn't wanted details, only to get a task off his mind. She turned her head slowly from side to side. Men — would they ever understand that functions involving important men and their wives, while intended to foster friendship, amounted instead to a battle between women intent on enhancing the prestige of their men. Had the ambassador caught on to the idea that friendships between cultures evolve from the meeting of women with common interests, untroubled for the moment by their men's struggle for dominance?

Maggie paused at Jenny's desk for a longer look at the photo of man and boy. How sad, yet Jenny seemed to be coping. Maggie turned to the door. Broken family — but a picture of the two Jenny had lost must prolong the grief. Pangs of sympathy coursed through her as she thought of her own sorrow, pictures of her mother, father, Betty, and herself. Now she had Irena and Benancio — family again and, longing for family pictures she'd destroyed, she went out to the street and strode away.

"Consulado Norteamericano, Señorita?"

Maggie pivoted to the curb and climbed into the rear seat of a taxi. "Miguel, how are you? I'd forgotten that you had a taxi company here, too. Will you be here tomorrow?"

"Veracruz tomorrow, and I'll go as far as Puebla tonight. When did you last see José?"

"Friday evening in Puebla." Was Miguel here to check up on José and herself? She told him what had happened in Puebla, including Adolf's breaking into her room. "Is something wrong?" she asked finally. "Why do you ask?"

"We were to meet here this morning," Miguel said.

"You mean he didn't show up? Do you know about his bullfights at the end of next week?"

He nodded. "Everybody knows." Miguel slowed down as they approached the Gutierrez gate.

"What about this?" she went on. "He's been conducting training sessions for groups of men on the Hacienda Buehler. The last group of four expect to be at the bull ring next week." Maggie thought he had not known, and that she'd surprised him.

"I got suspicious because they said they were just passing through, and men ranging thirty or more years apart in age aren't likely to do that. What would José train them to do? Fighting bulls is out, because the men range into the fifties in age."

Driving slowly, he circled a park before he spoke again. "Today Beno told me he asked you for a report on what José was doing."

"I wrote a note to tell him I couldn't spy on José. It's here in my purse."

"Good," Miguel said, sounding relieved. "He regrets asking you for it, and said that he would furnish fuel for that excursion you're planning. I stopped that, because —"

"That's already arranged," Maggie cut in. "It can't be tracked to him."

"Oh? I'll have to think about that. Frankly, Maggie, I wanted their support for my decision to send someone else in your place."

"Damn you!" She slapped a hand across her mouth to keep from screaming. Think-think, she told herself. He circled the park again before she felt she could speak calmly, but still her words snapped. "They refused, didn't they, Miguel? You supported me when we met with the ambassador, helped me convince him. I'm shocked. What got into you?"

"Yes, Maggie. I did support you, but other matters have cropped up. I'm convinced that we've lost José, that he's a double agent, a Nazi spy, and that he'll betray you."

"How can he betray me when he thinks I'm already out of it. He doesn't have a ghost of an idea that I'm on Ragnorak's trail. He doesn't know what I know about El Ragnorak. Nobody does, not even you. Back me up or not, I'm going."

Chapter 31

Miguel pulled up at the Gutierrez gate and leaned back to wait for Maggie to get out.

She opened the door, paused, closed it and said, "Maybe you'd better drive around the park one more time." When he'd pulled into the street, she said, "If I withdraw what I just said, may we talk?"

"Of course."

"Thank you. It would be easier to tell you what I've found out if I sit in front."

Miguel stopped the taxi. When Maggie was settled in the front seat, he asked, "What more do you have?"

"I've told you only a wee bit of what I should, whether I can continue on the assignment or not." She shifted so she could see him better. "I've wondered what side José was on, too. I think back to the time I first mentioned Ragnorak to José. His reaction banged my head against the Ford's windshield. Later, I knew he was lying when he told Beno and Irena he knew nothing about the man."

"I heard him from the bathroom" Miguel said. "He fooled me, too."

"If I report something about José to you, the FBI, and to Beno, head of Mexico's Security Council, am I a double agent?" She heard Miguel chuckle.

"No, because the council and FBI are working together," he said. "Outside interests might alter that, Maggie."

"Such as my feelings? I assure you I am not in love with José, but I feel a strong attraction because I think he's an exceptional man. He's troubled now, mentioned quitting the FBI and the bullring. Either way, he's afraid he'll be killed. He's beh—"

"Hold it there, Maggie. Killed? Who would kill him?"

"Bulls because he's losing his touch? Maybe the somebody who insists that he sign a contract extension to fight five more years."

Maggie related what José had told her about his contract, then got back to her Ragnorak assignment. "I've seen the boat Oso built. He's El Ragnorak's ex-helmsman. Remember Trece, Thirteen Rabbit?"

Miguel nodded. "Mechanic and my night watchman for a spell."

"Yesterday I took him from Irena's hacienda to get the boat's diesel engine running. The boat's afloat, provisioned and moderately armed. Now, here's the point. He's going to leave me on the job, she thought when he did not interrupt.

"A week ago, Oso gave me a list of places between Veracruz and the States where he'd taken Ragnorak. I'd asked the ambassador for detailed maps of Mexico's gulf coast, and got them today. I've had time to look at one, a U.S. Navy chart of the coast just north of Veracruz. It didn't even show an inlet where Ragnorak had a lot of diesel fuel cached."

"You said had?"

"Yes, not has. Oso knows where there's more," she said, and decided to feel him out by taking a different tack.

"Tell me, Miguel. If I should need back-up from the U.S. Coast Guard or Navy, is there someone I can contact, providing I can arrange a joint operation with the Mexican Navy?"

"The ambassador for our navy. I suppose you have it arranged with the governor."

"Heavens, no." Maggie heard Miguel chuckle, and was

surprised when he tapped his horn outside a gate. It opened and he drove in.

"You're home," he said. "You're doing a good job. I'll make no changes."

Maggie got out. "Thank you, Miguel," she said, and closed the door. She watched him drive away, then waited as her father's limousine entered. She went over to meet him and they hugged.

"You've got victory written all over you," he said. "You must have backed Miguel down."

"Yes. Nothing has changed. I believe he thought I should have a chance to back out. I told him I'd written a note to you explaining why I couldn't report on José."

"Miguel jumped me on that. We were discussing José's absence and I told him I'd asked you for a report." He wrapped an arm around her. "Come, let's find Irena."

How good that arm felt. More than words, it told her that she'd fulfilled his trust, and she slipped her arm around his waist. His request had caused her a lot of worry but that didn't matter. She'd done the right thing and, in that instant, felt Gutiérrez family bonds grow even stronger.

                    * * *

The air was cool, crisp, delicious from the smell of charcoal smoke as Maggie strolled to the embassy the next morning. The governor and Irena had left for the airport an hour earlier. She was thinking of the pleasant dinner she'd shared with them the evening before. Her father mentioned that José had attended the meetings and had received enthusiastic support for his committee's plan to block financial support from reaching foreign espionage agents.

Irena had answered a telephone call from the ambassador's wife, who wanted Maggie's help with a party like the one she'd attended in Veracruz. Irena had told her she'd send a list with Maggie of many of the city's influential women, and that five with an X beside their names would be especially good to work with. Maggie couldn't help laughing at Beno's comment about the five marked names as she checked in with the embassy guard.

"Good morning, Miss Magodon," the Marine said looking down at his uniform. "Is something out of order?"

"Oh, no," Maggie was quick to answer. "Last night my father said if I made telephone calls to five of the names on a list I'd have no social woes for the rest of my life. Funny the way he said it, that's all. Nice day, isn't it?"

"Yes, ma'am," the officer said as he stared straight ahead. "Might one of those names be Kevin O'Toole?"

"Mrs. Kevin O'Toole? I'll have to check. Nice to meet you, Kevin."

Hunker room. It's the ambassador's "get it done" room, Maggie thought as she turned the key to get in. Get what done? The files borrowed from her at the Veracruz consulate were on the table mocking, challenging her to organize Mexican commercial data into a system for predicting and combating Nazi espionage. Mocking? Yeah. She was just dying to get at those coastal maps to study Ragnorak's trail, but it was the data in those files which had caused the ambassador to bring her from Veracruz.

She rolled her chair — whee, it was on casters — to the table and started to check each file. She found notations on the borders, slips between pages and other hints on data which might be added and possible sources for data on the entire country.

She had summarized them and prepared a work plan when Jenny opened the door.

"I didn't know you were here," she said. "The ambassador just left for all-day meetings, but told me I'd find you here."

"Any messages?" Maggie asked.

"None, but your guide from yesterday has been looking for

you."

"My cicerone? That's what he called himself. He must have a name," Maggie said, and thought she shouldn't have asked when Jenny looked away.

"His mother must have reared him to fit the name," Jenny said, facing Maggie again. "It's Filbert Fitzwilliam. And he insists on being called by that."

"Nothing wrong with it." Maggie laughed. "His father had to be a wimp to allow it."

"Don't say that out loud, Maggie. Filbert, junior, it is, and a chip off the —" She giggled. "I'll say shaving off the golden brick. He's one of the few career diplomats to become a prestigious ambassador."

"Ooh-woo!" Maggie exclaimed. "I owe you a bushel for that warning. Anyhow, why was he looking for me?"

"He says you were assigned to work for him, but it's actually the opposite. He's been assigned to work with you. I suppose I shouldn't say this. Frankly, nobody can tolerate having him."

"Can you?" Maggie thought of a lecture she'd received from Kyna, who'd advised that she'd better learn to recognize hidden talents in everybody. She went on before Jenny could answer. "Can you think of anything he's good at?"

"Women seem to like him."

Was Jenny judging for herself? "What else?" Maggie asked. "Did he go to college? Where? His major? Outside activities? How long ago? Where has he worked? What org —"

"Stop, Maggie," Jenny said, and opened a file cabinet. "I've never heard anybody say a word about any of that. Let's look." She took out a file and laid it out on her desk. "Here's his college record, Dartmouth. He lettered in three sports."

"History major, Phi Beta Kappa," Maggie added. "Class treasurer one year, president the next. Geez! That and sports, too? I'd say we have someone to work on, Jen."

"Yeah, but he's such a bore."

"I had him as a sissy," Maggie said, "but not now. I've got a job for him — two jobs, and the ambassador has already volunteered your help on one of them."

Jenny sighed. "Said you'd — Oh well. Sometimes he makes me sick. He'll say or do something that makes me want to scream. I've been on pins and needles worrying about what you were going to do to me."

"The ambassador?" Maggie's mind flew to the time she'd been dressed as a maid when he dragged through the hotel lobby, and how sure she'd been that onlookers took her for a whore. "He's done it to me, too," she said. "I told him I might call his wife about arranging a shindig between American and Mexican women, no men allowed, and that I planned to ask you if you'd help, too."

"Is that all? Swell, I'd love to."

"Talking about me? Say the word and I'm your man." Cicerone strode in, sat down and lifted a leg across his knee.

"We might make use of all that energy and muscle at that. What do you think, Jen?" Maggie said, glad that Jenny had put his file back in the cabinet.

Jenny rocked her head back and forth pretending to study him, then giggled when he lifted his chin in a haughty pose. "He might just fit right in," she said. "Are you ready to get him started?"

"Certainly. Come this way, Cicerone." Maggie beckoned and, when he followed, she indicated her stack of files. When you get a desk set up for me close to yours, I'll come down and we'll get started."

"Ready right now," he said, and picked up the stack.

* * *

Two mornings later, Maggie asked Jenny if she might have a late-afternoon appointment with the ambassador. At five-fifteen, he marched into the hunker room with Jenny in tow.

"This very moment," he began, "my wife and five of the city's most worthy women are meeting to plan a get-together, no gentlemen invited, to take place between now and the first of the year. Cicerone, trusty stalwart that he is — You know, I had to look up that word in the dictionary when he used it on me last Monday. Didn't let him know it though."

"Maggie's mother gave us the names of the women," Jenny cut in.

"Cicerone offered to handle the publicity," Maggie offered.

"Report complete. So why am I here?" the ambassador asked.

"Not quite complete," Maggie said. "Cicerone is organizing the commercial data files and has made some good suggestions. Unless you have something else to discuss, we have nothing more except that I plan to leave for Veracruz today on the evening flight and return on Monday."

The ambassador laughed. "You have Al worried, Maggie. He called me today, asking me what I wanted you to do in Veracruz. What could I say except that you'd been burning both ends of the candle and deserved some time with your parents."

It was Maggie's turn to laugh. "Queenie — Sarah must have told him I was coming. I told her I'd like to stay at the consulate."

He went out the door. Jenny followed, then he looked back in. "Be very careful, Maggie," he whispered. "You're dealing with dangerous men."

"I will. That was the best staff meeting I've ever had," Maggie said. "Thank you."

Chapter 32

Maggie watched a tug maneuver a ship into one of the customhouse docks as she strolled onto the Malecon in the still of dawn. A rustling sound came from above her — coconut palm fronds stirred by the slight breeze, or bats roosting for the daylight hours. Then she heard a seagull scream. A sharp blast of the tug's whistle as it backed out into the harbor seemed to release gulls by the thousands, their scree deafening as they scattered over the harbor. Gitana and her cart would be coming soon, she thought as she sat down on a wrought-iron bench. She watched the tug moor against the Malecon seawall and waved at its captain.

"Hola, Señorita."

"Hola, Capitán," Maggie responded as the tugboat captain came off his craft. I've known him since my first days in Veracruz, she thought. Oso's wife appeared with her cart at the top of the seawall steps. *"Hola Gitana. Cómo se va?"* she called, thinking she'd known her, too, from way before Oso. These are my friends, she thought as they approached. She smiled. Gitana hadn't bothered to call out her wares. Why should she call to a vacant park?

"For you, *Señorita, buñuelos, bananas, cola. Usted también,"* you, too. Gitana nodded toward the captain, then laid a piece of newspaper on the seat beside Maggie and put down some of her goods.

They chatted and Maggie learned that Oso had been known

on the Malecon as *El Toro*, the bull, before the arrival of El Ragnorak, and that the captain had donated full tanks of fuel for Oso's engine. When he went back to his tug, Gitana told Maggie that Oso was taking a cargo of logs from Allende to Tuxpan.

"Pan fresco, naranjas dulces, bananas," Gitana called suddenly and wheeled her cart toward a group of people coming onto the Malecon.

Logs — It was her and Oso's code name for oil refinery and pipeline equipment, and dollars to d— *buñeulos* Gitana did not know they had a code. Might Carlos have received a message from Oso regarding oil production equipment? Maggie wrapped the remaining *buñeulos* in the paper and hurried to the consulate.

"Hola Carlos, cómo está?" Maggie called when she saw him at the consulate gate ahead.

"Bien-bien, y usted?" he answered, then waited and they entered the consulate together.

Ten minutes later, she headed for Enrique's garage to get Clank. She'd learned nothing from Carlos except that Allende was a small coastal village about a hundred kilometers down the coast from Veracruz with no connection to oil production. Before she left, she asked him to relay her respects to others on the staff and leave any messages for her in her room. He had received no messages from Oso, so Oso's run to Allende was probably no more than a break-in cruise for his boat.

How could she be sure? There just wasn't much she could be sure about now that she didn't have dollar numbers to work with. How could she have thought the whereabouts of Queenie's receipts was a problem? What was her rush yesterday? Why so important to come to Veracruz?

At least Clank was freshly polished, gas tank filled and ready to go. She drove toward Antigua with no real reason to go. She might stop and chat with Zita, but what good would that do?

She crossed the bridge over Rio Antigua thinking of Thirteen Rabbit's narrow escape from the *Hedda*. She'd had a good view of the Buehler hacienda dock. Why not take another look? She drove back across the bridge, turned onto the trail and went past the papaya grove. The trail was overgrown with weeds and hard to follow. Had she missed a turn? Oops! She stomped on the brake pedal. The trail disappeared in a wall of green at least ten feet high and extending right and left as far as she could see. Gaps in the vines revealed a chainlink fence, and it must have been there for months for vines to grow to the top.

The papaya farmer could tell her about that fence, and he would have done it months ago if she'd remembered her promise to take his two children for a ride in Clank. Better late than never, she decided, and backed Clank to the papaya grove.

Maggie stared. Vines had climbed to the papayas on pawpaw trees. Weeds covered the paths and the house was deserted. She squeezed her eyes shut, shook her head and looked again. There was no doubt. This was the farmer's house and grove, and he must have abandoned it months ago.

She thought of her first visit to Antigua with Adolf, Sara Williams and her guests. They'd seen a woman hanging laundry on a line close to the river mouth. The pole stilted shack had been on the same side of the river, so that unless there was another trail, the fence blocked access to it, too. It was worth renting a boat to explore, Maggie decided, but first she'd find out what she could in Antigua.

Maggie parked on the mooring tree plaza and ordered a cola in the Hotel Ceiba. She sipped slowly and, when the proprietor wandered by, beckoned for him to sit a moment.

"When I was here months ago I got some papayas at a finca across the river," she said. Nobody is there now."

"Sí-sí, papayas bien dulces, — very sweet," he said.

"Does he have another finca? Where can I find him?"

The proprietor shrugged. "Who knows. I saw him at the

Santiago Shipping warehouse a few days ago with Señor Buehler. I think he will not sell papayas." He looked at Maggie as if expecting her to ask why, then said, "He was wearing a white suit and a necktie."

Maggie laughed, too, but too quickly. She gotten herself into a lamebrain conversation. That look on the proprietor's face was suspicion, not question. She glanced at her watch. "Ai-yah, I am late,"she said, and put a peso on the table. "I will find another finca. When you see him again tell him I miss his papayas. *"Hasta luego."*

She hurried out, got Clank started and there was the proprietor looking over the courtyard wall. She hoped Zita could tell her more and turned north toward the cantina. "Oh, no. Clank, that man was suspicious. Get Zita in trouble — hun-uh." She *ah-oo-gah'd* twice to get Clank's approval, drove past the Cantina and circled back to the Veracruz road.

Coincidence? Maggie drove slowly, thinking back to that July evening when she'd encountered Adolf at the papaya finca. Catrina had been there, too, and she remembered that Adolf and the farmer were discussing something when they approached her from the house, and she with Thirteen Rabbit stashed away in the rumble pit covered with palms and papayas. She'd been nervous— geez — scared stiff more like it. Adolf had looked into the car but hadn't really searched it, and had made no move to prevent her from leaving when the farmer cleared her way. Hmm. For Rabbit's sake, it was good she'd had those young palms in the car, but Adolf must have wondered — thought she was crazy.

Maggie drove faster. She'd rent a launch to explore the Antigua river shoreline, but first she'd get whatever the farmer could tell her if she could find him at one of the Santiago warehouses. Why do that? According to Oso, Adolf had neither used the *Hedda* nor been on the hacienda after that day and no one had been closer to El Ragnorak than Adolf.

She glanced at her watch — gunned Clank. Might she catch the eleven-forty flight to Mexico City?

* * *

Maggie felt lucky to get a window seat, and luckier still when an old gentleman who spoke no English sat beside her. A simple *yes* response each time he addressed her was enough to discourage further talk and allow her to concentrate.

She thought of José's FBI assignment, to stop money from reaching Nazi espionage agents, and her own, to keep tabs on El Ragnorak. His trail had backtracked to suspicion of José. Had his led back to her? Were they both following a loop, and Ragnorak off on a tangent neither of them had picked up? Forget El Ragnorak, Maggie told herself. Might she get him on a collision course with herself by anticipating what Nazi headquarters wanted him to do?

Maggie's taxi waited while she snatched a bite and ate as she changed clothes, then dropped her at the embassy.

"What happened? I thought you were going to Veracruz today," Jenny said, when she saw Maggie come in.

"Hi Jen. Just got back. Good trip. Can you get Cicerone in here? Talk later." She went into the room, dropped her purse on her desk and returned to Jenny's office. "Sorry, Jenny. I had no business talking to you that way. Had a bundle on my mind, I guess."

"Oh, forget it, but thanks, Mags. I'll get the creature for you."

Grinning, Maggie settled down at her desk. Only Kyna had ever called her *Mags*. Might she come to like Jenny just as much?

"Jenny told me, 'find Maggie,' so here I am in Veracruz."

"Glad you did, Cicerone," Maggie pronounced the final 'e' as she swivelled to face him. "Peon, colleague, boss, emperor — distinguished title, whatever it means. You game to take on a project?"

"Italy, Rome, gotha — emperor, Caesar, Cicero, orator par excellence at your service. Whatcha got?"

Maggie laughed. "Pull up a chair. Any problems if we run a security check on you?"

"No, but you could be asking the wrong person."

"Okay. We can start and hope you clear before we have to wrap it up." Maggie looked up to make sure the door was closed. "First thing, I've got to be sure you talk to nobody about what you'll be doing — the ambassador, okay, but no one else."

"Got that." He nodded.

"We know the Nazis are building up their espionage force in Mexi —"

"I kinda gathered that," he interrupted. "There had to be a reason for compiling all that file data and collecting more. Boring, nonsense job gets you to wonder what's the point. Good job to bitch about."

Maggie laughed. "But not talk about." He nodded and she went on. "We have evidence that they'll be moving personnel during and after next weekend. If they do, there must be a reason, maybe to cause havoc of some sort."

"Like blow up a bridge?" He frowned. "Tomorrow's Friday. You mean the day after and Sunday?"

"The following weekend," Maggie said. "We've got a lot to do before then, but would you check with the military attaché to see if they got those coastal maps?"

Maggie stepped into the reception office, thumbed at the ambassador's door and lifted her brow. Jenny tipped her head to go in. Maggie entered and closed the door behind her. "May I have a minute, sir?" He looked up, nodded, and she asked, "This young man, Filbert, I —"

"I'm sorry if you can't use him, Maggie. I learned so much from his father that I — well, I — I thought you were in Veracruz."

"Just got back. No complaint, I just have a question. Filbert introduced himself to me as my cicerone, so I call him Ciceroney. Think he likes it. He has oodles of energy and that's just what I need. He guessed why we're collecting that economic data. If he's clear to work on counterespionage, he could save me a lot of time."

A buzzer sounded. He picked up the telephone, listened, then said, "Call him back in ten minutes, Jenny, and will you bring me Filbert's file?"

"Can you get a message to Miguel?" Maggie asked when he hung up.

"Price, our darkroom friend?" He gave her a quick nod.

"Just an alert. Four Americans, at least they speak American English, will be leaving El Ragnorak's training base next week and will watch the bullfights here that weekend." She paused when Jenny entered with a folder. "I know the person who's been training them," Maggie continued after Jenny left. "Based on his background, I suspect that the Nazis will place them in the States to handle money exchange, transfer and other financial arrangements."

"Ye Gods! Maggie. This midnight soon enough?"

Maggie gave him a quick smile. "And tell him my Veracruz contact is Gitana, the early-morning and late-evening vendor on the Malecon across from Mr. Williams's house. She's the only one who sells *buñuelos*." A sudden thought of her first night in Veracruz crossed her mind. "That instructor might be training those men for almost anything. He was once the intercollegiate fencing champion, and I happened to be a witness when he killed two men with a knife in less than a minute."

He knows who I mean, she thought when the ambassador leaned forward, his right fist punching slowly into his left hand. Presently, he opened the folder and leafed through it.

"There is a problem, Maggie," he said. "I have never known a man whose jaw flapped more incessantly. His father was quite the opposite."

Maggie grinned. "Have you noticed that when people discuss trifles he loads them with more. They think he's answered questions when he's only put their opinions back in their own mouths." She saw his lips purse and twinkles in his eyes.

"That he did get from his father." The ambassador laughed. "You're suggesting that he'll be mum if he has reason to be?"

"My life is in danger while I work on this project," Maggie said. "I'll feel a lot safer if he's aware that his life is at stake, too."

"Then work him into your team, Maggie. Anything else?"

Maggie stood up. "I may have to go to Veracruz next week, but I'll be back to see my torero friend in the ring. Have you seen a bullfight?"

"Oh, yes, it's part of my job at times. Politicos visit and go to a bullfight so they can be authorities on Mexico when they return to the States. Your four Americans may drop in to register, and may want help to get into the arena."

"I'm sure they won't need help, but I'll give Jen their descriptions. If they turn up, I may ask Ciceroney to keep tabs on them."

Chapter 33

Maggie felt the building rock, locked her maps in the cabinet and fled to the street.

"Did the ambassador get out?" someone screamed.

"He wasn't here," Jenny shrieked. "Maggie's still inside."

"I'm right here," Maggie called, and worked her way to Jenny. She heard a woman scream, and a man drawl, "Aw, that weren't nothin'.. Yokohama in twenty-three, now —"

"Did a call come through from Veracruz?" Maggie asked and, when Jenny shook her head, dashed back into the building. Grabbing a telephone, she joggled the earpiece hook. Dead.

Maggie took out the map set she'd made for Oso, rolled it tight and ran back to the street to find Jenny. "I don't know —"

"Louder. I can't hear you," Jenny said.

"I don't know when I'll be back," Maggie shouted, "Phone's dead, but if Carlos calls, tell him I'm on my way to Veracruz."

* * *

Dusk was falling in Veracruz when Maggie took a taxi to Enrique's garage to get Clank. Had Jenny been able to reach Carlos? She honked at the consulate back gate, drove in when it opened and dashed to the rear entrance.

"*Hola, Señorita* Maggie," Carlos whispered from just inside the darkened doorway. "Don't come in or you'll miss Gitana on the Malecon."

"Thank you, Carlos," Maggie breathed, hearing voices

inside and recognizing Adolf's. She wheeled away, told the watchman she'd be back, and ran to the Malecon.

Easy does it, she told herself. Adolf's driver might be killing time on a park bench while waiting to pick him up. She swung her arm at a bat and thought of Nolan's wild misses on that evening when he'd suddenly become human barely two weeks ago. She looked up and watched other bitsy critters flit out from high among coconut fronds and disappear.

"Mira, Señorita, look. That hairy man who looks like a bear is coming."

"Hola, Capitán." Maggie dropped her gaze from bats and coco-palms to the tugboat captain.

"Gitana says come back in a half-hour," the captain whispered as he ambled aimlessly past her.

"If that's his boat arriving, then I'm leaving," she called, rising. "He's pestered me for the last time." She saw running lights far out in the harbor — green left, red right — a boat approaching and, from the corner of her eye, a man gazing over the harbor about thirty paces away. He wore dark slacks, brown or gray — she couldn't be sure in the gathering darkness, and a cardigan sweater which could be beige in color. The garb marked him as a tourist, probably American, and he must have been following her since she left the consulate.

Might the cardigan man be one of Kyna's four? "Nice evening, but strange things happen on the waterfront at night," she said in English as she headed back toward the consulate. "Didn't I see you up at the Cortez mooring tree a few days ago? You here on business?"

"Yes," he said. "Good evening. It's quite a harbor, isn't it?"

"Beautiful harbor," she said, thinking that his statement was somewhat contrived. Kyna had described a prissy man who'd eyed her in the cantina a few days ago, and this must be the one. If Oso were coming, as the tug captain claimed, she couldn't take a chance that he'd be recognized.

"Will you join me for dinner?" he said, falling in beside her.

"Now that's a welcome idea," she answered. He had a resonant voice with an American accent, and probably knew where she worked. Maggie indicated the consulate ahead and to their left. "Have you registered here yet?"

"My papers are in the hotel on the square," he said.

"I suppose I could meet you there in about an hour," Maggie said. She dashed through the consulate gate, closed it, waved from the top step and saw him walk briskly to the corner and disappear. Uh-oh — Adolf's voice, and he was just inside the door. Maggie scurried down the steps and ducked into the shrubbery between the wall and building.

Crouching, Maggie worked her way around the end of the consulate and, approaching Clank, wondered if she might have caught the cardigan man off guard while he stalked Adolf. She'd have to think about that, but not now. She got her maps from Clank, then left the consulate grounds by the rear gate and strode back to the Malecon. Looking north and south, she saw the usual people lounging on cast-iron benches, strolling, chasing children, but no Gitana. Then she saw the tugboat captain sitting on his port railing, a cigarette dangling from his lips. He took a long drag, blew it out the right side of his mouth, got up and strolled out into the Malecon Park.

Oso must have moored the *Santa Margarita* against the far side of the tug, Maggie decided, and followed the smoke trail across the tug. It was there, and she jumped down onto its deck.

"This way, Señorita." Oso's voice.

"Noches, Oso," Maggie whispered as she entered the wheelhouse, then descended the ladder to a darkened cabin. She heard the hatch close, then light flooded the cabin and she burst out in a whisper, *Gitana, Trece, Oso,* and you must be Pacheco.*" She shook hands, then rolled out the charts. "This map shows the Tuxpan shoreline and sandbars. Oso, point out

the best place for me to meet you."

"Magnífico!" he said, and indicated an inlet. "We'll meet you here at sunrise on Tuesday next week. Now we must hurry."

"I'll be there," Maggie said. "Good luck." She followed Gitana to the deck and onto the tugboat. *"Noches, Capitán,"* she said to the captain and, when Gitana sat on the railing beside him, she sat down, too. She heard an engine cough, purr softly, and the captain's low voice.

"That's Trece's truck engine," he said. "It's quiet, so Oso uses it to get clear of the Malecon before starting the noisy diesel."

"He's very smart," Maggie said, and chuckled. "Captain, I'm glad you warned me about that American on the Malecon. He's been with José in Antigua for two weeks."

"American? No, Señorita — German, and he's been there for months. He knew Oso when he had a bushy red mustache. Gitana has more to tell you." He paused, and Maggie was about to question him when he added, "It's about a young man who talks too much."

* * *

Maggie sat at Clank's wheel with blabbermouth Julio, son of Zita, beside her. Gitana had persuaded her to take Julio to Mexico City to rejoin Zita's husband and the others on José's bullfighting team. The Americans had left the hacienda, she'd said, and Oso had seen the *Hedda* near *Barra de Tonala* down the coast. It was expected to return to Antigua the next day, leave on Tuesday for the Tuxpan and Tampico areas and not return until sometime in January.

"Why are you going to Mexico City?" Maggie asked. Julio stared straight ahead. She was about to ask again when he spoke.

"I am man. Driving an auto is man's work."

"Not now, Julio. I was surprised when your aunt begged me

to take you to the City. Why didn't you go with your father?"

Julio said nothing and, when Maggie stopped at the Hotel Posada in Cordoba, he got out and marched off with a dark sack over his shoulder.

"Julio, take this," Maggie called, holding up a basket of Gitana's pastries. "Be back here at six in the morning if you want to go on to Mexico City," she whispered when he came back to get the basket.

He took it, turned away, then looked right back. *"Gracias,"* he said.

She saw a crooked smile on his lips and thought he might have understood that shouting out their pre-dawn departure time would be an invitation for trouble as they left Cordoba in the morning.

* * *

Charlador — blabbermouth — flapjaw, and *fanfarrón* — boaster, egotist, Gitana had called Julio, and Maggie had come to agree with her before sunup the next morning. He'd begun when she asked if he worked on the Hacienda Buehler?

"I am *banderillero.*"

"What do *banderilleros* do?" Maggie knew very well what they did, but thought the question might loosen his tongue.

Silence again. He made her feel like a lamebrain. "Could I be a *bander* —"

He burst out laughing.

Sure, he thought her ridiculous, but she forced a laugh, too. "Do *banderilleros* ride horses?"

"Picadors ride horses. My brother is a *picador.* He's too slow to be a *banderillero.*"

The kid would have to be quick to jab decorated darts into a bull's shoulders. He probably had eyes set on becoming a torero, too. "My friend don José is a torero. Do you —?"

"Are you his woman?" Julio cut in.

Boy! did his eyes ever flash. "No, Julio. I am nobody's

woman, but we are very good friends. See these earrings?" She touched her right ear hoop. "Don José made them for me."

"Ah," he murmured, admiring the earring, then he frowned. "But you are *Norteamericana.*"

"Mexicana, and I will watch him fight bulls in the *Plaza de Toros* this Saturday and Sunday."

"Then you will see me, too." Julio was sitting up straight now and had turned to face her. "My brother rides my horse. Bulls cannot hurt Don José when we are in his *cuadrilla.*"

* * *

It was nearly midnight when the caretaker opened the Montoya gate, and Maggie asked him to put Julio up for the night. She'd had her fill of his stories about bullfights and José, but his chatter had helped pass the time while they waited for repairs on earthquake damaged roads. She roused him at six on Friday morning, early enough for him to point out features of the arena, corrals and entrances before she dropped him off at his uncle's house. He explained that if she brought beautifully decorated banderillas to José on Saturday, the guards would allow him to escort her to José's dressing room.

"Your car will be safe if you park it behind my uncle's house," he told her when he got out. "Beautiful señoritas will bring him banderillas. Yours must be the best and I will stick them highest into the bull's shoulders."

While in the area, Maggie bought four banderillas at a store Julio had indicated. She'd add decorations of her own, she thought as she drove to the Montoya house to change her clothes before walking to the embassy.

"Good morning. I'm back. Good trip, but I'm tired. How are you?" she greeted Jenny when she arrived at the embassy. "Any chance I can see the ambassador?"

"Hi, Mags." Jenny motioned toward the ambassador's door. "You'd best knock right now. Good luck."

Maggie knocked. The door opened. "Hello, Ciceroney.

Good morning, sir," she said to the ambassador, then sat down when he indicated a chair. "I plan to leave for Tuxpan and Tampico sometime this weekend."

"So soon?" The ambassador leaned back, fingers steepled across his chest. "Sudden decision, isn't it? Perhaps you'd better fill me in on your plans."

"Well, sir, I suppose you'll think my reasons are only gut feelings, but when events fall into a pattern with my hunches, I believe it's time to get a wiggle on." Maggie hesitated. Why hadn't she expected him to ask such a question? "Here's what I've got. Ever since El Ragnorak's arrival last July, a succession of groups have shuttled through Hacienda Buehler." She went on to reveal information and its sources. "To sum it up," she said, "activity at the hacienda has practically ceased, indicating that the groundwork for something else is completed. It makes sense to assume that months of preparation are directed toward a major event — a big bang. Cicero," she said, glancing his way, "have you shown him the locations of Ragnorak stops which don't show on the Navy's detailed maps?"

When he shook his head Maggie went on. "The *Hedda,* with Ragnorak on board, spent time since the Fourth of July at seventeen locations between Veracruz and the U.S. border which don't show on any charts or maps. El Ragnorak spent time at six of those three times or more, all in the Tuxpan or Tampico regions and one near the U.S. border. Ragnorak will leave Antigua for the area next Tuesday and is not expected to return for a month. That could mean that his plans include some sort of activity in the States."

"Hold it there a moment," the ambassador cut in. "Not expected to return for a month does not mean the same thing as expected to return at a certain time. Might it mean that whoever gave you the information simply did not know?"

"I suppose so," Maggie said. "Oh, you mean — he's gone — moved on, maybe to the States — replaced by a better man

— could mean anything, I've got to hurry. My colleagues left Veracruz yesterday, and I'll meet them at one of Ragnorak's hidden stops near Tuxpan. It's important to be there before —"

"If I may interrupt, sir," Cicerone said. "Maggie, you may not like this, but it's all set. I'm going with you."

"You're right. I do prefer to go alone." Maggie stared at the ambassador.

"His Spanish is atrocious but it will do. His German is impeccable. My support is contingent on his going with you." The ambassador paused to write a note. Handing it to her, he said, "FBI numbers — for memory only. Incidentally, they support your prediction."

Maggie glanced at the paper and returned it. "I know those numbers," she said, then heaved a sigh and popped out of her chair. "Come on, Ciceroney. We've got to get ready. I'll keep in touch, sir."

"Cicero," she said when they reached the outer office, "I can't go on calling you that. How about you go tidy up your desk, and you can expect a new name when you get back."

"I'd like to hear you fight that out with my mother," he said, grinning, and went out.

Maggie turned to Jenny. "Quick, does he have a middle name?"

"It's Filbert K. I'll look." Jenny pulled his file. "Kurt," she said a moment later, "his grandfather's name — mother's side."

"Fits him," Maggie said. Jen was grinning. "Kurt it is," she added.

* * *

"I am friend of don José Alvarado," Maggie told Julio's aunt when she parked Clank behind her house on Saturday. "Julio told me I could leave my car here until after the bullfights."

"I was expecting you," the woman said. "Will you have a cup of coffee?"

"I brought banderillas for don José's fights, two for today and two for tomorrow." Perhaps I —"

"Let me see them," Julio's aunt said. "We should take them to him right away."

Maggie had wrapped them with care after the Montoya caretaker's wife added a few spangles and bows, but she couldn't refuse the woman. Besides, it would be nice to have her as a guide.

"Qué marvaillosas son!" the woman exclaimed when Maggie unwrapped them. "Oh my. There's a tuft of your red hair on the end of each. You are so beautiful, and don José will be so proud. He made your earrings, too, didn't he? He will be happy to see you wearing them. *Vámonos.* We hurry."

Maggie went across the street to the arena with her, and soon learned that she was the wife of an arena director, and of considerable importance. Maggie watched her knock on José's dressing room door with plump knuckles, and just then felt herself spun around from behind and firm lips meet hers.

"Gracious!" she murmured, leaning back to make sure they were José's lips. "You never did that before." She sought his lips once more then, leaning back again, she said, "I brought banderillas to bring you good fortune, and will be in the stands to root for you."

"Ah, I hoped you would," he murmured. "You're wearing the earrings, and I made you a gift to match them." He unlocked his door. "Come in, all of you. You must meet my cuadrilla, Maggie. They know about you. May I present Margareta Gutiérrez y Magodon," he announced in a loud voice, then opened a drawer. He withdrew a package and handed it to her.

Maggie opened it and raised high a silver locket and chain for all of them to see. "It's exquisite, José, thank you," she said, throwing her arms about his neck.

"Let me fasten it," José said.

She handed it to him, turned about and felt tremors run up

her spine as he lifted her hair. She heard the faint click of its closing, a kiss whispered in her ear — "two safes," another kiss, the other ear — "Rag's and mine."

Time to get ready," a man shouted.

Maggie spun about for a final hug, then scooted out the door. Dazed, she found her way to the viewing stands. The embassy had reserved eight bullring seats for two visitors from the States, three men from the embassy, Kurt, Jenny and herself. She found her party just as two men entered the arena with long, straight trumpets and blazoned forth the start of the *corrida*.

Teams of *cuadrillas* followed, each led by one or two bailiffs in sixteenth-century costume. Behind them, the *banderilleros* were dressed in black knee-length tights, short jackets, lace shirtwaists and capes, all richly embroidered, and black hats, pink stockings and black shoes. Next came *picadors* on horseback wearing broad beige-colored hats and jackets, cream-colored chamois tights and boots. Toreros brought up the rear, stiff legged, strutting, their dress similar to that of the *banderilleros,* but more richly embroidered in silver, gold and colored silk.

"Don't tell me they get all dressed up like that to fight bulls?" the stateside visitor said bursting into laughter. "Bet they don't even work up a sweat."

Maggie squeezed tight her eyelids. Why was it that rude people had such loud voices?

"But aren't the colors grand — simply vibrant," Jenny put in, "and there's something to be said for a sports event that's not all sweat and grime."

Hurray for Jen, Maggie thought. No wonder she's the ambassador's secretary. And Jen was right. She'd forgotten how thrilled she'd been to see the ceremony as a child. Her eyes followed the action — *banderilleros* planting *banderillas* in the bull's shoulders, *picadors* herding, the matador maneuvering, gracefully dodging, the kill and, finally the procession around the ring by the torero and his cuadrilla to only mild applause. Her mind was on José, his wild embrace, and she couldn't help feeling that he'd been acting a role to impress others in the room.

She fingered the locket, remembering the feel of his lips, his mumbled message — safes, Ragnorak's and his. The meaning was obvious — combinations must be etched into the locket. Which safes? Might there be two on the *Hedda*? What about the one in his apartment? No, probably not that one, because he'd think she wouldn't know it existed. A burst of cheering brought her attention back to the bullring.

So soon? The second bull was being dragged away, and applause for the victorious torero indicated a performance superior to that of the first. When the torero and his cuadrilla left the arena, Maggie heard the drone of voices increase in anticipation of José's bullfighting demonstration. Tomorrow he would be featured in the final fight and pitted against the most ferocious of all bulls. Would it be his last, or had he signed an extension of his contract?

Suddenly she heard screaming — women — the señoritas Miguel had mentioned were on their feet in the central grandstand across the arena, and she popped to her feet, too. Good-gracious! Miguel had said she would, and he hadn't exaggerated. José, below and to her left, was strolling slowly to the center of the arena surrounded by his cuadrilla. Maggie just had to laugh. Rising from the band on his silken balled hat was a red ostrich plume extending to more than half again his height.

The *cuadrilla* stopped and stood at attention in the center of the arena, but José, loose of limb, went on to stand before the grandstand. Slowly, he bowed, lower, lower, then rolled his head from side to side, his plume flicking small dust clouds off the arena floor. He straightened, pawed dirt with his feet, then ran back to his *cuadrilla* to meet a bull charging from the bullpen gate.

Maggie gasped, then saw a small banderillero dash forward, José grasp his cape and tease the bull into tight circles around his own erect body.

Trumpets blared. The crowd quieted, and Maggie heard the bailiff describe the routines José — and the bull — would perform.

"I can't believe this," Jenny gurgled. "What's so wrong with bullfights?"

"Me neither," Kurt said, his chest still shaking.

Maggie looked out at José. He was standing alone in front of the grandstand, apparently waiting for the applause to subside. The bull and his *cuadrilla* approached him from behind. Suddenly the bull charged. Caught off guard, the *picadors* followed with pike poles leveled. The bull swung his great head up, his horn raking José and hurling him onto the sharp pike of a *picador*.

Banderilleros closed in, jerked out the pike and held José erect. *Picadors* reached down from their horses to support him, one on each side, and whisked him from the arena.

Maggie was already on her feet. "Meet me on the street — this way," she hissed to Jenny. As she left the stands, she heard trumpets blare, and the bailiffs announce the next fight. She dashed toward José's dressing room, saw a stretcher being shoved into an ambulance and ran to it. Looking in, she saw two men, one with a stethoscope pressed to José's chest.

"Dígame, Doctor?" the other one said. *"Está muerto?"*

"Sí, está muerto — he's dead," the doctor answered, and pulled a blanket over José's head.

Chapter 34

That body, the white face, just couldn't be José, but Maggie knew it was. She backed out of the doctors' way. Creepy — dreamlike — everything was in slow motion to Maggie as the doctors closed the ambulance doors and the ambulance drifted silent as the mist from the dressing room area.

Dragging her feet, Maggie followed. What a horrible way for José to break his bullfighting contract. Had he signed to extend it? She broke into a run as she recalled more of the doctors' words. "Don't announce the death yet" and, "let the news break on the radio tonight." Yet she couldn't wait. José was a U.S. citizen, responsibility of the embassy.

She saw Kurt and Jen waiting across the street and ran to them. "Emergency," she croaked. Was the voice she heard really hers? She cleared her throat and began again, but quietly. "Mum's the word. José's dead. I mean it. Don't tell a soul. It won't hit the news until tonight. He was a U.S. citizen. Jen, I've got to see the ambassador. My car's about a block away. I'll pick you up here and can seat five if necessary."

Maggie spun away, then forced herself to walk and not run to get Clank. Where was José's *cuadrilla?* They must have assumed that the medics would care for him? If so, they might not know of his death until the evening radio broadcasts.

"Embajada Norteamericana, Señorita?

Miguel — it had to be, and how come he dropped out of nowhere at any time and she never knew where to find him?

Maggie opened his taxi door and said as much as she got in. "You do pop up at strange times, and you must be sent from heaven. Did you watch José?"

"I just arrived. You sick? What happened?"

"He's dead, Miguel, a horn or picador's pike." Maggie took in a deep breath, then went on. "That's why I needed to see you. It's about a message. You see —" She reached back to undo the locket's chain clasp then told him how people were watching when José kissed her the message — "two safes" in one ear, and "Rag's and mine" in the other. She fingered each ear, then unclasped the locket.

"Where's your car?"

"Right there." She pointed, then indicated that he should drive around the block. "Do you happen to have a magnifying glass? I think we'll find two safe combinations etched into the locket."

Miguel pulled to the curb and stopped. "Where is José?" he asked as he searched a tattered briefcase for a glass. "Ah, here it is." He examined the locket.

"He's in the ambulance which was right ahead of me when you picked me up," Maggie said. "They're not going to admit his death until tonight's news on the radio."

"Of course not," Miguel said, and wrote on a notepad. "Four numbers might be combinations. Good pictures of you and José. Where do you suppose those safes are?" He returned the locket and resumed driving.

"On the *Hedda,* for one," Maggie said. "I'll go for that one. Then there's the wall safe in his apartment and one in his shop."

"Apartment? No, Maggie. I own the building and — "

"You do? Then you won't even be a burglar when you get that safe." She described its location, then added, "Wish me luck. We'll start the Ragnorak hunt next Tuesday after I meet Oso near Tuxpan. Here's where I get off."

"One moment, Maggie." He turned into an alley and pulled

to a stop. "Tuesday may be too late. Supposing José was murdered — famous matador killed by a bull. What better signal to begin an action, and it would be spread openly by newspapers and radio, the victims of their operation."

"O-mi-god! With sub-messages worked into detail updates," Maggie murmured. "You mean get Ragnorak quickest. Oh, one thing's in our favor. If it's triggered by the papers they'd have to allow a time gap for delivery."

"True, which means radio," Miguel said as she got out. "It's about two hours' flight time to Veracruz. We may get one safe before the public knows about José."

"Radio — The doctor said to break the news on the radio tonight. Two hundred miles, bad roads, but I'll be in Tuxpan tomorrow," Maggie said, and slapped the taxi roof to get them both going.

Maggie stopped Clank where Jenny and Kurt waited with one of the embassy men. Jenny got in beside her and the men climbed into the rumble seat.

Maggie thumbed over her shoulder. "Does his nibs back there know that the bullfighter died and that he was American?"

Jenny shook her head. "I doubt it. I didn't know he was American. I knew you were friends, but was he — ah — special?"

"I don't dare get into that right now, Jen. Just get me to the ambassador."

"What happens when we see him?" Jen said. "He's at a reception in that big building on the corner."

"I make sure he knows that José Alvarado was an American citizen, that he's dead, the FBI knows, and that I'm leaving at once to be in Tuxpan by tomorrow noon."

"How could you report it to the FBI so soon? You've hardly been out of my sight."

"It's done, Jen. I'll run in." Maggie pulled to the curb and got out. "Mind parking? Then you guys come in, too."

* * *

Maggie knocked, pushed the door open and, entering, saw a houseman quick-stepping her way and motioning her back out. From doors ajar behind him, she heard a woman singing — classical, maybe opera she did not recognize.

"I must speak to the American Ambassador," she protested. "It's very important."

"Ssssh." Finger to lips, the houseman shook his head and went on motioning toward the door.

She stepped left to go around him. When he blocked her way, she darted the other way into a long hall, then left on a cross-hall and followed the golden-toned voice to a doorway and felt the grip of a hand on her arm. She wheeled, mouth wide open to scream, but closed it when the houseman let go. Easing the door open, she peered past the accompanist and his piano, and saw the ambassador and his wife seated amid other guests.

She felt a hand grasp her shoulder, but she dipped, shook, and stepped through the door. Eyes — must be hundreds, seemed to pierce her before she could flash the ambassador a signal.

She persuaded the houseman to let her meet the ambassador alone in the foyer. When he came she told him that José had died. "They didn't want spectators to know during the fights," she added, "so the public will hear on the evening radio."

"Why are we concerned, Maggie? Why interrupt —"

"He was a torero, jeweler, silversmith, FBI and an American citizen. Your man, Price —" She went on with an account of her meeting with Miguel. "There's still more than two hours of daylight, so Kurt and I are leaving right now for Tuxpan." A knock sounded and she opened the door for Jenny, Kurt and the embassy man. "Ready to go?" She aimed a finger at Kurt. "Tuxpan by noon tomorrow?"

Kurt clicked his heels, saluted and marched out the door.

* * *

The zigzaggiest of the road behind them, Maggie and Kurt found rooms in a small hotel in Tulancingo with a guarded warehouse for Clank.

"Early start? Five okay?" she asked when the bellhop had left them. "With José out of the picture, Ragnorak may push his timetable up a day and our team won't know about it."

"Sure. Bang on the door. You think The Rag has a schedule?"

Weight on his right leg, the other slung across it with toe resting on the floor, Kurt was propped by a long arm against the wall beside her door. She smelled the man in him and stepped back. His relaxed manner and look of confidence gave her a sense of team-like oneness and assurance of success in their mission. "There's no if," she answered. "He has a detailed plan. Good-night."

* * *

"Why the change, Mags? Yesterday you insisted on driving," Kurt asked as they put Tulancingo behind them.

"Sitting would have been torture. I had to stay busy."

"I thought about that," Kurt said softly. "Was this bullfighter someone special? You didn't feel jealous of the screaming señoritas?"

Maggie felt a smile quiver her lips, then burst out laughing, "Thank you, Kurt. Asking me that put me back on planet earth. No jealousy. I was thinking that he deserved adulation, but not for the romance of their dreams. He was my best ever male friend. He made these earrings and locket for me and taught me so much. I'll admit to occasional thoughts of marriage to him, but the subject never came up and I would never have done it. Did I tell you he was American?"

"I probably didn't believe it."

"FBI, too, and so am I. He was —"

"Wait a minute. You?"

"Uh-huh. State, but on loan to the FBI. We were

colleagues on parallel but separate missions. Yesterday I told my contact agent where he might find critical information on El Ragnorak which we need. He may already have it, but he'll also have found records exposing José as a double agent." She shrugged. "If it hits the news, he'll be branded as a traitor."

"And you'd carry the traitor brand, too, and that worries you?"

"No." Maggie stared at him. He had to be teasing her, but it was still too dark to read any meaning from his expression. "I lay awake last night going over what I'd seen at the arena. Know what I thought when I finally went to sleep?"

She saw his head turn her way and went on. "His contract to fight bulls expired yesterday. I believe he had refused to sign a five-year extension, but agreed to one more fight — today."

"You mean, they advertise Alvarado and pack the stands. He'd agreed to a high payoff for one more fight. He shows, gets killed. The promoters get all that money and don't have to refund the spectators — fishy. So maybe it wasn't an accident?"

"Maybe." Maggie nodded. "Murder. At least there's one motive. Now supposing El Ragnorak has been financing José over the years. Nothing wrong — but is there? Ragnorak, a Nazi, is a master espionage organizer. He discovers that José is a member of Mexico's National Counterespionage Agency. Talk about motive, and his being FBI makes it even stronger."

"But Mags!"

"What's wrong, Kurt?"

"Thousands of witnesses."

"About twenty thousand, and what better setting for murder could anyone want?"

"I'd have been awake all night if you'd brought this up yesterday, Mags, but won't murder be hard to prove?"

"Proof? Who cares? We've gotta think strategy, staying alive, winning." Maggie paused, hoping that Kurt would say something to contribute to her own thinking, but he remained silent and she went on. "Think about it, Kurt, about what we should do — what El Ragnorak might do. I don't want to steer your thoughts. Perhaps I've already talked too much. Hmm — talked too much — the boy who talks too much. Hmm." She caught him looking at her sort of funny like.

"You off on another brainstorm tangent?" he asked. "What boy are you talking about?"

"He's small, quick, one of José's *cuadrilla*, a *banderillero*. Julio rode up from Veracruz with me last Thursday and I wondered why he hadn't gone earlier with his father. He worshiped José — wanted to be just like him."

"Right or left, which way, Mags?" Kurt broke in.

"Poza Rica, go right to Tecolutla," Maggie said. "We should be there in a half-hour, and I hope our guys are still there."

"You were telling me about talk-too-much," Kurt said.

"And getting to what he and his Mexico City aunt told me. His father is the superintendent of Hacienda Buehler in Antigua, Ragnorak's headquarters and José's training arena. He's very pro German, and runs José's *cuadrilla* as the head bailiff. His brother is on the commission which manages the bullfighting arena. That's where I parked during the bullfight. Another brother heads the drive to build an arena which will seat fifty thousand and be the world's largest."

"Might this José's contract be with one of those brothers?" Kurt asked.

Maggie shook her head. "I doubt it because he'd been under contract for years, ever since fighting in Spain." She leaned forward and pointed. "Look out there. That's our flagship, the *Santa Margarita.*"

"That scow?" Kurt blinked and hunched his shoulders. "You mean it? Our battleship? Well, son of a gun."

"Stop, Kurt. I'll get a newspaper." She read the headline from the car — "CHAMPION Torero KILLED." Both got out of the car and just then heard a radio blare forth— JAPAN BOMBS HAWAII.

Chapter 35

Maggie sagged back onto her seat, Pearl Harbor, *Arizona* sunk, surprise attack, the voice of President Roosevelt blaring forth, beating on her ears. "Japan, I was wrong," she murmured — "not the Nazis, but Japan."

"Same thing," Kurt burst out. "You thinking what I'm thinking?"

"Ragnorak knew it was coming so he murdered José yesterday instead of today."

"Yeah," Kurt said, "but we're just guessing. Maybe he wasn't murdered."

"It doesn't matter now, Kurt. The attack right at the time of his death, intentional or not, will erase José from public interest. I can't let it distract me from what we've gotta do, so —" She sucked in a deep breath. "Think about it. Our job was to find out what the Nazis plan to do by tracking Ragnorak and reporting what we discovered. War changes that. We'd be too late. We've got to complete our job within one or two days."

"Yeah — staggering!"

Maggie motioned for him to move on. "I'm hungry and all those seagulls say there's a cantina close by. No matter what I say or do, let on that you think I've lost my mind."

"Hmm — might be fun." Chuckling, Kurt got the car going.

"Well." Maggie laughed. "Don't be too obvious. Maybe like you wouldn't want your wife to catch you at it."

"You mean that's who we are?"

"You're kidding, of course. No. We're exactly who our identification papers say we are — embassy — collecting trade-with-the-States data. Park beyond the boat."

She got out with her clipboard and approached a man counting sacks of beans as they were off-loaded from the *Santa Margarita.* "*Hola. Buenos dias, Capitán.* How much to take me to Tampico?"

The man pointed at Oso in the pilot-house.

"*Capitán,*" Maggie said, and felt a wave of relief when Oso stepped onto the dock and scowled, a sign that he was going along with her pose as a stranger. "I need a ride to Tampico. How much?"

"Take the bus at Tuxpan."

"The bus doesn't go to all the shoreline villages. How much?"

Oso shrugged. "Five hundred pesos."

"*Estás loco.*" She waved him off, saw Kurt headed for the cantina and followed. "*Desayunos — dos, por favor,*" she shouted to a man hunched over a blaring radio as they took seats at a table. "I ordered two breakfasts," she told Kurt. "Can you understand what's on the radio?"

"Some, but the announcer talks too fast. Horrible!"

"Come see the cabin," a voice rumbled from the entry, "private, three hundred pesos."

Maggie saw Oso standing at the entry. "Fifteen minutes," Maggie said. She waited for the waiter to serve and leave, ate a bite, and went on. "There's one way to catch up before Ragnorak's big bang. Get into his safe and steal his plans."

"Talk about losing your mind." Kurt paused, then stared into her eyes a long moment. "You're loco."

"Can't argue the point." Maggie stuffed all that was left of her breakfast into her mouth and rose. "Come after you pay the bill."

Outside, Maggie squinted into the morning sun, located Oso, and crossed the dock. Kurt emerged from the cantina. She beckoned, then followed Oso into the *Santa Margarita*.

He faced her as she got off the ladder. "Señorita, we must catch him now or lose him. You can't go with us."

"Okay, have it your way," she said. "If you don't want me on your ship when you attack, I'll let you be heroes and rescue me off the *Hedda*.

Oso just stared at her. Dear God! He was huge.

"Perfect!" Kurt exclaimed as he stepped off the ladder. "Ravishing flaming-haired dream-girl rescued from Nazi spy. I'll write the —"

"Cut it, Kurt," Maggie broke in. "These guys don't understand your kidding and—"

"You would."

"I said stuff it. This is serious. " Maggie faced Oso. "You heard the news? We're at war." Oso nodded, and she said, "Gitana — Zita said the people at the hacienda think El Ragnorak will not come back to Antigua. That means his work is done, his organization ready. We can expect bridges and dams to blow up, oil well fires, wrecked trains, all sorts of terrible things unless we get the *Hedda* log book and his plans. It doesn't matter if he escapes. I've got to get onto the *Hedda* and into his safe. Where's Trece? Oh, I forgot." She waggled a thumb at Kurt. "That's Kurt. He works with me and can speak German. Where's Trece?" "*Buenos,*" Kurt said and grasped Oso's hand.

Oso shook it and answered Maggie without looking at Kurt. "Our cargo from Veracruz to Jolzitlan was an engine. Trece told the engineer who came with us to install it, that it was just like the *Hedda's* engines which he had worked on. The engineer wanted Trece to install it. Hmpf!" Oso snorted. "No grease under his fingernails."

"He's installing the engine?" Maggie said. "On the

Hedda?"

"They'll pay him one thousand pesos," Pacheco cut in.

Oso added, "He'll stay with the *Hedda* until we meet him near Tampico."

"Swell, and meet me, too," Maggie said. "Somehow, I'll get on the *Hedda*. Where is Jolzitlan?"

"Not far," Oso said, turned to a narrow desk-like shelf and began to sketch. "It's on this side of the *Rio Nautla* at the river mouth. Drive across the river to Nautla, then rent a launch to get back to the boatyard."

* * *

Kurt slowed to a stop on the Nautla plaza and Maggie got out. She pulled her backpack from the rumble seat, said goodbye to Kurt and felt her spirits sink as Clank faded from sight.

Alone like biblical Daniel, she'd taken the first step into the lion's den — Ragnorak's lair. She remembered the photo in his stateroom, the signature — *Ragnorak Holz*. Dear God! Jolzitlan was named after him, but spelled the Spanish way. That's where she was going — where she had to charm her way onto the *Hedda* — into his lair.

How might she approach El Ragnorak — convince him to take her aboard? What did she know about him? Nothing, really, except that he was subject to outbursts of vicious fury. It must be fear, the black reward, which held his organization together. There must be ways to gain his favor other than by blind loyalty and obedience.

News of Hawaii, bombing attacks, casualties, broke into radio music coming from a window, and was suddenly shut off. Somebody didn't care, but from all about the broadcast sound increased, and she wondered how people were reacting in the States? Had President Roosevelt spoken to the nation — declared war?

If not, he surely would, but she couldn't wait. She cocked her cap to the side, shrugged on her knapsack, and set off for the river.

* * *

The fueling station and boatyard had been in operation only a short time, the launch owner told Maggie as they left Nautla. When she pulled a clipboard from her pack to take notes he started to talk, and she pumped him for the information she needed about Nautla, its commerce and aspirations. He told her, too, that the grand house where El Ragnorak lived at Jolzitlan had a magnificent view, but it had been abandoned after the docks were washed away by a hurricane.

"When was that?" Maggie asked.

"Twenty years, and only a caretaker there. The owner returned and blasted a wide passage to a cove where new docks are located."

"Does he have a family? Wife? Children?" Maggie asked. "Is he polite? What sort of man is he?"

"*Muy agradable, sencillo, también* — pleasant and straightforward. We are proud to have him here again." The boatman swung his launch into the entrance to a cove. "He was once very handsome, but now —"

Maggie glanced his way, caught his shrug and noticed the bow of a cabin cruiser protruding from between two platforms. "I would like to meet him," she said, dreading the thought of it.

"*Muy bien.* He will thank me for bringing him such a pretty woman."

Uh-oh. Had the boatman done this before? What might have happened to the women? "I will thank you, too," she managed to say as she heaved her pack onto a landing.

"*Hola, Señor Holz,*" he called just then. "I bring you a guest."

Maggie looked up and her breath caught. El Ragnorak was waving to the boatman from the top of the steps. She debarked, climbed up and held out her hand. "*Mucho gusto, Señor Holz,*" she said waving toward the cruiser, and went on in Spanish.

"Isn't that cruiser the *Hedda*? Her bow is raked under almost the same way. Excuse me. I'm Margaret Magodon."

"How do you know the *Hedda*?"

"*Pues, Adolfo,* Adolf Buehler is a very good friend and I've been on the *Hedda* with him many times. It's the nicest cruiser I've ever seen."

"Governor Gutiérrez's daughter."

"*Verdad Señor,* by adoption, but he is my real uncle."

"You honor me with your visit, and you will be my guest for dinner. Come."

"Thank you," Maggie interrupted, "but I'm not dressed for dinner and I only have work clothes in my knapsack." As she indicated her pack on the landing below, she saw the launch headed for a landing across the cove. Why hadn't she asked what the launch was delivering? El Ragnorak's countenance — she looked away from his hollow eye socket — forced his name, Mr. Holz, to mind as a piercing whistle came from two fingers in his mouth. He waved, pointed, and Maggie was surprised by the gentleness of his voice when he spoke.

"Chico, will you please take Miss Magodon's luggage to the guestroom with the Gulf of Mexico view?"

She saw a boy snatch up her pack and run off. Her host's back was to her for a moment and, when he faced her again, two eyes bulged from deep within their sockets. Which might be the glass one? Tempted to comment, she smiled instead.

"Now to show you our facility," the man said. "You are right. The cruiser in the slip is the *Hedda*. Two cruisers, or one twenty-two meters or less in width can be serviced in the slip, and we are preparing a separate drydock."

"What about fuel?" Maggie asked. "Can you pipe it in?"

"Not yet, but soon."

He showed her an existing oil storage tank and preparations for another, and answered all her questions. She picked up her clipboard to take notes as they passed the guestroom, and he said from the open doorway, "I would be delighted if you use this room tonight."

"Will you excuse me?" she said and, suddenly trembling, ducked into the bathroom. — "Will you come into my parlor, said the spider to the fly." — El Ragnorak — The man had a certain charm about him, and she'd come to do exactly what he had invited her to do — work her way into his circle. Did she dare accept his invitation — enter the spider's web? She thought of sailors, hundreds, dying in Hawaii. Really, her job, she had no choice.

He was still in the doorway when she emerged. Turning slowly to take in the room, she said, "How could I possibly choose a Nautla hotel over a room like this. If you're willing to put up with me in my grubby work clothes, I'll be most happy to accept."

"Fine, that's settled," he said. "Now, suppose we dispose of all you need to know over here on the balcony. Would you care for coffee, tea, something else?"

She hadn't noticed a man in a white suit close by, but when her host raised two fingers, she recognized the *Hedda* steward. *"Hola,"* she said smiling, and with a quick bow of her head. "I believe I'll have the same as—"

The steward grinned, hustled off and served them both Coca-Colas when they were seated.

"Remarkable memory," Holz said, cocking his head back at the departing steward. "How more can I help you? What are your plans?"

"Take the bus to Tampico," Maggie answered quickly. "We came — my partner from the embassy and I arrived from Mexico—" She broke off when he lifted a hand.

"You might consider going with us in the *Hedda* instead," he said. "Excuse me a moment."

The spider weaving its web, Maggie thought as she watched him go to the door. She hadn't accepted his invitation, but how could she turn it down after considering stowing away as a means of getting aboard? Too easy. What had she done? What was he planning to do with her? He'd sent her pack to a bedroom. Might that mean he intended all along to have her stay — or not escape? Had the pack been searched? Probably. She'd seen the *Hedda* but no workmen. Come to think of it, other than the errand boy, steward and Ragnorak, she'd seen nobody and had not noticed because of his charm and open responses to every question she asked. She'd been a fool to think she might outwit a man famous for his treachery and cunning. Well — Maybe so. Tangled or not in the spider's web, she hadn't shown signs of alarm and might even be alive because of it.

"Daybreak tomorrow," Holz told her as he resumed his seat. "The engineer plans to start the new engine at midnight. Breakfast will be aboard the *Hedda* at seven tomorrow. If you'll excuse me, I'll take you to your room and return in about an hour to escort you to dinner."

Maggie, showered and dressed in a china poblana, was ready when Mr. Holz tapped on her door at six o'clock. "Our meals are simple here," he told her as they crossed the hall to the dining room.

It lacks a woman's touch, was Maggie's first reaction on entering the room, but she couldn't fault the steward's efforts. Exquisite furniture was cheapened by the plain plywood wainscot, and paintings of European castles crowding the walls. They were probably priceless, but looked out of place in a dining area, and there were no flowers. Her host was most courteous and, when she complimented the steward on preparing such a delicious dinner, his lips spread slightly and his seeing eye shone.

But he put down his fork and sat straight in his chair when she asked about progress of the war in Europe.

"The war in Europe is a European war and should not

concern other countries," he stated. Her mention of Japan's
Hawaii bombing brought a similar response: "Spats between
children ought not be noticed."

"When thousands die it's hardly a spat," she countered, but
backed off and asked what plans he might have for the future of
Jolzitlan.

The topic consumed the evening until ten o'clock when he
walked her back to her room. "Be sure to keep your door locked
until I come for you in the morning," he advised, then clicked
his heels and turned away.

Maggie locked her door and made sure the balcony door and
shutters were secure before going to bed. She was tired, but
questions flooded her mind. What would she do if denied
passage on the *Hedda* at the last minute, and what if Thirteen
Rabbit were not the mechanic installing the engine? She'd
come up in an elevator, but how far? She got up and peered out
to the balcony — nobody, so she went out and, across gulf
waters, gazed along a shimmering path to the rising moon. Then
she looked down, saw a rocky shoreline and lines of breakers
about as far down as from her eighth-floor apartment in St.
Louis to the street. Leaning far out, she saw no balconies
below, only rocks. Her room was on the face of a bluff, or cliff.

Why hadn't she been more nosy? She leaned out again and,
looking up past the narrow overhang, saw stars and, farther east,
clouds, then a star moving. It grew brighter, came lower — a
small airplane. It was barely above her level when the roof of
the balcony on her left hid it. Moments later, the soft purr of an
engine stopped.

"Think, Mags, think," she mumbled as she went inside and
locked the door but tipped up the window shutters to admit
moonlight. Sitting on the edge of the bed she listened. The
sound of the surf was muted and with it, she heard something
with a steady rhythm, then came a low voice from outside her
room. Barefoot, she went to the door and, on tiptoes, peered

through the peephole. She felt her chest tighten. The cardigan man she'd seen on the Malecon— the prissy one of Kyna's cantina four, was in the center of the hall whispering to a uniformed guard. She tiptoed to bed, lay down, popped back up. She had to do something to quiet the thumping in her chest.

What might cause that rhythmic sound? It had a beat familiar from her past and suddenly she had it — the old steam engine at the power plant two blocks from home in Torreón. At once, she recognized another faint noise, wheezy and intermittent while it sounded, with irregular periods in between — St. Louis again, her apartment elevator three doors down the hall. This elevator had stops at different floors. This was no simple Ragnorak residence on top of the bluff. It had its own steam powered electric plant, airstrip, boatyard with a slip wide enough to berth a submarine and water deep enough to take it. What else? What might she discover in the light of dawn?

Chapter 36

"Sí, sí. Estoy despierta," Maggie called when a knock on her door wakened her. She reached for the bedside lamp.

"Ten minutes, Miss Magodon." It was El Ragnorak's voice.

"I'll be ready." She turned on the bedside lamp and glanced at her watch — three o'clock. She'd expected a call at six. Was this a ploy he used to assert his authority?

She dressed in an emerald-green cardigan over a men's khaki shirt, khaki skirt, green socks and saddle shoes. She gathered her hair at the neck and put on her St. Louis cap with the visor pointed up at a sharp angle. She met her host in the hall and, thank God, his glass eye was in its socket. Her cap must have tickled him, for he even smiled at the sight of it. Without a word, he picked up her knapsack and neither spoke nor let it go until he dropped it on the bed in the guest stateroom on the *Hedda.*

"I apologize for the early departure," he said, turning on the light and indicating a steamer blanket at the foot of the bed. "It will be cold on deck." He clicked his heels. "Until breakfast at seven."

"Thank you," she said, and sat on the bed thinking to set more details of Jolzitlan in her mind. Starting at her bedroom door, she'd taken six steps to her right and a right turn into a hall about eight feet wide — probably three meters. From there she'd taken one hundred and thirty-one steps to the elevator in a northerly direction roughly parallel to the shoreline. "Oops," she muttered, rising. The *Hedda* was moving and she hoped there was still enough moonlight to see how the cove was laid out.

Maggie snatched the blanket off the bed, doused the light and shut the door. The engine room was straight astern. Was Thirteen Rabbit on the other side of the door or even aboard? She had to discuss strategy with him, but would miss seeing details of Jolzitlan unless she looked right now. The helmsman was speaking English into the tube to the engine room when she reached the pilothouse.

"Tiene que hablar Español," came back in Thirteen Rabbit's voice, and she heaved a relieved sigh.

"He said to speak Spanish," Maggie interrupted. "Good morning. My name is Margaret Magodon." Now Rabbit knew she was aboard.

"Tell him the tide's ebbing so go slow — one engine."

Maggie translated, then said, "I thought the cove was deep enough for a submarine."

"Had one in here last week— minor repair. Not on this side, though. Channel between rocks here, and moonlight's — feel it? Scraped one, but not enough to rouse the gaffer."

"Jolzitlan was a surprise to me." Maggie said. "I have a good map of the coast but it doesn't show."

"It's part of Nautla, and charts of the harbor before the world war show it," he said as the cruiser cleared the alcove and picked up speed.

"Voy atrás. Sorry, I forgot you don't speak Spanish," Maggie said. "I'll see more from the afterdeck. Talk to you later."

"Hey. It's cold back there. Take the blanket."

"Thanks," Maggie said picking it up. "I supposed you were Afrikaans but you speak American."

"Definitely Afrikaans, South African citizen, but twenty-four years and all my education in the States. It didn't wear off overnight."

Maggie dallied at the window a moment to make sure Thirteen Rabbit had time to get to the afterdeck, then felt thrilled by his gusto, when he clasped and pumped her hand.

"You must signal me when we pass the *Santa Margarita,*" he said. "Five minutes later I will sink the *Hedda* and Oso will — "

"No. The *Hedda's* log, and Nazi plans are in his safe. I must get them. They are much more important than the life of Ragnorak."

"No. Ragnorak first. Who cares about paper?"

"Then trap Ragnorak but don't sink the boat."

"Impossible. I am one. They are four."

"No, Trece. We are two. They are one busy, three sleeping. Who are they?"

"Steward, guard, helmsman. Steward is the radioman."

"Can you cut off power to the radio?"

"*Sí.*" He raised three fingers. "Main switch, fuses, battery terminals."

"Where will Oso meet us?"

"He'll wait three kilometers off Tecolutla. When he sees us coming, he'll go north. Five minutes after —"

"Look," Maggie cut in. " The moon has set. It will be darker before sunrise. He might not see us."

"Oh." Rabbit looked out over the gulf.

"Think about it, Trece," Maggie said softly. She'd caught him in a flaw so he might accept another scheme. "Do you know where the safe is?"

"The lamp table — port side aft in the pilothouse."

"*Muy bien,*" Maggie said. "Meet me here in fifteen minutes." He moved toward the hatch. "Wait," she whispered. "When we catch them, how do we tie them?"

He lifted the lid of a cockpit bench and pulled out a line. Drawing a knife, he cut it into four lengths, gave her two, then went below.

Maggie followed a moment later wondering if it was possible to lock the cabin doors.   Tiptoeing down the passageway, she saw that they all opened into the rooms and she couldn't block them closed. She looked again. Latch handles on the two bow cabin doors were four to five inches apart. Tied together, neither door could be pulled open from the inside. The steward and guard would be trapped. With the helmsman occupied, Thirteen Rabbit and she would be left to confront El Ragnorak.

Maggie beckoned Thirteen Rabbit from the engine room and indicated the closeness of the handles.   He nodded understanding, and both returned to the engine room.

"When I see the *Santa Margarita,* I'll bind the latches," she said, and drew back as a crooked grin spread across his face. Even the darkness in the passage could not conceal the wildness in his eyes as he raised both hands and slowly clenched his fists.

"Mira," he said, shaking them. "Now I have the power of Volcán Orizaba."

"I suppose I could rustle up some coffee," she said when she returned to the pilothouse.

"I have a thermos. Talk," the helmsman said. "I'm getting sleepy."

"Did you go to college?"

"I did. Master's degree in naval engineering."

Maggie saw something to port and toward shore, but asked, "Why did you go back to South Africa?"

"Curiosity. I was born in Windhoek. Dad died and I — That's private, take another tack."

"I'll see what I can do about the coffee," Maggie said, sure they were overtaking the *Santa Margarita.* She retrieved rope from her cabin, fashioned a bowline knot, looped it around the two door latches. Another loop then she pulled the rope tight and secured it with double half-hitches. She got the other rope, then opened the engine room door.

"The *Santa Margarita* is close, about three hundred meters," she told Rabbit.

He pressed a large potato-size gray object with a dangling cord in her hand. "When this fuse burns to here" — he indicated a knot in the cord — "throw it high over the water, then shout: 'fire in the engine room.'"

No, she thought, but he'd lit the fuse. She scrambled up the ladder, through the lounge to the afterdeck and drew back her arm. A glance at the fuse showed the sparkle still had inches to go so she lowered her arm and waited — waited. Finally she heaved it high off the port side and dashed to the down ladder. The engines died as she saw the lounge flare with light and, through hands over her ears, heard a piercing boom. Then she shouted, "FIRE , FIRE — ENGINE ROOM."

She waited, smelling smoke. A light came on down in the passage and she saw a shadow flit by as a door banged, bounced and banged again. Then she heard a thud, metal on metal, another thud and a dying wail — silence. Finally, a whisper reached her.

"*Bien hecho, Señorita. Qué lástima. Creo que está muerto el hombre.* I think the man is dead."

Maggie heard the bow cabin doors rattling and shouted. "Steward, guard, we had a bit of trouble out here but everything is under control. Stay in your bunks until we clean up the mess and find a way to let you out." She repeated what she'd said in Spanish, French, Italian and Portugese, then rejoined Thirteen Rabbit.

"The helmsman is armed," Thirteen Rabbit whispered. "We should wait for Oso."

His voice and grin told of victory. Of course he would wait for Oso, show him the engine room deck — blood — the body, bloody, too, and ready for sharks to complete the revenge for their friends. Let them have El Ragnorak, she thought. She had to have plans from his safe.

.   "Open portholes to let out the smoke," she said, "then help me look for a safe in Ragnorak's cabin."

Thirteen Rabbit beckoned, led her to the master stateroom door and indicated the far bedside lamp. "The safe in the pilothouse is above that lamp. Maybe it has a chute to the cabinet above that lamp."

Maggie forgot about fresh air and looked in the cabinet. She dialed one of the three combinations from her locket and heard a faint click. "Eureka, it works," she murmured, pulled open the door and muttered, "He emptied it." She spied the red leather-covered logbook and took it out, then found two black packets just like the one she'd seen José put in his safe. There was a small notebook, too. Maggie took them to her stateroom, shoved them into her knapsack, then approached the engine room.

"Trece," she whispered.

She opened the door a crack and peered in. No Rabbit — no Ragnorak, but dawn light was coming down from an afterdeck hatch way to the aft. El Ragnorak must have gone out that way. She saw the light disappear, then Thirteen Rabbit crawled into the engine room.

"I'm going up to the pilothouse," Maggie said. Surprised when he made no attempt to stop her, she took one step, another, then another. "Hey, you up there in the pilothouse, it's just me. I'm coming up, I'm not armed, so I don't expect to be shot." She heard him laugh.

"You're the last person I'd have taken for a pirate," he shouted. "I don't get paid to fight pirates. Damned if I can figure out what happened. Heard a bang then the diesels died. You got friends on that scow? I don't see any crew."

"Véngate Trece," Maggie called out. "Tell Oso to come aboard." She found the safe in the corner and opened it with the same combination she'd used on the one below. She looked

down through a chute to the other one.

"Hi, Mags. How in blazes did you do it?"

"Kurt, tell you later," Maggie called back. "Oso, there's one Afrikaaner here who may be okay and another locked in a cabin below. There's a steward, too, and I don't know what language he speaks. Tend to them, please. Come below, Kurt, I need your help.

"Sit," she said, closing and locking the door when he entered. "I've been hoodwinked, sucked in. I was so proud to get onto the *Hedda,* that I got careless and let what we needed slip right past me. I spent last night in Nautla, well— Jolzitlan, which doesn't show on the map. I had a chance to prowl, but didn't because I was too confident of finding what we need on the *Hedda."* She opened her knapsack and removed the safe contents. "That's all there is. Can you get the FBI on the radio?"

"Probably if you have access numbers. Write it out, but short."

* * *

On Tuesday afternoon, December 9, at four forty-seven, Maggie pulled Clank to a stop at the United States Embassy in Mexico City. "Take off, Kurt," she said, "Look who's coming."

"Jen," he called, and scrambled out to receive her charge. He lifted her, spun her around and they trudged arm in arm into the embassy. Maggie climbed out, too, locked Clank and broke into a run when she saw Irena and Governor Benancio Gutiérrez appear at the embassy door. Maggie rushed into Irena's hug and felt Benancio's arms encircle them both.

"Somewhat on the fun side to have a pirate daughter," he said after they'd shared a tender moment. "Let's see if the ambassador will let us in."

"Can't we just go home?" Maggie begged.

"Very soon." He wrapped an arm around each, and they entered the ambassador''s office.

Maggie looked about the small group: Kurt and Jenny in the corner whispering, five from the embassy staff, a military attaché, a Mexican Navy representative.

"Hello, Victor," she said raising her hand. "For those who don't know him, meet Commander Victor Dalpica, Mexican Navy." There was another man, gray-haired in a beige suit and red necktie. He wouldn't be an embassy man because they just did not dress that way. Then there was the ambassador, her parents and herself.

"Everybody seated?" The ambassador glanced about. "We have a strange situation. Two people with separate stories to tell accomplished a fantastic feat and, I'm sure they don't even know what they did. All of you have reason to know what happened and will understand why nothing will be distributed to the press. I remind you, we are at war. Price." He indicted the man in the beige suit. "You have all the details. Fill us in."

Price — Maggie racked her brain. Who was he? Oh, of course— Miguel.

"I only have details of the wrap-up. You'd have to get the complete story from Maggie. Hello, Maggie. My congratulations." He looked away from her and began.

"Maggie's been in Mexico only six months — eventful months. I'll give you a short summary. The intelligence community had lost track of a notorious Nazi spy. During Maggie's first week in Mexico, she identified him here. She accumulated evidence, identified his associates, read his thoughts, anticipated his operations and provided the information leading to major Nazi espionage failures this past Saturday, Sunday and Monday. I'll be specific. Forty-one Nazi espionage agents were captured, including the chief of their North American operations. More than a million dollars in cash intended for agent expenses was confiscated, as well as millions in assets intended for sale to provide cash for future espionage expenses. We got explosives, incendiary devices, a boatyard which had already serviced a submarine. Papers other than money, consisted of plans and schedules for the demolition of transportation facilities, dams and power plants. Maggie," he faced her, "The third lock combination you gave me last Saturday opened the Ragnorak safe at Jolzitlan. Just as you predicted, it contained all the plans I mentioned. Did you know that Ragnorak was returning to South Africa when you nabbed him? His replacement had taken control just that day. Thank you, Maggie."

"Thank Kurt," Maggie said. "He and the radio did it. If he hadn't been on the spot and able, we would have been too late. We were both sorry to miss President Roosevelt's declaration of war. Now it's your turn, Kurt."

"Your stage though, Mags," he said. "You're doing swell."

"We were blessed by having a young Guatemalan diesel wizard on the team, a burly Afrikaans boat builder, a Mexican seaman, a taxi driver, many others, like a waterfront vendor woman and a cantina cook. Very special were my mother and dad — Irena and Beno." She stood up, sat on the governor's knee and leaned over to kiss Irena on the cheek. "Ma, let's go home," she whined into roaring laughter.

*   *   *

Maggie climbed steps to the Veracruz Malecón, turned and waved, then headed for the consulate.

"Consulado Norteamericano, Señorita?"

"Miguel," she said softly and sat down, not even bothering to see who was seated on the bench. "I got your message. Didn't you say to meet tomorrow?"

"One day more to think about it. Are you looking for a job?"

"Me. No. Why?" Maggie turned and stared at him.

"How's your visit going?"

"Swell. That was Oso, who just let me off." Maggie laced her fingers behind her head and stretched out her legs. "He doesn't have to hide anymore. Because we're at war with Germany, he likes Oso better than his German name. Makes him feel tough— macho. You own José's plant, don't you? What's with the new name, *Plateria Alarcón?"*

"His sister. By the way, Maggie, there was a cruiser, the *Hedda,* I believe. You delivered its crew to our navy. What about it?"

"Yes. I did. You trying to get me to talk? Try again. We were well outside the three-mile limit when I last saw it. Does it matter? It was owned by Ragnorak Holz and registered in Cape Town, South Africa. Are you asking in an official capacity?"

"Hardly. Mrs. Williams expects to use it frequently now that Adolf Buehler is moving to the Antigua hacienda."

Maggie sighed. "I might as well tell you. We were northbound east of Tuxpan when there was a loud explosion. Ragnorak tore through to the engine room. He was six-feet-seven, you know, and split his head open on the header over the engine room door. The *Hedda* didn't run again. You might be interested to know that Oso has two new marine diesel engines with drive shafts and propellers. He's building two more boats like the *Santa Margarita,* and says we don't owe him a single centavo in exchange for risking his boat."

Miguel laughed. "I suppose his boat works will come out with a cabin cruiser one of these days."

"I wouldn't be surprised, but not until after the war when he can get engines for it. Incidentally, I'd better come clean on this. We didn't turn the *Hedda* helmsman over to the FBI agents. It happens that he's a naval architect and a close friend of Oso's brother, the one Ragnorak murdered. I think he was glad we played pirate. Why did you ask if I was looking for a job?"

"José's safe contained a lot of incriminating evidence — double agent. Newspapers reported that his body was shipped to El Paso and buried by the family. That was news to the family. FBI thinks he's alive in Ecuador. Thompson reports that the embassy books and accounts for a project there are the worst he's ever seen. Interested?"

Maggie stared at a column of ants tracking across the flagstones.

"Well? What do you think?" Miguel asked.

"I'm mad — furious. José gave us the safe combinations, his with that phony evidence, the *Hedda's*, and the Jolzitlan safe that yielded the major windfall. He knew he'd been exposed, knew they planned to kill him. If he's alive, those bullring doctors are liars, and if I ever go to Ecuador, it'll be to prove he was a hero, not a traitor.